UNBORN

EVA BARBER

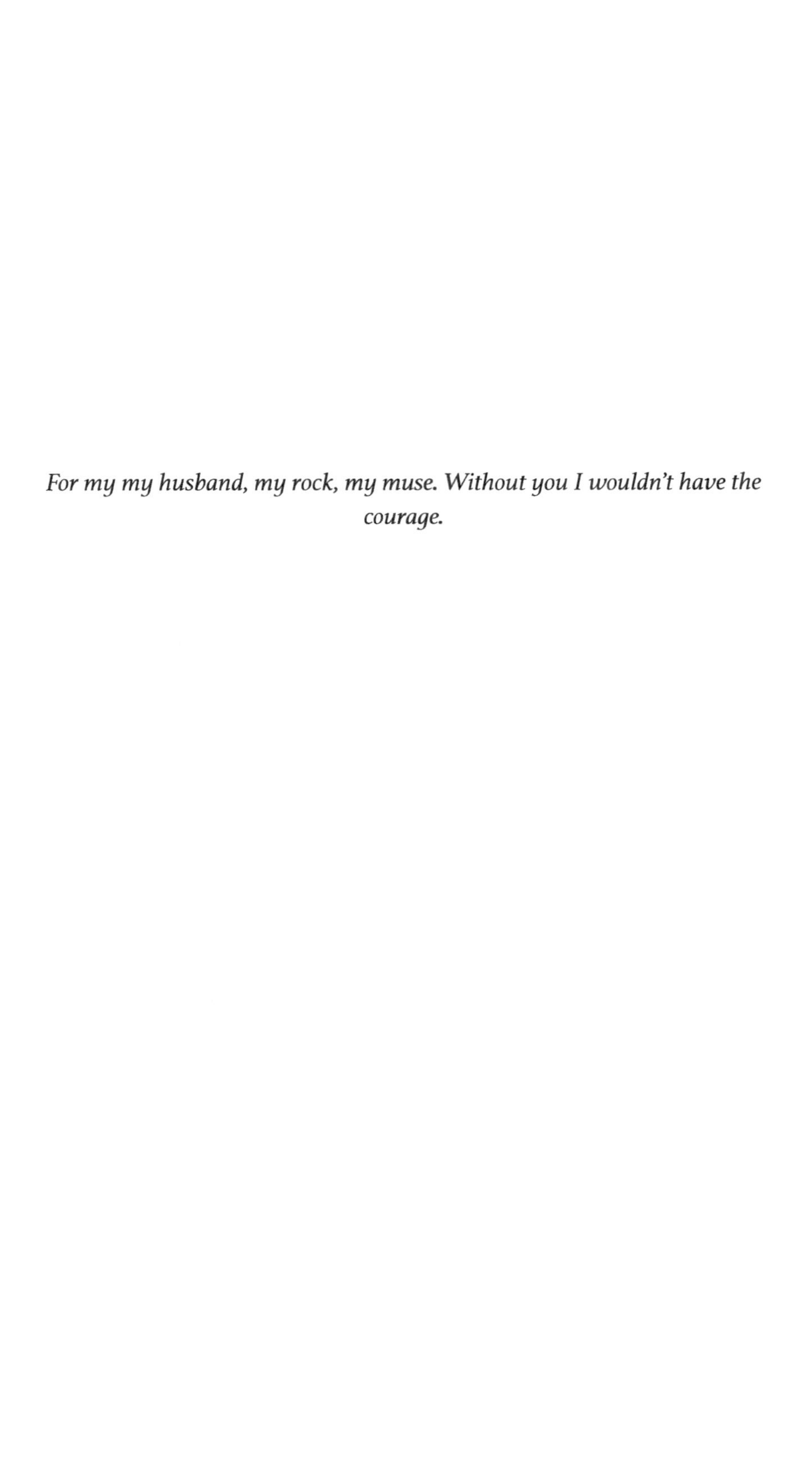

For my my husband, my rock, my muse. Without you I wouldn't have the courage.

CONTENTS

PRAISE FOR UNBORN

Bold, thought-provoking, and deeply humane, Unborn is a standout work of speculative fiction that lingers long after the final page. Eva Barber's Unborn is an ambitious and emotionally read that fuses speculative science with myth, family drama, and a meditation on destiny.

-Book Viral

Unborn is an atmospheric and thought-provoking read for anyone who enjoys stories about family, identity, and the intersection of science and the fantastical. Fans of speculative fiction with a strong emotional core, think The Midnight Library meets The Giver, will find much to love here. It's a slow burn, but one worth savoring.

-Literar Titan

1

FOREST'S TREASURES

SEPTEMBER 1999

When my parents found me in the early fall of 1999, they didn't know their lives were about to change. They didn't know what I was or where I came from. I could have had a tail and horns; it wouldn't have mattered. The instant my mother saw me lying helpless and alone in the middle of the forest, she poured into me the love she'd kept pent up for years. A love so powerful and selfless that no force in the world could keep her apart from me. Many years later, she told me a powerful sense of purpose had swept over her when she saw me. Destiny put her on that path that day, she said to me.

My parents often walked the windy forest path, loving this forest where trees were old enough to remember Ivan the Terrible, but recently even their favorite walk had turned into another reminder of their woes.

That late summer afternoon, my parents weren't holding hands or smiling. Long gone were the times they'd walked this path, holding hands with their hearts filled with hope. It had been years since Sasha, my mother, had caressed a bump on her belly, talking to it softly and imagining the life ahead. Each time her belly flattened, she felt immense grief, guilt, and lost hope. It was becoming harder for her to rekindle the courage to continue and keep it alive long enough to try again. But my mother never gave up. Her confidence wavered, but her strength and determination grew each time she lost a baby. And with it grew her love and longing to hold a child to her chest. For years now, her hope had lain buried deep inside, waiting for the right moment to awaken.

Sasha walked ahead of her husband, my father, Lev, paying no attention to the early fall's yellows and reds, softened by the afternoon sun as it filtered through the leaves. Lev kept his hands deep in his pockets, keeping his slender body hunched as if he didn't want to tower over his wife. He had his entire attention focused on her.

When the sun suddenly hid behind clouds and a gust of wind chilled the fall's moisture-laden air, he sped up; his hand leaped out of his pocket trying to reach her. As if sensing it, Sasha lurched forward and covered her head with a wool hat. Lev quickly shoved his hand back into his pocket and kept shuffling his long legs behind Sasha.

They walked in silence until Sasha stopped at an ancient oak tree and stood there, frozen, staring at the ground. Her eyes opened wide as she tried to understand the sight before her.

Lev caught up with her and touched her shoulder. "What is it? Sasha?"

His touch startled Sasha. She woke from her trance and kneeled on the soft earth blanketed by a deep layer of leaves.

Lev's eyes drifted to the ground, and when he realized what was before him, his knees gave out, and he collapsed to the ground beside her. Their eyes met and then reverted to the forest floor where a newborn baby lay, covered by a blanket of leaves. The baby was alive and asleep. The leaves quivered as the baby's small chest moved with tiny breaths.

Sasha blinked and then removed her coat and spread it by the tiny figure. She laid the baby on it, carefully brushed the leaves off her, and then lifted the corners of her coat to bundle the baby, but stopped, holding the coat open, staring at the perfect little girl. Perfect, except she didn't have a belly button. There was no sign of an umbilical cord—only smooth, pale skin. Lev gasped and glanced at his wife, but she disregarded him, clenched her teeth, and, wide-eyed, studied the smooth belly until the baby stirred and moved its tiny arms. She then pursed her lips, wrapped the newborn in her coat, and picked up the little bundle from the ground.

Lev glared at Sasha and opened his mouth, as if wanting to say something, but she hardened her eyes, avoided his stare, and walked in the direction they had come from, holding the precious cargo tight to her chest. Lev stood alone by the oak tree, watching as Sasha walked away with the baby. He drew a deep breath, about to bellow in protest again, but watching Sasha clutch the baby to her chest with desperation and tenderness, exhaled and caught up with her. He draped his coat around her shoulders, and they walked in silence back to their house at the forest's edge.

2

OLESYA

SEPTEMBER 1999

The house showed signs of neglect. The porch steps creaked as Sasha and Lev climbed them. Weeds had taken over the flower beds, and the gray wood of the house and picket fence was visible through the peeling white paint. A large willow tree captured most of the yard, and its delicate leaves danced, whispering secrets with the slightest wind.

Lev opened the front door for Sasha. The sun was low on the horizon, casting long shadows on the house so that even the blue flower boxes that adorned the blue-shuttered windows appeared dim. He exhaled before following Sasha inside, closing the door as if it almost weighed more than he could manage.

Sasha dashed straight to the cheerful bedroom with its sturdy homemade furniture embellished with brightly painted details and soft throws.

Gently, Sasha laid the baby on the bed and then pulled out onesies, cloth diapers, and a colorful, soft blanket with little white stars out of a carved wooden closet. Sasha smiled when the pink onesies fit the girl as if they were made for her. She wrapped the baby in the blanket while soothing her with her gentle voice. After she was done, she picked her up as if she were picking up a flower and, afraid to bend its delicate petals, held her in her arms a little distance away from her chest. Then, as the baby felt her warmth and her beating heart and sank deeper into her arms, she pressed her to her chest lovingly but gently. As she gazed at the girl's face, her own face changed. The thin lines around her mouth disappeared, replaced by a smile, and her eyes brightened as if a cloud had lifted off them. "Malenka," she whispered. "Malenka, moja."

Lev leaned against the door, watching, hesitating before asking. "You kept them?"

"I tried to give them away, but something always stopped me," Sasha said, caressing the baby's tiny finger. "Where are we going to put you, little one? We will keep you close so we can get to you quickly, right? Is that what you want? What are we going to name you?"

Lev leaned against the doorway and ran his fingers through his thick brown hair. "We are not keeping it."

Sasha ignored him. She whispered something in the baby's ear and smiled.

"We should report it. Let someone know," Lev continued, seeking Sasha's attention.

"It's not an 'it,'" Sasha sighed. "It's a she. Let who know? Why do you think someone dumped this baby in the woods? Dumped her like garbage with no clothes, no blanket, nothing." Sasha spoke louder. "Do you think that someone wants this baby back? Think about it. Someone wanted the baby dead, but they didn't have the guts to do it."

"What about the...?" His words trailed off as he pointed at the missing belly button.

Sasha shrugged. "What about it? I don't know. She is alive and looks healthy." Sasha paused and furrowed her brow. "I am afraid of what someone might do to a baby like this if we tell anyone about her. Somehow, I doubt that she'd be reunited with her loving family, if she even has one."

"Maybe they were scared? Or perhaps they'll think this through and come back?"

"Scared of what? Lev, she is just a tiny baby. Being scared does not justify leaving the tiny thing to die in the woods."

"How would we know how to care for her?"

"We do not need to know anything except how to love her. If we tell someone, she may end up in a hospital or research facility or someplace even worse, probed and examined all her life. We are not telling anyone."

"What is she? We know nothing about her."

"We know she is our baby girl and that this was meant to be. We were supposed to find her. And be her parents."

"I'm scared, Sasha."

"Everything is going to work out. You'll see." She added hesitantly, "We can't lose her too. I can't lose her."

Lev glanced at Sasha. Her eyes had regained their intense blue color and shine. His Sasha had come back to life. She hadn't seen her so happy and full of life in years. No one ought to take that away from her.

"Should we give her a name?" Lev asked.

Sasha smiled. She glanced out the window, stroking the tiny girl sleeping in her arms, and her eyes rested on the willow tree.

"How about Olesya? The girl of the forest," Sasha said.

Lev nodded. He took the tiny hand and whispered. "Olesya. Our little forest girl. Our little secret."

At that moment, the baby opened her eyes, which were completely black—there was no distinction between the color of the iris and the pupil, and the white sclera stressed the darkness even more. Lev and Sasha glanced at each other, and their hands touched. They smiled at their daughter and then at each other.

Lev called his boss at the nuclear plant on the outskirts of Belyaska, asking for a few days off. He ran errands for Sasha, who gave him a list of baby necessities to get. After he had finished his errands, he paced the small yard, hoping to loosen the knot in his stomach, telling him to go back to the oak where they had found Olesya. The foreboding sensation that he had missed something important in the forest persisted and grew stronger. On the third evening, he couldn't wait any longer. Sasha was feeding the baby when Lev tiptoed out of the house, closed the front door quietly, and stood there for a while with his ear glued to the door. Then he crept down the stairs.

As Lev neared the path into the forest, he looked around before running toward the oak tree. When it was almost within his sight, he stopped suddenly and ducked behind a tree. Two, armed men holding machine guns stood in front of an enormous white tent set up near the oak. Bright lights inside the tent outlined dark silhouettes moving within.

Lev's heart thrashed in his chest as he stepped back, placing each foot slowly and carefully, trying to avoid touching sticks or crunchy leaves with his feet. Once he reached a safe distance, he turned around and ran fast, looking over his shoulder.

Lev opened the front door and tiptoed into the house. Sasha sat near the window overlooking the backyard, feeding the baby, whose black eyes focused on her. He lingered in the entryway, considering telling Sasha what he'd seen, but a cowardly voice whispered. *Not now. Just look at her. Don't spoil this moment.*

The scene resembled an old painting of the Madonna and her child. His Sasha was glowing. The soft afternoon light painted her unbraided hair with golden streaks and added shine to her blue eyes. Lev forgot to breathe for a moment as his heart filled with emotions he hadn't experienced in years. He couldn't tell her then. Instead, he kissed Sasha's cheek, glancing at the little girl, who met his gaze and smiled, squinting her black eyes. Lev's chest constricted.

Each time Sasha changed Olesya's diapers, her eyes inadvertently rested on the spot on her belly where the belly button should have been. She had inspected that area with a magnifying glass and gently ran her fingers over the girl's delicate skin but found no answers. On the fifth day, Sasha left the house, telling Lev she had to run an errand.

Before entering the hospital, she put on her white nurse's uniform, pinning her keycard to her pocket. Then, she confidently strode along the empty hospital corridor. With a key she fished out of her pocket, she unlocked the medical supply room, throwing furtive glances in both directions before entering. Inside, she searched through cabinets and drawers until she found a small glass bottle, surgical scissors, and a syringe. She stuffed everything in her side pockets and smoothed them out.

Relieved no one saw her leave the room, Sasha ran to the exit, but before she reached it, her coworker, Petra, rushed around the corner, bumping into her.

"Sasha! You're back! So glad. Are you feeling better? How is Lev?"

"Oh, yes. I am doing much better. Lev is doing well, too. I'll be back next week."

Pietra wanted to continue the conversation, but Sasha walked past her, smiling nervously. "I am in a bit of a hurry. I have an appointment. Talk to you next week," Sasha said, and left without looking back.

3

BELLY BUTTON

SEPTEMBER 1999

Sasha and Lev's kitchen was cozy and full of country charm, like the rest of the house. The colorful clay pots, stacked on wooden shelves, bathed in the warm glow of a wicker and brass chandelier, while dried herbs and garlic hung around a window adorned with blue and white curtains.

On his way back from work, Lev smiled in anticipation of seeing Sasha and Olesya. He ran into the house, surprised to see it enveloped in darkness. At this time of the evening, Sasha usually sat in the chair by the window, feeding the baby. Upon noticing the kitchen light, Lev smiled and walked toward it. The smile on his face faded when he saw shiny surgical instruments in metal trays arranged on the burly wooden table. With gloved hands, Sasha filled a syringe from a small glass bottle. His mouth dropped open in astonishment. Olesya was lying on the tabletop, kicking her legs in the air with her little belly exposed.

"Sasha! What are you doing?"

"What needs to be done. The sooner, the better."

"What needs to be done?"

"I'm going to make her look...normal. I think I can make it look just right."

"Are you out of your mind? It may kill her."

"I will not kill her. I know what I'm doing. It's superficial, skin-deep. I'll numb her belly so she won't feel a thing," she said. "I'm saving her life."

Then, she pointed at the instruments with her eyes. "You can help."

Lev hesitated. The fierce determination and the silent plea in her eyes dispelled his misgivings instantly. "What can I do?" he asked, washing his hands in the kitchen sink.

"You can hand me the instruments when I ask. Can you tell their names?"

"I think so. Knife—no, scalpel. Scissors, forceps…"

"Good enough."

Sasha used forceps to take a piece of gauze from a glass jar and dipped it in a container filled with yellow liquid. She dabbed it on Olesya's belly while talking to her. Olesya, looking content, had her black eyes glued to Sasha's face.

Sasha selected vegetables from the stand and placed them in her shopping cart. Before pushing the cart into the aisle with baby formula, diapers, toys, and other baby necessities, she looked around. The possibility of running into someone who might recognize her in an aisle with baby paraphernalia suddenly frightened her. She realized she was unprepared to explain the baby items in her basket without raising suspicion. Her mouth was drying rapidly as she tossed a few items into the cart and hurried to leave the aisle, looking over her shoulder. As she was leaving the aisle, a middle-aged woman, a neighbor from two blocks away, Natalia, appeared out of nowhere, like a ghost.

"Sasha! How are you?" Natalia said, smiling. She snooped inside Sasha's cart and, noticing the baby formula and diapers, glanced at Sasha and continued talking, albeit slower, as if she were expecting an explanation. "I've heard you've been sick."

"I'm doing better. I had a cold that would not go away." Sasha said, placing her hand on her chest to quiet her pounding heart. "Lev's cousins are visiting with their new baby. I've got to get back—they are on their last diaper."

The woman smiled. "I understand. It was great to see you. Say hello to Lev for me."

Sasha hurried to the cash register. She glanced back at her neighbor, who was still looking at her. Sasha gave her a faint smile, paid, and fled the store.

Sasha was telling Lev about her shopping experience while putting away groceries. But this simple task seemed more difficult at that moment, and she kept misplacing and dropping the items. Lev stood nearby, holding Olesya, who was sleeping on his shoulder.

"I don't think she believed me. She didn't buy my story about your cousins. I didn't know what else to say. I was very careful not to be seen. She just appeared out of nowhere."

"This will continue happening. We can't stay here, Sasha."

Sasha continued putting cans and bottles into the cupboard above her head. The seriousness of Lev's tone frightened her. "I know. What are we going to do?" she asked, knocking over a bottle with her trembling hands.

"You remember what my cousin Lech said one time?"

Sasha met Lev's eyes and slowly nodded, but she did not seem pleased. Not that she didn't like Lech. Quite the opposite—she adored her husband's first cousin, who looked and behaved just like Lev. Funny, spontaneous, and smart, Lech was impossible to dislike. It was the company he kept that bothered her. Recalling the eerie feeling after meeting one of his friends, she wanted nothing to do with him. Excuses piled on top of each other in her attempts to avoid Lech. Fortunately, he lived in Moscow—too far for frequent, casual visits.

"Remember when he offered us—"

"Why can't we just move to a big city?" Sasha did not want to hear it and interrupted harshly, but with a plea in her voice. "We could disappear in a big city. We could go to Moscow or Saint Petersburg? There are so many people in big cities. Nobody would notice us there."

Lev was quiet, gathering his thoughts. He kept his eyes on Sasha, who immediately sensed that something was troubling him.

"What is it, Lev? What? Tell me!"

"I went back."

"Back where?"

"To where we found her. It was a couple of days later. I wanted to make sure we missed nothing."

Sasha tapped her fingers on the counter. "And?"

"I think the military was there. Government and all."

"You think? What do you mean, you think?"

"I saw men holding guns, guarding a white tent set up by the old oak. I couldn't see what they were doing because I ran away quickly. Nobody saw me."

"You sure?"

"It's been two weeks. Someone would've contacted us by now if they had seen me. I was careful."

"Depends on what they were looking for."

"Come on. What else would the military be doing there? Of all the places?"

"It might be a coincidence."

"Not likely. Maybe she is their experiment. They came back to get her, but she wasn't there. They will start looking for her, and we can't hide her forever. People will start asking questions, and I couldn't think of a good lie to tell them, given what happened. They will come for her and for us. I think we've reached a point where we must decide whether we want to keep her or come forward."

"I thought we'd already decided that. We are keeping her." She glanced at Olesya, sleeping peacefully in Lev's arms. "Just look at her. She is our baby. She is perfect. Do you see how happy she is? Do you see how happy I am? You are worried, but I can also see that you are happy. I see the way you look at her. And I think it's too late to come forward. They would most likely imprison us, or worse."

"Then we must leave. I don't see any other option but to contact Lech. We could disappear in a big city, but not forever. You know that, Sasha. Someone will eventually find us. Lech could help us get out of here with his connections."

"I'm sure he could," she said, rolling her eyes.

Hearing Lev's story, however, Sasha realized that contacting Lech was the only way they could keep the baby and save her life. Perhaps even their own.

4

SERGI

SEPTEMBER 1999

They didn't call for a taxi. Lev wanted to walk instead, hoping to ease his anxiety and placate his conscience before the meeting. They walked through a dark alley in the run-down outskirts of Moscow, frequented mostly by people conducting shady business late in the evening or at night. Night fell on the street; the wind carried the smell of stale fried food and marijuana.

Lech was Lev's first cousin on his father's side. Both in their late thirties, they looked alike, shuffled their long, slender legs the same way, and moved their light brown hair out of their eyes with similar quirky movements. They even sounded alike when they argued. And when that happened, their intelligent brown eyes glistened with the same intensity and wit.

Lech's stride was confident, while Lev tried to hide his apprehension, but his uneven gait betrayed him. He shoved his hands into his pockets and looked around. From the corner of his eye, he noticed movement in the darkness and darted forward. Lech sped up too to catch up with his cousin.

At last, Lech stopped at an imposing black door, reinforced with huge metal bars. He glanced at Lev. "Let me do the talking. I know him well."

Lev exhaled. "Sure."

Lech knocked on the monstrous black door, which opened slowly to reveal a tall, muscular man staring at them suspiciously. When Lech was about to say something, the man averted his gaze and directed him inside without a word.

They entered a cavernous, dark room ruled by dust and shadows and smelling dank and moldy. An enormous desk surrounded by rickety old chairs dominated the center of the dingy room. Another tall, muscular man stood in the corner. He also appeared to be a bodyguard. When he saw them enter the room, he raised his burly arm and pointed to the chairs without even a glance, but Lev sensed he was ready to spring at them if they even looked at him the wrong way.

The cousins sat and waited. Lev self-consciously glanced around, wondering if anyone would notice the beads of perspiration on his forehead, hear his heart pounding, or notice his eye twitching.

Lech glanced at his cousin, elbowed him, and gave him a reassuring smile.

The dark silhouette of a tall and muscular man moved toward them without a sound. He sat across from them at the imposing desk and turned on a small desk lamp, which illuminated his strikingly handsome face and emphasized his incredible blue eyes. Never had Lev seen such intensity in someone's eyes. He expected a thug but found a man whose eyes beamed with intelligence and curiosity. But there was something else in his expression. Something impossible to grasp because it only surfaced for a second. But Lev noticed and shuddered. Yet, he could not look away from him.

Lech touched Lev's arm and started the conversation in a friendly and even tone. "Good evening, Sergi. Thank you for meeting with us."

Sergi only glanced at Lech, barely acknowledging him. He turned his entire attention to Lev, focusing his penetrating eyes on him. Under his stare, Lev's hands trembled.

Finally, Sergi addressed him in a rich and pleasant voice. "I understand you need help to get to the United States?"

Lev cleared his throat to respond, but Sergi did not wait for the response.

"Your baby is a newborn, right? Why would you want to leave your country and face the unknown with such a young baby?"

Lech interjected quickly before Lev had the chance to respond. "They're thinking about the future. And it's better for the baby. It will get used to the new—"

"I didn't ask you. I asked Lev," Sergi interrupted calmly with an icy tone, focusing his eyes on Lev.

Lev struggled to get his voice to obey him. "We want to give a better life to our daughter."

"But that is not the entire reason, is it, Lev?" asked Sergi.

"No, but I'd rather not talk about it. It's personal."

Sergi kept his inquisitive, laden with suspicion gaze on Lev. This time it was Lech who shifted in his chair.

Sergi extended his hand. "Do you have it?"

Lev hesitated for a moment, then with a shaking hand and a wretched look on his face passed a small package wrapped in brown paper to Sergi. With a deliberately slow move, Sergi reached for the package, not easing his stare, then got up and silently disappeared as if he were just an apparition. The cousins remained seated, glancing at each other for reassurance. After a few minutes, Sergi returned. He didn't sit but stood facing Lev and staring at him for a long moment before he finally spoke.

"Looks like you are going to be a cowboy in great big America. You've got yourself a deal. You will get passports and visas in a few weeks," he said, sounding amused.

"How do I know you'll keep your word?" Lev asked, but the instant he did, he guessed no one would ever answer the question.

"You don't," said Sergi. "But then again, you don't have a choice, do you?"

Sergi left the room. Lev moved as if he wanted to follow him, but the bodyguard was suddenly at their side, glaring and pointing at the exit. Lech grabbed Lev's arm. Lev resisted momentarily, but then let Lech lead him out through the door. Once outside, Lev exhaled and hung his head. His stomach threatened to revolt right there in the alley as Lev faltered, fearing he had made the wrong decision.

"He sounded like he suspected something," Lev said in a trembling voice. "Is he dangerous? Could he go after us?"

"He suspected nothing, Lev. Sergi is very intuitive. Sensing you were hiding something, he pried, but he had no way of knowing what. He makes you feel like he knows all about you because that's what he does. Trust me, Sergi didn't even try to find out. You'd know if he had," Lech said and paused, glancing at Lev. "Yes. Sergi can be dangerous. But he would not hesitate to risk his life to protect someone he cares about. We served together. I don't think he'll try to harm you or your family."

Lev sighed. "I hope you're right, but I feel like shit."

"I get it. But you must forget about it for your sake. And that of your daughter and Sasha's. It's done. With time, it'll become easier. You saved someone's life today. Do you still think the price was too high?"

5

BLACK SHARD

AUGUST 1793

In the summer of 1793, ten-year-old twins—a boy and a girl—were playing with rocks on a Paris city street. Sebastian and Zoe wore rags and lacked shoes. Uncombed blond mops and layers of dirt hid their delicate faces.

Their blue eyes sparkled at the sight of a shiny horse-drawn carriage pulling to the curb, and a middle-aged man stepping out. The man flaunted his wealth with his new carriage and clothes full of intricate brocade embroidery. He didn't seem very comfortable in his fashionably tight clothes. His round belly seemed as if it were about to burst out of his gold-infused vest. Before he reached the jewelry store, stopping midway to wipe his red, sweaty face with a silk handkerchief, the merchant flung the door open, bowing deeply and inviting his soon-to-be customer inside his store, squinting his small, greedy eyes.

The twins glanced at the wealthy man and exchanged looks but continued playing, watching the door.

Moments later, the man emerged from the store. Zoe approached him and extended her little hand, asking for money with exaggerated, sad eyes. With an angry gesture, he swatted her away. She persisted and stopped in front of his carriage, blocking it. Relenting, he retrieved a coin purse from his coat pocket and extracted a coin. He examined it and, dissatisfied, put it back. He pulled out another smaller coin, extending his hand toward Zoe. Zoe reached for it, but the wealthy man pulled his hand away.

"Now, now, little girl. Not so fast. What do you say?"

Zoe jumped, grabbed the coin out of his hand, and ran away. She stopped a few feet away and grinned at him.

"You ungrateful little bitch. You come back here and say a proper thank you," he screeched, pointing his finger at Zoe, his round face reddened with anger.

Zoe stuck out her tongue at him, grinned, and ran down the street, skipping.

Zoe sat on a wooden box in the attic, staring at the door. The straw bed with worn-out blankets and pillows provided little comfort or warmth during the winter, and a few old wooden boxes served as the only furniture. Two sad, mangled metal buckets sat in a corner. This miserable attic was where the twins had lived for the last two years. And that was an improvement over where they had slept before, since their parents' death during the revolution. The children had stumbled upon the attic while fleeing from a gendarme, who'd been chasing them for stealing a truckle of cheese. Their new hideaway was difficult to get to and partially hidden by treacherous stacks of wooden boxes. They were safe here, being the only ones able to navigate the barricade with their small and lean bodies.

Zoe waited for her brother's return, wondering what was taking him so long. Often, his tardiness was a sign of mischief. They had little to eat during the last few days. Lately, the begging on Parisian streets offered very few coins, and falling asleep with empty bellies wasn't easy. Sebastian always aspired to be the big brother and to take care of Zoe.

While she was sitting on the box waiting, Sebastian burst in, trying not to grin.

"What did you do? Show me," Zoe demanded.

Sebastian pulled a purse out of his pocket, smiling.

"You did not! Sebastian! Why did you do that?"

"He was mean. And rich. And we're hungry. He won't miss this stupid purse."

"He'll come after us."

"Zoe, there are so many coins in here. We can go somewhere else."

Torn between anger at her brother for stealing and the hope of filling their bellies with food, she snatched the purse from him and poured the contents on the bed. There were about twenty coins of different sizes. Zoe gazed at the coins, and then a wide grin lit up her face.

"The old, fat miser deserved it. Let's get some food," she said.

Sebastian smiled and nodded. Enthused, the twins scrambled out of the attic.

Zoe and Sebastian sat on a log, sharing bread and a chunk of cheese. Startled by a sudden loud noise, the twins jumped off and looked around, and spotting fire and smoke in the distance, they exchanged a look and ran through the forest until they reached an opening. They stood, jaws dropped, gawking at the smoke and fire billowing out of a large depression in the ground. A small stream ran through the depression. Suddenly, black shards burst out of the fire, reflecting the sun and the fire in a portentous glow as they fell into the stream.

Zoe, mesmerized by the shards, jumped into the stream and cried out. The water was hot. Not giving up, Zoe ran along the stream, searching for the shards. When she saw one, she reached for it and missed. She tried again, slipped on the rocks, but got up and continued searching. She searched and searched and finally laid her eyes on it, this time grabbing and gripping it tightly. Instantly, she cried out, staring at her clenched fingers with horror as they remained closed despite her efforts to open them. Zoe collapsed onto the grass-covered bank, curled herself into a ball, and cried in pain. Blood dripped from her hand.

Sebastian, frozen, watched as his sister moaned in agony. "What is it, Zoe? What is wrong?"

After a few moments, Zoe sat up abruptly. Her eyes flickered open and slowly met his brother's. Her eyes were no longer blue. They were deep and black now, as if the pupils had expanded, taking over the irises. Sebastian took a step back.

Zoe observed Sebastian while her hair changed color and texture, becoming thick, black, and wavy. Zoe smiled and then laughed. She opened her hand and motioned for Sebastian to come closer.

Sebastian hesitated. "Zoe, your eyes? Can you see? What happened to you? Are you hurt?"

Zoe smiled. "No, I'm not hurt. I'm well. I'm better than well. I feel wonderful. Come here. Your turn."

Sebastian approached Zoe slowly. She grabbed his hand and tried to put the shiny black shard covered in her blood in his. Sebastian glanced at it and pulled the hand away.

"What's the matter? Don't you trust me? Give me your hand. You must do it. We must be the same again. It only hurts for a while, but it is worth it. It's wonderful afterward."

"Is it still you, Zoe?"

"Of course, it's me, silly. Come here."

Sebastian hesitated, but extended his hand, palm up, and shut his eyes. Zoe dropped the shiny black object in his trembling hand and closed his fingers around it. And just like his sister had before, Sebastian flopped on the grass and curled into a ball, moaning in pain.

Zoe lay on the ground by Sebastian, wrapped her arms around him, and whispered in his ear. "The pain doesn't last long. And then, after it's over, you'll feel amazing. It's as if the world became more beautiful and clearer."

The twins couldn't sleep that night. They sat on their dinky bed and whispered to each other, even though no one could hear them. Zoe, mesmerized by their new looks, couldn't keep her eyes off Sebastian and kept stroking his wavy hair while sharing the strange new sensations her body and mind were experiencing. Sebastian nodded—he felt them, too. The dingy attic seemed more colorful, as if a magic wand had sprinkled it with new and deeper shades of color. Distant and faint the night before, the smells and sounds coming from the open window overwhelmed them with their strength and variety. They smelled the food cooking and freshly washed laundry mixed with the odors of homelessness and decay. They finally fell asleep in each other's arms just before twilight streaked their tiny windows with silver dust.

When they woke up the next afternoon, they discovered their bodies had changed even more while they slept. Sebastian's sleeves, too short before, now barely reached his forearms. His worn-out pants were a few inches shorter now. Zoe's dress, formerly mid-calf, was now above her knees. With their newly gained height came strength. Sebastian stared at his sculpted, muscular forearms with awe.

"I'm starving," Sebastian said after the initial shock passed.

"Me too," Zoe whispered, and then, looking at her worn-out, dirty, and now too short dress, added, "I want new clothes."

Sebastian gaped at her with his mouth open.

"You need new clothes, too. And shoes. We need clothes and shoes," she said and stomped her foot.

"But we don't have enough money for clothes and food."

"We'll get some. Let's go," Zoe said and grabbed his hand. "Come on, let's go shopping."

"Get your hands off me!" Zoe shouted, dropping the clothes she hid under her dress as the merchant dragged her back to his store. As she fought him, trying to free herself from his grip, he grabbed her hair.

Zoe cried out more out of humiliation than pain. Sebastian had already left, unaware that his sister, instead of following him out of the store, had stopped to grab a hat from the stand, which fell, alerting the merchant. Despite his sizable belly, the man crossed the store in two quick strides and grabbed her arm. Hearing Zoe's scream, Sebastian ran back, and seeing his sister in the clutches of the merchant, ran into him with all his strength, screaming at the top of his lungs. The merchant staggered, and his grip on Zoe's arm and hair loosened. Zoe was free. But instead of running, she clenched her teeth and, glowering, thrust her hands at her pursuer.

The twins watched in shock and awe as a silver ball formed in Zoe's palms, then spun out of her hands in silvery-blue waves and hit the man in the chest. He fell to the ground with a pitiful little cry and landed on his back. The children looked at him as he remained motionless on top of a pile of scattered hats and clothes. His eyes stared blankly at the ceiling. A feather, displaced from a hat by the commotion, landed slowly on his nose, but he didn't move.

"Is he...dead?" Zoe whispered.

"I don't know," Sebastian answered, kneeling hesitantly by his side. "He's not breathing, Zoe. What do we do?"

Zoe didn't answer at first. Then she said through her clenched teeth. "Nothing. We take our clothes and run."

"We can't just leave him?"

"Why not? What can we do? Why didn't he just let us take these stupid clothes? I would have. Greed killed him, not us."

Zoe calmly picked out a new dress, shoes, and a hat scattered by the dead merchant, glanced at Sebastian, and strolled out of the store nonchalantly. Sebastian stayed, staring at the dead man. Then he inspected his hands, and after a moment of indecision, he thrust his hands forward. The clothes flew off the wooden shelves and racks and swirled around him after the bluish-silvery wave hit them. Sebastian gawked at the spectacle with his mouth open, then grinned.

6

RECRUITING

OCTOBER 1865

I n the fall of 1865, Zoe sat on the sofa, engrossed in a book. Her stunning black eyes scanned the pages fast. Barefoot, she wore a simple white sleeveless dress that unfolded in smooth waves on the Persian carpet. Although slender, she didn't lack strength. Her well-defined muscles showed through the delicate material of her dress. Two big black dogs sat by her side, relaxed but watchful, ready to strike anyone who dared to approach their mistress.

Sebastian came running through an oversized French door. The dogs perked their ears, but they stayed at Zoe's side. While he crossed the enormous room with an effortless, springy stride, his black, wavy hair moved, exposing his handsome face and eyes as arresting as his sister's.

He approached Zoe and asked, narrowing his eyes, "Why aren't you ready?"

"I don't want to go to another party. They are all so terribly boring."

"It was your plan."

"You are right," Zoe said, but continued to sit and stare out the window.

"We'll do it, won't we? Or have you changed your mind?"

"No. I haven't."

"What if he says no?"

"He won't."

Zoe watched Sebastian shift his weight and lift one eyebrow, but after a moment, her lips twitched, and she smiled. "I'll get ready. You know me so well. You can talk me into anything."

"Right. It's the other way around," he mumbled.

Zoe was already leaving the room and didn't hear his comment, but she would have agreed with her brother. Since their change, Zoe's attitude had changed. Both siblings perceived the unfairness of the world, but unlike Sebastian, she wanted to do something about the corrupt governments, the power-hungry politicians, and the wealthy people who swindled and scorned the poor. When she realized the full power of the black shard, she convinced herself that she had found it for a reason. It was her destiny to make the world better; she had told Sebastian. Sebastian didn't dissuade her from her ambitious plans but didn't take part in planning, hoping it was merely a phase Zoe would outgrow.

But instead of outgrowing it, Zoe's resolve grew, and Sebastian grudgingly agreed to help. Since he stole the purse from the rich man, he had done it many times. At first, he was hesitant and careful, but then it became easier with time. Zoe didn't protest at first, but one day she stopped him and told him her plans. No more petty thefts, she told him. From now on, they would do things differently. They would find the right people to join them. In exchange for the benefits the shards offered, they would gain money, power, and people they could trust and grow their empire.

In a richly decorated nineteenth-century palace, people were engaged in an elaborate group dance—the cotillion. The women's long dresses blurred together in a multitude of colors as their part-ners spun them on the dance floor. Others stood observing the dancers, some wishing they were dancing, some glad they didn't have to step on other people's toes and could keep their own intact.

Zoe and Sebastian lingered in a corner, talking to a young man in his late twenties. The man gazed at Zoe with fascination and nodded in agreement while she spoke with what seemed genuine inspiration and sincerity. She grasped his hand, leading him out of the ballroom. She held his arm, still talking while they passed through several corridors illuminated by candles glimmering from the gold chandeliers. Sebastian followed them, looking left and right, but nobody paid attention to their departure or bothered to see where they were going.

Outside, the dense fog greeted them with gray swirls dancing around the gas streetlights. The few dim lights flickered, disappearing and reappearing in the mist, revealing the outline of the two-horse carriage. Sebastian stepped forward and opened the door. The man hesitated.

Zoe climbed inside the carriage and leaned out, smiling. She held out her hand and pleaded. "Come on, Henry. Let's continue our conversation in a more comfortable place."

Henry looked into her eyes, took her hand, and entered the carriage. Sebastian jumped gracefully onto the coach box alongside the driver. The black horses neighed, shaking their manes, and hauled the carriage away along the dark cobblestone street.

Henry, Zoe, and Sebastian stood by the window at Zoe and Sebastian's estate, each holding a glass of red wine and enduring a long and heavy silence before Zoe broke it.

"Henry, do you know why we have chosen you?"

"Because I can offer you money and political power."

"That's just part of it. There're many people who have money and power. We chose you because of your high moral standards and intelligence. Money and power are important, but not as much as your integrity. We chose you to join us in creating a better world because you are a remarkable human being."

Henry stared at Zoe's face, then focused his wise brown gaze on her black, bottomless eyes, searching, probing. He didn't seem to doubt her sincerity, but seemed to need extra convincing and reassurance. "I believe you, but I'm not sure. And...I'm scared."

"What are you scared of?"

"I'm afraid of changing my mind. I'm terrified of the irrevocability of it all. What if I don't want immortality anymore? What if I want to be a regular human being? Can I go back?"

"I understand," Zoe said. "We were children when it happened, so we didn't think about it and didn't realize what we were getting into. No, you can't go back. Not that you will want to. Trust me. I can tell you how it is afterward. You are still you, but stronger, healthier, and full of energy. Look at me! Look at us. We are seventy-two years old, but we appear and feel as if we are still in our twenties. That's not all. Your mind will be sharper, you'll be able to focus better, notice things you've never noticed before, hear sounds no other human can hear, and remember everything. I swear to you, you will not regret it."

"Are there any downsides?"

Zoe cleared her throat. "I can't think of any."

"There is another benefit if you're a man," Sebastian said, smiling mischievously.

Henry gazed at Zoe and then Sebastian, considering what they had told him. "I will do it, but under one condition."

"What?" Zoe asked.

"Mary, the love of my life, must come with me."

Zoe frowned while contemplating his request. "Deal. If she is your girl, she must be special too."

7

NIGTHMARE

JUNE 2005

On a summer morning in 2005, in a small suburban house in Walla Walla, in the evergreen State of Washington, the crisp early light found a small opening between the curtains and left bright streaks on the walls of a tiny but cozy bedroom filled with books and toys arranged neatly on shelves. Drawings depicting stars, planets, suns, and moons adorned the walls, complementing the curtains covered with stars and moons. A six-year-old girl lay deep in her silver-blue spaceship bed, on which the girl's father had painted white and yellow stars. A large telescope stood in the corner, facing the window. It was apparent that the little inhabitant of this adorable bedroom had already developed strong, starry interests.

Thick black waves of hair surrounded the girl's delicate face. Her eyes twitched in her sleep. Olesya was stirring in her bed, moaning. She woke up sobbing and crying for her mother.

"Mama! Mama!"

Sasha ran into the bedroom and held Olesya close. "It's all right, baby. I'm here. Everything is okay now. You're okay. It was just a dream," Sasha whispered.

Sasha held Olesya in her arms, gently stroking her head and wiping her tears away. The girl stopped sobbing and calmed down.

"Did you have a bad dream?"

"Yeah."

"Was it the same dream?"

Olesya was silent at first, trying to remember. "It was a little different."

"Do you want to tell me about it?"

"The woman was different. She had a bigger belly this time. And... and she...everything was black. And the man found me again." Olesya grew upset recalling her dream.

The recurring dreams were only scary after she'd first woken up. As she thought about them throughout the day, apprehension gave way to curiosity and a sensation that her dreams had a meaning that she hadn't grasped yet.

"It was just a dream, baby girl. Just a dream. Let's get up and have some hot chocolate."

The anticipation of her favorite morning drink pushed the dream aside. "With marshmallows?"

"With marshmallows and anything else you want in it, my princess."

Olesya jumped down from her bed and grasped Sasha's hand.

"Will Daddy be back today?"

"No. Not today, malenka. In two days," Sasha said, showing two fingers to Olesya. "One, two. Two short days."

"Yeah. One, two."

Sasha sat the girl and her book by the kitchen table while she prepared hot chocolate and pancakes for Olesya. She loved the mornings off from the local clinic where she had been working since they had moved from the Seattle suburbs to Walla Walla three years ago. She could devote as much time to her daughter as she wanted. Not daring to entrust anyone with Olesya's care, she alternated with Lev, whose flexible schedule at the nuclear plant in Richland allowed him to help take care of their baby girl. Now that Olesya had started school last September, the mornings alone with her daughter were few, and Sasha cherished them with her entire soul.

8

MONSTER

OCTOBER 2012

On a late October afternoon, middle school-aged children gathered in small groups, talking, laughing, and throwing paper balls at each other, waiting for the teacher to arrive. Olesya sat alone in her chair, deeply immersed in a book.

The teacher, Matt Crawford, a slender man in his thirties with a mop of unruly brown curls and dark-rimmed glasses, arrived. "Hello, children. You can sit now. It is time for some science, kids. Time to have fun!" he shouted cheerfully.

Children settled into their chairs, but some still carried on quiet conversations, ignoring the teacher.

"Today, we will learn about something exciting. Last week, we learned about...Who can remember what we talked about last week? Yeah...last week feels like ages ago, but perhaps someone remembers? Anyone?"

An embarrassing silence enveloped the classroom. Some children stirred in their seats, pretending to search eagerly for something in their bags, or looked embarrassed. Some just stared at the teacher innocently.

Matt sighed, scanned the classroom, and rested his eyes on Olesya. "Olesya? How about you?"

31

"We learned about atoms," Olesya responded. "That they are the smallest things that everything is made of. And then you said at the end that they are not the smallest and that you would tell us next time."

The teacher smiled. "You're correct as usual. Today, I will tell you about the smaller things inside the atom. Isn't that exciting?"

"Yes!" Olesya exclaimed.

Matt glanced at the girl and smiled, but his smile faded and turned into astonishment when he noticed the book she was reading. He walked toward her desk and picked up the book.

"May I?" he asked after he had already taken the book. *The Spider That Made the Cosmos Web* by Edward Purginger. He leafed through the book, adjusted his glasses, and glanced at Olesya. "This is brand new. It's just been published. How...? Do you understand what it says?"

She nodded, wrinkling her forehead. "It's in English."

The young teacher nodded broodingly, slowly put the book back on her desk, and returned to his desk, scratching his soft curls.

Children watched her with smirks on their faces. One boy sitting two rows behind her whispered loudly. "Know-it-all, brown-nose."

Olesya heard the boy but ignored him. It wasn't the first time a boy—or a girl—had tried to engage her in a quarrel. She had learned ways to escape their sharp tongues and prying eyes and to ignore their insults. Never quick enough with a clever retort, Olesya stayed silent and learned to be invisible. She cowered in her seat and hung her head.

You can't see me. I'm invisible. You can't see me.

The boy did not give up. At twelve, as the cool kid, he gave the impression that he was above caring about good grades and made a point of punishing brown-nosers whenever they made themselves too visible.

"Hey, weirdo. I am talking to you."

The boy tried to get Olesya's attention by throwing paper balls at her and chanting in a whisper. "Weirdo, weirdo, weirdo."

She ignored it until the boy, seeing no reaction, threw a pen at her, cutting her neck and drawing blood. A wave of sudden anger settled on her chest, pressing hard on it. With her eyes open wide, laboring to inhale, Olesya tugged at her chest, trying to get the weight off. When she heard the boy's spiteful rants continue while she struggled to breathe, her anger grew and the pain in her chest intensified, becoming unbearable. She spun and instinctively projected her hands forward. She blinked, thinking she was imagining things that weren't there. A silvery-blue globe formed in her hands, morphing into a wave when it surged out of her hands and hit the boy in the chest. The weight lifted instantaneously. She could breathe again, but the boy fell off his chair, and confused, he sprawled on the gray vinyl floor while the children laughed at his clumsiness.

Olesya scrutinized her hands. Her slender hands looked no different, and yet she had caused his fall without touching him. She fought the urge to repeat it, sensing they would consider her an even bigger freak. She had to forget this had happened and bury it deep in her memory, so she hunched back in her seat and buried her eyes in her book.

Upon returning from school, Olesya ran into the kitchen, threw her school backpack on the floor, and buried her face in Sasha's apron, sobbing quietly. Sasha, who stood by the kitchen sink washing vegetables, hugged Olesya with her hands dripping water, waiting for her daughter's sobs to subside.

"What is wrong, malenka? Did they bully you again?"

"Am I a weirdo?"

"Of course not. What makes you say that? Did someone say that to you?"

"Why am I different? Am I a monster, Mama?"

"You're not a monster..." Sasha's words trailed off as Olesya pulled out of her embrace and darted to her room.

Sasha sighed deeply and leaned against the kitchen counter. She then took her apron off, wiped her hands on the towel, and headed toward her daughter's room.

She knocked and called softly, "Malenka." She went inside and walked toward Olesya, who lay curled on the bed. Sasha sat by her daughter and stroked her head. "Listen to me. Everyone is different. No two people are alike in the entire world. Being different is not something you should be ashamed of. It's something you should be proud of. There will come a time when more people will appreciate your uniqueness. Ignore those who do not understand you and know that you are special. In a good way. In a very good way, malenka."

Olesya considered telling Sasha what had happened at school, but something stopped her. She turned her face toward her mother.

"It's okay, malenka moja. Everything will be okay," Sasha said, wiping her daughter's tears. Olesya sat up and folded into her mother's arms. Sasha stroked Olesya's head, rocking her gently. Before she left her daughter's room, her attention shifted to a large drawing that hung on the wall facing the bed. The more she stared at it, the more alive the web-like, colorful structure on a dark blue background seemed. "Is it new?" She asked, pointing at the drawing.

"Yeah. Do you like it?"

"I love it. It's so colorful and so different. What is it?"

"Cosmic web. It's the universe—"

"Wow! It is...beautiful..."

"This is how dark matter shapes the universe. You see, Mama. There is this invisible stuff everywhere. It's called dark matter, but it is not really dark. It's just invisible because it doesn't interact with light. But that is what our cosmos is made of. It's its backbone."

Olesya's eyes shone as she shared what she had learned from the book she had just read. Sasha listened, nodding. Her eyes gleamed too, listening to her daughter talk passionately about what was important to her.

～

Olesya survived middle school without further incident. The boy avoided her from then on. He called her a witch several times, but always from a safe distance, glaring and making a cross with his fingers. He never came close to her again, not even to make fun of her.

In high school, she developed a better strategy to stay unnoticed by joining a group of nerds. Well, she didn't really join them, as they didn't form an organized group. All the kids in that group did their own thing but stayed together for the same reason: protection from being singled out and bullied. She hasn't developed long-lasting friendships among them, but was safe to immerse herself in her studies and not be on the constant lookout for bullies.

Once though, she almost fell onto a path that would have put her in the spotlight her whole life. During her first weeks in high school, she tried different sports, and although she excelled in them all, they didn't spark any special interest until she tried track and discovered that running gave her wings. However, she soon learned it was something she would have to do on her own, unseen by others. Because she ran faster than anyone else. Much, much faster. When she tried track initially, she outran her peers by half a lap without even realizing it. Her classmates stopped running and just stood and watched her with their mouths open. She was glad nobody had phones to film her that day.

The coach and the principal tried to convince her to accept a prestigious scholarship and train for the Olympics. She declined. They wouldn't stop trying to convince her, seeing such amazing potential. Sasha stormed into the principal's office, demanding they leave her daughter alone. Olesya didn't know what Sasha had told them, but they stopped asking her. She was relieved and grateful that her mother hadn't persuaded her to take the scholarship, and she wondered why. Olesya didn't know then that Sasha had her reasons for her daughter not to be exposed to the attention of the media, doctors, and countless locker rooms.

9

SARA

NOVEMBER 2022

On an early November afternoon, Sasha, Lev, and Olesya stood in their living room, shrouded in melancholy and sadness. Olesya was leaving again to start her job at the University of Washington. She had returned home for two weeks after finishing her doctorate. But their time together quickly ended when the university snatched her for an important project.

Sasha wept silently, trying to smooth a non-existent wrinkle on Olesya's blouse or smoothing Olesya's long ponytail, stretching to reach it, as her daughter towered over her.

Lev leaned against the doorway between the kitchen and the living room, trying not to cry.

"My little genius is a doctor. Not just any doctor. A doctor of physics. My little Olesya." Sasha's voice broke with emotion.

"Mama, stop it. I'm not that smart. Not really. Just lucky and curious."

"You are the smartest person I know."

"I'm lucky, Mama. I love physics. It's all I can think about. It comes naturally to me, so it is luck. I even feel like I'm cheating a bit."

"Cheating? Nonsense. You've always had your nose in books. Luck has nothing to do with it. You like it. Sure. But you also study. All the time. I tried to get you to go outside to play with other kids, ride a bike, and be mischievous. Remember? You'd go outside for a minute and then sneak back in. That physics lab is lucky to have you."

Tears flowed freely from Lev's eyes.

"Dad, I'm not going very far. I'll visit often. I promise. Daddy? Don't cry. You'll make me cry."

"We're not sad, honey, but proud and happy for you. We're thrilled. My heart wants to jump out of my chest. I love you so much, baby," Lev said, in between sobs that ripped through his chest. "I was just hoping it wouldn't happen so soon."

Olesya arrived at the quantum physics lab at the UW for her first day at work as a leading researcher. After getting her visitor's badge from the receptionist in the lobby, she followed the signs to the ADMX Research Lab. Her destination was a sizable double door, by which she stood, straightening her blouse and her pants, reading and rereading an oversized sign above: ADMX Research Experiment, Department of Energy.

Olesya delayed opening the door, mustering all her willpower to stay composed. She needed to make a good first impression and not mess up this opportunity. This was her dream job. Before opening the door, she breathed in deeply and exhaled.

She took a few shaky steps inside the large lab and stopped, admiring the equipment stacked wall to wall, floor to ceiling. This task relaxed her and restored courage to continue. The physics lab was her environment; where she felt most like herself.

Several people, most in casual clothes and some wearing lab coats, stood by the electronic equipment or sat at desks scattered around the room.

A woman around fifty, who was talking to two other people at the far end of the lab, noticed Olesya and waved, nodding and saying something to her colleagues. The woman Olesya had guessed was Sara Mowen, the head of the quantum physics department and in charge of the ADMX experiment. Smiling, she approached Olesya with her hands outstretched in a welcoming gesture. Her shoulder-length blonde hair, tied in a ponytail, bounced as she walked, and her jeans and T-shirt spoke of casual comfort. A web of fine lines, suggestive of a ready sense of humor, surrounded her sparkling blue eyes.

As Olesya gawked at Sara's comfy T-shirt, her hand wandered inconspicuously to her blouse and unbuttoned the first two buttons.

"You must be Olesya. I am delighted to have you in my lab. I loved your paper on the compressed dark matter dimensional explosion. Kudos to you for being brave and imaginative. I couldn't put it away. I read it three times."

"You didn't think it was over the top?"

"One of the reasons I hired you, kiddo."

"Thank you. Doctor Mowen?"

"Sara. Call me Sara. There is no need for formality in my lab. They are just a waste of time and effort. We're all equal here. Well... unless someone screws up."

Sara burst into a wholehearted laugh. She stopped laughing and covered her mouth with her hand when she saw Olesya's expression. "Just kidding, kiddo. You can screw up. Just don't screw up big." Another laugh escaped her lips.

Sara's laughter eased Olesya's apprehension, and she relaxed enough to unclench her teeth and study Sara's face and body language, captivated and comforted by her genuine laughter and no-nonsense and unabridged approach. She found herself immediately drawn to Sara, as if she'd known her forever.

"Don't worry, kiddo. You'll get used to me. Everyone eventually does. Come on, I'll show you around. Pick a spot to call your own. We have had several desks available since last September. You know, the funding is so spotty that I can never fill all the vacancies. I'm so happy that I could afford you. At least for now." Sara laughed again.

Olesya followed Sara, who pointed out each piece of equipment and explained each one's function, although Olesya recognized most everything.

Sara glanced at Olesya. "Why am I showing this to you? You're already familiar with all the equipment, aren't you?"

Olesya nodded. "Most of it. But not all."

"Next time, speak up. Don't be too modest and don't be afraid to hurt my feelings by telling the truth. I'd rather not waste time talking if I don't have to."

"I will. I don't enjoy talking if I don't have to, either."

Sara regarded her intently. While Olesya held her gaze, something passed between them. Whether it was understanding, mutual respect, or fondness, or all combined, Olesya was uncertain, but when a tingling warmth spread through her chest, easing the tension in her shoulder and temples, she knew she had reached her home. She had felt apprehensive when offered this position, afraid her stiffness could alienate her new colleagues. Instead, she found herself in the company of a genuine, open-minded, and brilliant physicist.

"The support staff will set you up with everything you need once you pick your spot," Sara said and began to walk away, but paused only after a few feet. "You know, you arrived just in time. We're getting new microwave-detection equipment. It may be just possible to detect our dark friends soon. We are all very excited. Perfect timing. Welcome to our Axion team."

10

THE WOMAN IN WHITE

MARCH 2023

The party was in full swing. People held conversations, sipped drinks, and nibbled on appetizers served by khaki-clad staff. The entirety of the enormous room was filled with natural light, which filtered softly through the outside greenery before reaching the oversized windows. Olesya walked through the living room so slowly that she was barely moving. Muffled sounds of laughter, glass clinking, and faint music reverberated through the space in an unnerving dissonance.

A young man dressed in white was trying to get her attention. The guilt of not remembering him gripped her stomach. She stopped, trying to say something to him, but her dry mouth produced no sound.

A hand touched her shoulder. It belonged to a striking woman in a white dress that appeared as if it had come straight from a Roman statue. Her thick black hair cascaded over her slender shoulders in black waves. Olesya couldn't look away, mesmerized by the large black eyes staring at her intensely from the white apparition. The woman was nearing the end of her pregnancy. She said something unintelligible and extended her hand, trying to reach Olesya's face.

The young man suddenly appeared next to Olesya and intercepted the hand.

Olesya noticed a pendant on the woman's chest. Hanging low from a golden chain, barely fitting between her full breasts, it seemed too heavy for her or her outfit. Inside the pendant, a shiny black object sparkled, pulling Olesya in. She desperately wanted to touch it. She reached for it, and a piercing and intense whisper broke her stare. The woman was glaring at her, whispering. Suddenly, she understood her words.

"Go back. Go back," the woman whispered.

The whisper intensified and slowly transformed into a loud, piercing shriek. Olesya, transfixed by her eyes, couldn't look away. The woman's mouth was open wider than it should be.

Heavy and motionless, like a stone statue, Olesya fixed her eyes on the creature, watching her open mouth grow wider, longer, and darker. The darkness from her mouth extended, blanketing the woman's entire face. Then it spread into the room, enveloping it in darkness and changing its shape. The walls elongated, matching the woman's mouth. People didn't seem to notice, still engaged in conversations and laughter while the darkness swallowed them whole, one by one. Olesya's limbs became too heavy to move and escape the creature's pull.

The woman was now almost entirely enveloped in darkness. As Olesya's hands and then her body started disappearing into the thick darkness, her chest constricted under its pressure.

Suddenly, a hand grabbed her arm. The man dressed in white came to her rescue. She winced as his iron grip tightened on her arm when he yanked her from the woman's encroaching blackness and then hurled her toward a blinding light.

Olesya woke up gasping for air. She breathed in and out when she realized she was in her minimalistic bedroom and her recurring nightmare was over.

Olesya had furnished her bedroom and the rest of her apartment with modern furniture in light colors. There were no knick-knacks and no personal touches except for one photo of Olesya and her parents. In the photo, she stood between her parents on a lakeshore. Sasha and Lev both smiled, their arms wrapped around their daughter. Olesya was not smiling, but her eyes sparkled with joy. Her head rested on Lev's shoulder. The small family appeared close and happy.

She stayed in bed a while longer, taking a moment to relish the fact that she was secure in her apartment. The dreams were getting more intense and more frequent. As a child, she had them only every six months. Now, in the last year, the nightmares tormented her monthly. They had gotten so intense that one morning she had even considered a visit to a shrink, but as the day progressed, she'd felt foolish and dismissed her worries.

It was time to go to work. She dropped her feet into her slippers and shuffled to the bathroom. Her reflection in the mirror displayed dark rings under her eyes. Tired and shaky, Olesya stood still in the shower while the hot water warmed and relaxed her body.

She lathered her skin with soap and grimaced when she got to her arm. Her neck didn't stretch far enough to see the painful spot on the back of her arm, so she stepped out of the shower, dripping water on the tiled floor, as she hurried to the mirror. Unable to see anything through the fogged glass, she swore and yanked on a towel, tearing the hook out of the wall.

"That is just great!" She yelled at the wall.

She shuddered after examining the wall to discover she had pulled the sturdy-looking holder from the equally sturdy wall, as if it were a mere pin. Then she wiped the glass, glanced into the mirror, and gasped at the reflection of her arm. The four dark spots, spaced as if a hand had grabbed them. She tried to wipe the black spots away and cringed.

Olesya closed her eyes and recalled the young man from her dream, trying to remember which arm he had grabbed. She draped the towel around herself and proceeded to the living room, where she collapsed onto the sofa, indifferent to the water dripping from her wet hair and creating puddles on the floor. In her mind, she pictured the young man who had freed her from the white ghost in her dream, but his features hid behind a dark shadow. She had always believed she should know him. Not only from her recurring nightmares, but from somewhere else entirely. Someplace she'd long forgotten about.

Somewhere in the apartment, her phone rang, sending a jolt through her. She jumped up and scrambled to find her cell.

It was Sara, her boss, sounding out of breath. "Olesya? Where are you? Are you okay? You're never late. Well, I don't give a you-know-what that you're late, but get here soon. Something exciting happened."

"Hi, Sara. I'm sorry. I had a headache and slept in. I didn't realize it was so late. Be there in twenty."

"Okay, sleepyhead."

Olesya rose from the couch. Now that Sara had brought her back to reality, she felt silly overreacting about a dream. Sure, it was more a nightmare than a dream, but it was not real, as her scientific mind tried to convince her. She had probably bruised her arm somewhere and forgotten about it. It had probably become tender when she tossed in bed, and her mind had incorporated it into a dream. She dressed hastily and fled the apartment, not bothering to clean the watery mess.

11

WE DID IT!

MARCH 2023

Olesya entered the lab, surprised to find it empty. Remembering the excitement in Sara's voice, her pulse quickened as she hurried to the far side of the room to access the haloscope. The door to their most complex and expensive piece of equipment stood partially open.

The haloscope converted axions—the still hypothetical dark matter particles—into photons with its strong magnetic field, thus making them visible and verifiable. Everyone was very excited when they had installed the long-awaited new and more powerful microwave detection reader—MD reader for short—two months ago. They hoped the new reader would detect the photons and prove the axions made dark matter. They'd all celebrated their new instrument with champagne right here in this room, although it was against university policy. Sara didn't care that she could have gotten in trouble with Human Resources. Practically everyone had dreamy eyes, hoping the experiment they had been working on for twenty years would finally produce results.

With her heart pounding, Olesya entered the large, concrete-encased room where her coworkers gathered around a giant screen.

They pointed at the screen with feverish excitement, gesticulating and talking loudly over each other.

Sara noticed Olesya and rushed to her side. Her T-shirt was crumpled, and her uncombed hair piled in a messy bun. She caught Olesya's curious glance. "Yeah, I slept here. I had to. I had a feeling. Come and look at the MD reader. See for yourself. It's a historic moment."

Sara grabbed Olesya's arm and led her to the monitor. "Here. Tell me what you see."

Olesya scrutinized the numbers and graphs on the screen. She took her time, not showing emotion, while Sara waited, biting her lip and shifting her hands in the pockets of her jeans. At last, Olesya, certain of her evaluation of the results, regarded Sara with astonishment.

"Well?" Sara asked impatiently.

"It is definitely photons we detected. We finally know what dark matter is. You were right all along about the axions. This is unbelievable. You know you are a genius, Sara?" Olesya said.

"I'll take it. I feel like a genius today. We've been at it for twenty years, but it was worth it. Every minute."

"Maybe now we'll be able to figure out why dark matter is disappearing." Olesya said, looking into the distance with eyes full of hope and wonder.

"Now we tell the world," Sara said with dreamy eyes.

THEY DID IT!

MARCH 2023

The ambient light crossed the modern, bright kitchen, streaking the table where Zoe, leaning over her laptop and inhaling the aroma of coffee from a steaming cup in front of her, read the news. She gasped upon seeing the headline: *University of Washington makes the greatest discovery of the century, proving dark matter exists!*

The article continued: *The axion has been a candidate for the dark matter particle for nearly twenty years. A team of scientists from the University of Washington, led by Doctor Sara Mowen, will share their discovery and what it means for humanity.*

Without finishing the article, Zoe jumped from the table, knocking over her coffee. She didn't bother picking it up and darted upstairs. She ran fast, skipping steps, yelling the entire way to her brother's bedroom, which she bolted into without knocking.

"Sebastian! Sebastian! You've got to see this. Wake up. Wake up, damn it! They did it! They actually did it! They found it!"

Sebastian rubbed his eyes. "What? Who? Slow down. Found what?"

"Dark matter. They figured it out. Come on. We don't have much time. We have to fix this fucking mess before it gets out of hand."

Tall mahogany bookcases lined the four walls of the vast, windowless chamber. A majestic wooden table governed the center of the room, and masterfully carved chairs surrounded the wooden giant. Each chair was unique, carved into a different animal, with a head raised above as if to guard whoever sat in it. Sparse lighting left the four corners in misty darkness and made this old and mysterious room appear even older and creepier. This library served as Zoe and Sebastian's headquarters, where they met with others like them.

Several people sat at the table, and more were coming through the carved wooden doors. They seemed to know their places at the table and greeted each other with nods as they sat. Everyone in the room shared a few similar features. Just like Zoe and Sebastian, they all had black, wavy hair and dark eyes, and they all looked like athletes with their slim but muscular bodies. Seven women and twenty men sat around the table, conversing, and occasionally glancing at the eleven empty seats.

Silence, pregnant with anticipation, filled the air when Zoe and Sebastian appeared and sat at opposite ends of the table. Two wooden tigers guarded Sebastian's head. The head of a lion guarded Zoe's left side, and on her right side a lioness bared her teeth, daring anyone to approach. Zoe, who looked regal in her purple dress, tapped a gavel on the table, and everyone turned their heads toward her.

Zoe addressed her audience in a calm but assertive tone. "We have called this special meeting to address an important issue concerning everyone here."

She pointed a remote control at one wall. A giant flatscreen TV descended from the ceiling. She turned it on and continued speaking.

"I hope everyone is aware of recent developments in Seattle."

The TV showed Seattle television news footage, headlining the discovery and showing a photo of the ADMX team. Zoe stopped the prerecorded news on the team photo. She zoomed in on a woman's face—Olesya's face. Glancing around the room, Zoe scanned the faces with probing eyes.

"Does anyone recognize this woman?" Zoe asked.

Everyone looked at each other and then at Zoe and shook their heads.

"Why?" one woman asked.

"Look at her. Closely."

All heads turned toward the TV, then toward Zoe.

"You don't know her?" a man asked.

Zoe shook her head and pursed her lips.

"She looks like one of us. Is she? You haven't—" a man asked.

"No! That is why I am asking you," Zoe interrupted. "Who did it and how? I will find out if any of you did this. Better tell us now."

An uncomfortable silence filled the room as people shifted in their seats, glancing at each other and then at Zoe.

Sebastian glared at a man to his right. "Taylor, was it you?"

Taylor shook his head. "No. I wouldn't know how."

Sebastian stood up, stretching his lean and tall body in a cat-like move, and approached everyone seated at the table, asking the same question. No one said yes.

"Everyone. Somehow, we missed her before. Henry, find out who she is and follow her everywhere she goes," Zoe said.

She turned to a woman seated to her right. "Mary, find out everything about her relatives, friends, and coworkers. Anyone you can find who knows something about her."

"Should we bring her in?" Henry asked.

"No. Just follow her and report. Wait for further instructions. The meeting is over. Thank you, everyone. Till the next time." Zoe tapped her gavel on the table.

People started getting up and leaving, saying their goodbyes.

After everyone left, Sebastian walked to Zoe. "Do you think any of them did this?"

"No. But I had to ask and look them in the eyes to see if anyone blinked."

"Do you think there are other fragments like ours out there?"

"We searched. Remember? We found nothing."

"Perhaps in a different country? If it had happened to us, it could've happened to other people."

Sebastian observed his sister while she got lost in her thoughts.

"Don't you find it strange that we hadn't noticed her before?" Zoe asked.

"Could it be that she just looks this way? A coincidence?"

"A coincidence?" Zoe asked, turning her head toward Sebastian. Their faces were almost touching.

She observed him searchingly, then touched his cheek. "You didn't do it, did you, Sebastian?"

"How can you even ask?"

"It's been a while. It must be terribly boring to be around the same people all this time. Once you find someone you care about, they get old and die. No special one to share your life with."

"I didn't. And how would I? Did you? It must be even more boring for you."

"What's that supposed to mean?"

"You know what I mean. You've always been more adventurous and curious. I just follow your lead."

"If you stop getting me out of trouble, Mister Dependable, I'll be a quiet little hen and follow your lead."

Zoe nestled her head on Sebastian's chest. He wrapped his arms around her and kissed her tenderly on the head, sighing in resignation.

13

EXPLOSION

APRIL 2023

Monday morning, four days after the discovery of the nature of dark matter, Olesya squirmed in her car, stuck on the freeway. The traffic came to a complete stop, and sirens wailed in the distance, cutting the morning air like a pair of sharp scissors. She sighed and checked her watch, drumming her fingers on the dashboard, realizing she was late for work. Sara wouldn't care, but Olesya liked punctuality.

Her phone rang. Her car intercepted it and, on the line, people yelled, sirens wailed, and Mindy, the lab technician, sounding upset, shouted over the noise. It surprised her to hear Mindy, who was usually calm and joking around while fixing their lab equipment, sounding scared and upset. Olesya clutched the steering wheel.

"Olesya! Olesya! Can you hear me?"

"I can hear you. What's going on, Mindy?"

"Oh my God, Olesya. Oh my God. This is horrible."

"What's horrible? What happened, Mindy?"

"The lab is gone. Our lab is gone."

"What do you mean, gone?"

"Gone," Mindy said, sounding distant. "There was an explosion, and there's nothing left. The entire wing of the university is gone. The

50

entire building is gone. Nothing left! Only fire and smoke. There are fire trucks and police everywhere. It's horrible."

"Was anybody hurt?" asked Olesya, sinking deeper into her seat.

"I don't know. The building was already in flames when I got here. The police cordoned off the building. There are a few of us here waiting to talk to them, but Sara isn't here. She's usually the first one to come…"

"Do you think that she…"

"I don't think so. I overheard the cops saying that the explosion happened early in the morning. They said around four. Even Sara doesn't come to work that early. She's probably sleeping in today," she said and added in a low voice. "I've got to go. They want to talk to us now."

Olesya stared into the traffic ahead of her. She slumped into her seat, foreseeing that this might derail their discovery and destroy Sara. She had worked her entire life toward discovering dark matter.

14

PETER

APRIL 2023

A detective from the Seattle police station called, asking Olesya to come downtown and make a statement. He said it was a formality that everyone who worked at the lab had to go through.

Olesya had been expecting this after what Mindy had said. She was eagerly awaiting it, hoping to hear that they had found Sara safe and unharmed. Having received no messages from her in a couple of days, Olesya was worried. Not that they talked to each other daily, but she thought that Sara would have reached out to her by now to discuss recovering their research and continuing it. And she missed Sara. After calling her several times, getting no further than her voicemail, the knots in her stomach had gotten worse.

The police station was a modern glass building nestled among restaurants and businesses in a vibrant modern city that had risen to fame after a well-known producer filmed a blockbuster movie here and for its thriving music scene. From rock to grunge, Seattle's cafes, clubs, and other venues were always packed with music fans.

A uniformed police officer directed Olesya to a small room with a mirror covering one wall and a camera mounted above. A small, oval table in the center of the room had a water pitcher, plastic cups, and a box of tissues arranged neatly in the middle. She sat in a chair facing a woman in her early thirties and a man in his early forties.

"I'm Detective Peter Amberlite. Let me know if you need anything. Would you like a glass of water?" the detective asked in a rich and melodic voice, the timbre of which could loosen stomach knots.

"No, thank you. I'm fine."

"I'm sure you are aware of why you're here, but I must follow the protocol and tell you. At approximately 4:00 a.m. on April 4, there was an explosion at the Quantum Division of the ADMX Research Lab. You are here because you work there, and we must talk to all the employees to find out the circumstances leading up to the explosion. This conversation will be recorded unless you have any concerns. Do you have any concerns?"

"No, I don't. I understand you must talk to everyone."

"Thank you. Would you state your full name and your position at the lab?" Peter asked.

"My name is Olesya Solensky. I'm a senior research scientist. I started working at the lab approximately six months ago."

The detectives sat quietly, observing her. Olesya's hands became clammy under the intense stare of the woman detective, and she discreetly wiped them on her pants, shivering more imagining the wet stains, and worrying they won't dry before she had to leave.

"I'm Detective Laila Mayfield. Olesya Solensky," Laila said very slowly, playing and dramatizing with each word... "You started in that senior research scientist position six months ago. Is that right?"

"Yes."

"Does everyone start as a senior scientist when they first get hired?"

"I don't know. Never hired anyone."

"Right. Dr. Sara Mowen hired you."

"Yes."

"Were you her favorite employee?"

"Pardon?"

"It's my understanding that not everyone starts as a senior scientist, especially right out of college. I'm trying to understand your relationship with Sara Mowen."

"My relationship? Sara is my boss. If she hired me as a lead scientist, she must have had her reasons. Maybe because she was impressed by my dissertation. I really don't know. Why don't you ask her?"

"I understand your lab made a major discovery. A life-changing discovery. We are talking Nobel Prize level. As a senior scientist, you are second in command. The recognition, fame, and financial benefits following a discovery of this magnitude would be significant. I can imagine this could be an incentive to eliminate your rivals. Wouldn't you think so, Olesya?" Laila pressed.

Peter glanced at his colleague, and Olesya detected slight surprise in his eyes. Maybe even annoyance.

Olesya fidgeted in her chair and turned to Peter for clarification. "First impressions count, baby. Never underestimate your instincts," Sasha had ingrained in her. At first impression, Peter instilled a sense of security despite being her interrogator. "I am not following. What are you asking me?"

"When did you last see Sara?" Peter asked before Laila asked more questions.

"Friday evening. We had a party at her house, celebrating our discovery."

"I understand you were the very last to leave Dr. Mowen's house. Correct?" Peter asked.

"I think so. Why are you asking me this? Did something happen to Sara?"

The detectives sat in silence, observing her reaction.

"You were the last person leaving Dr. Mowen's house. Why? Did you wait for everyone to leave so you'd be alone with her? Did you have a disagreement? Were you jealous of her accomplishments, wishing it was you who was in charge and made the discovery?" Laila kept pressing.

"Are you mad? You have no clue. We are a team. It doesn't matter who is in charge. This is bigger than some small-town beauty contest.

If Sara had won the Nobel Prize, I would have been thrilled. She deserves it more than anyone I know. And why are you talking this way to me?"

"We have not been able to locate Sara. She is not at her house and is not answering her phone," Peter said.

"Nooo..." Olesya said, picturing Sara's burned body and cries for help. Sara had become her friend. With Sara, she had shared her wildest research ideas without being ridiculed. With Sara, she had eliminated the boundaries of her approach to scientific research. They were looking forward to the next chapter of their research on dark matter.

The possibility that she might never see Sara again dropped on her, as if the roof were collapsing on her. She sat unmoving, like a statue, staring at the wall past the detectives.

"No one has seen her since Friday. You were the last one to see her," Peter continued.

"Was she inside? Inside the building when it happened?" Olesya's voice trailed off, reluctant to finish asking and hear the answer.

"We are not entirely sure, but so far we have found no bodies from the building," Peter answered.

Olesya exhaled. "Did you check her beach cabin? She sometimes goes there to chill out."

Laila raised her eyebrows. "Why chill out? Was she stressed?"

"She didn't seem to be, but I don't know."

"We checked. She's not there either," Peter said.

"You don't think I had anything to do with her disappearance?" The young woman's belligerent questioning morphed Olesya's worry about Sara into an irritation, which unexpectedly eased her stomach-clenching dread.

"We are questioning everyone," Laila said with a smug expression, enunciating each word deliberately slow.

"It sounds more like an interrogation than questioning," Olesya said.

"Thank you, Olesya. That'll be all for today," Peter said with genuine sympathy.

"Do not leave town until we say it is okay," Laila added sternly.

"Let us know if you must leave town. We will work something out." Peter said, smiling as if he were trying to smooth things over.

"Where were you on April 4 at 4:00 a.m.?" Laila did not want to give up interrogating Olesya.

"Asleep in my bed."

"Can anyone confirm that?" Laila asked, smirking.

"Yeah. My vibrator."

Laila sent her a reproachful scowl. Peter almost chuckled and pretended to clear his throat to hide his grin.

15

GRAY CAR

APRIL 2023

Clutching the dry cleaner bag to her chest as she left the store, Sasha instinctively scanned the road both ways before getting back into her small SUV. She had developed this habit right after they had left Belyaska. The irrational fear that someone was watching her—following her—had constantly been lurking in her mind since they left Russia. The fear of being found. No one had ever followed her, as far as she could tell, but she was still watchful.

"You are being paranoid," Lev kept saying. "It has been a long time."

Her next stop was the bakery, where she bought a bag of baked goods. She smelled the bag full of rolls and smiled to herself. Sasha always bought the poppyseed rolls for Lev. Sometimes she went to great lengths to find them when the neighborhood bakery was out.

She loved seeing him devour the rolls, which he never grew tired of. Their smell reminded her of young Lev with a mouthful of poppy-seed rolls and another dozen rolls in before him. Never had her stomach hurt so much from laughing as when she watched Lev trying to shove yet another roll into his already-full mouth while

57

trying to talk and smile simultaneously. Chunks of the rolls had spewed out in messy white globs and ended up on the table and chairs and Sasha's hair as he laughed with her.

That was when they were young and full of hope and dreams. It was before the miscarriages, the tears, the pain, and the lost hope, and before their escape from Russia. They laughed at nothing and everything back then. They still laughed, but there was always a hidden worry creeping into their subconscious. Lev tried to minimize the threat for Sasha's sake, but they both remembered how resourceful and unrelenting their former government could be when motivated to find someone.

Sasha scanned the road, set the bag with the rolls in the back seat, and drove to her next stop: the grocery store. She absentmindedly pushed her shopping cart around and put random items in it, sensing something was wrong but couldn't put her finger on it.

Suddenly, she realized what was wrong. She was being followed. The same gray car parked behind her at the dry cleaners, the bakery, and now at the grocery store.

She raced to the cash register, pushing her squeaky cart and getting in front of other shoppers. Ignoring their angry stares, she paid and walked out of the store.

This time, she didn't look both ways, but got into her car and started driving. Only then did she dare glance in the rearview mirror, spotting the gray car two cars behind her. She gasped because she was certain it was the same car she had spotted after leaving the dry cleaners and the bakery. The same gray sedan had parked across the street from the grocery store. She was convinced it was that very car, but not sure if it was a coincidence.

Sasha merged onto the freeway, drove past her usual exit, and moved to the left lane ahead of a big truck without signaling. The gray car tried to move into the left lane, but there was not enough room between Sasha's car and the semi. The next exit was coming up. In the last second, Sasha, clutching the steering wheel, crossed two lanes and exited the freeway. The gray car did not make it.

Sasha exhaled. She could barely hold the phone with her shaking hand when she called Lev.

~

Olesya sat at a corner table of Café Kristina, holding a coffee cup, deep in thought, when her phone rang. Startled, she reached for the phone and, recognizing her mother's voice, answered with a sigh, knowing her mother had been worried about her since the explosion.

"Hi, Mama."

"Hi, baby. How are you? Have they found out why your lab exploded yet?"

"I'm fine, Mama. No, they haven't."

"Can I come and see you?"

"Mama. I'm okay. No reason to drive several hours to see me. I'll see you in July to celebrate your birthday."

"I really would like to see you now." She heard something in her mother's voice that made her pause. Her calm and level-headed mother sounded frightened, making her think it was more than just anxiety caused by the explosion.

"Mama, are you okay?"

"Yes, sweet girl. I'm okay."

"Dad?"

"Dad's fine. I want to see you, malenka. You know I don't mind driving. I love you."

"I love you too, Mama. If you really want to come, you know I always want to see you."

~

Olesya unlocked the front door and let Sasha in. Sasha smiled and hugged her girl. When a sob shook Sasha's slim chest, Olesya pulled back from her mother's tight grip and studied her face. With new wrinkles and more gray hair, Sasha appeared older and tired.

"Mama, what's going on?"

"Nothing. I'm okay, baby. I could use some tea. Let's sit down for a moment."

Olesya disappeared into her small kitchen, made tea, clanking the pots and cups, then carried the tray to her bright, modern living room and set it on her small and empty coffee table. Sasha settled on the couch, looking out the window. Olesya sat by her mother and handed her a steaming cup. Her normally easygoing and composed mother seemed sad and worried. Her hands trembled slightly when she took the tea from Olesya.

"Mama. What's going on? I can tell that something is wrong. I know you."

Sasha put the teacup on the tray and grabbed Olesya's hands. "It's the explosion. I was so worried about you."

Olesya observed Sasha, not believing a word. "Mama. Tell me, please. Are you sick?"

"I'm fine. Dad is fine too. Everything is fine. I just wanted to make sure you weren't hurt."

"I'm fine, Mama. I told you. It's over. No one got hurt."

"Was the explosion an accident? What did the police say?"

"They didn't say. Maybe they don't know, or they don't want to say anything while they are still investigating it. I don't know much more, Mama, but I'm okay."

The next morning, Sasha got up early and looked out the window of Olesya's kitchen. The gray shadows of early morning slid across the street, and Sasha shuddered. She shook her head, tiptoed to the living room, and watched Olesya sleeping on the couch.

Sasha quietly made coffee and poured herself a cup. She settled at the kitchen table, opened Olesya's laptop, and started reading the news, occasionally glancing at the couch and smiling. Suddenly, the smile left her face, and the blood drained from it.

Sasha got up, knocking over the coffee cup, which tumbled to the floor and broke, spilling coffee on the white tiles. The sound woke Olesya. She jumped up from the couch and rushed to her mother.

Still groggy with sleep, she sounded raspy. "What's going on? Mama? Are you okay?"

Sasha stood still, visibly shaken, staring at the laptop. Olesya followed her mother's eyes and landed on the laptop.

Sara's smiling face peered below the headline. "Doctor Sara Mowen, the ADMX project manager, is still missing. The police aren't sure whether the disappearance is related to the recent explosion at the research lab..."

"You said no one got hurt," Sasha whispered.

"No one got hurt, Mama."

"What about Sara, your boss?"

"Just because they don't know where she is doesn't mean she got hurt. They didn't find her body in the building. She might have gone somewhere on a whim. Sara is spontaneous."

Olesya saw panic in her mother's eyes. Distraught, Sasha rubbed her hands nervously. Having never seen her strong, pragmatic mother acting so scared and helpless, she felt a sudden need to protect her. Something was wrong. Something was very wrong.

"You didn't even know her. I'm okay. Nothing happened to me," Olesya said calmly, even though her heart was pounding so loud she heard it.

"You could've been in the building, working late. I could've lost you," Sasha whispered.

"But I was not. I'm here. What's up with you? You've been acting strangely. Tell me!"

Sasha opened her mouth to speak, but said nothing and bent down to pick up the pieces of the broken cup from the floor, avoiding Olesya's stare.

"Mama, leave that. What are you afraid of?"

Sasha kept picking up the broken pieces. Olesya touched Sasha gently on the arm, but she brushed her off. Olesya stepped away. Her mother never brushed her off. The next question barely passed through her clamped teeth.

"Mama. Do you have cancer?"

Sasha became still and then lumbered up from the floor and slumped onto the sofa, crying. She used the kitchen towel to wipe her tears, looked at her daughter, and patted the seat next to her. "Sit with me, baby. I have something to tell you."

Sasha told her only half of the story. The half where Lev sold government secrets on the newest technology of nuclear designs to Uncle Lech's friend Sergi Orlov to get passports and visas to immigrate to the States. Back then, regular Russian citizens could not get passports unless they had a reason deemed important enough by government officials to travel abroad. The government issued passports only to its agents and the best athletes who competed internationally and brought medals back home. It was also nearly impossible to get visas to the States, much less work visas like Sasha and Lev got from Sergi.

Sasha implied she never trusted that 'Orlov guy', as she called him, sneering at the memory of him. She told Olesya that the Russian government treated escapees as traitors and would sometimes search for them relentlessly, especially if they sold government secrets, as Lev had.

Then Sasha told Olesya that someone was tailing her, and that she was worried they had targeted Olesya by setting a bomb in the lab where she worked.

Olesya showcased a calm and indifferent expression for Sasha's sake, while anger and hate at people who threatened her mother stirred deep inside her, building up in her gut as Sasha told her story.

After Sasha finished and gazed at her daughter, Olesya took her mother's hands. "Mama, I don't think the Russian government had any involvement in the explosion. It's most likely faulty wiring or gas lines. As for the tailing, it may just be a coincidence. You saw a different gray car three times. You've never been good at recognizing cars, Mama. We left Russia ages ago. You mustn't worry so much."

Sasha met Olesya's eyes and nodded. Then she leaned deeper into the sofa, and her face relaxed as though she had let go of an overwhelming weariness along with the secrets she had held onto for a long time.

"You're probably right, baby. I worry too much."

"Just stay home and don't worry," Olesya said, patting her mother's hand. "Has anyone followed you here?"

"No. I was being careful, watching all the cars behind me as I drove."

16

THE PHOTO

APRIL 2023

It was mid-morning when Olesya started pacing her living room. She had grown restless from the interruption of her routine, her work, and her exercise regimen at the gym, just two floors below her lab. Since the explosion, just like her coworkers, Olesya had been on paid leave. Given the unprecedented occurrence, the university was at a loss about what to do with its employees. The ongoing police investigation prevented the lab's reestablishment. Olesya struggled with her inability to work and start the efforts to salvage their research. Needing a routine and to make things seem normal, she continued to go for a daily run. The speed, the rush of air on her face, and the burning muscles relieved her anxiety, and following a routine eased the stress that had been robbing her of her sleep since the explosion.

And now, her mother's visit had added more tension and unsettled her even more. After Sasha left, Olesya contemplated calling her father but procrastinated, delaying a conversation about the treason he had committed for his family. Her desire to discover what had happened to the lab and uncover who had tailed her mother, and why, only grew in intensity, but she didn't want to involve her parents. Even though the involvement of the Russian government in the explosion of an American science lab seemed far-fetched, something in her subconscious was nagging her to pursue this lead. Her stomach tied into a tight knot when she remembered Sara was still missing. Did the people who tailed her mother kidnap her friend? But why, and what was the connection to her mother?

While she was taking a shower after her run, a memory resurfaced so vividly that she had to hold on to the showerhead not to fall. She recalled a rushed visit to a remote cabin in the woods and meeting her Uncle Lech, who had just arrived from Russia, and the hushed conversation late at night between her parents and Lech. They had thought she was asleep, but she had just awakened from her nightmare and lay overhearing their conversation about the Russian government, people disappearing in Siberia, and Sergi Orlov, whom they spoke of in fearful voices. She was only nine, but she grasped that they had shared grave secrets and didn't want her to know about them.

Now, while Olesya finished her shower, she formed a plan. Then she dressed and hastily departed from the apartment. She hopped into her Jeep and started the four-hour drive to her parents' house in Walla Walla. There was something she needed to find in her parents' house without them knowing.

She called her mother and found out she had a double shift at the clinic, and her father was in Kentucky consulting on the design of a new nuclear plant. Olesya had nearly hung up, but a nagging thought since her last nightmare made her blurt out. "Mama, am I an only child?"

"What? Why?"

"No reason. Forget I asked. Bye, Mama."

The moment she arrived at her childhood home, Olesya dashed straight to the hall closet and removed the sheets and towels from the upper shelf. After she had cleared an area high by the ceiling, she pressed on the wall. It opened to a secret compartment. Her father had a knack for carpentry and was a master of concealment. If she hadn't known it was there, she would never have guessed. She smiled, remembering running into him while he was installing it. He had tried to hide it from her, but Sasha had said not to worry, insisting the girl was too young to remember. Olesya forgot nothing, but her mother didn't know that then.

Inside the compartment was a locked metal box, a little rusty on its sides.

Olesya searched her parents' bathroom for something to open it. She glanced in the mirror, and instead of her own face, she saw the face of the young man from her dreams; his mouth repeating two words: "Help me." He looked like her, only his face was thinner and paler. The box rolled out of her hand and landed on the tiled floor, breaking the lid off and spilling the contents. Olesya didn't even notice the mess she'd caused, transfixed by the face.

"Who are you? Where are you?" Olesya cried out in the mirror. "How can I help you if I don't know where you are? Tell me where I can find you."

His image disappeared, and her own pale face stared at her from the mirror. She backed away and slipped on a pile of old photographs scattered on the tiles. Staring at the photos, she remembered why she had come here. She kneeled and searched for a specific one and finally found it. It was a photo of a cabin in the woods in the remote part of the Okanogan-Wenatchee Forest that belonged to her Uncle Lech. She'd only been there once, when she was nine years old. Since then, her parents had never visited Lech, and Lech never came to see them. They had never talked about him since that time, and she had never asked why.

She turned the photograph over.

"Bingo!" she exclaimed. She remembered Lech saying he'd left directions to the cabin. And sure enough, she'd found handwritten directions to the cabin on the back of the photo.

Olesya drove her Jeep along a narrow, curvy road, checking the scribbled directions, until she finally turned onto a dirt road obscured by vegetation. She drove for a while and arrived at a cabin that looked like the one in the photo. She hesitated only for a moment before knocking. Lech opened the door. His eyebrows went up initially, but then he pushed the door open wide and welcomed her with a warm smile.

"Olesya."

"Uncle."

Lech's cabin was not large, but it was cozy. There was a wood stove in the corner, a country-style kitchen table, and four chairs. The small kitchen had the appliances and the counter space to make a holiday dinner. Olesya remembered their Christmas together in this cabin when they visited that one time. They made a family of snowmen, laughing and throwing snowballs at each other.

Lech emerged from the kitchen holding a tray with two steaming cups. He was older, but just like her father, he had aged gracefully. Still slim, Lech also had all his brown hair intact, with just a hint of gray at his temples. He put the cups on a small coffee table facing the sofa.

"Hot coffee."

"Thank you," Olesya said, taking the cup and holding it in both hands. "My mother told me my dad had traded government secrets for our freedom."

"Ah. She did," Lech said, probing her with his keen eyes.

"He was trying to improve our lives. I understand and don't blame him," Olesya said, her words fading. She procrastinated in asking him the next question. She stared inside the cup as if getting inspiration or courage and took a long sip of coffee before she spoke. "I must ask you something."

"Anything, Olesya. Just ask. You and your parents are my only family, and I would do anything for you."

"I need to learn everything there is about Sergi Orlov. Mama said you two were close friends."

"We were army buddies. Close? No, nobody's close friends with Sergi. He's complicated...and a bit of a loner."

"Tell me everything you remember. What he likes, dislikes, and what drives him. I want to know all his favorite places. What women does he like? Anything you can think of."

Lech tilted his head. "Why do you need to know that?"

"Someone followed my mother. I want to know who and why."

"What makes you think it has any connection to Sergi?" Lech's voice sharpened.

"Who else would follow my mother?"

Her uncle didn't answer right away, but observed her with penetrating eyes. "You're not going to do anything stupid, are you, Olesya? Sergi is dangerous, but the Russian government is even more so, and Sergi might even be in cahoots with it. He is ambitious, and, as smart as he is, he realized early on that being part of the government can lead to immense power and wealth."

"I just need information. To protect myself and my parents. What does he look like? Describe him. I need details."

Lech studied her for some time. Olesya sensed he was trying to decide whether to tell her anything or to warn her parents that she was contemplating doing something reckless and dangerous. Her uncle didn't know her personally, but she guessed her parents appraised him of her life regularly and that he was aware she'd think things through before jumping into danger.

She suspected he recognized her determination as something more substantial and permanent, and not a fleeting moment of anger, because he relented.

Lech sighed. "All right. I don't think I can persuade you otherwise. But be careful. He is very smart...brilliant, really...and can be dangerous. He can sense a trap a mile away."

Lech wandered to a small bookcase, removed a few books, and searched for something in the back. When he turned around, he held a small box, similar to the one her parents had stashed in the secret compartment, and opened it, searching for something. When he found it, his face changed, and his eyes lost their clarity and softened. He handed it to her after a long moment of staring at it. Then he cleared his throat.

"One remaining photo from the special forces training. It was a while back, but I doubt he has changed much."

Olesya took the photo and stared at the face of the man who played such an important part in her parents' and her life. Shockingly handsome, Sergi stood by Lech, their arms around each other's shoulders. His piercing blue eyes pulled her in like magnets and into a memory of a different time and place. She saw herself sitting on a blanket spread over emerald-green grass and a blond man with piercing blue eyes staring at her from above, with the wind blowing the trees behind him. A chilling shiver traversed her spine as the powerful feeling of recognition and unsettling familiarity brought on by Sergi's eyes became stronger the longer she kept staring at the photo. Lech watched Olesya with growing concern.

"Be careful. He is...he can be very charismatic."

17

THE SUSPECT

APRIL 2023

She didn't sleep well, dreaming of drifting in the air in a circular room and trying to escape it. Every time she thought she had found a way out, Sergi's face appeared, sending her scurrying away. Once she realized sleep would not return, she climbed out of bed and made coffee, trying to forget her dream.

She was brushing her teeth when the doorbell rang. Surprised because she never got visitors, she spat the toothpaste out and slowly approached the door, expecting the worst—news of finding her parents or Sara injured or dead. She peeked through the peephole and saw the distorted image of detectives Peter and Laila standing in front of her door. Her hands trembled as she opened it.

"What happened? Did you find Sara?"

Peter answered quickly and in a gentle tone. "No. But we'd like to ask you a few questions."

"Come on inside."

"We would like you to come to the station instead," Laila said coldly.

"Why? Can't we talk in here?"

"No, come with us," Laila said, businesslike.

"Okay. No problem. I've got to get my jacket and my keys. Be right back." She said, as calmly and indifferently as she could, while her heart wanted to jump out of her chest.

If something had happened to my parents or Sara, they would have told me already, she reassured herself.

Laila drove the unmarked police car. Olesya stared out the window, uneasy, guessing why they were taking her to the station. The anxiety grew stronger as they drove.

Peter kept turning and glancing at her. She sensed his glances and held his gaze. It was then that she truly noticed his deep blue eyes. Kind and honest; calm on the surface like the ocean before a storm, but hinting at a restless passion locked inside. Peter had eyes you could get lost in. And she almost forgot about her worries, forgetting even that she was in a police car driving to be interrogated by the woman detective who seemed to have a grudge against her.

Then Laila turned and gave her a disdainful look. The kind of look that made you believe you were guilty, even if you were not. Olesya averted her eyes and kept them glued to the window until the ride's end. The knot in her stomach tightened as she explored the reason behind the effect Peter's eyes had and Laila's hostility.

Peter opened the door to the police station for Laila and Olesya and then disappeared somewhere. Laila grabbed Olesya's arm and held it in a powerful grip while escorting her to the interview room. Olesya eyed her arm and then Laila.

"Is this really necessary?"

"Yes, keep walking. This way," Laila's tone chilled the air.

Laila opened a small interview room. The windowless room did not inspire confidence, painted in a gloomy dark gray with a shiny black table in the middle and a mirror spanning one wall. Laila pointed to a chair and then sat across the table and stared at Olesya in silence. A few seconds later, Peter walked in and sat beside Laila. Smugly, Laila pushed a box of tissues toward Olesya.

Olesya pushed the box back at Laila a little harder than was necessary. "Why am I here?" asked Olesya.

Laila opened her mouth to speak, but Peter interjected. "We want to ask you to participate in a lineup."

"What? What do you mean?"

"It will just take a few minutes. You line up with—"

"I know what a lineup is. Why?"

"A credible witness observed a woman matching your description outside the physics department minutes before the explosion," Laila said, glaring at Olesya. She didn't even try to hide her suspicion and dislike.

"This is insanity. I was nowhere near the lab that night."

"We have a witness who saw a woman fitting your description. Don't you think that is strange?" Laila asked, enunciating every word deliberately and carefully, and by doing so, she iced her tone even more.

"You're just throwing accusations at me, hoping they'd stick? Why would I destroy the research if I wanted to take credit for the discovery? Why get rid of my rival then? How does this make any sense? Why would I do something so dumb?"

"That's what we are trying to find out. Why? Perhaps it was a subterfuge? Maybe you tried to sell it to the highest bidder?"

Olesya shivered as if a gust of cold air had blown in her face. She glared at Laila, trying to come up with an appropriate comeback and say something clever that would get the detectives off her back, but her mind was blank. Laila's suspicions and accusations were getting serious. Olesya realized this was over her head and she needed help.

"I will say nothing or take part in any lineups until I speak with my lawyer," Olesya said.

Peter leaned back, appraising her. "Do you have a lawyer?"

"No. I've never needed one. But I'll get a lawyer. A good one. One who will call you out on your shady police practices and your bullshit. So, since I won't be answering any more of your questions, I'll be leaving. Now." Olesya stood up, glaring back at Laila.

Peter nodded in agreement, but Laila did not hide her disdain and disappointment. She picked up a file from the table and slammed it down.

Peter clenched his jaw.

"It would be better for you if you cooperated with us willingly.

Hiring a lawyer makes you look guilty. It won't be the same anymore," Laila snapped.

"No more talking. Lawyer," Olesya replied.

"We must follow all leads, Olesya. This is just a formality that we must go through. A few minutes and it'll be over. Come on. I'll escort you outside," Peter said, getting up.

Peter walked with Olesya to the exit, leaving Laila still sitting at the table, shaking her head. Olesya turned her face to Peter. Peter watched her with sympathy and gentle attentiveness, as if Laila's conduct embarrassed him.

"Any word on Sara?" Olesya asked.

"No. I'd have let you know."

Olesya followed Peter with her gaze, expecting something more.

Peter understood her unspoken question. "There have been no bodies recovered from the building, and there won't be," Peter said quietly, searching her eyes.

Olesya sighed with relief but blinked under Peter's stare. "Thank you, Peter."

After Olesya left the station, Peter turned around and approached Laila, who was talking to another detective. Peter waited for her to notice him, but she acted as if she's not noticed him.

"Laila. Can I talk to you?" Peter finally asked, clearing his throat.

"Can it wait?" Laila sounded uninterested.

"No."

"Why do you look so angry?"

Laila followed him to his office, which he had upgraded to from a cubicle along with his rank as a senior detective two years ago. He shut the door behind her.

"Nice performance there, Laila."

"Thank you?"

"It would have been nice to know ahead of time that we were playing good cop/bad cop. I would have been all sugar and honey."

"She is guilty, Peter. She did it. And even if she didn't, she knows something. I can feel it. Instinct tells me—"

"Instinct? You have been on the job for how long? Six months.

Instincts? You develop them through years of experience, sweat, tears, and hard work. Don't give me that bullshit."

Laila folded her arms and glared at him, tapping her foot. "I can have instinct without experience. That is what instinct is. Gut feeling. And my gut tells me she is guilty or knows who did it."

"Because of your gut feeling, we might have lost our chance to have a real conversation with her. She is wary now. Any good lawyer, or even a mediocre one, would laugh at us. We have nothing on her or anyone else. We still don't even know if the explosion was intentional or accidental. From now on, I will interview her, and you will follow my lead. You will sit quietly and observe and not make a peep."

"You can't do that."

"Sure, I can."

"What if I don't oblige?"

"Well, I can simply tell Margaret you didn't work out as a detective. I can tell her you would be better off at a different job. Not everyone can be a detective. Your probationary period is not over yet. Don't forget."

"You would not."

"You don't think so? Take your chances. I don't want a partner with whom I must argue about every little thing. Looks like you and I are not in harmony. Not yet, anyway. Close the door on your way out."

18

ORDINARY COUPLE

APRIL 2023

Zoe sat down in a white leather chair at a small desk by an oversized window, scrutinizing an old black-and-white photograph and tracing the face of a young man with her fingers when her phone rang. She picked it up without looking at it and kept looking at the photo.

"Hi, Henry. What have you got?"

"Not much. Nothing interesting anyway. She goes to the university, the grocery store, and she must really like her coffee, as she is a frequent guest at downtown coffee shops. Normal stuff. She doesn't seem to have friends or a boyfriend."

"But there is something. I can hear it in your voice. What is it?"

"The cops questioned her. Twice."

"Anything else?"

"Nothing else for now. Oh, her mother visited her. Should I continue following her?"

"Yes." Zoe dropped back into her chair, gazing into the distance, past the Japanese garden and past the meandering stream. She sat quietly for a few minutes, thinking. She then reached for her phone and pushed a button.

"Hi Mary. Anything on Olesya Solensky yet?"

"She was born in Belyaska, Russia. Her parents immigrated to the States when she was just a few weeks old. Sasha, her mother, is a nurse and works at a local clinic in Walla Walla. Her father is an engineer. He works at a nuclear power plant in Richland. Ordinary couple."

"Do you have photos of the parents?"

"Yes. I am emailing them now."

"Thanks. Anything else?"

"Not yet."

"Keep me posted. Ah. I almost forgot. Dig up her birth certificate. Thanks."

Zoe slowly put her phone away and opened her laptop. She typed "Belyaska, Russia" into a search engine, finding very little information. There were no photos, restaurants, places to see, population details, or even hotels. She searched some more, but nothing came up.

Zoe opened her email and found Mary's photos of Sasha and Lev. Her eyebrows knitted when she studied their faces. Sasha had dark blonde hair and blue eyes; Lev had brown eyes and brown hair. They looked nothing like their daughter. Or the other way around—Olesya did not look like her parents.

Zoe fumbled for her phone and pressed a few buttons. "Have the plane ready for tomorrow," she said and listened for a moment. "Belyaska, Russia."

19

LINEUP

APRIL 2023

I t was a sunny and hot April day. Temperatures above eighty degrees Fahrenheit were unusual for the Pacific Northwest at this time of year.

Olesya wore a white, short-sleeved blouse and light khaki pants. She was sweating just walking the few blocks to the police station from the parking garage. Olesya's lawyer, a well-groomed and well-dressed man in his early fifties, accompanied her to the station. Baffled and slightly envious, Olesya eyed her lawyer, who wore a suit and tie but didn't seem uncomfortable, as though the heat didn't bother him. He still appeared immaculate and energetic. Although glad he looked presentable for the cops, Olesya felt her cheeks flush, eyeing his dark, constraining attire.

When they reached the station, Olesya's lawyer swung the door open for her.

She grabbed his arm. "Richard. Are you sure I have to do this?"

"Yes. You do. Otherwise, we would have had to jump through more hoops. But it's not a big deal. It's just a formality to get them off your back. Once you do, they will have to back off. You were not there that night, so you have nothing to worry about."

"They have been treating me like a suspect from the beginning. Especially that woman detective. I don't know why."

"They have been playing good cop/bad cop? Not very inventive and immature. It tells me that their backs are against the wall."

Olesya and Richard sat on a bench and waited for someone to escort them to where they needed to be.

Peter appeared after a few seconds as if he had been waiting for them.

"Olesya! Thank you for coming," Peter said, smiling.

Olesya's shoulders tensed, peering past Peter. Just imagining the surly look from Laila caused her hands to get clammy and her heart to beat faster.

"Detective Laila had another engagement today," Peter said, as if he had read her mind. "Please follow me. This won't take long."

Peter directed Olesya and her lawyer to a narrow hallway and opened another room where a woman in a police uniform was waiting. Noticing the woman's pursed lips and the official uniform, Olesya had a cornered animal's desire to run away.

"I will take it from here, Peter. Thanks," the officer said, inviting Olesya into the room in a practiced manner.

When Olesya walked inside, her hands started trembling, her body shook, and her lips twitched. She failed to understand her sudden, primal fear. She was innocent, and yet she felt guilty.

"When you enter this room, you will stand where I tell you to stand. You will be told when to turn right and left. Otherwise, stand still and face the mirror on the wall. You will not talk to or interact with other people in the room. Questions?"

"No, let's get it over with."

The officer led Olesya to a room where three other women stood facing a large mirror. Despite their young age, the slim brunettes appeared worn-out and subdued. Olesya stood amidst the lineup and stared at the floor for a few harrowing seconds, willing her hands not to tremble and her lips not to twitch. And when she faced the mirror, she was calm and composed, knowing Peter watched her from the other side.

Across from the mirror, in a dark room, Peter, Richard, and an older man stood facing a glass window spanning an entire wall. Below the window, a small table held a console with a row of buttons. The four women gazed at them from the opposite side of the window. Each woman held a large black number.

The door opened, and Laila entered, avoiding Peter's eyes. Peter balled his hands into fists, but said nothing to her in the witness's or the lawyer's presence. Laila stood by the window, her eyes moving between the older man and the mirror, avoiding Peter.

Peter pointed to the window and addressed the man. "Please take your time and let us know if you recognize the woman you saw on April 4 at 4:00 a.m. on the street facing the UW's physics lab by calling her number. You must be sure of your selection."

"All right." The man kept his hands in his plaid jacket pockets while throwing quick glances at the women.

"They can't see you. It is confidential. They don't know who you are," said Peter.

"All right."

The witness studied the women from left to right. He still didn't seem comfortable. "I'm not sure," he said.

"Take your time."

"I just don't know."

As Peter pressed a button on a console, the women turned once more, but his witness shook his head.

"I don't know. I saw her for only a second. I paid more attention to my dog. You know, the reason I was out is that Astor, my dog, had to go," the witness said, lowering his voice and winking at Peter. "You know, he had the runs. He must've eaten something bad, poor fella—"

"But if you had to choose?" Laila asked with a sly smile.

Peter sent Laila a scolding glance.

"I would say it would be number three. But, like I said, I'm not sure. She just comes closest," he answered.

Olesya was the one holding number three. Laila smiled triumphantly.

"Are you sure?" Peter asked.

"No, I'm not. But if I had to pick one."

"Thank you for your help." Peter pressed another button, and the door opened to an officer waiting outside. Peter said to the officer, looking at the witness. "Escort the gentleman outside, please."

"Richard, please wait outside for a moment?" Peter asked.

"Sure. I'll wait." Richard sounded cross.

Soon after Richard and the witness left, Peter glared at Laila and opened his mouth to speak, but she beat him to it.

"What? No statement?" Laila asked, appearing enraged. "You just let him go without confirming what he'd said?"

"Yes. He was not sure. We don't push witnesses to choose. It was something you should've been aware of already. This was very unprofessional, Laila."

"He picked her. You are not going to dismiss it, are you?"

"What is it with your dislike of her? Is it because of the one that got away? The first case you were on? That woman accused of murdering her daughter...what was her name? Sam? Samantha something. Is that it? You are fixating on her because she reminds you of her? Or is it personal? Has she stolen one of your boyfriends or girlfriends, or whatever? Why do you hate her so much? It is obvious, and it doesn't come across as just a good cop/bad cop scenario. It goes deeper than that."

"What the fuck? Are you for real? I don't know her, but I sense she is guilty as hell. She is slick. She is manipulative. Have you ever looked her in the eyes? They are malevolent. He recognized her. I could see that he kept looking at her. It was obvious!" Laila said and backed up a step, searching Peter's face. "But you didn't see that because she's got you fooled. What, do you have a crush on her?"

"Watch it. I warned you!"

"Or what? Gonna whine to Margaret about me? You know I can talk to her too and tell her you're behaving unprofessionally because you have feelings for the suspect."

"Stop! Last warning. Or you will find yourself somewhere else. And Olesya is not a suspect, only a person of interest, just like all the other lab employees. I will interview Olesya without you from now on. And I do not have a crush on her...I do not!"

"You will regret it. She is evil," she snarled.

Peter shook his head and left the room, shutting the door with a thud. Laila uttered a frustrated sound and wrapped her head in both hands.

Olesya and her lawyer sat on one side of the table, speaking in low voices, waiting for the detectives to arrive. The door opened, and Peter walked in. Olesya glanced past Peter and exhaled, relieved that Laila was not with him. Peter sat across from them.

"Do you have results from the fire marshal yet?" Richard asked with confidence and wit.

"Well, kind of."

"Kind of? Do you have it or not?"

"According to the fire marshal, there is no evidence the explosion was man-made," Peter droned.

"And yet you've harassed my client, questioning her repeatedly, and putting her through the lineup without the evidence the explosion was intentional?"

"There's no evidence that it wasn't."

Richard glowered at Peter, as if he were trying to assess his truthfulness or mental state.

"The fire marshal found no natural cause, eliminating the obvious faulty wires or broken gas lines. Until we are certain of what caused it, we must explore all the possibilities and interview everyone. And if we must do it repeatedly, we will. A woman matching your client's description had been observed at the scene shortly before the explosion."

"Unless there is more evidence of foul play, I must ask you to stop contacting my client."

"Another issue requires your client's cooperation."

"Oh?" Richard sounded concerned.

"We are also investigating the disappearance of the lab employee."

"The missing woman? Sara Mowen?"

"Yes, Olesya was the last person to see her."

"Do you have evidence of foul play?"

"Not yet."

Olesya's heart was racing hearing Peter confirm Sara was still missing. She'd hoped they'd found Sara safe and unharmed and that the heaviness deep in her stomach would finally lift. She realized her suspicion that her friend's disappearance was her fault was irrational, but couldn't shake the impression that she was at the center of what had happened: the explosion, Sara's disappearance, and her mother's tailing. If she knew the reasons, perhaps she could find Sara.

Peter observed Olesya.

"My client answered all your questions to the best of her ability. She's told you what she knows and has nothing to add. Do not contact her again without new evidence. And when and if you do, go through me." Richard got up, motioning for Olesya to follow.

Peter angled his head, gazing at her. "Thank you for your cooperation, and I am sorry if the lineup was uncomfortable. If you think of anything that might help us find Sara, this is how you can find me. Anything. Anytime."

Peter gave Olesya his card, ignoring Richard's glares. Olesya nodded and took the card but said nothing, in a hurry to leave. The humiliation and the stress of the lineup left her with an odd desire to cry, shout, and laugh all at once. What she didn't desire was to talk to anyone, especially Peter. She fought the unexpected urge to gaze into his eyes and left without even a glance in his direction.

20

BILL, PLEASE

APRIL 2023

Olesya slammed her laptop with a sigh. Her search for Sergi Orlov did not produce results. As if he didn't exist. She fished out the photograph her uncle had given her and studied his face for a long time, then asked in a high-pitched voice. "What do you want from me?"

She didn't believe the Russian government was after them, sensing this pursuit was personal. Sergi was after something. For a moment, she'd entertained the thought there was a connection with the information her father had sold to Sergi, but then dismissed it. It was many years ago. What her dad gave Sergi was now outdated and irrelevant. She'd have to tail her mother's followers to find out why they stalked her. Perhaps they would even lead her to Sara.

Olesya crammed some clothes into a small backpack and then walked to the door, but she remembered something and ran back to the closet, taking clothes out and throwing them onto the floor. Finally, she found the electric taser her father had given her following a brutal attack on a woman jogging in Ravenna Park, where she usually ran. She tossed it into her pack and glanced at the pile of clothes and shoes on her bedroom carpet and hesitated. Her hands clenched and unclenched, desperately wanting to put away the clothes. But she adjusted her backpack, pictured herself cleaning the mess while she ran downstairs, skipping steps to the parking lot and her Jeep, heading to Walla Walla.

When she arrived in her hometown, she rented a hotel room and an inconspicuous silver sedan, leaving her Jeep in the hotel's underground parking lot. She decided not to call her mother, fearing that her phone, her mother's phone, or both were bugged. A small convenience store nearby offered a small selection of burner phones. She bought one and drove to her parents' house, parking the sedan two blocks away.

She spent the rest of the afternoon and into the evening in the car, but saw no strange gray cars or people on the street. Starving, not having eaten anything since breakfast, and desperately needing a bathroom, she drove off, planning to return in the morning.

A neighborhood pub seemed like a good idea: one in an old Western style where she could disappear among strangers and get something hearty to eat. The place was busy, but several stools were available at the far and dark end of the bar. She made herself comfortable on one and ordered a cheeseburger and fries, which she seldom ate, as she was trying to follow a vegetarian diet. *Tonight is not a vegetarian night,* she convinced her guilty conscience, and her mouth watered in agreement.

Most people were watching a baseball game playing on large monitors scattered throughout the large pub. Some played pool, some darts, and some just talked, but nobody paid any attention to her. The food made her sleepy, and her head started bobbing until someone sat on the empty stool next to her. Olesya adopted an unavailable and disinterested attitude to avoid being picked up by an adventure seeker, as it frequently happened whenever she ventured out into a bar by herself. She continued reading the news on her phone, waiting for the bartender to bring the bill.

Her drowsiness vanished, and her pulse raced as she heard the man beside her order a drink, speaking with a heavy Russian accent. Olesya flagged the bartender with a nearly invisible hand gesture, imploring him to hurry with the bill.

"What are you drinking, young lady? Can I buy you a drink?" Her stool neighbor asked.

"No, thank you. I'm leaving," Olesya answered, without looking in his direction.

She paid the bill with cash and left the bar tense, but faking coolness, and avoiding looking at her neighbor. Outside, she exhaled deeply, reasoning with herself that it was just a coincidence. Many Russians lived in Washington State, and many lived in Walla Walla.

She peeked through the window, only seeing his wide, muscular back and shaved head through the window that was fogged on the inside with the warmth of the people and the steaming food.

Recalling the description of the car that followed her mother, Olesya searched the parking area for a gray sedan but saw none among the SUVs and big trucks. Exhaling, she walked to her rental car, but instead of leaving, she sat there, waiting for the man to leave the bar, hoping to get a good look at him and maybe even follow him if he appeared suspicious.

After half an hour of waiting, she could hardly stay awake. The drowsiness brought on by the greasy cheeseburger and fries returned with a vengeance. Thinking fresh air would wake her up, she put her taser in her pocket, left the car, and walked around the parking lot. That is when she saw him come out of the pub, accompanied by another man. Muscular and clothed in black, they walked shoulder to shoulder, like great black cats on a hunt. They seemed heavy, but their steps were surprisingly light and springy.

When she heard them speak Russian, she became more suspicious, and her hand wandered to the taser in her pocket and wrapped around it. She didn't take it out. She could handle one of them, she thought, but not two. They appeared as though they would not be easy to overpower, even with this super-powerful taser that her father must have gotten through some not-so-official channels.

She ducked behind a big truck and watched them cross the street into a vacant bank parking lot. They vanished from her sight in the dark. Olesya, hiding behind trucks, snuck across the street and then planted herself flat against the building, and soon a gray Lexus pulled out of the darkness. Olesya peeled herself off the building and had just enough time to memorize its license plate before the Lexus turned suddenly and headed straight toward her. She jumped sideways, but not far enough to avoid it. It hit her on her side and sent her flying into the ditch.

The Lexus drove off with its wheels squealing. Olesya picked herself up and hobbled to her car, holding her side. She drove to where the Lexus had disappeared, but she saw no cars. She refused to give up and drove around the area in circles, searching while thumping her hand on the steering wheel. An hour had passed when she finally accepted that they were gone and pulled over to the curb. She rested her head on the steering wheel and exhaled, rubbing her side. *I fucked up. They've spotted me and are aware now.*

21

THE CRATER

APRIL 2023

Zoe's private plane landed at a small, decrepit airport in Belyaska, Russia. The door opened, the steps pulled out, and Zoe stepped out. Carrying a small backpack and wearing a comfortable hiking outfit, she looked as if she was headed for a safari in the Russian tundra.

A green Jeep-like car pulled up, and a young man jumped out and greeted Zoe. Just like Zoe, he had black, wavy hair and black eyes. Elliot was her trusted ally in Russia and other Slavic nations. He spoke most of the Slavic languages, having been born in Prague and having a knack for languages. His forte was finding information and diplomacy, resolving conflicts with the help of his sense of humor, good looks, and charming personality.

He handed Zoe a set of car keys. She shifted her glance from the green car to Elliot, doubting his better judgment. The old machine had more dents and chips than paint. One door was gray and patched with something unappealing. "Really?"

"You told me to get you something to blend in. In this Lada, you won't get any attention from the locals. It's great off-road and has a lot of power. I got you a room at the local hotel. Not great. Well, that is an understatement, but it's the only one in town."

Zoe took the keys from Elliot ostentatiously and rolled her eyes. She threw her backpack onto the passenger seat. The car started right away and sounded powerful. Zoe rolled the window down and waved at Elliot.

"It runs. It will do. Thanks, Elliot."

"Stay out of trouble," Elliot said, and waved back.

The next morning was cloudy and laden with chilling moisture when Zoe opened her ground-floor hotel room. Before she stepped outside, she glanced right and left. In desperate need of paint and repairs, the one-star Baikal Hotel appeared old and neglected. The "k" was missing from the sign by the entrance, and the colors had faded until they blended with the slate clouds above. Moss covered the roof, while tape and cardboard patched many of the windows. Not much pavement remained in the parking lot, giving way to weeds, which filled the many cracks and reached for more.

Zoe, wearing a hiking outfit and carrying her small backpack, was locking her door, ready to head for her car, when a woman rolling a screechy cart with cleaning supplies nearly bumped into her, stopping just inches away. The woman was in her forties, wearing a dirty blue apron and a scarf with bright red poppies on a black background. She looked at Zoe with eyes and mouth wide open.

Zoe questioned her with her eyes, but getting no reaction, shrugged, walked toward her car, and drove off while the woman stood frozen, watching her.

Zoe drove through a run-down residential area in the small town, which seemed to have been forgotten by time. The heavy clouds magnified the town's gloom and neglect. Houses where people still lived cried out for repairs and paint, but most were deserted and crumbling. What was the reason so many houses were boarded up and forsaken in one town?

The smartphone alerted her she had arrived at her destination— a small abandoned house, which was Sasha and Lev's old home. The glass was long gone from the windows; the paint had mostly peeled from the walls, and the caved-in, mossy roof rendered the old residence gray and dismal. She walked around the crumbling structure, struggling through the chest-high weeds. She tried to go inside, but the front porch rotted away. When she peeked through the windows, she saw dark emptiness, smelling of mold and decay. A raven dashed out of the window and flew toward the forest, revealing an overgrown pathway.

Zoe obeyed her intuition and followed the shiny black guide, moving through the thicket effortlessly like a cat on the scent of prey, and soon she found herself in an old forest. She ambled for a bit, but not seeing anything of interest, she turned to go back. Noticing a clearing ahead out of the corner of her eye, she turned around to explore it. When she reached it, she gasped at the sight.

She stood on the rim of an enormous crater that extended several miles across and nearly 250 feet down. Devoid of vegetation, the crater's jagged black and gray rock looked uninviting and threatening. The eeriness of this dark chasm dropped goosebumps on her arms that prickled her flesh like icy needles.

"I'll be damned."

Zoe walked along the edge, snapping photos, straining to see the bottom, and seeking a way down. The edges were too steep, and the rock was too sharp to descend alone and without climbing gear. She continued walking along the edge with her eyes glued to the crater and nearly collided with an eight-foot chain-link fence topped with double barbed wire. Intrigued, she tried to peek inside, but green metal strips woven into the fence blocked the view.

Zoe followed the fence, looking for an entrance, and stopped, noticing a gate. A heavy padlock secured the gate against unwanted visitors. She rummaged through her pack, taking out a lock pick. It took her only a few seconds to unlock it and open the gate. She entered cautiously and looked around. The ground was disturbed, with trenches filled with monitoring equipment and a concrete building hinting at hasty construction with mismatched concrete blocks and metal sheeting.

She started walking toward the building but paused, hearing a deep growl. A huge black German Shepherd ran toward her, his white teeth bared in a deep growl.

Zoe, startled by the noise, stood alert and ready, but seeing the dog, she relaxed and waited. The dog continued running toward her. His growl intensified, and saliva dripped from his mouth in a white foam. He jumped at her, resting his enormous paws on her chest. But she didn't lose her balance; she stood still and calm even though his huge white fangs were only an inch away from her face. Locked in a stare at each other, they stood in total stillness. Then the dog stopped growling, dropped, and licked Zoe's hand.

"Hi, friend," she said to the dog.

She touched the dog's head. The dog responded by inching closer, wanting more attention. He sat by her side, looking at her with his big brown eyes, stirring dead leaves and dark soil with his tail.

"My friend. You have three choices. You can stay here, come with me, or you can be free," Zoe said, pointing at the open gate.

The dog stared at her as if he were considering his options. He got up, gave Zoe another tail wag and a toothy smile, and bolted to the gate. At the gate, he looked back. Then he was gone.

Zoe smiled and continued surveying the area, snapping photos of the building and the monitoring equipment. Then, she walked around it, looking for an entrance. The windowless structure had one door that was locked with a keypad. She inspected the unfamiliar and electronically complex keypad and shook her head in disappointment—she lacked the skills to open it without triggering an alarm that might bring in the owners of this secluded compound so close to the ominous crater.

Zoe's private jet awaited at Belyaska Airport, with steps extended and the door open. Elliot stood leaning against his car and scrolling through his smartphone, and seeing her arrive, met her halfway to the airplane.

Zoe gave him the keys and a thumb drive. "Hi, Elliot. Here. You can have this piece of shit back."

"You didn't like your ride?" asked Elliot, grinning. "What's this?" Elliot asked, holding up the thumb drive.

"I found something, but I need your help. I need more information. It's all in there. Find out as much as you can and let me know. ASAP! Oh, and I want the report in person."

Zoe walked toward the plane, which ascended shortly after she climbed inside and slid into her leather seat.

A woman in her forties entered the Belyaska Police Station. The uniformed officer managing the reception area waved her into the office of Detective Roman Saranski, as the worn-out sign on the door announced. His large, red, potato-shaped nose stood out in his pale, meaty face. His longish yellow hair resembled a pile of soiled straw on top of his balding head, as if he had recently awakened from a night of disturbed sleep in a barn.

He motioned for her to sit. "How is the hotel business these days?" he asked.

"I'm surviving."

"What can I do for you, darling?" asked Roman.

"I have seen a stranger who doesn't belong here," she said, pouting.

"You did? Who did you see?"

"I saw a strange woman staying at Baikal. I took a good look at her when she was leaving her room."

"Strange how?" His eyes sparkled upon hearing Svetlana's story.

"She had the weirdest eyes I've ever seen. They were so dark and creepy. The way she was dressed and looked, I gathered she was from somewhere far away. She didn't belong here."

"What did she look like?"

"I can do better than that. I took a photo with the phone you gave me."

"Smart girl. Show me."

The woman fumbled through her purse, found the phone, and passed it to him. He glanced at the photo and nodded with approval, squinting his beady eyes. "This is good, Svetlana. Very good."

He selected a few bills from a drawer and handed them to her. "You know what to do if you see her again?"

She nodded, snatched them, and left, stashing the bills in her purse and holding it close to her belly. She scooted out of the station with a big grin on her face.

Roman grabbed his cell and dialed without looking at the dial pad, which would have been fruitless anyway, as the numbers had rubbed off years ago. He talked to someone in a subservient tone. "This is Detective Saranski from Belyaska Police Station. A trusted resident reported a strange woman with black hair and eyes staying at a local hotel. I have her photo." Roman listened for a while, nodding his head.

"What's that? A terrorist? Will do. Right away, sir," Roman said and then listened, nodding. "Just the local area? Will do. Will do. Thank you, sir. Thank you very much."

22

GRAVEL MINE

APRIL 2023

Zoe and Sebastian sat at one end of the table in their library with only a few of their most trusted members by their sides. Mary sat close to Zoe, and Henry sat by Sebastian. Two others huddled by Henry and Mary. They kept quiet, glancing at the main entrance as though expecting someone. Then Elliot came through the door, Zoe exhaled, and the others focused their attention on her.

"Elliot. Thanks for coming. What have you got for us?" Zoe asked.

He handed a small external drive to the man sitting next to Mary. Mark, one of Zoe's oldest confidantes, plugged it into a computer. The screen was already up and, after a short while, displayed the photo of the compound Zoe had found in Belyaska.

"I didn't find much," he said.

Zoe regarded him with cold eyes. Elliot seldom failed to find information.

"Oh?" Sebastian sounded disappointed.

"We don't have anyone in the Russian Foreign Intelligence Service anymore since the plane crash a few years ago."

"Do you have anything?" Sebastian asked coldly.

"What makes you think it has something to do with the feds?" Zoe asked.

"The keypad. It's standard FIS. And according to the labels on the monitoring equipment, it belongs to FIS too."

"Thank God for bureaucracy." Zoe smirked.

"What are they monitoring for?" Sebastian asked.

"Radiation. Heavy metals. Biomolecules."

"What metals?" Zoe's eyes sparked with interest. She approached the screen and zoomed in on the monitoring equipment.

"I don't know," Elliot said, shrugging in a frustrated and apologetic gesture. "Everyone is tight-lipped and dismissive about this area and the entire town of Belyaska. I tried all my sources, practically everyone I know in that area, and got nowhere."

"That's interesting. What about the Solenskys' neighbors? Family?" Zoe asked, continuing to gaze at the screen. "What do they say about them?"

Elliot let out a gigantic sigh. "No close family. The father's cousin, Lech Solensky, lived in Moscow, but he vanished without a trace years ago. I tracked down two neighbors and Sasha's coworker at the hospital."

"And?" Zoe asked impatiently.

"The neighbors described them as a quiet, ordinary couple who were nice, hardworking, and kept to themselves. Nobody knew anything about a child or Sasha's pregnancy. Nobody heard about Olesya Solensky."

Everyone became quiet and watched Zoe as she turned around and walked back to her chair. She sat staring into the distance, gathering her thoughts, tapping her fingers against the table.

"What about the crater? What do the locals say it was?" Zoe asked.

"They all say it was a gravel mine that stopped operating years ago because of an accident."

"A gravel mine? How can anyone think that? Looks nothing like it," Zoe said, raising her eyebrows.

Sebastian walked over to Zoe, seized the remote from her hand,

and zoomed in on the crater. He stared at it for a moment, then shook his head. "I agree. It looks nothing like a gravel mine. Looks like a bloody crater!"

"No one remembers it operating, but they insist it was a gravel mine," Elliot continued, nodding in agreement. "No one seemed suspicious. Of course, there are no records of the mine or the crater. It is as if this giant bloody hole in the ground does not exist. And the people in that town are...strange. Well, the whole town seems strange."

"Strange how?" asked Zoe.

"Well, it is like all the people in town are keeping a secret. I can't explain it, but it felt like they all belonged to a different century. They look at you strangely. The town was creepy, and I am not easily creeped out."

"Hmm. I noticed that too," Zoe said pensively.

"The cousin...is there a death certificate for him?" Sebastian asked after a pause.

"I have found none. Like I said, he disappeared without a trace," said Elliot.

"And you think that the Russian government might have played a role in his disappearance?" Henry asked Zoe.

"The thought crossed my mind. Given where the Solenskys lived, it is possible," Zoe said. She contemplated for a while, then turned toward Mary. "Did you find her birth certificate?"

"I found a copy of her birth certificate that she submitted to schools in the States. It's a fake," Mary said, grimacing with distaste. "It states she was born in Belyaska on September 20, 1999. However, there is no record of her birth in Belyaska or anywhere else in Russia."

"Hmm. We are going to have to do something different," Zoe said. "When are you going back?" she asked Elliot.

"I'm not in a hurry. Unless you need me to go sooner."

"Yes, I want you to fly back ASAP. I need you to set up a meeting for me."

FIND HER

MAY 2023

Peter was sitting at his desk when a uniformed police officer knocked on his door.

"Come in. What is it?"

"There is a woman at the front desk reporting her daughter missing."

"Send her to Missing Persons." Peter sounded slightly annoyed.

"Well, I thought you should listen to her, since you are investigating the disappearance of Sara Mowen."

"Oh?"

"It is Sasha Solensky. She claims her daughter has disappeared."

Peter got up so quickly that his chair tipped over and landed with a loud crash. "I will go get her. Thank you, Andy." Peter felt embarrassed at sounding annoyed.

As Andy left his office, Peter was right on his heels. He saw a woman standing by the front desk, her trembling hands clutching the counter. "Olesya did not get her looks from her mother," he mumbled to himself before approaching her.

"Sasha Solensky?"

"Yes. Who's asking?" Sasha replied resolutely.

"I'm Detective Peter Amberlite. I'm investigating the explosion at the lab where Olesya works. Please follow me to my office."

Sasha sat across the desk, focusing her blue eyes on him so intensely that Peter felt pressed into his chair. The red and swollen eyes emphasized the paleness of her face.

"Tell me what happened," Peter asked.

"Olesya, my daughter, is missing," Sasha said, her voice failing her.

"Why do you think she is missing?"

"I've been trying to call her for three days. It's not like her not to call me back. She always does. I've filled her mailbox with my voice-mails. I couldn't take it anymore, so I drove to her apartment. She wasn't there."

"When was the last time you spoke to her or saw her?"

"I visited her a week ago."

"Did she seem distraught? Different?"

"Well, I think the explosion upset her. But she didn't seem especially down or anything."

"She might've lost her phone."

"She would've let me know somehow. Olesya is very responsible and caring. She's my entire world. And now she's missing. Find her, please." Sasha started crying again.

Peter observed Sasha with genuine sympathy. Her slight Russian accent grew stronger as she became more upset.

"Could she have gone away with her friends or a boyfriend? Perhaps she's having a good time with her friends and forgot to call you," Peter said.

Sasha's eyes seemed even more pained.

She shook her head. "Olesya doesn't have any friends. Or a boyfriend."

"She must have someone she confides in?"

"Me and her father. But mostly me. You must understand something about Olesya. She's brilliant. School and work are her life. She's not very good at social interactions. Not that she's shy; she just doesn't seek friends. And people rarely choose her as their friend."

"How so?"

"She lacks the patience to engage in conversations not centered on her work or interests. Small talk. Come to think of it, she was getting along with Sara, though. I've heard her laugh when she was on the phone with her."

"Really? That's good."

"Yeah, that surprised me, too."

"Where is her father now? Isn't he worried?"

"He's away for work. I didn't tell him. Didn't want to worry him yet."

"When you were in her apartment, did you notice a suitcase missing? Clothes and things like that?"

"No. I told you; she wouldn't go anywhere without telling me. Something happened to her. Her car is still at the apartment."

"I'll look into it. I promise. Give me your contact information. Here is my card. Call me anytime if anything comes up. Could you write your number down for me, please?"

Sasha wrote her number on the pad Peter placed before her. She finished and regarded Peter with her solemn eyes. "Did you find her boss? Sara?"

"No. Not yet."

Sasha seemed as if she were ready to burst out crying. Peter eyed the box of tissues, ready to push it thoughtfully her way, but Sasha, instead of crying, straightened her back and glared at him with eyes as cold and unforgiving as a steel blade. "It has been two weeks since Sara went missing, and you haven't found her. But you had time to harass my daughter in the meantime. Now she's missing too. I'll find my own way out of here."

Peter slumped in his chair and sighed with frustration, looking out the small window onto a modern, colorful glass building across the street until Sasha's note sparked his attention. He grabbed the pad, scrutinized the note, and shook his head in astonishment when he saw below Sasha's number, scribbled, with the letter "X" crossed out and replaced with a "Y," a license plate number. He tore the page from the pad, grabbed his coat, and dashed out of his office.

Peter placed the piece of paper on the desk of a young officer. "Matt, run this for me, please. ASAP. Call me as soon as you find out."

Peter ran toward the door, but stopped, remembering something, and waved at the two detectives talking to each other nearby. "Have you seen Laila?"

Both detectives stared at Peter, rubbing their chins. "I don't think I've seen her today or yesterday. I thought she was doing something for you."

"For me?"

"That's what she said the other day; she left in a big hurry."

"The other day? What day was that?"

"Tuesday. Three days ago."

"Three days ago? Is that the last time you saw her?"

"I think so."

"Do me a favor and ask around if anyone else has seen her. Call me the moment you know something."

"Sure thing," he drawled and added hesitantly. "So she's not doing anything for you?"

"I've got to go. Call me if you see or hear from her," Peter answered as his stomach constricted in panic. He pulled his phone out and called Sasha.

"Sasha? Please don't hang up. Can you let me into Olesya's apartment? It's important," Peter pleaded, and then listened to Sasha and started shaking his head. "I'm only going to look around and won't take anything without your permission. I promise. I might notice something you've missed."

Peter listened and smiled lightly. "Thank you, Sasha. I'll be there in half an hour."

24

DUNGEON

MAY 2023

Olesya woke up disoriented, with a headache throbbing at the base of her skull. She touched her head and felt stickiness but could not see very well in her confusion and the murkiness surrounding her. Once her eyes had adjusted to the darkness, she discovered she was not in her bedroom but in an unfamiliar place that smelled old and musty. She tried to remember what had happened and recalled her disappointing trip to Walla Walla. Two straight days of sitting two blocks away from her parents' house and following her mother to work proved fruitless except for the humongous bruise on her hip. She never saw the gray Lexus again. She returned to Seattle to talk to Peter, prepared to beg for any information he was willing to share with her regarding the explosion or Sara's disappearance.

But she never got around to talking to Peter.

The last thing she recalled was walking on the sidewalk across from her apartment right after she had returned from Walla Walla. *I led the Russian thugs right to me.*

Olesya sat up, fighting nausea. A few feet ahead, a faint flickering light outlined the iron prison bars and cast their shadows on a dusty stone floor. The old mattress and the worn-out blanket and pillow gave off the stench of mold and something sweet and metallic. She immediately thought of blood and rolled off the mattress, letting out a tiny shriek and an expletive.

She jerked up when she heard a faint voice. "Olesya? Is that you? Are you okay?"

"Sara? Is that you?"

"Yes, it's me. Olesya, are you hurt? I saw them carrying you. I was afraid you were badly hurt or dead."

"Are you okay? Have you been here all this time?" The relief that her friend was alive made her forget for a moment that she was in confinement.

"I'm okay, considering. You know, I'm not sure how long I've been here, not having a watch. I've lost track of time. That's a new one for me." Olesya heard Sara laughing.

Even now, she can still laugh.

Suddenly, the spooky place seemed brighter. Sara was alive and still laughing.

"Where are we? What's this place? It is like an old dungeon. Who are the people who brought us here?" Olesya couldn't contain her anxiety.

She heard Sara shuffle closer to her cell and whisper. "I'm not sure, but I think they blew up our lab."

"Why?" Olesya whispered back. She walked to the bars and wrapped her hands around them.

"I don't know. I think it has to do with our research," Sara whispered.

"But why?"

"I don't know, kiddo. I'm just guessing from what she asked me about."

"She? Who is she?"

"The woman who kidnapped us."

"A woman? What woman?" Olesya raised her voice, and Sara shushed her. Was she from the Russian government, one of Sergi's cronies, or someone entirely different?

"I don't know who she is," Sara whispered.

"Have you seen her? What the hell does she want from you? Or me?"

"I saw her once. Briefly. They walked me to some enormous, dark room that reminded me of a giant, old library, and she asked me a few questions, but I couldn't see her very well, though she was tall and dark. She wanted to know everything about our research and if I'd saved any data on the cloud. It sounded like she didn't want the results to be out there. That is why she destroyed the lab."

"But why? It makes no sense. We'd shared our findings with the entire world," she said and then paused. "I guess they won't be shared with anyone now."

"I don't know."

"Did she hurt you?"

"No. But the food at this establishment sucks." Sara hesitated, then lowered her voice even more. "She also asked about you."

"About me? What did she ask?"

"She asked if I knew who you were."

"Who I am? I don't understand. I'm a nobody."

"I told her you were brilliant, but that is not what she wanted to know."

"What did she want to know?"

"Something strange. She asked if I knew who you were and if...if I made you."

25

YOU ARE MY NIGHTMARE

MAY 2023

Olesya woke up hearing Sara's jolly voice, feet shuffling, and metal clanking.

"Oh, wow! A bowl of…something brown. I bet you had to go all the way to Paris to get this gourmet dish. You are spoiling me. But don't wait for the tip. The service wasn't great."

"Don't get used to it. You may not get it tomorrow," a man's voice replied.

Olesya heard a dish clanking on the stone floor. Seconds later, her cell opened. Two men were standing by the entrance to her cell.

"Let's go! Get up!" one man said.

"Where are you taking me?"

"You'll find out soon enough. Move it!"

Olesya rose from her mattress and studied the two men for a second. They appeared strong and agile. She'd have to wait for another chance to escape.

She grew claustrophobic, sandwiched between the two men as they walked through a narrow, winding corridor, passing other cells that vanished into darkness. The dim, flickering lights on the walls stirred shadows and moldy whiffs from the dark corners. Carved in old stone, the place looked like an ancient dungeon. She felt the breath of the guard on her neck and shivered.

The passage ended at stone stairs leading to a heavy wooden door reinforced with metal bars. As they approached, the doors opened into a dimly lit room. The man behind Olesya pushed her inside, and a bookcase concealed the door that closed behind them.

Behind the ironclad door, the tall room turned out to be a library, where gold-engraved books, giving off a musty scent, filled every corner. A majestic table surrounded by carved chairs dominated the heart of the library. A couple, a man and a woman, sat at the table observing her.

Sebastian's mouth dropped when Olesya entered. Zoe motioned for the guards to leave the room. They disappeared without a sound through a large, carved double door on the other side of the room.

"Come closer," said Zoe, her tone commanding.

Olesya heard Zoe's authoritative tone and stepped back. The woman's features hid in the shadows. The few sparse lamps on the walls provided little light, shrouding the table and the people who sat by it in ghostly obscurity.

"You are the crazy bitch who kidnapped my friend and destroyed our lab? Who the fuck are you? What do you want from me?"

Zoe rose from her chair and approached Olesya. Olesya could see her now and cold chill spread from her neck to her spine when she recognized her. She stepped back, pressing against the bookcase while an ice-cold calm descended upon her. She felt her face slacken with dread, and soon after Zoe's eyes brightened.

"You know me? How?"

Olesya couldn't find her voice.

Sebastian walked toward them. "How can you tell she knows you?" Sebastian asked.

"I saw it in her eyes. She recognized me."

Olesya flailed her arms, fighting for balance, as the blood abandoned her brain, leaving it in eerie chilliness, and with blurry vision. Sebastian clasped her hand and led her to a seat at the table. She didn't protest.

"Sit down and have some water. You look like you were about to faint."

Sebastian poured water into a glass and set it down before Olesya. Then, he approached his sister. Zoe and Sebastian stood facing each other. A while after the change, they realized there was yet another benefit to their transformation—they could talk to each other without using words. As Olesya watched them communicate silently, an unsettling sensation of déjà vu pushed her stomach contents uncomfortably close to her throat. She shivered, not sure if from fear or the chilly dampness of the old library.

"She is beautiful and looks just like you. She could be our sister," Sebastian said.

"Don't be foolish. She might look like one of us, but she is not. Obviously, she can't be."

"She is not in good shape," Sebastian said, glancing at Olesya, and his lips curved into a sympathetic arch. His eyes softened, resembling black velvet.

As Zoe observed Sebastian, her expression hardened, and her lips twisted into a disdainful grin. "She seems beautiful to you. Do you like her?"

"Come on. I don't even know her. But she doesn't look good. Perhaps we should call Brown?"

"She doesn't need a doctor. She is well enough to talk."

"Olesya! Look at me!" Zoe yelled and snapped her fingers in front of Olesya's face.

"Where do you recognize me from? Talk!"

Olesya hesitated while searching Zoe's face. Yes, that was the woman from her recurring dreams. She was staring at her nightmare.

"From my dreams," said Olesya.

"From your dreams?"

"Since I was a child, you have been in my dreams. You were my nightmare."

Zoe stepped back. "What was I doing in your nightmares?"

"Screaming and pulling me into your darkness."

"My darkness?" Zoe grimaced. "Who are you? Who made you?"

"Who made me?" Olesya tapped her chin, trying to understand the question. "My parents?" She said slowly, to buy some time. It occurred to her that this woman might be crazy, and she should indulge her rather than antagonize her.

"You really don't know, do you? I guess I'll have to ask your parents."

Here it was again. The feeling from a long time ago, she thought, was behind her. The building anger and the weight on her chest that needed release. Olesya jumped up from the chair and darted toward Zoe. When she was near, she thrust her hands at her nightmare, shouting. "Leave my parents alone!"

Zoe staggered backward but didn't fall.

Hit by an echo from the past, Olesya leaped back into her childhood when she pushed the boy off his chair without touching him.

Zoe didn't seem surprised. "Is this the first time this has happened to you?" she asked, piercing Olesya with her bottomless eyes. "No, it is not, but you can't control it," Zoe guessed.

Zoe thrust her hands at Olesya. The familiar silvery-blue wave headed her way and hit her chest before she could react. She fell hard onto the stone floor.

"Who are you? What do you want with me? And what the fuck was that?" Olesya cried out, more out of humiliation than the dull pain in her chest. Zoe didn't push her hard.

Sebastian hurried to Olesya to help her up. She brushed him off.

"Olesya. Calm down. We are just trying to understand where you came from," Sebastian said calmly, pleadingly. "You said you recognized my sister from your dreams. We just want to understand where you are from. Look at us. The three of us. What do you see?"

Olesya stared at Sebastian and then shifted her gaze to Zoe, taken aback that she hadn't noticed the remarkable resemblance before. She saw Zoe's face in her dreams, but her mind had dismissed the likeness.

"We look...similar. Like we're related somehow," Olesya whispered.

"We're not related. But I'll find out who made you," Zoe snapped.

"And that was kinetic energy that you and I possess. It can be a powerful weapon if you know how to control it."

Zoe let out a sigh. "I'm not getting anywhere with her. She knows nothing. Not even that she was not like other people, or that she possessed this immense power."

Zoe knocked on the double doors. Two guards entered as if they were waiting for the knock.

"Take her back," Zoe barked.

"No! Let me go. Let Sara go. Why are you keeping her? What do you want with her, you sicko bitch?"

The two men started walking toward Olesya. She thrust her hands at them. Nothing happened. Disappointed, she stared at her hands while one man grabbed her arm. She flinched and tried to free her arm, but he only gripped her harder and dragged her through the hidden door.

Olesya screamed through her gritted teeth. "You'll pay for this! The cops will find me. You'll see!" The monster door shut behind her, cutting off her screams from her intended audience.

On the way to her cell, Olesya was quiet, trying to understand what had happened and why her powers hadn't worked on the guards at all. It was time to understand what was happening to her body. Was it anger that fueled it? Was she not angry enough?

When the guards pushed her into her cell, her friend was already asking her question after question.

"Are you okay? What happened? What did they do to you?"

"I'm okay. She did nothing to me, but I sensed she was dangerous. We must get out of here!"

"I've inspected every goddamn inch of this cell and found no way to escape. The walls are thick and sturdy. I've spent weeks in here, and not even a mouse found its way in here to keep me company."

Olesya stared at her hands as if she were seeing them anew. If she could control her anger and funnel it into a deliberate and precise attack, she might be strong enough to overpower the guards.

"What time do they usually bring food?" Olesya asked.

"I'm not sure. I'd guess around eight in the morning and then three in the afternoon. Why? You're not planning anything foolish?"

"We must try, Sara. I'm creeped out by this place and that woman. I'm afraid she might be crazy. She seemed to think that I was hiding something. When the guards come, distract one of them. I think I can overpower one of them. One at a time."

"Overpower? How? That sounds insane, Olesya. You are not a fighter unless you are keeping a secret from me. Do you have a black belt in martial arts or something like that?"

"Something like that," Olesya said. "Trust me. We must try."

Olesya was pacing her cell when she heard Sara's cell door open. She stood still in the center of her cell, waiting for the guard to come.

"Hey. Wait. There is something strange in my bowl. Gosh, it is gross! Come here and see. Tell me what this is," Sara said, sounding genuinely distressed.

"I don't see anything. You are imagining things."

Olesya's cell opened, and the other guard entered, carrying a bowl of food. He put it on the floor inches away from Olesya's feet.

"Here it is. See?" Sara asked.

"There is nothing here!" the man answered, sounding annoyed.

Olesya concentrated, building up anger at the kidnappers, and thrust her hands forward, sending the guard flying onto the bars. He hit his head and cursed. The other guard came running, and when he saw his buddy on the floor, reached for his gun with one hand, extending the other to his buddy while glaring at Olesya.

"What the fuck?" he yelled.

She thrust her hands forward, but the guard only staggered, remaining on his feet. The other guard got up, holding his bleeding head.

"Are you all right, mate?"

"I am okay," he answered, glowering at Olesya. "Crazy bitch!"

26

THE INFORMANT

MAY 2023

Zoe stepped out of her private plane at the small airport outside the city limits of Moscow. Elliot greeted her and swung open the door of a black SUV. She slid into the back seat. Elliot got into the driver's seat and drove with the ease of someone who has been driving for years and enjoys it. He took corners fast but with expert smoothness.

"All set? No problems?" Zoe asked.

"He is ready for you," said Elliot. "He is not..."

"One of us? No, he's not."

"Why?"

"Some people should only have one lifetime."

The SUV drove through the streets of Moscow. Zoe looked out the window, admiring the old buildings they passed on their way. No matter how hard she tried to be prepared and to avoid it, nostalgia always snuck up on her when she came to Europe. She missed European cities, the old rivers, and the countryside. But only some-times. Other times, they suffocated her with their oppressive history, as if the old sorrows and sufferings surfaced from the deep stains embedded in the old stone to torment her. In those moments, she wanted to run away screaming. But there were days like today when the sun was out, bathing the old buildings in soft light, enhancing their elegance and beauty rather than hiding them in tired shadows, and the trees were in bright spring foliage, so that the melancholy brought on romantic overtones instead.

Zoe had left Europe because it was easier to disappear in the States, she'd told her group when she moved her headquarters to a town northeast of Seattle. But there were other reasons, too painful to discuss. Only Sebastian and Mary were aware of them, and Elliot suspected it.

Elliot drove, ignoring Zoe. He knew her well enough to approach her when she was in her nostalgic European mood.

They arrived at an old gray building and drove through a massive metal gate flanked by Russian flags, stopping by an enormous double door. Two uniformed men escorted Zoe and Elliot inside.

They entered a big, high-ceilinged room lined with portraits of Russian leaders and windows spanning the entire length of one wall. A majestic desk with legs skillfully carved into lion feet proudly displayed a lustrous gold samovar. Zoe sighed with admiration, having a penchant for samovars, and then shifted her gaze to a small, bald man sitting in a red leather chair, his shiny head barely visible behind a colossal desk. Two sizable lion heads carved on each side of the chair made him appear even smaller. But the small man didn't know that—he couldn't see himself. He got up and greeted Zoe with an exaggerated bow. She fought not to laugh at the comical gesture. Fear mixed with respect and admiration reflected in the man's small gray eyes when he gawked at Zoe, inviting her to sit.

"It's a pleasure to see you again, Zoe," he said, trotting back to his chair.

"Pleasure is mine, David. What have you got for me?"

"This is top secret." David shifted in his chair.

"That is why I am here. You have my full attention, discretion, and appreciation," Zoe said with a pleasant but commanding voice, putting the emphasis on the last word.

"It is a rather complicated story. I'll let you talk to him to avoid messing up the details. My English is not good enough for this," the man said and picked up, with some difficulty, a large old-fashioned dial-up phone, laced with gold.

Before he dialed the number, he glanced at Zoe nervously. "Tread carefully with him. He is...he can be...unpredictable and dangerous."

Zoe and Elliot waited for a few minutes. When the man entered the room, Zoe's mouth dropped for just a second, but she collected herself and greeted the man who would give her the information she needed and who might even be of service to her. "I'm Zoe," she said, extending her hand.

27

ALIEN MUSHROOM

MAY 2023

When the guards brought Olesya to the library, one of them sported a black eye and a bandage on his head. Olesya tried to adjust her T-shirt and smooth her hair, which now fell onto her shoulders in messy waves, while she glared at Zoe.

"What happened to you?" Zoe asked the guard.

"She tried to escape. Powerful little witch threw me on the bars like I weighed nothing. If Sam hadn't shown up..."

"I see you've been busy abusing my staff. You need to learn how to control your power. Sit down, Olesya," Zoe said in a firm but pleasant tone, dismissing the guards with an imperceptible hand gesture.

"I'd rather stand. Wouldn't want to infringe on your hospitality."

"I have something important to tell you. You should sit down. I don't want to pick you up off the floor."

"You won't have to. Say what you want to say. What did you do to Sara? Where is she?"

"She's fine. You'll see."

"What do you want?"

Zoe observed Olesya, gathering her thoughts. She sighed. "Oh, hell! I am just going to say it. You are...unborn."

"What!? Are you insane?"

"You were not born like other people. Your parents found you in a forest."

"What a bunch of crap! And how do you know that?"

"From my reliable sources," Zoe said slowly, hesitating, observing Olesya as if evaluating the impact of the revelation.

And the impact had almost brought Olesya to her knees. She searched for a chair and slid into it. She didn't want to believe Zoe's story, but doubts started creeping in.

"There is more," Zoe continued. "You have a brother."

"A brother?" Olesya sucked in her breath to keep her emotions in check. Her brain argued this was a preposterous lie, but her entire being welcomed the idea of a brother with a sudden burst of tenderness and affection. The pale face of the young man she saw in her dreams and in the mirror flashed before her eyes.

"He was found in the same area your parents found you, but he was less fortunate. The Russian government found him and has held him captive since."

"Why would they do that?"

"Because he is special. Just like you. They are still trying to understand what he is and what he can do."

Olesya hunched in her chair, suddenly drained. What Zoe said confirmed what her intuition had been telling her all along. She was not like other people.

"What am I, then?" Olesya whispered, as if afraid of the answer. "Who are my parents?"

"You don't have biological parents. Not in the sense that other people do."

Zoe sat down next to Olesya and covered her hand with her own.

"I understand how hard this must be for you, but you'll be okay," she said. There was a strange softness in her voice that surprised Olesya.

Without removing her hand from under Zoe's warm and firm hand, she asked in a tone of voice she wished wasn't so wimpy and needy, "Why are you being so nice to me suddenly?"

"I realized you know nothing, and that nobody made you threaten me or my work."

They were still for a long time. Olesya didn't remove her hand from under Zoe's. She spoke softly; her eyes burned with tears that hesitated to roll down her cheeks.

"All these years I suspected I was different. There were times I didn't dare look in the mirror. I tried to figure out how I differed from everyone else. Different from my parents. And not just in looks are we different. They are outgoing and social, and I prefer to be alone. School counselors kept telling my parents that I was autistic. I just laughed at their incompetence. Watching other children play at the park one day, I asked my mother why I didn't look like her. Do you want to know what my mother said?"

"What did she say?"

"She said that I was the spitting image of my grandmother and changed the subject. She offered ice cream and pushed the question aside. I was a child; I never met my grandmother, so I believed her," she said, sighing. "And I couldn't pass on ice cream."

Olesya paused, remembering her mother. Telling Zoe about her mother relieved some of the heaviness that had descended on her chest when she learned she had a brother. The heaviness had mutated into an immense sadness, pervading her entire body. Zoe waited.

"Who am I?" Olesya finally asked.

"I'm going to tell you as I heard it," Zoe said. "A meteor crashed in 1951 in the woods near Belyaska, Russia. The government investigated and circulated propaganda that a gravel mine exploded, leaving nasty chemicals in the area, and advised people to stay away. Many years later, during their routine visit, and I suspect right after your parents found you, the government found a baby on the forest floor. They took the baby and kept it a secret. Experimented on him, tormented him."

Olesya shuddered. "Why experiment on him? Why keep him a secret?"

"The baby boy was different. He didn't have a belly button. The government searched the area and discovered mass graves of Russian officers killed by the Nazis. They also discovered a massive underground fungal organism. A new species that shares over eighty percent of DNA with humans. They found other babies, but none were alive. The theory is that something in the meteorite induced the fungi to create your brother out of the DNA of the murdered officers and the meteorite—"

"Are you saying that I'm a fucking mushroom?!" Olesya exploded.

"I don't know what you are."

"What was that thing in the meteorite?"

"They don't know."

"But you do. Don't you?" Olesya asked, cocking her head to the side.

Zoe didn't answer.

Olesya had a sudden epiphany, leaped to her feet, and exclaimed. "You are wrong about me! I am not unborn. I have a belly button!" "You do? Really? Can I see it?"

Olesya unbuttoned her shirt with hasty moves and opened it in a showy, triumphant gesture, pointing at her belly button. "See? Here it is."

Zoe examined Olesya's belly button and looked up at her with a quizzical expression. "Have you ever looked at your belly button?" Zoe asked cautiously.

"Not from up close. Can't really see your own belly button. Why?"

"It doesn't look like a belly button. It looks like a scar."

Olesya stretched her neck, trying to see her belly button. Zoe put her finger up in a moment of recollection, darted to a dark wooden cabinet in a shadowy corner, and after a minute of shuffling things around, she pulled out a hand-held mirror. She handed it to Olesya. "Here. See for yourself."

Olesya saw the reflection of her belly button, and Zoe was right. It was just a scar. She put the mirror closer to her belly button and played with the different angles and looked again, but her belly button remained just a scar. "How have I never noticed this?"

"Your mother is a nurse. I think she might have made this scar to make it seem like a belly button to protect you."

There was a long silence after Zoe spoke.

"So I'm a mushroom. Or an alien. An alien mushroom. Are you a mushroom too?" Olesya giggled and then started laughing uncontrollably, hysterically. Then the laugh changed to a sob when she realized the strand of normalcy, which she had so desperately held on to, had suddenly gotten thinner. She was not normal. She was a monster. Lost in self-pity, she sobbed quietly while Zoe waited for her to calm down.

When Olesya's sobs subsided, Zoe continued in an even and calm voice. "You're not a mushroom. And neither am I. I'll tell you about me and my brother and how we became who we are. But I have conditions."

Olesya stopped sobbing and wiped her tears with her dirty sleeve. "I do too," she said, perking up. "Where is Sara? Your thugs took her from her cell when I was asleep, and she hasn't come back. What did you do to her?"

"Sara's fine. I swear. You'll see her soon."

"What are your conditions?"

"Everything I'd say to you will remain between us. Forever. You cannot say anything to anyone. Not even your parents. And you join us."

"Join you? What does that mean?" Olesya snorted at this ridiculous proposal.

"We are the keepers of peace. Protectors of—"

"What a bunch of horseshit!" Olesya spat. "You kidnap people and keep them prisoner and probably kill them, too. You destroy knowledge. There are so many wars everywhere now. Just turn on the news. Keepers of peace, my ass! You're deranged! You destroyed our research. Why?"

Zoe, unfazed, continued explaining. "There are reasons for it. We have to make sure certain knowledge does not end up with the wrong people. Some people will stop at nothing in their quest for power. We've worked for many years to achieve power; we distribute it to a limited few and replace them if they abuse it. If it weren't for us, wars would be worse. Much worse. We've destroyed many potential dictators whose intention was the global eradication of certain peoples."

"Right," Olesya said slowly, thinking the woman was indeed mad. "Who is 'we?' Your brother and you? Or are there more of you crazies out there? Like a secret society?"

Zoe nodded. "We don't advertise ourselves but work in the background, unseen, unheard, unknown. I guess you could say we are a secret organization," Zoe answered patiently.

"Whatever. Did the Russian government send you to get me?" she asked, observing Zoe's reaction.

"No! Why would you think so?"

"No reason," Olesya said. "Do you know where my brother is?"

"No."

"Your informant didn't tell you?" Olesya asked, sneering.

Instead of getting angry, Zoe got flustered and couldn't speak. Something in Zoe's voice assured her she did not know where her brother was, but she was certain Zoe was not telling her everything.

"It's complicated. Some of my informants—"

"Don't trust you?" Olesya baited Zoe.

Zoe observed Olesya. "All right. Fine. I will tell you my story, and then you decide for yourself."

"What if I don't join you? Are you going to kill me?"

"We have a code of conduct and laws we obey. We don't kill people who don't deserve to die. And you don't deserve to die, do you, Olesya?"

Olesya suddenly felt all her muscles ache and a wave of tiredness spreading to her arms and legs. *Indulge the bitch. Why not?* But part of her was curious. Sensing a connection to this complex and powerful (and possibly mad) woman, she wanted to learn her story.

"Knock yourself out."

"I was born in 1783 in Paris, France, six years before the start of the revolution. Sebastian was born only a few minutes after me. They guillotined our entire family during the revolution. Left alone with nobody to take care of us, we had to beg and steal on the streets of Paris to survive..."

Olesya watched Zoe as she told her story. She was too tired to ask questions or protest, but her eyebrows rose in disbelief when Zoe mentioned her birth year. With her head cradled in her hands and her elbows on the table, she kept still, listening to her story, gazing into Zoe's black eyes as if looking into her own.

28

THE CAMERA

MAY 2023

Sasha was looking out the window in Olesya's living room, as if hoping her daughter would suddenly materialize, while Peter rummaged through Olesya's belongings.

"Tell me again about the car that followed you," Peter asked.

"I've told you. It was a gray car," Sasha replied, gripping the window frame.

Peter glanced into Sasha's eyes. In Olesya's bright apartment, they appeared even redder and swollen. "Do you recall what kind of car it was?" He asked gently.

"I'm not sure. I couldn't see the insignia, and I'm not good with cars."

"And you didn't see the driver?"

"No. The windows were dark."

"And you have absolutely no idea who might have followed you?"

"No, I've told you already," Sasha said, averting her eyes.

"You should tell me everything. You want to find your daughter?"

"Of course I want to find my daughter. Why would you ask me that?"

"I have been doing this for a while. I know when people are not telling me the entire story."

Sasha watched Peter searching Olesya's drawers. "I have to talk to my husband first," she finally said.

"The sooner you tell me everything, the sooner I can find your daughter, Sasha. I think I'm done here. Thank you."

Her blue eyes darkened in reply, but she nodded as she headed for the door.

Peter and Sasha left Olesya's apartment. Peter walked her to her car, said goodbye, and waved as she drove away. He felt he should console her somehow, but glancing at her face, he sensed she didn't need a stranger's pity.

Aside from a convenience store, there were no other businesses on Olesya's block, just this apartment complex and a small city park across the street with a sidewalk running parallel to it. Peter walked toward the store and entered. A young store clerk with a mop of blue hair and large silver earrings sat by the cash register, scrolling through his phone and bobbing his head. Peter showed him his badge.

"I'm Detective Amberlite. Investigating a missing person. I need to see your surveillance footage."

The clerk's jaw dropped. "How did you know we have a surveillance camera? I thought nobody could spot that thing after I did such a sweet job of camouflaging it."

"Why did you hide it?"

"Because it has been stolen or vandalized a few times before. I can't keep on replacing them damn cameras. I don't even know why they do it. This store has never been robbed or vandalized. Someone is just having fun playing practical jokes. How many times can Joe replace the camera before Joe gives up?"

"Interesting," said Peter. "Can I see it?"

Joe didn't seem to understand what Peter was asking for.

"The footage? From the camera. Can I view it?" Peter repeated.

"Oh, yeah. Sure. Come on in. It is in the back room. I can show you now, since we are the only ones in the store right now."

Peter followed him to a small room toward the back of the store that served as a storage, kitchen, and office area. The clerk typed his password into his laptop and showed Peter how to operate the video software from the camera. Peter eyed the rickety plastic chair and then slid carefully into it, gliding the laptop toward him, cringing at the squeaky noise it made on the wobbly metal table.

"You got it?"

"Yeah. I can handle it."

"I can't stay. I'll be at the front counter. Wouldn't want anyone robbing me with a cop present," the clerk said, chuckling. "Yell if you need anything."

"Thank you, Joe," said Peter.

For two hours, Peter observed people coming and leaving on the 14-inch laptop screen that was speckled with unidentifiable white and yellow dots and smudges. Some customers loitered in the store, some bought some things and talked to Joe before leaving, and some just hurried to get whatever they needed and get back on the road. Peter slouched by the small table, resting his head in his hands. His eyelids were becoming too heavy to keep open, and blinking didn't help. Peter rubbed his eyes, and when he opened them and glanced at the screen, his heart skipped a beat. Now wide awake, he disconnected the laptop and held it under his arm. He walked fast without stopping, but turned toward the clerk.

"I am borrowing the laptop as evidence. Someone will call you for information to give you a receipt later today or tomorrow. We'll return it when we don't need it. By the way, I didn't see your camera. I just took my chances."

Peter waved. The clerk smiled.

29

THE LEXUS

MAY 2023

eter leaned over the computer technician's shoulder as he finished enhancing the surveillance footage.

After the technician was done, Peter asked. "Can you zoom in more?"

"Not much. This is not a very sophisticated system, and I've already maxed the resolution."

Peter pointed at the screen. "There! Stop and zoom in."

He didn't blink once as he traced a black SUV pulling over to a woman walking on the sidewalk. The SUV stopped, and two men jumped out. One ran behind the woman and hit her on the head. She turned and faced the camera as she collapsed. Peter gasped, recognizing her. The second man grabbed Olesya to support her, but her head slumped and hit the metal frame (Peter cringed at the sight). The other man opened the back door and shoved the unconscious Olesya into the back seat.

"Get the license plates," said Peter through his clenched teeth, and turned to leave. "Find me if you see anything else," he said to the technician as he was leaving.

"I think I just did," the technician said. "There's another woman. Different car, though."

"What?! Let me see." Peter spun around and crossed the room with such impetus that he barely stopped before bumping into the technician. Then, his face tensed as he watched him zoom in on the second woman's face. It was Laila. She ran after the SUV that had taken Olesya. After the SUV was gone, Laila stopped running, pulled out a phone, and called someone. While she talked on the phone, a gray Lexus pulled up close to her, and two men shoved her into the car. She didn't have time to react and defend herself.

With shaking hands, Peter glanced at his phone. His face dropped when he saw a missed call from Laila made three days ago. "She called me. I did not see it until now. I messed up."

"Fuck!" he shouted.

Two other detectives approached him, jutting their chins toward Peter.

One detective asked. "Did she leave a message?"

Peter shook his head and ran into his boss's office without knocking. Captain Margaret Benson sat at her desk, typing something on her laptop. The afternoon light filtered through the slits in the blinds, making her silvery strands shine, accentuating her black curls. A captivating woman in her fifties, Margaret had an aura of approachability and openness about her. "Oh, please do come in," said Margaret, sarcastically but friendly. She looked up and removed her reading glasses, and gestured for Peter to sit. When she moved her head, her dark brown eyes sparkled with curiosity and humor.

"We have a situation. Some thugs kidnapped Laila. We have CCTV footage of her abduction. I'm pretty sure that her abduction is connected to the disappearance of Sara Mowen, Olesya Solensky, and the explosion at the physics lab."

The friendly smile faded from her face. "Oh, no. Laila was abducted? Are you sure there is a connection?"

"Yes. Laila was following Olesya and was kidnapped shortly after Olesya and taken away in a different car, which may or may not mean different kidnappers. It's too soon to say."

"Why was she following her? Did you ask her to?"

"No, I didn't ask her. I don't know why she was following her.

Perhaps she had found something and went on a hunch. She called me, and I...I messed up. I didn't see her call until today. We could have been on it three days ago. If something happens to her—"

"It was not your fault. She should have checked with you before acting on a hunch. You are her superior. Hunch or no hunch, we have protocols for a reason."

Peter lowered his gaze to the floor. "I should've checked on her. I really messed up," he whispered.

"I know you feel bad. I would too if I were in your shoes. But it's not your fault. For now, though, we need to get everyone together and get moving on it."

"Will do. Thanks, Margaret."

Peter left her office and shouted. "Everyone to the conference room! Margaret will join us shortly and will make an announcement."

Detectives and uniformed officers walked to the conference room, somber and agitated. They sat in silence, exchanging heavy glances, waiting.

Margaret came and got right into it. "Some of you must have heard what happened. Laila Mayfield was kidnapped. Peter thinks it may be related to the kidnapping of Olesya Solensky, Sara Mowen, and the explosion at the physics lab. We are going to take this very seriously and devote all our resources to getting our officer back and finding the other two missing women. Anything you need, just ask. Overtime, more people, resources. Amberlite will oversee the investigation, and I will handle the press when it comes down to it. The less we tell them for now, the better chance we have of finding Laila. That is all for now. Get to it! Good luck, and thank you! You've got this!"

Peter took Margaret's place up front and faced his colleagues.

"The CCTV footage is all we have for now. Olesya and Laila have been kidnapped by two different groups in two different vehicles, a few minutes apart. I have a hunch that Laila's kidnapping was unplanned. A chance kidnapping. She was in the wrong place at the wrong time. But this is just my hunch. I may be very wrong. I want you to search for any CCTV footage in the area. I don't care how many men it takes or how long it takes. Search all of them. On all side streets, businesses, and even private residences. Anything you can find. This is your primary goal for now. The gray Lexus looks like the car that followed Sasha Solensky. She wrote the license plate numbers for me to check, but they turned out to be bogus." Peter paused for a few seconds, gathering his thoughts. Then continued. "We need to dig into Sara Mowen's private life further than we've done so far. Marty, you are on it. The rest of you search for CCTV and run the plates of the car that got Laila. Get to it. Thanks."

Peter singled out a junior detective in his thirties. Dark-haired and slim, Matt seemed younger than he was.

"Matt, please find the contact information for Lev Solensky. Find any information on Olesya's parents, family, and friends. I want to know the circumstances of their immigration to the States. Previous addresses, work information, anything you can find about them. If you find anyone who knew them in Russia, talk to them. Neighbors, friends, family members," Peter said.

"In Russia, sir?"

"Yes. In Russia. We have translators, don't we? Find their friends, coworkers, neighbors, or any living family."

"Yes, sir. On it."

As he was leaving the station, Peter dialed Sasha's number. No answer. He left a message asking her to call him back urgently.

30

THE OLD FOREST

MAY 2023

Olesya woke up to the sound of birds and opened her eyes to a forest canopy. Disoriented, she looked around and discovered she was lying on a soft bed of damp leaves. Everywhere around her, she saw enormous trees whose crowns were so tall; they faded into the sky. She was in the middle of an old forest. Olesya stood up and, feeling dizzy, held on to a tree to stabilize herself before taking a few wobbly steps.

Her feet eventually felt like her own after walking for a while. The setting sun painted golden spots on the trees as if it were guiding her. So she followed her golden guides until she noticed an overgrown pathway that led to a dirt road. She started walking in one direction, then changed her mind and walked the opposite way. It was getting dark. Tired, she sat on the scraggly grass alongside the ditch to rest, but before she realized it, she fell asleep.

A strange, screechy voice penetrated Olesya's dream, and then the wrinkled face of an old woman greeted her as she woke up with one leg in the ditch. The ditch stretched between an unkempt, scraggly field, surrounded by trees, and a road riddled with potholes. Everything seemed fuzzy and strange, as if she were still dreaming, except for the cold she felt, wearing only a hoodie and cotton pants dampened by the morning dew. Oddly, the front of her clothes seemed dry.

The woman wore an old parka and a colorful scarf tied under her chin, appearing to belong in a different century. She kept asking Olesya questions in a strange language. Olesya shrugged in frustration, not understanding her. The crone waved toward an old hatchback parked on the road. A moment after she had finished waving, a heavy man rolled out and walked toward them. He also wore an old parka and a funny hat with rabbit's feet dangling by his ears. The scruffy man seemed surprised and not very pleased when he saw Olesya. He thundered something in the strange language, pointing at her. The woman repeated her question and watched her expectantly.

Olesya replied hoarsely, "I don't understand you. I'm sorry. Where am I?"

The couple exchanged glances. They talked for a while, eyeing her suspiciously, and then the old woman gestured for her to come with them, pointing at the car. Olesya hesitated, but after glancing at the road that appeared abandoned, she followed the odd couple to their car.

The rusty red hatchback of mysterious make had seen better days. Inside, worn-out seats gave off a moldy stench, and the cracked windshield was patched together with duct tape. The ancient machine started with noisy clanks and blew out a cloud of black smoke that hung to the back window as they drove. Olesya's hope of getting warm in the car didn't materialize, as the heater didn't work, only buzzed as the broken fan tried rotating. She sat in the back seat, shivering and hoping they were taking her toward civilization and a heater.

The man drove, glancing at her in the rearview mirror. The immense bags under his eyes enhanced his menacing stare.

They drove through a small, deteriorating town. The houses or shacks were old and barely held together, barely stood erect, crying for better days and better owners. People stood outside smoking cigarettes, glowering at them as they passed.

The driver parked on a street bordering a gray building flanked by unfamiliar flags. He got out and held the door for Olesya, staying close to her. The old woman got out and walked to Olesya's other side, touching her arm with a hand covered with red, gnarly knots.

Olesya shivered, feeling uneasy and slightly annoyed at being herded by the odd couple, but the cold and thirst were a powerful enough incentive to go inside with them.

The couple had brought Olesya to a police station. Like the rest of the town, the station had seen better days. Dark streaks and stains covered the walls, which were no longer of any discernible color. The furniture appeared old and well-used. A young officer in a worn-out uniform greeted them in the same strange language. The man and the old woman talked simultaneously, gesticulating while pointing at Olesya. The young officer listened, watching her suspiciously. He held his phone close to his mouth and talked to someone.

A man in his forties led the couple aside and gave them a few bills. They pocketed the money, bowed to the man, and headed for the door. Before they left, the old woman turned and gave Olesya a toothless, menacing grin.

31

THEY LEFT

MAY 2023

Peter parked in front of Lev and Sasha's house, stepped up to the front porch, and knocked on the door. He knocked again, and when no one answered, he tried the door. It was unlocked, opening without one squeak. He walked through the hallway to the living room, announcing himself loudly.

"Sasha? Lev? This is Detective Amberlite. I need to talk to you. It's urgent. I left you a message. Anybody here?"

Nobody answered. The house lay in silence. Peter walked through another hallway and stopped, noticing family photos on the wall. The first photo was of Olesya wearing a high school graduation gown, looking rather stiff and serious. In the next photo, Olesya stood between her parents, who had their arms wrapped around her, smiling. Olesya was serious, but her eyes seemed happy. Next was a photo of a younger Sasha, cradling tiny Olesya in her arms, Lev in the middle, and another man, who bore a remarkable resemblance to Lev, stood with an arm around Lev's shoulder. Sasha wasn't smiling or holding on to Lev, but appeared tense.

Peter stood there, gazing at the photo, forgetting why he was there. Startled by the sudden noise of an ice maker dropping ice in the eerily quiet house, he shuddered and then continued to the bedroom. The room was in disarray, as if someone had packed in a hurry. Some clothes were still in the closet, some lay strewn on the bed, but most were gone. The drawers were open and mostly empty. Peter walked to the bathroom and saw a similar scene: open cupboards and drawers, mostly empty. His pulse quickened as he walked to the garage. The neatly organized two-car garage was empty. The cars were gone.

"They left," he whispered. Then shouted, realizing Sasha was gone and couldn't tell him anything. "They goddamn left while their daughter is missing! They left!"

His voice reverberated through the empty garage, mocking him. Peter walked back to the hallway and yanked a photo from the wall. He stepped out onto the front porch. An idea crossed his mind as he looked up at the porch ceiling. He stood like that for a while, staring at the ceiling, then left.

32

THE ROLEX

MAY 2023

The door to Peter's office was open. He sat hunched over his desk, staring at his laptop. The dark rings under his eyes, the stubble on his chin, and the crumpled candy bar and potato chip wrappers strewn across his desk spoke of sleepless nights away from home and a lack of cooked meals.

Matt knocked lightly on his door. "Got a moment?" he asked.

"Come in."

"The man in the photo is Lev's first cousin, Lech Solenski. Lech lived in Moscow until 2009, when he disappeared. I couldn't find any accident reports or his death certificate. No trace after 2009. Lech was their only living relative."

"Damn!"

"Sasha and Lev immigrated to the States in 1999 on work visas. Sasha is a skilled nurse in high demand. He is a nuclear engineer and, likewise, in high demand. I found nothing suspicious about them. They are ordinary, quiet, hard-working people."

"Hmm, thank you, Matt," Peter said absentmindedly, rubbing his forehead. "Wait. The cousin might have followed them to the States. Check that for me, would you?"

"Yes, sir," Matt said, nodding at Detective Marty Evans entering Peter's office.

Marty's intelligent hazel eyes shone, betraying his excitement. "We found something on CCTV footage in a small convenience store in Arlington. The gray Lexus parks in front, and get this...a guy comes out—"

"Let me see." Peter jumped up from his chair, his weariness gone.

"We enhanced the video for you. You can clearly see the face of the guy."

Peter followed Marty to his neatly organized cubicle. On a computer screen, a tall, muscular man wearing all black was buying Snickers. He handed a bill to the cashier, and his impressively large gold watch, studded with diamonds, flashed.

"The guy has a sweet tooth, apparently. Lucky for us. Maybe we'll finally get a break," Marty said.

"Run facial recognition on him. See if you can find out what kind of wristwatch he is wearing. Looks expensive and custom. Might lead somewhere. Is the Lexus the same as the one used to snatch Laila?"

"Looks the same, but the license plate doesn't match and is also fake."

"Great work," Peter said, turning around before leaving in a hurry.

Two hours later, Peter leaned on Marty's desk, peering at his laptop.

"We got lucky," Marty said, excited. "This is a special-edition rainbow Rolex. We traced its purchase to a store in LA and found that a certain Boris Minski bought this watch two years ago. No luck on facial recognition, though."

"A Russian," Peter said, as if he'd just had a revelation. "Thanks! Great work!" he exclaimed as he rushed toward Margaret's office.

"Margaret, I need your help."

"Anything you need."

"I need help from Interpol. We may have found out the identity of

Laila's kidnapper by tracing his Rolex that he had flashed in front of a convenience store camera. I think he is Russian. His name is Boris Minski, but we can't find anything else on him. We ran facial recognition, but got nowhere. Interpol might have something on him. He matched both videos, so he is definitely the man who kidnapped Laila!"

"I'm on it. That is fantastic! First clue," she said, looking Peter up and down. "Peter, you look like shit. You need to get some sleep."

"I can't right now."

33

APPLE JUICE

MAY 2023

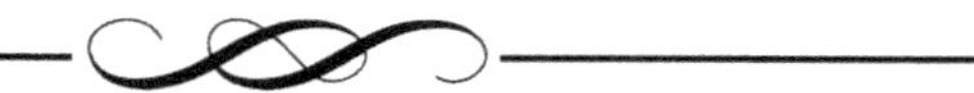

Olesya sat at a small wooden desk, scrutinizing the shabby police station. Bored and dejected officers sat behind their old wooden desks, from which old tower computers scorned her with their tired gray screens as if asking her what business she had in this hellhole. Everything seemed to have been grayed by time and stained with nicotine. The stench of stale cigarettes, dampness, and some other, better left unidentifiable odor, permeated every corner of the building. But the heater worked, and she relaxed her muscles, tense from shivering.

A man in his forties, wearing wrinkled clothes and with the tired, gray face of a chain smoker, sat across from her with a grunt. Soon after, a young woman wearing a flowery dress came in and walked straight to Olesya. Her blonde braids wrapped around her fresh face. When she smiled, she seemed even younger and out of place in the dingy police station, where disillusioned older men wasted their lives shuffling musty papers.

"My name is Olga. I speak little English. Detective Sokolov ask question. I translate. What is your name?" the young woman said with a strong Russian accent and not-so-good English.

"I don't remember my name. I don't remember who I am," Olesya said.

On his yellow, crinkled pad, the man wrote what Olga had translated and asked another question.

"Where are you from?" Olga translated.

"I don't remember. I woke up in the forest and can't remember anything."

Olga translated what Olesya said into Russian. The man threw Olesya an odd glance and asked another question.

"You hurt?" asked Olga, with a sympathetic expression on her face.

"I don't think so. Where am I?"

"Belyaska," Olga said, surprised.

"Belyaska. Where is Belyaska?"

"Russia. Belyaska in Russia. You are in Russia."

He asked another question.

"Show hands," Olga translated.

Olesya didn't understand the question. She shrugged.

Olga showed what she wanted with her own hands. She brought her hands forward and turned them around. Olesya imitated Olga. The man seized Olesya's hands with his chubby fingers stained with nicotine and examined them. He nodded and said something to Olga.

"He say no... Do not know word. No...no lines."

"No signs of restraints?"

"Oh, yes. Restrain. Spaciba. Thank you! He wants photo. Perhaps you missing. Your parents or husband looking for you. Okay?"

Olesya nodded. The man waved at a uniformed officer, who came and snapped a photo of Olesya with a digital camera.

"We put photo in computer and we wait. Okay?"

Olesya nodded. The cop left his desk and walked away, not saying a word.

"You want tea? Russian tea good."

"Sure. Thank you!"

Olga smiled and left the room. A few moments later, she returned carrying an ornate silver tray with an exquisite porcelain tea set. She put it in front of Olesya with an inviting gesture. The tea's rich and pleasant aroma invaded her nostrils. She glanced up at Olga and thanked her with a nod. Then she took a sip. The tea had a flavor that matched its rich, earthy scent. She sipped the tea, admiring the intricately painted design of the cup and the sugar bowl portraying a boy kneeling before a girl and handing her flowers. Accepting the flowers, the girl smiled shyly. The teacup depicted the same girl sitting on a bench, sad and alone, which tugged on Olesya's heart as if she were the abandoned girl.

The tea setup and Olga seemed unreal, like an enchanted, colorful apparition in a black-and-white movie that was yellowed and worn-out by nicotine and time.

Olesya, captivated by the tea setup, was unaware she had become the center of everyone's attention. Suddenly, the air became heavy, settling around her like thick fog. She looked up to malicious stares from middle-aged, angry Russian males. A man with crimson cheeks pointed at her, yelling. Olesya saw several men approaching her, closing in on her, surrounding her.

A vision of the young man's face from her nightmares appeared before her eyes. "Run! Run, Olesya! Run!" she heard him yell, even though the sound was only inside her mind.

She jumped up and ran to the door, knocking over the tea tray. A man stepped in front of her, trying to stop her. Olesya thrust her hands at him, and he fell. She stepped over him and dashed out of the police station. Noticing trees in the distance, she ran toward them in a straight line, jumping over fences. The cops ran after her, trying to catch her, but they were no match for her. She allowed her body to do what it did best and let her long legs carry her, loving the wind in her face and the way everything blurred around her as she zipped through the alleys and then fields.

Olesya stopped right before the forest and looked back. Nobody was behind her. She sat on a rock to rest and to think. She closed her eyes, recalling the image of the young man urging her to leave the station. "Why did you tell me to run from there? I came here to find you. Where are you?" she cried out, hoping he would answer.

Instead, a woman's voice startled her. When she opened her eyes, she saw a stout woman wearing a dirty old coat and a flowery scarf tied under her chin. She waved her hand, which seemed too big for her body, while staring at Olesya with piercing, shrewd eyes that disappeared under thick black eyeliner. Then she smiled, revealing several missing teeth, thumped her chest, and repeated her name. "Svetlana, Ja Svetlana."

Svetlana pointed at something in the distance and made an inviting motion. Olesya traced the woman's finger to a barely visible shack obscured by trees.

Why does she want me to go with her? What does she want?

As if reading her mind, Svetlana massaged her arms, pointed to her coat, and then to Olesya's inadequate clothing.

Ah, she thinks I am cold. Maybe she just wants to help me. A good Samaritan? Although her body was still radiating heat after running, she realized she'd soon be cold and opted to go with the woman.

Svetlana talked and gesticulated as they made their way to the small, decrepit house. There was not much paint remaining on the uneven walls. The cracked windows, lined with plaid blankets on the inside, were barely held together with brown tape on the outside. But the roof was even worse off. Its shape was no longer discernible under a mass of brown and green tarps tossed on top of the roof in a disorganized heap.

Svetlana opened the door and invited Olesya into a dark, cluttered mess smelling of fried food and ancient dust, and led her to the kitchen, which, although messy, had a large window letting in the afternoon light. Svetlana pointed at a wooden chair. Olesya sat on the edge of the rickety old chair, expecting it to collapse at any second.

A big man wearing a stained shirt too short to cover his white, jiggling belly strode into the kitchen, sending an annoyed look toward her. He then stopped and stood before Svetlana, waiting for an explanation. She said something that appeased him. He walked away with a grin on his face.

Svetlana put an empty plate and a cup in front of Olesya. Suddenly thirsty, she pushed the cup forward, nodding. Svetlana grinned, opened a rusty yellow fridge, and pulled out a jar of yellow liquid. She held the jar ready to pour the liquid into her cup, but Olesya, not liking the looks of it, covered the cup with her hand. Svetlana, noticing her hesitation, grabbed an apple and pointed to the jar.

Ah, it must be apple juice. I hope it is.

Olesya nodded and moved her hand, uncovering the cup.

Svetlana poured the liquid into Olesya's cup. Olesya took a small sip. She liked it enough to empty the cup. Svetlana clapped her hands, giggled, and then brought over a cookie jar. She opened it, proudly showing it to her. Olesya salivated at the nutty and fruity scent, grabbed one, and bit into it, surprised at how tasty it was, with a spice evoking a memory of her childhood. She relaxed, eased into her chair, and glanced out the window at the yard full of fruit trees.

It must be windy, she thought, looking at the trees that moved strangely. When the kitchen tilted, she realized it was not the wind and tried to get up but fell on the floor like a sack of potatoes.

"You drugged me. You witch," Olesya said, slurring, looking up at Svetlana, who grinned at her from above.

Olesya passed out. Svetlana marched into the living room, giggling and clapping her hands. She picked up a piece of dirty paper with torn edges from a small, cluttered table. Zoe's face stared out from the black-and-white flyer, which announced in Russian. "Wanted: Dangerous American terrorist. Contact authorities. Reward one million rubles."

Svetlana picked up an old-fashioned dial-up phone, yellowed by time, and dialed the number from the paper.

34

SPECIMEN 290

MAY 2023

In the middle of a large, windowless room full of medical equipment, monitors stacked along the walls, and cabinets full of jars of indistinguishable floating pink chunks, stood a raised metal examination table. Bright lights from humongous round ceiling lights that resembled flying saucers illuminated a woman's body lying on the table. Sound asleep, Olesya had needles in both of her arms and was tended by two women in lab coats, masks, and surgical gloves. They extracted blood from one arm and pumped serum into the other.

The glass doors opened, letting in two men in full surgical attire. Doctor Obolenski, a thin man in his late fifties, walked in first with an air of superiority about him. The only visible parts of his face were his tired gray eyes, which stared from behind thick-lensed glasses between his mask and surgical cap. Much younger, the other doctor appraised the room with enthusiastic blue eyes. Young Doctor Sputnik followed his older colleague into the room with a fervent stride.

"Good morning, Tamara. How's she doing?" Doctor Obolenski asked the nurse.

"She is a truly remarkable specimen. We've found benzodiazepines in her blood, some bruising on her right side, and recent head trauma that has almost completely healed. Otherwise, she seems perfectly healthy," Tamara answered in a mechanical voice, as if reciting from a medical book.

Doctor Obolenski opened Olesya's eyelids and examined her eyes with a tiny flashlight he fished out of his front pocket. Doctor Sputnik stared at Olesya's face with fascination.

"Supposedly, she woke up in the woods with no memory of who she was or where she came from. She spoke only English," said Doctor Obolensky.

"Do you think she overdosed on benzodiazepines?" Doctor Sputnik asked Doctor Obolenski.

"There is an injection mark on her arm. It may have been intentional," Tamara said before Obolensky could answer.

"That would explain the memory loss," Doctor Obolensky said slowly.

"Look, Gregory. She looks remarkably like Specimen 290. The resemblance is astounding, as if they were…twins."

"I've noticed that. We're going to run a genetic comparison, but I already have a strong suspicion of what we're going to find."

"Do you think they are related somehow?"

Doctor Obolensky sounded noncommittal at best. "We'll see."

"This is so exciting. I am so glad you let me take part in this experiment. Thank you," Doctor Sputnik said.

The older doctor glanced at the younger man with an odd expression in his tired eyes. "Don't thank me yet. Nobody stays here long. I've been here for two years. That is the longest anybody has ever worked here."

"Oh? They fire them or what?" Doctor Sputnik asked, sounding worried.

"I don't know. Never met any of my predecessors. Let's get started."

Meanwhile, Olesya was asleep and dreaming of the young man, oblivious to the surrounding conversation. In her dream, he was facing away from her, and she only saw his black, wavy hair covering his neck. Then he turned and screamed. "Find me, Olesya. Hurry!"

"Who are you?" Olesya asked.

"I'm Specimen 290. You must find me. You need to hurry. I will not last much longer."

"Where are you? Where can I find you?"

"Here. I am here. Wake up, Olesya. Wake up. Before it's too late."

Olesya woke to see four sets of probing eyes surrounded by surgical masks and caps. She croaked a question, "Where am I?"

"You are in a hospital. You had an accident. Hold still and don't move. You don't want to hurt yourself even more," Doctor Obolenski answered in English with a thick Russian accent while placing his hand on Olesya's chest.

Olesya's heart started pounding as his hand pressed heavily on her chest.

"What accident? I don't remember any accidents. I want to get out of here, please," she said, and tried to sit up, but they overpowered her.

Tamara injected her with something. Olesya passed out.

She dreamed of the young man again. At first, she couldn't understand his barely audible voice, but as his voice got louder, she understood he was urging her to wake up.

Olesya woke and sat up, discovering herself lying on a hospital bed in a small room, alone. Other than a shabby side table, a rusty sink, and a free-standing closet, the space was barren and depressing. Fueled by anger, remembering the doctors and nurses overpowering her and injecting her with something, she yanked the needles stuck in her arms. Blood dripped from her veins onto her white hospital gown, but she ignored it. She stood but had to cling to the bed so as not to collapse, weakened and drowsy from the drugs still wreaking havoc in her system.

After a few deep breaths, she managed to get to the closet and open it. To her disappointment, it was empty except for a broom and a metal bucket. She headed for the door, but when she reached out to open it, she discovered the doorknob was missing. The window was not an option either, covered by heavy metal bars fastened to the wall with sturdy bolts. Discouraged, she grabbed the broom like a weapon and waited for someone to come.

The door finally opened, and a man wearing a white lab coat, studying a medical chart tied with a rubber band to a brown clipboard with all four corners chipped off, entered the room. Olesya attacked him with the broom, breaking it on his head. He staggered, but the broom was not substantial enough to inflict much damage. She hurled her arms forward forcefully, tossing the man across the room, noticing that the waves produced by her hands had more color and seemed sharper this time. He landed by the bed, hitting his head on the metal bars. The sound of a breaking skull sent a shiver down Olesya's spine, and her eyes glazed over in horror as she saw blood spill onto the white-tiled floor.

She stood frozen, watching the blood drain from his body. So much blood. She had never seen so much blood. She would have stood there much longer had it not been for the young man's voice, sounding desperate and weak.

"Where are you?"

"I'm coming!" I might not have any powers left after this, she thought, and seeing the broken broom, picked it up and inspected it. The broken end was sufficiently sharp to use as a weapon, she hoped. She left the room and tiptoed barefoot down the dark corridor.

"Where are you?" she whispered.

"I'm here." His voice came from behind a door down the corridor. She tried the doorknob, but the door was locked.

"Shit!"

Her stomach knotted, realizing she'd have to touch the body of the man she had killed to search for the keys. She inhaled, turned around, and ran back to search the body. Grimacing and averting her eyes from the pool of blood, she searched his pockets, finding syringes, pills, and *yes*! A set of keys. When she got up, her disobedient eyes drifted to the floor, where pieces of brain floated, looking surprisingly like cheese curds in the pool of crimson. She covered her mouth, fighting nausea, and ran back to the locked room. With hands shaking, she tried several keys, finally finding the one that fit. She drew a deep breath and entered.

The room had a barred window, a closet, and a side table, resembling the cell she had woken up in. The difference lay in the amount of medical equipment that was attached to a man's body, which lay motionless on the hospital bed.

Olesya's heart sank, dreading the worst. Perhaps she was too late, and he was already dead, and she'll never get to know him. She approached slowly and touched his hand, which felt cold and wet to the touch. His skin was ghostly white, almost translucent. His eyes slowly opened at her touch. They were black, almond-shaped, framed by thick black lashes, and looked just like hers. He recognized her, tried to say something, but no sound came out. Only a faint breath escaped his lips, which also looked like hers, only much paler.

Olesya removed the sensors from his head, the needles from his arms, and finally, the sheet covering his body. Her hand curled around her lips to stifle cry, seeing how thin he was.

She searched the closet to find some clothes or a blanket, but found none. Instead, she covered him with the bedsheet and tried to pick him up. She shuddered when, instead of muscles, her hands, and arms encountered sharp bones. He groaned in pain.

"I'm so sorry, but I have to pick you up to get you out of here."

While she tried to lift him up again, a dark figure entered the room. Noticing him from the corner of her eye, she grabbed the broken piece of broom from the bed and attacked, but the dark figure intercepted her makeshift weapon.

"Wait. Hold on, Olesya. I'm Mark," said the dark figure. "Remember me? You met me at Zoe's headquarters…the old library just before you left for Russia. We talked about it. Remember?"

Holding onto the broken broom, Olesya shook her head, trying to break the last of the cobwebs from her mind. The man wearing black clothes and a black knit hat held onto the broom with one hand. With the other, he removed the mask from his head.

"Took you long enough," she said sourly, giving him a sideways glance.

"There are three other men with me. Here, put this on."

Mark fumbled inside a small backpack and pulled out a black hoodie, black pants, and a pair of black tennis shoes, which he handed to her. Olesya wore the clothes on top of her white gown. The clothes and shoes fit perfectly.

"Your men must carry him out of here. Tell them to hurry."

Another dark figure entered the room and effortlessly lifted and carried him out. Two other men in black were waiting outside and moved forward quietly and vigilantly, like predators, immediately after Olesya and Mark emerged from the room.

They passed through empty corridors. A man wearing a blue uniform and golden-red insignia on his arms rounded the corner and gawked at them with his mouth agape. One of Mark's men delivered an expert, quick blow to his temple and lowered his limp body to the ground before he uttered a sound. They continued until they reached the elevator. Before the elevator door closed, a man in a lab coat carrying a silver case squeezed inside. Olesya tensed, but neither Mark nor the two men seemed alarmed and greeted him with a nod. He stripped off the lab coat and a blond wig, revealing his wavy black hair. Then, he reached up to his eyes and removed his contact lenses, as Olesya stared in confusion as his blue eyes became black, and Sebastian's face materialized from under the disguise.

Sebastian grinned, winking at her.

Olesya stared at him, and the silver case. "What're you doing here? It wasn't part of the plan."

"Taking care of business," he answered, smiling. "A precaution Zoe thought we should take."

"She did, didn't she?" Olesya said, glancing at the case.

The elevator carried them to the first floor. As they exited the elevator, Olesya saw the bodies of two uniformed men sprawled on the floor. Mark led the small group to a back door that opened to the outside. A large SUV was waiting for them with the doors wide open. The man carrying Specimen 290 placed him in the back seat. Olesya sat beside him.

Sebastian and Mark stayed outside the SUV and faced the building. They looked at each other with knowing glances, nodded, then thrust their hands at the massive structure, and quickly got into the car.

As they drove off, an explosion annihilated the building behind them. Fire and black smoke rose high from the rubble and trailed after them as they drove away. Olesya didn't expect it, but wasn't surprised. She didn't pity the people who had died in the building. They were monsters who imprisoned and tortured her brother.

"You found me," the young man said in a weak voice.

"You speak English. What's your name?"

"I am Specimen 290."

"You don't have a real name? Like Anthony or Michael? They didn't even give you a name?" Olesya gripped the leather seat with both hands and clenched her teeth so hard they hurt. Her nostrils flared as she tried to breathe through her nose.

"I think not. They always referred to me as Specimen 290."

"You are my brother?" Olesya asked after a considerable pause. She already knew the answer. She sensed it the moment she was near him and saw him, but she had to ask.

He nodded. Being near him, she felt a strong, almost physical connection to him, as if he were pulling her in. She sensed his pain, his surprise, and his relief when he saw her. They were brother and sister, not born to any parents, but somehow related to each other and connected by a force strong enough for him to reach her across land and ocean, protecting her in her dreams, and beckoning her to come and save him.

An immense sadness mixed with guilt overwhelmed her at seeing his emaciated and tortured body. Surprisingly, she also felt hope and a new sensation stirring in her chest—love for her brother. Her sibling. Never had she felt this whole, this strong, and this focused, having her brother's inner strength by her side. His body withered with neglect and abuse, but his inner strength remained untouched.

35

THE SWANS

MAY 2023

Sergi's opulent office at the edge of Moscow was hidden in a clearing by a pond surrounded by tall firs and birches. Outside, a pair of graceful white swans moved their long necks in their courtship dance. Inside, a large crystal chandelier cast colorful streaks on the gold-laced, intricate wood molding and on the thick Persian carpet, while the marble-sculpted faces of Russian leaders guarded the room from all four sides. The bookcases held books stacked unevenly, appearing to have been read rather than just decorating the room. An imposing, ornate desk sat by an enormous window overlooking the pond. Russian flags and other national insignia hinted that this office belonged to a high-ranking government official.

Sergi sat in a leather chair, gazing at the pond, lost in his thoughts. His cool eyes became softer and more melancholic when they rested on the pair of swans. He did not need to hide his emotions, not playing to an audience, and instead observed the two swans with a woeful hunger, as if envying their dance and closeness. A knock on the door interrupted his daydream. When he turned his chair toward the door, his eyes reverted to their usual intense coldness. Sergi appeared stronger and even more arresting, as if life had gifted him profound secrets that deepened his soul and reflected in his eyes.

"Come in," Sergi said in his deep, melodic voice.

A man wearing a black suit and tie came in and said apologetically, "I have bad news."

"What is it?"

"The Kropotkin Lab was destroyed. There was an explosion. Specimen 290 is gone."

Sergi's eyes became two steel knives, but he didn't lose his temper as the man must have expected, clutching the door with one foot in the air as if readying for immediate evacuation.

Sergi responded in a calm voice. "How is that possible? The lab was protected by the highest security available. How could this happen? Who did this?"

"We have no details yet, sir. Everyone is dead. All cameras were destroyed."

"What about the girl?"

"She's gone too. They didn't find her body either."

"They must have left a clue. Find them. Now!"

"Yes, sir."

After his assistant left the room, he picked up his phone and dialed a number.

"The plan worked. What now?"

Sergi's eyes flashed with surprise, and his face became tight and pale as he listened. He said nothing for the rest of the conversation. When it was over, he stared at the phone for a long second, set his jaw, shoved the phone into his pocket, and then gazed at the swans with a pained grimace, as if battling an internal struggle. Sergi opened a book in front of him and took out a photograph. He looked at it for a long time with the same longing he observed the swans with. Then, he sighed and put the photo back in the book, which he slammed shut. He stood up abruptly, straightened his back, and clenched his teeth. His eyes shone like two blue diamonds.

36

LAILA
MAY 2023

On a dark road in the industrial area of south Seattle, police cars, fire trucks, and ambulances with flashing, pulsating lights parked in tight rows. Police officers were finishing putting up yellow crime scene tape when a car arrived at the scene at high speed and skidded to a stop, stirring up dust and scattering gravel. Peter rushed out of the car, ran past the yellow tape, and stopped where two men in Tyvek suits, masks, and gloves kneeled on the ground. They saw Peter and moved aside to give him space, exposing Laila's body covered with dried blood, lying in the ditch. Her face, discolored and swollen, just like the rest of her body, had been beaten up. With tears quickly filling his eyes, Peter fell to his knees; his knuckles turned white as he knotted them into tight fists.

"I swear to you, I will find the son of a bitch who did this to you. I'm so sorry, kid."

Peter glanced expectantly at the man in a Tyvek suit. As if responding to Peter's unspoken cue, the medical examiner, Dr. Gary Lawson—a small man in his forties sporting a sizable curly mustache —dropped to his knees beside the detective.

"Multiple stab wounds to the chest. Tortured. Seven fingernails are missing."

Peter cringed as Gary explained Laila's injuries.

"I will have the preliminary autopsy report by tomorrow afternoon. I will work all night if I need to."

"Thank you." Peter got up and, as he shuffled into his car, tears rolled from his eyes. He whacked the steering wheel in frustration and then started sobbing.

"This is all my fault. I'm so sorry, Laila, so... sorry. Forgive me. I let you down," Peter said between sobs tearing through his chest.

THE PERP

MAY 2023

Peter sat at his desk, looking haggard. His chin had not seen a shaver in a few days. He appeared tired and upset. His phone rang, and he answered it half-asleep.

"Amberlite."

"I have news from Interpol. Come into my office," Margaret said briskly.

Peter perked up and hurried to Margaret's office.

"What?" Even his voice sounded tired and hoarse.

"The perp is a paid assassin for the Russian government. Apparently, he has been on Interpol's radar, wanted for human trafficking, murder, and countless other felonies, which Interpol didn't want to disclose."

"Where is he now?"

"If they had known that, they would have snatched him already. They don't have his current location, but are willing to work with us if we share what we have on him."

"Isn't that nice?" Peter's tiredness sharpened his sarcasm. "They don't have any clue where to find this guy?"

"They told me he spent some time in LA, Chicago, and New York. We can start there. They don't know what he's doing in the States.

They suspect the usual: kidnapping, murder, but gave no specifics. We ought to hold a press conference and circulate his photo."

"It will only spook him," Peter said. "I'm not sure if this is the right way to go. My intuition tells me there is a connection between Olesya's parents and Laila's death—perhaps even the explosion—but I can't figure out what it is. They were tailing Sasha because she knows something. She was scared and was about to tell me something, but she wanted to talk to her husband first. And then she and her husband disappeared. They are running from something or someone. Perhaps from the Russian government."

"But why?"

"If I knew that..." Peter started saying, massaging his neck before having an epiphany.

"What? What is it?"

"Sasha's coworker in Russia mentioned they tried for years to have a baby."

"How is that relevant?"

"I'm not sure. But I have a hunch that it is. Somehow."

"Keep digging," Margaret said, sighing. "I trust your intuition. But we must seriously consider the press conference. It may be our only chance."

"Give me a day."

"One day, Peter. I'll give you one day. Under one condition."

"What?"

"Go home, shave, change clothes, and get a few hours of sleep."

"But that will eat into my day. Unfair."

"Okay," Margaret said. "You've got twenty-four hours plus the eight hours for sleep. Now, get the hell out of here and go home before I change my mind."

38

BURYING THE HATCHET

MAY 2023

The SUV carrying Olesya and her brother arrived at the airport and pulled up in front of Zoe's jet. Mark, Sebastian, and the third man, Brandon, positioned her brother on a portable hospital bed and connected him to the IV. Olesya sat in a leather chair beside him and, holding onto the bed, fell asleep the moment the jet took off.

She woke up, sensing his stare. She patted his hand and smiled. "You'll be okay now."

Mark and Sebastian sat together, talking in hushed voices. The other two men sat on the other side of the plane. Although they were asleep, they still appeared vigilant, like cats.

Well trained.

"Fasten your seat belts. We are landing in ten minutes," the captain announced from the cockpit.

Sebastian kept glancing at her, smiling. Olesya held his gaze, nodded, but didn't smile.

The plane landed on Zoe's private landing strip, near several open hangars housing smaller airplanes and two helicopters. Workers in blue uniforms were busy maintaining the planes and choppers. The extensive area was enclosed by a cyclone fence topped with barbed wire.

A black van pulled out of a parking lot and parked by the extended steps of the jet moments after it had landed. The van door opened, and two men pushed a gurney out and rolled it toward the plane. Brandon and Mark were ready to pick up her brother to carry him out, but Olesya stopped them.

"Wait," she said, and beckoned Sebastian. "I want to get a taxi."

"You are kidding?" Sebastian said, raising his eyebrows. "What are you going to do with your brother? He needs medical attention. Zoe has nurses and a doctor waiting for him. I thought my sister had told you all that."

"I'll take him to a hospital."

"Suit yourself, but what are you going to tell them?" He asked with a little boyish grin.

"The truth," Olesya said and swallowed hard, realizing how naïve she sounded. Nobody would believe her. Worse, she may end up being accused of harming him and get sent to jail.

"Your choice, Olesya. But you are being an idiot," Sebastian said, and added with a canine smile. "I promise I won't bite."

Olesya was kicking herself for not thinking this through when she made the plan to rescue her brother. She had thought she could just take him to her apartment and didn't expect he would need so much medical help. And now she found Zoe was better prepared. She didn't trust Zoe and didn't want to be indebted to her, but her brother required immediate help; otherwise, he might not make it. She couldn't take him to the hospital. No loving mother had attempted to make a fake belly button for him.

"All right," she grumbled, nodding.

Brandon disconnected the IV, and together with Mark and Sebastian, transferred him to the gurney and into the van.

The massive metal gate opened when the black van approached it. The tall stone wall stretched as far as Olesya could see. They drove along a long, paved driveway until they reached a colossal, modern house. Enormous windows, unburdened with curtains, radiated inviting light from the inside. Two men rolled the gurney out of the van as soon as it stopped. Olesya walked by her brother's side, holding his hand.

"I am with you. I won't leave you," she said to him.

"Where are we?" he asked.

"Sebastian's house. But don't worry. If it is not safe, we'll leave."

A large double front door opened onto a large, brightly lit hallway, from which French doors led to an enormous, modern living room. Olesya stepped back, recognizing this room from her dreams. Sebastian walked toward a massive staircase enclosed in glass and yelled. "Zoe, we're here!"

"I know. I'm coming," Zoe shouted from a distance.

Zoe arrived, accompanied by her two black dogs. They walked by her side and sat when she stopped, assessing the newcomers with their wise black eyes. Sebastian and Mark started rolling the gurney toward an elevator at the far end of the hallway, but Olesya grabbed Sebastian's arm to stop them.

"Wait. Where are you taking him?" she asked him.

Zoe gave Sebastian a sign to wait and faced Olesya. "They are taking him to his room, which is right next to yours. Two nurses will take care of him twenty-four hours a day until he recovers. I also have a physical therapist, and a doctor will be here any minute."

"I am going with him to make sure he is okay," Olesya said sharply. Zoe's dictating tone unnerved and annoyed her.

"Olesya, this is my home. This is where I live. I trusted you enough to share my home with you, which I rarely do," Zoe said in a softer tone. "Sure, go check on your brother and come down when you're ready. I'll be waiting in the living room when you're ready to talk."

Olesya thought for a second, then nodded and let go of Sebastian's arm. She surprised herself with how much she enjoyed holding onto him. It was comforting and electrifying at the same time. For the first time in her life, a man's touch didn't sting her skin or tense her body.

She followed Sebastian and Mark, pushing the gurney to the elevator. In the elevator, Olesya glanced at Sebastian. Now, she had the chance to take a good look at him and studied his face. He had the bright, generous smile and the ease of someone comfortable in his own skin. He glanced at her, appraising her with his intense eyes and a faint smile. She looked away, unable to read him.

The elevator opened to two nurses waiting for them. They appeared professional and friendly. When they assumed control of the gurney, Olesya didn't protest, trusting the nurses the instant she saw them. She followed them into a large, bright room with a high-tech hospital bed and medical equipment.

The room, smelling of freshness and flowers, was furnished with taste but was welcoming and designed for comfort. Olesya glanced at the walls, recognizing the paintings as French Impressionism, guessing they were originals. The chairs seemed so comfortable and inviting that she got a sudden urge to fall into one of them and relax her tired body. She couldn't help but admire the giant vase filled with a mountain of flowers, wondering how many hours it had taken to arrange it into a work of art. While she admired the room, the nurses positioned her brother on the bed, checked his pulse and temperature, attached an IV to his arm, connected him with stickers and wires to blinking monitors, and moistened his lips with water. At first, he was uneasy, but he relaxed as the nurses gently looked after him. Olesya watched in silence as his expression changed from frightened to relaxed. She approached the bed and touched his cheek.

"How are you?" Olesya asked.

He smiled, but barely.

"Will you be okay if I leave you for a while? I'll check in on you later. My room is right next to yours," she said.

He nodded slightly.

"Does he have any way to call for me if he needs to?" Olesya asked the nurses.

"Yes. All he must do is push this red button." One nurse pointed to the small contraption on his chest. "Here, have this," she added, handing her a small gadget. "It will light up when he presses the button."

"We will be with him until the doctor arrives. I'm Silvia, and this is Maria," she said, glancing at the other nurse.

"Don't worry, we'll take good care of him," said Maria, looking at Olesya with compassionate brown eyes.

Olesya turned around to leave the room and jerked, seeing Sebastian standing behind her. She hadn't heard him approach, and she didn't like that.

"Everything to your liking?" asked Sebastian.

"Don't know yet."

He glanced at Olesya's petulant face and laughed, as though delighted with her attitude. His laughter surprised her because it reminded her of Sara's spontaneous, real, and beautiful laughter. *Someone who laughs like that can't be evil, can he?* She wondered, eyeing Sebastian curiously.

Sebastian took her hand. She didn't protest. Her hand in his felt somehow familiar. For a moment, she felt like a little girl, safe, cared for, and guided by a parent. A warm sensation of well-being spread through her chest, and not wanting it to stop, she kept her hand in his.

"Let's go downstairs, little sister."

From no siblings to two brothers in one day?

Zoe was sitting in a chair, holding a glass of wine, when Olesya and Sebastian came downstairs. Her dogs were asleep by her side and moved their ears, but didn't bother to open their eyes. Zoe observed Olesya and Sebastian walking in together and pointed to a chair next to her.

"Sit by me, Olesya. Please."

Olesya sank into a plush seat next to Zoe.

"What can I get you to drink?" asked Zoe.

"You mean alcohol? I don't drink alcohol."

Sebastian raised his eyebrows. "At all?"

"Well, no. I've had beer or wine a few times, but normally I don't drink alcohol. Just doesn't taste good. And I hate losing control."

"Would you make an exception for me? I want us to bury the hatchet and have an honest conversation, and wine is the best tongue loosener I know," she said and smiled. "Besides, this wine is superb, aged to perfection. I promise you'll love its flavor and taste. Much better than anything you've previously tried," Zoe said, holding out a bottle of wine with a fancy French label as a peace offering.

"I'll try some. Not too much," Olesya protested as Zoe filled her glass almost to the top.

"You'll love it and beg for more."

"Are you going to drug me again?" As soon as Olesya said that, she regretted it. *What's wrong with you? Weren't you supposed to act friendly? Remember Grandma saying that you get more bees with honey than with vinegar?*

"Drug you? What do you mean?" Zoe sounded surprised and even wounded.

"You injected me with too much benzodiazepine."

"Have you forgotten that it was your idea in the first place? You said it had to look real so no one would suspect you."

"The dosage was a little higher than I remember discussing. It took me a while to remember things. What if I couldn't remember at all?"

"You are very strong. I had to give you enough to look convincing, and I checked with Dr. Brown first. He assured me you'd remember everything within twenty-four hours. We got your brother out. That is what you wanted, isn't it?"

"I also don't remember planning to be dumped in a forest with not even a blanket. An animal might have attacked me, someone... anyone might have killed me, or...worse," Olesya said. It was as if someone were in her head, directing her to sound petulant. She breathed deeply and ordered the testiness to back off.

"We couldn't place you smack in the middle of town, could we? The stakes were too high to risk it. I recognized you were resourceful and would get where you needed to be."

"You followed me?" Olesya asked Sebastian.

"I put a second GPS locator in your shoes besides the one in your arm. I was worried there for a while," said Sebastian, nodding and grinning. "I had trouble catching up to you after you escaped from the police station. You don't run. You fly."

"Did you cover me with a blanket in the forest, and when I fell asleep by the side of the road?" Olesya asked.

Sebastian smiled, glancing at Zoe, who grimaced upon hearing this.

"She was shivering. We sent her out without warm clothes," Sebastian said.

"Thank you."

The little gesture of covering her during the night swayed her opinion. She trusted him more than she trusted his sister.

Zoe shook her head and sent a reproachful look toward her brother.

Olesya finally accepted a glass of wine from Zoe, inhaled its aroma, and took a sip. Surprised, she took another sip. Zoe smiled.

"I'll leave you two alone so you can girl talk," Sebastian said and left.

Disappointed, Olesya lingered on him as he was leaving.

"Does Sebastian live with you in this house?" Olesya asked after he had left.

"Most of the time. He travels a lot," Zoe said, sighing. "Sebastian has wanderlust in his nature, pulling him in many directions. He's searching for something or someone, but he refuses to talk about it. But he always comes back home to check on me and make sure I'm okay."

"What is in the case Sebastian brought back?"

Zoe laughed. Her laugh, although as spontaneous as her brother's, lacked something, and Olesya thought it was sincerity. Zoe was even more beautiful when she laughed. Olesya wasn't ready to trust her and forbade herself from liking her. She had to know what Zoe wanted from her, believing she'd rescued her brother with strings attached.

"You miss nothing. It is research," Zoe said, her voice still thick with laughter.

"Is that why you had gone there in the first place?"

"No. But I won't lie. It was important. But the main reason was to reunite you with your brother. As a twin, I would have suffered a miserable void if my brother had ever separated from me. I sensed the same void in you when I first saw you. Even though you didn't know you had a brother, you missed him. Am I wrong?"

Olesya shifted in her seat. Zoe's perceptiveness was dangerous. She would have to be more careful and hide her emotions better. "Yes. I felt a void. I have seen him in my dreams since I was a child, but I didn't know who he was. He was trying to protect me."

"Protect you from whom?"

"From you," Olesya said and took a big sip of wine, and this one went to her head instantly.

"From me? But how could he have known me?"

"I don't know. In all my dreams, you were trying to pull me into your darkness, and he always pulled me away."

"I don't want to hurt you. It is just dreams. He probably tried to warn you about the men who are after you."

"What men?"

"The men who kidnapped you and transported you to that lab. My first visit to Belyaska had triggered their attention, and they had been on the lookout since then. Because we look so much alike, they thought you and I were the same person. They belong to a special branch overseen by a new guy who rose to a high rank in the government out of nowhere. His name is Sergi Orlov."

When Olesya heard the name, the room swirled around her. She directed her attention to the glass of wine in her hand, pretending to inhale its aroma so her eyes would not betray her. Zoe ought never to realize that she had a personal vendetta against him. Her intuition told her to keep that a secret from Zoe.

"Created to protect the president, this branch had too much power and resources, with no control over it," Zoe continued, throwing curious glances at Olesya. "Now, he is more powerful than the president. Sergi appropriated the research and your brother. But he wants you too. Super smart and power-hungry, this man is dangerous. In addition, he is backed by a billionaire who is a complete nutcase, obsessed with space and other nonsense."

"How do you know all that?" Olesya asked in a steady voice.

"I have informants in all governments. And we intercepted his top mercenary as he was following your mother."

"My mother? Why would he follow my mother?"

Olesya struggled to stay calm. Zoe observed her.

"For leverage? I don't have a clue. He never got to your mother. We got to him first."

Olesya didn't respond. She clutched the wineglass with her hands, which twitched with a mind of their own, wanting to bridge the short distance between them and squeeze the truth from Zoe's throat. Olesya took a sip of wine, hoping to drown her murderous thoughts.

"So he never got to my parents?"

"No. But he kidnapped, tortured, and killed the detective investigating the explosion and Sara's disappearance."

"No! Who? Peter? Did he kill Peter?" Her hands shook; a drop of wine landed on her jeans. She ignored it, staring at Zoe.

Zoe's eyebrows went up. "You like him."

"Is he dead?" Olesya pressed her hand to her chest as if something heavy had hit her and was trying to suffocate her.

"No, he tortured and killed the other one. The woman detective."

Olesya got up from her chair and crossed the large living room to reach the window with some difficulty. The wine had gone to her head, and even summoning her entire willpower to walk in a straight line didn't help—she still swayed with each step. She gripped the window frame and looked out into the blackness of the night. The wine and the news about Laila amplified the urge, with an ardor she hadn't experienced before, to find Sergi before he hurt someone dear to her and to find out what he wanted from her.

Zoe observed her calmly, but her black eyes were anything but calm. Olesya ignored Zoe's stormy eyes focused on her as she thought about Peter and how he had barely escaped death and that it was her fault. A heavy silence dropped on the room as the two women sat engrossed in their thoughts.

"Who is the guy who followed my mother? What's his name?" Olesya broke the silence, avoiding Zoe's stare. She was shocked to hear her words sounding far away, as if someone else were saying them.

"Boris Minski. You mustn't worry about him anymore. He is dead."

"You killed him?"

"Unfortunate boat accident. He wasn't careful."

"Why did you follow my mother?" Olesya asked, turning around and looking at Zoe with unyielding eyes.

"I wanted to find out if there were any others like us. I wanted to understand how you and your brother were made. You were made differently, and yet you seem the same as me and Sebastian."

"Why? You have your own way of making people like you. Like you did in the past. You possess your group, your army."

Zoe sank into her chair. Olesya realized she had touched on a painful subject.

"You said you wanted to bury the hatchet. Be honest with me," Olesya said, trying to keep her voice steady and affable, heading back to her chair on rubbery legs.

"I can't make more like me," Zoe blurted.

"What do you mean? You told me all about the fragment that you found, how you chose people with integrity, money, and power to help you make the world a better and safer place."

"It broke," Zoe said, sounding irritated. "It emitted a blue light and disintegrated in my hand many years ago. Since then, I've lost people and couldn't replace them."

"Lost? How? I thought you could live forever."

"I'm uncertain how long we can live naturally. We still succumb to accidents. We get killed in cars and planes. Our bodies can heal wounds better and faster, but not fatal ones."

"Did you find any fragments in the lab?"

"No, Sebastian searched everywhere."

"It's possible there weren't any."

"I doubt it. I have a bad feeling."

"Have you tried having children?" Olesya asked and regretted the question immediately.

"Enough!" Zoe stood, flashing her hurt and furious at Olesya, and started walking away without looking at her.

"In my dreams, you were pregnant."

Olesya had found an unhealed wound in Zoe and felt the need to scratch it. The wine amplified the strange desire to hurt Zoe.

Zoe turned quickly. Olesya readied herself for an attack, but Zoe did not attack. She seemed pained and left the room. Olesya's arms slumped as she collapsed into her chair. She grabbed her glass and finished her wine in one big gulp.

Why did you do that? Is that how you convince her you trust her? And how is that working out for you? Idiot.

39

ALEXANDER

MAY 2023

Olesya woke up in a comfortable bed in an unfamiliar bedroom, and this time, she didn't immediately remember where she was. The luxurious bed and the silk sheets, as soft and light as feathers, hugged her body gently. Waking up in unfamiliar places seemed to be her life lately. Oddly, though, she felt rested. She had slept through the night without her usual troublesome and vivid dreams, which she attributed to the wine she had guzzled last night.

Remembering her newfound brother, she leaped out of bed, dressed hurriedly, and rushed to his room.

Propped up by a soft pile of pillows, he sat upright, gazing with puppy eyes at the nurse feeding him. He seemed to like the nurse's attention. Olesya came closer, and only then did he notice her, and his eyes smiled at her.

"You are doing better," Olesya said.

He nodded between spoonfuls. She sat by his bed, studying his face, waiting for the nurse to finish and leave. The nurse was finally done and left.

"I'm happy you are with me," Olesya said.

"I thought I'd die without ever seeing you."

"We should think of a name for you. What do you think?"

"I'm not familiar with many names."

"Did you spend your whole life in a hospital bed?"

"No. I remember reading books in different languages in school and watching television."

"You attended school?"

"School? No, I didn't go anywhere. The teachers came to me. Many over the years. Then the teachers stopped coming, and the nurses and doctors poked me more with needles and attached me to machines. Took my blood. A lot of blood. I became weak and couldn't walk, so they strapped me to the bed and locked me in a room."

"How did you know I existed? How did you reach me so far away?"

"Since I was a baby, I've always felt a connection to you and seen you in my dreams. I tried to talk to you, the man tried to grab you, and the dream ended."

"What man?"

"A man was trying to take you somewhere. I didn't know where, but I sensed it was somewhere dangerous."

"It was a man who was after me, not a woman? Are you sure?"

"Yes."

"What did he look like?"

"I never saw his face."

Olesya sat contemplating what he had told her. Who was the man in his dreams? In her own dreams, it was Zoe who tried to pull her into her darkness, not a man. Was it Sergi? Was it Sebastian? Or someone altogether different?

Her brother touched her hand as if he had read her thoughts. She glanced at him, wondering just what he was capable of. She held his hand to her cheek, and a powerful wave of emotion overwhelmed her for a moment. Not letting go of his hand, she laid her head on his chest and heard his heart beat in unison with hers.

He stroked her hair. "My sister," he whispered.

"My brother," she whispered. "You need a name. Do you have a favorite book? A favorite person you read about?"

"Alexander the Great."

"You've got big shoes to fill, Alexander, but I am sure you'll manage." Olesya laughed through tears that came without warning. "Alex for short?"

"Really? Can I be Alexander?"

"You can be anyone you want. You can be Alexander the Greatest."

Olesya laid her head next to Alexander's. They stayed like that for a while, holding hands and enjoying being together.

40

THE LAB

MAY 2023

Olesya walked outside, taking in the natural beauty of Zoe's estate. The area surrounding the house featured a Japanese-style garden, while the rest of the property remained in its natural forested state, providing a haven for birds and other wildlife. Olesya spotted the garden from her bedroom window and thought this would be a perfect spot to clear the cobwebs left by the wine and help her plan the next move in this game of cat and mouse. She needed to do research but didn't have her phone or laptop and, not trusting Zoe, didn't want to use hers.

Zoe sat beside her.

"Are you okay?" Olesya asked without looking at Zoe.

"Yes, I'm fine."

"I'm sorry about yesterday. I had too much of your wine."

"That is all right. I overreacted."

"Although it may not seem like it, I appreciate your help in rescuing my brother. Thank you."

Zoe nodded.

The two women sat in silence for a long time. Olesya didn't want to start the conversation, waiting for Zoe to break the silence.

"I need your help," Zoe finally said, sounding nervous. "I've asked no one for help before, but big trouble is on the horizon."

"What big trouble? The Russian guy? Sergi?"

"He will not stop until he finds you. But that is not the worst of it. His authoritarian ambition craves ultimate global power. He will stop at nothing to get it."

"How can I help you? I have no idea how to fight. And my brother can't even walk."

"You are powerful, Olesya. You just don't realize it yet. But I don't need your fists. I need your brain and your knowledge. Your fire."

Olesya nodded to appease her.

"I want to show you something," Zoe said, sounding mysterious.

A few moments later, Zoe and Olesya rode in silence in the back of a black SUV. They stopped before a sizable industrial building. A large sign on the building stated, "Brie Logistics Center." Zoe and Olesya got out and approached the door. Zoe scanned her iris and placed her hand on the scanner by the door, which then opened soundlessly.

Inside, the building was bright, modern, and clean. A tall hallway with elevators leading to an upper floor occupied the center of the building. The first floor was what the sign outside announced—a storage and distribution hub. Boxes and containers with labels that were impossible to read filled shelves stacked from floor to ceiling.

Zoe and Olesya entered the elevator, where an electronic raised her heartbeat panel displayed buttons for two floors. The panel lit when Zoe touched it, revealing an additional electronic screen hidden underneath the upper one. When Zoe pressed a button, and the elevator went down instead of up as she had expected, Olesya grabbed the steel bar to steady herself as a sudden suspicion that Zoe was taking her to another dungeon made her knees wobble.

"Seventh floor," announced a computerized female voice.

When the elevator opened onto a bright corridor, Olesya's shoulders relaxed. Zoe led them through the corridor and opened a double door while looking at Olesya with an enigmatic smile. For a moment, she thought she was dreaming, seeing her physics lab, only much larger and with more and newer equipment.

"Your research is here. I didn't destroy it. I just didn't want it to end up in the wrong hands."

"What is this place?"

"For outsiders, it's a logistics center. For scientists like you, it's heaven. All the equipment you want. No limitations. Plus, salaries and bonuses that no one else can match."

"What about recognition? Scientists are human beings. They crave recognition for their achievements. How are they getting recognized while hiding in a basement?"

"They recognize each other. It has never been a problem."

Olesya shrugged, but said nothing.

"Come with me. I want you to meet someone," Zoe said with an odd smile, and led her toward a room behind a glass door at the far end of the lab.

With her back to them, a woman focused on her monitor, seated at a high-tech glass desk with countless screens and equipment blinking in multicolored lights, was typing something on the keyboard. She turned her head, hearing Zoe and Olesya enter, and Olesya let out a deep sigh when she saw her face and the sparkling blue eyes. Sara had transformed her appearance, looking almost like a different person. She'd cut her hair short and dyed it a different color. But that is not what made her appear different. Sara always seemed happy and full of life, but Olesya had never seen her looking so radiant and energetic.

"Sara?" Olesya asked softly, afraid her voice might dispel the apparition.

"Welcome to my lab, Olesya. For the second time," Sara said, laughing.

"What are you doing here?" asked Olesya.

"I work here, and I love it! For the first time, I don't worry about funding or equipment. I request all I want, and the stuff just shows up, and I can concentrate on my work. Don't have to write project proposals and wait and wait and then have them denied and have to start all over again," Sara said, adding, glancing hopefully at Olesya. "Are you going to join me?"

Olesya gazed at Sara with mixed emotions. There's nothing she wanted more than to work with Sara, but not under Zoe.

Zoe's face tensed as she studied Olesya's face.

"I'm glad that you're okay," said Olesya.

Zoe and Olesya sat across from each other in the back of Zoe's luxurious SUV, driving back to Zoe's estate.

"Will you help us?" asked Zoe after a long silence.

Olesya was quiet, looking out the window, while Zoe waited patiently.

"I need to take care of a few things first," Olesya said.

"How much time do you need?"

"I don't know."

"We might not have much time."

"Look, Zoe. I have been through a lot. I just found out that I am a freak and that I have a brother. And you are pushing me to help you play God."

"I'm not playing God. I have a responsibility to stop someone extremely evil from destroying our planet."

"Wow! Stop! This sounds preposterous! Destroying the planet? How?" Olesya glanced at Zoe to check if she was joking.

"I am scared that Sergi will act soon. We didn't find any fragments. I'm certain he has them and will use them to do something terrible after what we did."

"Use them how?" Olesya asked.

"The fragments are powerful and can do a lot of damage. I will tell you everything after you come back."

"Okay. I won't be long. Will you take care of my brother? By the way, his name is Alexander."

"Of course. I will take care of Alexander."

Olesya sat on a chair next to Alexander, who, supported by countless pillows, sat upright in his bed. He received the news of her leaving for a few days surprisingly well. Olesya noticed his cheeks had gained some color. She described her parents, her life, and her struggles to fit in.

Alexander took her hands in his. "You know, there was always something missing in me," Olesya said. "Some kind of essential part, and without it, I couldn't lead a normal life. I didn't know then that my second half, my brother, was out there, waiting for me to find him. I didn't know then that he would complete me."

Olesya felt tears roll down her cheeks, but she ignored them, leaving her hands in her brother's.

"My sister. I am so much stronger when I am with you. I've never felt so powerful and...whole and happy. Until now, I had never known hope. It was just an abstract concept."

Olesya shared with him everything she'd learned about Zoe and Sebastian. When she described the twins' telepathic communication, his eyes sparkled with interest.

"I think we can do that too," Alex said.

"What makes you so sure?"

"Because I reached you and you heard me. I sensed you existed, and so did you, so in a way, we communicated in this way already."

"How would we do it?"

"Not sure. I could only do it when I was unconscious or dreaming."

The sound of someone knocking interrupted their conversation. Olesya waited a second before opening the door. Zoe stood outside, looking unsure of herself. "Am I interrupting? I can come later."

Olesya opened the door and invited Zoe in with a welcoming gesture. "No, come in."

Zoe entered and focused her attention on Alexander. "I am glad that you are here, Alexander. I hope you get your health back soon,"

Zoe said. She was polite and shy, which surprised Olesya and triggered an immediate suspicion Zoe was up to something.

"Thank you, Zoe," Alexander said. "Thank you for rescuing me and for everything you've done for me and my sister."

"I am glad I could help. Tomorrow, a physical therapist will evaluate you for treatment. If you're ready. By the way, your English is superb."

"I watched a lot of television. Worse, I had conversations with it when no one was around."

Zoe smiled at him. Olesya looked away to conceal her distaste at the tender expression on Zoe's face.

Don't you use my brother to get to me.

"I'm ready," said Alexander, and then continued after a pause. "Can you help us with something?"

"Sure. What?"

"Olesya told me you can speak with Sebastian without using words. Can you tell us how?"

"Zoe doesn't have time to teach us," Olesya cut in.

"I can tell you how I do it. It's not difficult but requires patience and practice." Zoe ignored Olesya, looking past her at Alexander.

Alexander smiled again. "Thank you, Zoe."

When Olesya noticed the warmth in Alexander's eyes when he stared at Zoe, she experienced a jolt of jealousy. She'd just found her brother. Her other half. And now Zoe wanted to take him from her?

41

AWAKENING

JUNE 2023

The spacious exercise room seemed even larger than it was because of the floor-to-ceiling mirrors covering most of the walls. Exercise equipment filled half of the giant room; the rest was open and lined with thick mats. Through a glass door, the swimming pool shimmered emerald blue and reflected in the mirrors. Alexander was held by a contraption in the ceiling, attached to a harness that hugged his torso as he gripped the horizontal bars with his feet touching the floor. Ned, a stocky man in his thirties and Alexander's physical therapist, stood by him, giving him encouragement and instructions.

"You are doing great! Keep going. Move your body to the left. You got it! Excellent!"

Zoe entered the exercise room and stood by the door, watching him struggle. Sweat glistened on his forehead, and his jaw clenched in pain when he made even the slightest movement with his feet. Zoe gave Ned a nod and left the room. Alexander noticed she had left, lost his concentration, and stumbled. He glanced at the door, but Zoe didn't return. His shoulders dropped.

Four days later, Zoe stood by the door to the exercise room, observing Alexander and Ned engaged in their daily physical therapy session. Alexander was still very thin, but his cheeks were fuller and his muscles showed definition. She watched in awe as he walked without help—the harness was loose, not supporting him. Ned regarded his patient with disbelief.

Zoe came to the exercise room every day over the next few days, observing the sessions, amazed at Alexander's perseverance and the progress he made. She didn't need to do that. Ned gave her daily reports on the progress of his patient's recovery. But her legs carried her to the exercise room every day as if they had developed a will of their own. She didn't try fighting them too hard, either. She never came in, just stood at the door, not wanting to be seen by Alexander, watching him. As her eyes landed on his slender hands or his lips, her stomach felt strangely light and alien. This time, he glanced at her and smiled before she left. Zoe hesitated but entered the room and smiled back at him.

"Amazing. Soon, you'll be running."

"Thanks to you, Zoe," Alexander said, sending Zoe an unmistakably flirtatious glance.

Zoe felt flustered, surprised, and slightly annoyed with herself that her reaction was to flirt back rather than scold. Instead of being detached and cool, she grew nervous when he looked at her and yet couldn't peel her eyes off his face. She smiled nervously when his gaze landed on her lips, averted her gaze, but then glanced back, craving his glances. It had been a while since anyone had looked at her that way, or she noticed anyone viewing her as anything other than a leader. It had been a while since anyone had sparked her interest in that way. She tried to scold him with her glare but smiled instead. She tried to avert her eyes, but they didn't listen and reverted to his eyes and lips. Just as exotic as his sister; his sensuous lips and bewitching eyes held her gaze captive, demanding her attention.

As Alexander's body started to recover and strengthen, his starving soul craved its own nourishment. His whole being has been waking up. Zoe was oblivious to the fact that Alexander was secretly observing her from the corner of his eye whenever she came. When she was near, he pushed harder and gripped the bars so tight his knuckles were white, pushing his legs to move faster, while his black eyes shone with awakening passions and hunger for emotions.

At one point, Alexander beckoned her to find his eyes. When she looked into his eyes, and they told her she was beautiful, a thunderbolt traversed her entire body, awakening her. And she realized in that instant that she had been in an emotional slumber for an eternity. She panicked and left. Although disappointed she'd left, this time he smiled, sensing he'd caused her trepidation. If she didn't give a damn, she wouldn't have left.

During the evenings, they dined together, sitting at opposite ends of a huge dining table, and ate their food in silence, stealing furtive looks at one another. Zoe couldn't wait for dinnertime, constantly glancing at the clock. But when she finally took her seat at the table, her hands trembled when she cut her food, and the only thing she desired was for the dinner to end. As soon as he started walking on his own, Alexander came to the dining room long before dinner was served, waiting for her. He wandered the rooms of Zoe's modern mansion, searching for her in more intimate settings instead of the stuffy formal dining room.

And he finally found her in the kitchen one day, making coffee and munching on a muffin. Not expecting him, she struggled to maintain her composure. Alexander stood shifting his gaze between her and the muffin, and then his face exploded into a smile. "Can I have one of these?" He asked, pointing at the muffin. His smile, which made his face look even more alluring, eased Zoe's nervousness and the tension between them. She smiled back and moved the plate of muffins toward him.

Moments later, they sat at the kitchen island, eating muffins and talking. Their conversation, awkward and strained at first, eased into a natural and then enthralling one, broken by laughter and loud exclamations. Under Alexander's goofy smile, her nervousness crumbled and vanished. His hunger for a conversation with another human being and his curiosity reminded her of being this curious and hungry for life before, and dissolved the rest of her hesitation. The conversations over sweet treats with coffee for Zoe and milk for Alexander became their morning routine. After a while, Zoe no longer avoided him but sought his company as much as he did hers.

While Olesya visited her parents and Uncle Lech, her brother's friendship with Zoe blossomed and morphed. When he craved another being and their closeness to fill the abyss in his soul, denied of human contact and warmth. In her absence, Zoe filled the void. Alexander couldn't escape her strong and charismatic personality, and neither did he want to.

42

THE HIDDEN CAMERA

JUNE 2023

Olesya entered her apartment and hastily packed a few things, then sprinted down the stairs while calling her mother's cell. No answer. So she dialed her dad's cell. No answer. She hopped in her Jeep and headed for their house, hoping Sasha had left her a clue.

On her way, she stopped at a small shopping center and entered an all-in-one store. She grabbed a pair of oversized sunglasses and a baseball cap from a stand, added bottled water and a chocolate bar, dumped them on the counter, and paid for them with cash.

Once Olesya reached her parents' neighborhood, she parked her Jeep a few blocks away. By now, she was certain Zoe was not following her mother, but Sergi's thugs might still be after her. She put on her sunglasses and baseball cap and proceeded to the house, scanning her surroundings. It was a workweek in the suburbs, and the afternoon remained quiet, resting before children returned from school and parents from work.

Climbing the porch steps, she glanced around once more before trying the door, which, to her surprise, was unlocked. She entered the house and noticed signs of hasty packing. She went straight to the secret compartment in the closet and retrieved the metal box. Inside the box, she found a note from Sasha. *We're celebrating our anniversary with your uncle. We're okay.*

Relieved, she smiled and left the house in a hurry.

She nearly bumped into Peter while she was leaving her parents' house, but she evaded his arm and ran past him.

"Olesya, you are alive! Olesya, please wait! Don't run. I need to talk to you. I just wanted to make sure you were okay. Please," Peter cried out, sounding desperate.

She hesitated. She stopped, glanced back, and saw distress in his eyes. "What do you want?"

Peter pointed at the porch steps and made an inviting gesture. "Sit with me for a moment? Please. I will not try to stop you. I just want to talk."

Olesya nodded and waited for Peter to sit before joining him on the porch steps.

"Are you aware that Laila Mayfield was murdered?"

Olesya nodded.

"After Laila's murder, I was worried that you were dead, too. You can't imagine my relief when I saw you on the video," Peter said, his voice quivering.

"What video?"

Peter pointed to a hidden camera lens sticking out of a wooden box attached to the porch ceiling. He had painted it blue to match the house's color. On closer inspection, it was obvious it was an add-on, but who looks at the porch ceiling?

"You did that?"

"I learned a camera-hiding trick from a certain Joe. I didn't want the department involved because of the jurisdictional difficulties, so I improvised and installed the camera a week ago, and on a hunch, drove here today to check it. From this day forward, I will never doubt my hunches ever again," Peter said, smiling. "I wanted to find the bastards who killed Laila and kidnapped you. Aware that your mother had a tail, and suspecting a connection to the kidnapping, I had to try."

Olesya nodded, impressed with his vigilance, sensing it wasn't solely for professional reasons. She considered telling him about the Russian mercenary intercepted and killed by Zoe, but decided not to. The less she told him, the less dangerous it was for him. But he already knew about Boris. Without embellishing the gruesomeness of the murder, he divulged finding the body of the Russian mercenary in the lake and how this had driven him into desperation, having lost his only lead.

"How did you escape?" asked Peter after a lengthy pause.

"I didn't escape."

Peter's eyes opened wide.

"Look, it's complicated. I can't tell you anything right now. My parents' safety is at stake. I'm okay. Thank you. Perhaps I'll explain some of it later, but I must go now."

"Your parents' safety? What do you mean?"

"My parents are safe," Olesya said, seeing a growing concern in Peter's eyes and his detective senses kick in. "I just don't want anyone to know where they are."

"I can help you—"

"I don't need help. I'm okay. Really, Peter."

He observed Olesya for a while and then relaxed his hands. "Do you know where Sara is?"

"She is fine," she said hesitantly. "She is happy. I can't tell you where she is because she doesn't want to be found, but nobody is holding her against her will."

"Thank you for telling me that." Peter cleared his throat before continuing. "If you ever need anything, you know how to find me. I mean anything. Not necessarily within the police's scope of business. As a friend. I mean it, Olesya."

She watched him, contemplating telling him everything and sharing her burden. But his safety and the fear that he would try to stop her from leaving made her reconsider. Instead, the yearning yet insecure girl inside her searched his eyes. Without realizing when or why, she began to like and trust this man more than she usually allowed herself to. When she imagined his face and his eyes, her heart beat faster, and she longed to be with him. She looked into his eyes long enough to know he felt the same.

But she lacked the courage to jump into anything that was beyond her reach of understanding (and therefore control), and she didn't have the time to dissect her feelings just yet. She brushed his hand with the tips of her fingers and then jumped up and ran to her Jeep, carrying with her the shape of his lips and the expression in his eyes when he looked at her.

She glanced back. Peter sat on the porch steps, looking forlorn. At that moment, her heart contracted in a painful grip. He would never know how much she wanted to run back and embrace him. Driving to Lech's cabin to visit her parents, she envisaged Peter; then her thoughts shifted to Sebastian and ended in Sergi's blue eyes that had burned themselves into her mind. She sighed deeply while clutching the steering wheel. *There is something seriously wrong with me.*

43

THE NEW PRESIDENT

JUNE 2023

Olesya spent a few days visiting her parents in Lech's cabin to make sure they were safe. Originally, she planned for a day or two, but reconsidered, noticing how pale and thin her mother was. So she stayed longer, playing board games, taking long walks in the woods, and getting to know her uncle better. Finding Alexander filled a void Olesya had experienced her entire life. Despite the insecurities about Sergi and Zoe, Olesya felt stronger and more focused than ever before. Sasha must have picked up on that because after a few days, the lines on her face smoothed, and her blue eyes regained their shine. Olesya left the cabin, leaving her parents less anxious.

On her way back to Zoe's estate, Olesya pulled into a small gas station, filled her Jeep with gas, and then walked to the convenience store. Absentmindedly, she grabbed a bottle of water and a granola bar, paid for them, and left the store. She paused while returning to her Jeep, trying to remember and visualize something she had seen in passing in the store. And when she realized what it was, it almost brought her to her knees.

She ran back to the store and found the newsstand. The *Seattle Times* headline exclaimed in big black letters. *The Russian government is undergoing drastic changes. President Vasily Potanin died in a car accident near Moscow. A hushed emergency meeting of the Russian Government resulted in the selection of a new president, Sergi Orlov—a controversial choice...*

Olesya felt her face cool as blood withdrew from it. She dropped the water bottle and the granola bar as she gazed at Sergi's face, which was staring at her from the newspaper stand. His eyes were no longer piercing blue—they were black. His hair was no longer blond —it was black and wavy. Smiling malevolently, he seemed hungry. Hungry for power.

Olesya left the store, climbed into her Jeep, and sat there for a while, looking out of her side window, staring at the dry landscape of the eastern Washington prairie. She sighed, pulled out her phone, and called Zoe.

"I need to learn how to ski and learn Italian and the best way to do it is to go to Italy," she said to the phone. "Yes, I know. Just saw it. I talked to someone who knows Sergi and I have a plan. I'll be back in two hours and we can discuss it."

44

GREAT BRITAIN

DECEMBER 2023

The light but persistent snow, typical for this time of the year in Piedmont, Italy, promised a good skiing season. Olesya had just returned from a skiing lesson in the Alps with her instructor, whom Sebastian, an avid skier himself, had recommended. She'd been here for three months, mastering skiing and Italian, which she'd learned even faster than skiing. The ski instructor, impressed with her quick progress, said she was a natural and half-joked she was good enough to compete in the Winter Olympics.

Exhausted but in high spirits from the adrenaline still rushing in her veins, she sat in a booth in a dimly lit bar with a laptop in front of her and headphones on. Her lips moved, repeating Italian phrases. She had been a frequent visitor to this cozy Italian hole-in-the-wall because it was usually empty at this time of the early evening. She typically came right after training to get a snack (they had great pizza), study, and occasionally eavesdrop on nearby conversations to learn the melody of the language. That evening the bar was not full, with only a few people sipping drinks or playing pool, and a group of soccer aficionados watching a game on an enormous TV. Olesya glanced up from her laptop when occasional loud shouting or cheering bypassed her headphones.

An intense, high-pitched sound interrupted the soccer game. Olesya removed her headphones and glanced at the TV. A terrified news anchor announced in Italian with a trembling voice. "We interrupt this program for a special announcement from the Quirinal Palace. We have a confirmed report that...that England is...gone. The entire island is gone. Scotland and Wales are gone too. Our helicopter crew is transmitting footage of...of...where it used to be while we are waiting for satellite images..."

The TV showed a wide expanse of water and the outline of Ireland. There was no sign of England, Scotland, or Wales. "As you can see, Ireland is still there...North Sea...to the east, the English Channel... Celtic Sea...No Great Britain..."

The horrified anchor kept talking, but his voice was breaking with emotion. "The entire island is gone. There is no outline, no debris, nothing indicating what happened. We have received no reports of explosions. Currently, there are no signs that this was an attack. However, it's difficult to imagine what natural phenomenon could have caused the disappearance of an entire island...so...so quickly, with no warning. The European Commission is dispatching investigative and first-response teams. There are rumors of a mass evacuation of Ireland. We can already see boats arriving at the..."

Olesya bolted from her booth and walked closer to the TV. As she stood in front of the TV, immobilized by horror, her fear and shock morphed into anger and determination. Everyone at the bar stood still, staring at the TV, terrified and panicked. Except for the news anchor transmitting the horrifying news story, the room was so quiet that she heard people breathing in between the breaks in the broadcasts.

"You motherfucker! You are dead, you motherfucker!" Olesya yelled, rolling her hands into fists, forgetting about other people in the bar.

She returned to her booth without realizing that everyone was staring at the strange American, cursing loudly in English. She grabbed her phone and called Zoe.

"We must do it now," she said. Olesya listened for a while, shaking her head.

"No, we have to do it now!" She shouted into the phone. "He will go there now. According to his army buddy, it's his celebratory tradition. I suspect he's a creature of habit, like a typical psychopath. If we don't do it now, we may not get another chance anytime soon," she said and listened, shaking her head. "It doesn't matter how I know. I just know."

Shoulders pushing back, muscles tightening, she listened for a moment and then said impatiently. "I am ready. I have to be."

45

THE RESORT

DECEMBER 2023

The Alpine ski resort was in an area that was hard to reach. High in the mountains and remote, the area lacked ski lifts; therefore, it also lacked crowds. One had to climb up the steep, ice-and-snow-covered slopes before they could ski. And the climb was long and arduous. Only a few came here: those who took skiing and the adrenaline rush to the extreme and had the ability and guts.

Inside the log building, the ceiling-high stone fireplace burned hot with wood, radiating warmth and coziness. Burgundy red leather chairs, emollient with ambient lighting, and sofas so deep one might be in danger of disappearing in them if small enough. The warmth of the old wooden walls and paintings depicting winter landscapes completed the scene of a welcoming ski retreat. While the bartender arranged bottles and glasses on shelves that were attached to mirrored walls, the bottles reflected the light onto the windows, streaking them with color, feigning Christmas lights.

Two other staff busied themselves with bringing in firewood and wiping surfaces while watching the door as if waiting for someone. And they didn't wait long for the door to open, letting icy air and three men inside. They seemed to know this place and the staff, greeting them loudly and ostentatiously in Italian. Two of the men carrying four bags disappeared up a massive wooden staircase.

The third man was Sergi. He gave his coat to one of the staff and sat in a chair facing the fireplace. The bartender had started mixing drinks as soon as the men arrived, vigorously clanking ice in the shaker. Sergi sank into the comfortable chair, but instead of enjoying the crackling fire, he crossed and uncrossed his legs, and shallow sighs escaped his lips. The bartender rearranged glasses on the shelf, and one caught the light, and as if guided by a fairy, the bright beam bounced toward Sergi, brightening his eyes and easing the tension in his shoulders. He uncrossed his legs and glanced at the door; his eyes shone with excitement and anticipation. As red flames from the fireplace reflected in his black eyes as he tapped his fingers on the burgundy arm of his chair, his face lit up with a mysterious smile.

46

HURRY!

DECEMBER 2023

Zoe waited by the elevator, tapping her foot and looking at her watch. She yelled toward the staircase. "Alexander. Hurry! We've got to go!"

The elevator door opened, and Alexander came out carrying a backpack. He was not only walking without help, but his steps were light and energetic. He appeared healthy and fit. A slight tan had replaced the whiteness on his face. His black, wavy hair, so long it touched his shoulders, framed his face, slightly shadowing it and making his features seem even more exotic and mysterious. His face brightened with a radiant smile, seeing Zoe.

"I am here. Right behind you," he said.

Zoe pretended to be annoyed with him, but she couldn't help but smile back. It was apparent that she was fond of him, though she tried ineffectively to hide it. He ignored her feigned annoyance and put his arms around her.

"We have little time. We are cutting it close as it is," said Zoe, but smiled and eased into his arms.

"She's going to be okay," said Alexander with conviction.

"How can you be so sure?" Zoe pulled out of his arms and looked at him.

"I can...I can see her in the future. She is alive."

"What else can you see in the future?" Zoe asked, narrowing her eyes.

"It is not like that. I can't see the entire future. I can only see bits and pieces, and only of Olesya. Since we've been reunited, I can catch glimpses of the future. Her future. At least, I think it's the future."

"Hmm. How far in the future?"

"Not sure. She didn't age, but I can tell she's older. Why?"

"No reason. Just curious."

"Are you sure? You look worried about something."

"I'm fine, drop it."

Alexander angled his body away from Zoe. "What is it?"

Zoe waved her hand in a dismissive gesture. "Sorry, I'm just worried about her."

47

ANANKE

DECEMBER 2023

Sergi sat in the chair, sipping a drink and reading a book: *The Prince* by Machiavelli. His two bodyguards talked in low voices, immersed in the deep sofa cushions, sipping their drinks and glancing at the door from time to time.

Soon after, the outside door flung open with a loud thud, and three women entered through a snowy cloud that twirled around them as they stood in the opening for a moment, as if to make an impact. The snow slowly dissipated, and in the doorway stood three beautiful women. Dressed in flashy but classy clothes, showing just enough cleavage, with perfect make-up, and wearing high heels, they gave the impression of high-end working girls. With their arrival, the atmosphere in the room transformed and electrified. The two men jumped up and greeted the women, taking their coats and ordering drinks, shouting at the bartender. The women laughed and greeted them in melodic Italian. Sergi remained seated but turned his head and glanced expectantly at the new guests. He appeared calm, but his hands gripped the arm of his chair so tightly that the tips of his fingers were becoming white.

Two of the women made themselves at ease on the sofa, tossing their heads and letting their hair swing and bounce around their faces.

The third woman, wearing white fur, a white dress, and shiny black heels, moved slowly toward Sergi with extraordinary poise and grace. She removed her coat and nonchalantly threw it at one of Sergi's bodyguards without checking where it landed.

The third woman's shoulder-length hair swayed in honey waves when she walked toward Sergi. Once he looked at her, he couldn't look away and held her honey-colored gaze. And so they stared at each other for a long while, saying nothing, each transfixed and immobilized.

"I believe you are waiting for me?" she said finally in a melodic, deep voice in perfect Italian.

Sergi got up from his chair, his eyes focused on the golden goddess, whose magnetism he couldn't and didn't want to escape. He didn't hide his awe at her beauty and her magic, and her poise.

"You would be right in believing it," said Sergi in perfect Italian. "I've waited for you for a long time," he said, not caring that his voice didn't obey him, cracking with emotion as he spoke.

The moment she sat in a chair across from Sergi, the bartender approached her and kept staring at her, speechless. Sergi noticed it and smiled, clearing his throat.

"What can I offer you?" the bartender asked.

"Santi Brunello. Thank you. What's your name?"

"Frederico," the bartender replied.

"Thank you, Frederico."

"If you need anything else, just let me know," he said, not moving away as though he were prolonging his stay at her side. Sergi glanced at him, and Frederico returned to the bar, casting furtive glances at them.

"What can I call you?" Sergi asked the woman.

"You can give me a name. Your own name for me—for tonight. To make it very special."

Sergi sat for a while, contemplating while keeping his eyes on her. "I can name a few. Ananke—the goddess of inevitability," he finally said. "Or Apate—the spirit of deception. Perhaps Lynx—the goddess of love. Which one are you?" Sergi asked, his piercing black eyes on hers.

"None of the above, but you can call me anything you want. You can just call me Isabella and avoid any senseless connotations." Her voice hinted at annoyance.

Sergi heard it and smiled. "No, I think I will call you Ananke."

She accepted her imaginary name with a shrug. He clasped his drink tightly, then set in on a table nearby with a clank and sank his eyes into hers. He sucked in air through his nose, filling his broad chest, and looked at her intently as if he were about to ask her something. Something profound. She felt it and its inevitability. Her pulse quickened as she waited for the question, wanting it and dreading it at once. But the question never came; the moment was interrupted by the bartender bringing the wine. She exhaled and welcomed the distraction. The moment was gone. Would he ask her again? Enveloped in a shroud of competing emotions—relief and regret—she sat gazing at the flames. Buying time.

Frederico opened the bottle and poured a glass. "Let me know if there is anything else I can do for you."

"That will do for now. Thank you!"

She sat watching the fire lick the blackened stones, then looked at Sergi, who was already composed and smiling with a smile that drilled right into her heart and felt like it was opening a wound that never quite healed.

"Did he just wink at you?" Sergi asked when the bartender left.

"I don't think so. Why would he?" Ananke said and changed the subject. "What can I call you tonight?"

"You can call me Sergi, which means 'the Protector'."

Great! Another self-proclaimed protector! She silently sneered, but asked Sergi, smiling. "What are you protecting?"

"What needs to be protected: the order of the world as it was designed a long time ago and since forgotten. The world belongs to the strong and courageous," he said.

He still had a peculiar expression, charged with anticipation, as if searching her face for an answer. An unspoken question hung in the air.

Is he going to ask? Tell me something?

"Are you one of the strong ones?"

Sergi glanced at her and laughed. "What do you think? Do you think I'm strong?"

She faltered momentarily before replying, spellbound by his spontaneous laughter that transformed his face into that of a mischievous boy, and one that seemed so familiar. "I don't know. You appear strong. And you have high aspirations," she said slowly and added hesitantly. "What will happen if you fail?"

"I will not fail, Ananke. I will protect the world for the strong and the bold, so that the world can survive. And you. I will protect you," he said calmly, but his eyes betrayed restrained passion.

"I'm not sure if you can protect me, Sergi," she said, and fell silent. Something in his laughter and his eyes triggered a strong feeling of déjà vu. She had been here before. She had sat in the same chair, talking to him. And she knew him. She knew this man as well as she knew herself, even though this was the first time she had met him. Her heart thrashed in her chest; her mouth was dry, and her hands became clammy. She glanced into his eyes, sensing similar emotions in him.

What the fuck? What's wrong with me?

Later that night, Sergi and Ananke entered his hotel room. He closed the door and approached her. He faced her and gazed into her eyes. She met his gaze and held it. Sergi touched her cheeks, pulled her closer, and found her lips, kissing her softly. She kissed him back and, without realizing it, folded into his arms with ease as if she'd done it many times before. But she didn't think about it, or anything else, as all her thoughts and worries were gone in an instant. She felt as if she had entered a different world. A world she had either forgotten or the world that awaited her in the future. But a world that was deeply hers and deeply entwined with this man. She didn't care about anything else but this moment. This was so unlike her, and yet she had never felt freer, more open, uninhibited, or alive.

Later, when he was lying on his back immersed in a deep sleep, Ananke lay on her side, her head supported by her elbow, inspecting a birthmark on his chest, which she had first seen when they were making love. The sizable mark resembled a sun with spreading rays that covered his entire ribcage. She rested her head on his chest and fell asleep, dreaming of a faraway land. Sitting on a checkered blanket, she stroked the tips of brilliant green grass when a hand covered hers. It was a man's hand, and it felt familiar, but she couldn't put a face to it. She tried to look up at his face, but her eyes refused to budge.

Ananke opened her eyes to the sound of Sergi closing the bathroom door. She sprang out of bed, grabbed a GPS pin from under the pillow, and opened the closet carefully. After she inserted it into his ski outfit, she hurried back to bed and pretended to be asleep. Sergi emerged from the bathroom and stood by the bed, looking at her in her pretend sleep. A heavy cloud of sorrow draped over his face when he gently touched her hair.

"My little forest girl," Sergi whispered in Russian. "See you later. I hope."

Her heart started beating faster when she grasped what he had said. Her mother used to whisper it to her when she assumed she was asleep. Curious, she looked it up in a dictionary but never understood what it meant. She found it odd that her mother would call her that, as she had never really spent much time in the forest. She understood its meaning now, and apparently so did Sergi.

48

SLALOM

DECEMBER 2023

Sergi, wearing his ski outfit, left the resort. He stopped and glanced up at the window of his hotel room. Ananke looked down at him. He waved and smiled. She stood motionless. His bodyguard opened the door of an SUV. Sergi had his foot inside the car, then changed his mind and darted back toward the hotel, glancing at the window. He stopped just before he reached the door, changed his mind once more, and slid inside. The bodyguard closed the door and got into the driver's seat. They drove off onto the blinding white road ahead.

A few minutes later, Ananke left the building, dressed in a ski outfit and carrying a small backpack. She waited outside for only a short while before a white SUV pulled up to her. Frederico came out and handed her the car keys. He shook her hand and placed her pack in the back seat.

"Tell Zoe I said hello," he said.

She nodded, started the car, and drove off into the snowy veil, following the car ahead.

Olesya, wearing a helmet and glasses with skis on her back, was working her way up a steep mountain covered with snow and ice. Each swing of the ice pick was precise and quick, as though she'd done it all her life. She fished a phone from the front pocket of her ski jacket, removed a glove with her teeth, and checked the GPS signal. The signal was getting closer. She just needed to climb a little higher.

She climbed, stopped, and looked up. Then she veered off to the side, avoiding a straight pass at the GPS signal to remain unnoticed, and climbed to the signal, which had stopped moving. She took one last step up and saw the GPS lying on the snow, abandoned. There were no footprints, no ski marks on the snow. A rocky overhang concealed the area above. With her heart beating lightning fast, she climbed down a few steps, around a rock face, and climbed back up to another spot to look for Sergi. She looked around desperately but saw no sign of him.

That was your only chance, and you blew it. Now what?

She heard a noise and instinctively bent down. She felt a thump on her head, but her helmet absorbed most of the impact. Through a cloud of snow, she saw the back ends of skis. She quickly slid her skis on and skied down the slope. And soon, she spotted puffs of snow ahead and assumed it was Sergi skiing fast. Then he disappeared from her view. She stopped and pulled a gun from her side pocket. Noticing a rocky outcrop to her left, she proceeded toward it when she heard a snowy crunch behind her, followed by a sudden pop from a gun equipped with a silencer. She felt a push and a dull pain in her back. She spun around and fell on the snow on her back and saw Sergi standing with a gun pointed at her.

"Really? In the back? You coward!" Olesya said, gasping for air, waiting for the pain and surprised the shot didn't hurt as much as it should have. Did he damage her spine? No, her legs moved. While she stared at him, a myriad of emotions and questions flashed through her mind. Why was he looking at her this way? Was that sorrow in his eyes, or was she dying and hallucinating? She remembered her uncle's warning. "He can be very charismatic...he can be dangerous..."

"Sorry, my little forest girl. Stay here for now. Don't follow me." Sergi had grasped the ski poles, twisted his lean, muscular body to take off downslope when he heard a man's scream. He tensed, took his glasses off and strained his eyes looking toward the scream's origin.

Olesya, hearing the scream, shoved her doubts away, regained her focus, and slammed into his legs with her skis. He lost his balance and tumbled down the steep slope while grabbing Olesya's ski at the last moment, pulling her down with him. White fog enveloped them as they tumbled. Only a part of a ski occasionally protruded from the explosive snow flurries.

At one point, Olesya stood upright, balancing on one ski. Sergi tried to grab her, but she pushed him away and skied down the slope. Her gun was gone. She looked back. Sergi had gotten up and was gaining on her, being a better skier and still having two skis. He skied past her and punched her hard in the face as she stared at him. She landed hard on her back. Stunned but determined, she got up and pushed herself down the steep incline, catching up to him. Her willpower grew as time was running out—she must kill him before they reached the bottom. Olesya held on to him fiercely as they tumbled to a flatter area.

Sergi got up first. Olesya was still disoriented and sat up slowly. He removed his ski and landed a blow to her head with it. Her helmet had come off, and the blow landed directly on her head. Her forehead started bleeding, but she didn't lose consciousness.

"I told you to stay put," he bellowed, then pleaded. "Don't follow me, and stay here, please. I must tell you something—"

"No way! You monster!" She interrupted, grinning a devilish little smile, crying and laughing at once as she thrust her hands toward the mountain of snow above them. "Protect yourself from this, asshole!"

"Listen to me," he stopped mid-sentence, hearing a loud thundering noise. He moved his head toward the noise, and instead of surprise and anger, there was sadness and resignation in his eyes as the white dust started swirling near giant cracks in the snow. Avalanche was heading their way. Olesya laughed. Just before the snow covered them, Olesya and Sergi locked eyes. The haunting look in his eyes shook her entire body in a powerful spasm.

Zoe and Alexander stood on a small plateau a hundred feet lower than Olesya and Sergi, observing their fight. They scurried to the side to evade the avalanche heading their way. One of Sergi's bodyguards lay on the snow with his arms outstretched; his blood had turned the surrounding snow crimson. The avalanche covered his body and the blood, restoring the blinding, clean whiteness as if nothing had happened there.

After the avalanche passed, Zoe and Alexander ran up to where they had last seen Olesya and Sergi. When they got close, Zoe thrust her hands forward and pushed some snow aside. When she thrust her hands the second time, she pushed some more, but not enough. She thrust her hands again and cleared little snow this time. She glanced at Alexander.

Alexander stood motionless with his eyes shut, concentrating. Finally, he extended his hands slowly toward the pile of snow. Nothing happened for a moment, and then the snow began to stir and rise. At first sluggishly, barely noticeable, then the enormous masses of snow lifted off and swirled up, dissipating high in the air. He continued until they saw a dark figure in the snow. Sebastian came skiing down the slope just as Zoe and Alexander brushed the remaining snow off Sergi's lifeless body. He was not breathing. Zoe checked his pulse, retrieved a knife from her pocket, and sliced his throat with one quick move.

"Just in case."

Sebastian looked around. "Where is Olesya? She was right beside him. Where is she?"

Alexander searched around frantically for signs of his sister, and not seeing any, started clawing at the snow with his bare hands. "Olesya! Olesya! Where are you? Answer me. Olesya!"

"I knew you shouldn't have let her do this alone. I knew it! I told you so. Olesya! Olesya! Where are you?" Sebastian yelled.

The three were frantically digging in the snow with their hands, calling Olesya's name, when her barely audible voice sounded behind them.

"Stop yelling. My head hurts."

The three of them turned to face Olesya, who could barely stay upright on her trembling legs. Streaks of blood from the wound on her head had stained her hair, dyed the color of deep honey; her eye was swollen shut, and her shoulder appeared dislocated. Her torn ski outfit revealed a black Kevlar vest underneath. The shock and fear slowly ebbed from their faces as they stared at her.

"You are alive," Zoe said and approached her as if she wanted to touch her. She stopped, noticing Olesya's shoulder. She circled her, assessing her condition and narrowing her eyes, inspected her Kevlar vest as if she were looking for something.

With the adrenaline leaving her body, Olesya shivered from the chilliness penetrating her through the torn jacket, exhaustion, and feeling deflated from having accomplished what she had set out to do. "Yeah, barely," she said, pointing at Sergi but avoiding looking at his body. "Is he dead?"

"Yes, very," Zoe said.

"Make sure," Olesya said to Sebastian. Then she mustered her remaining energy and turned to Zoe. The uneasy feeling that something didn't add up in Zoe's story had grown since last night. When she had learned about the disappearance of Great Britain, her immediate suspicion fell on Sergi because of what Zoe had told her about him and the Russian government. But after last night, she was not so certain anymore and needed reassurance she hadn't just killed someone for something they didn't do. "You owe me an explanation. You promised to tell me everything if I committed. I'd say I committed. Speak!"

"Now? You look as if you are about to collapse. Let's take care of you first."

"No. Now. Sergi might be dead, but we are not done. You know that. We must find the black fragments the Russian government stashed somewhere and make sure Sergi's successors don't destroy us all. If you don't tell me now, you will never see me again. I'll deal with this shit myself."

"Okay," Zoe said quickly.

"How can you be so sure it was Sergi or the Russian government that disappeared Great Britain? It might have been some kind of freak accident that nobody had figured out yet."

"I told you, I have informants everywhere—"

"I don't give a damn about your informants. I want to know how it happened. How was he able to disappear an entire island? Can you do that? Is that why you're so sure he did it?" Olesya asked, trembling from exhaustion and anguish.

"'I'm not sure exactly how. My fragment was gone before science advanced enough for us to study it. That is why I need you and Sara to continue the research."

Sebastian noticed Olesya was in pain and could barely stand. He sped up the storytelling and interrupted his sister. "It happened to people."

"What happened to people?" Olesya asked impatiently while touching her head and wincing in pain.

"It didn't always work. Some people disappeared when we tried the fragment on them. They just vanished in front of our eyes," Sebastian explained.

"Many years had gone by before we figured out whom we could transform," Zoe added.

"How did you figure it out?"

The twins exchanged a knowing glance, and then Zoe continued. "For the next few days, we searched for more fragments down the stream and the river and found none, so we suspected they had washed down to the ocean. We searched—"

Olesya clenched her teeth as her pain intensified.

Sebastian interrupted Zoe's slow rant. "Instead of fragments, we found two puppies. Two little black puppies. We took care of them," Sebastian said.

"How is that relevant?" Olesya interrupted.

"They showed us who we can change. At first, we didn't understand why the dogs growled at some and not others. Then we noticed the dogs had growled at those who disappeared and had licked the hands of the people we could transform."

"Are the dogs…?" Olesya asked.

"Yes, they are the same dogs. They must've found the fragments like we did. They have been with us ever since," Sebastian said.

"I'm not sure how they disappeared the entire island, but you are right. If we don't find the fragments, they will send us back into the darkness, the entire United States, as Russian enemy number one," Zoe said.

"Back into the darkness? What do…"

Olesya collapsed without finishing her question. Sebastian picked her up and carried her to their SUV. Zoe and Alexander stayed behind, eyeing Sergi's body.

"What are we going to do with his body?" Alexander asked. "If we leave him here, nobody will find him in this remote area until spring, and even then…"

"It's probably better to leave it here," Zoe said slowly. "If nobody finds him for a while, there'll be fewer chances of anyone connecting Great Britain's disappearance to Sergi. It'll all blow over, hopefully."

Zoe opened the door to Olesya's hotel room and peeked inside. Olesya was sound asleep in her bed, sedated by Dr. Brown after he had set her shoulder and dressed her head wound. After assessing Olesya, Brown had assured Alexander that his sister wasn't concussed. He said the wound was superficial and would heal fast. Zoe sneaked inside and carefully closed the door behind her. She searched and found what she was looking for—Olesya's dirty and torn clothes and the Kevlar vest lying on the floor.

Zoe examined the clothes and the vest and gritted her teeth. She approached the bed and stared at Olesya. Her hands folded into tight fists while she stood watching Olesya's chest rising and falling. Then she left, walking down the hallway until she found a garbage bin where she threw Olesya's torn clothes and the vest.

49

GROWING SOLDIERS

DECEMBER 2023

At two o'clock in the morning, the outskirts of Moscow disappeared behind a heavy fog, interrupted only by a handful of working streetlights. Thirty-one figures entered through a hole cut in the chain-link fence and ran toward a concrete building at the far end of a parking lot. One of them unlocked the front door with an electronic device, and the dark figures entered the building. Their silhouettes moved through unlit corridors soundlessly and with purpose, taking down armed guards on their way as if they were lifeless puppets.

Then, the group split into three. Olesya's group included Zoe, Alexander, Sebastian, Mary, and five other of Zoe's black-eyed and black-haired people. When Olesya's group approached a locked door with a red "Authorized Personnel Only" sign in Russian, Mary grinned lightly and opened it in a few seconds. Sebastian and Alexander entered the room first.

"Holy shit!" Sebastian exclaimed.

"This can't be real…" Alexander said, his face white.

There were incubators stacked against the walls, floor to ceiling. In the middle of the room stood a giant glass and metal container, divided into lower and upper parts. In the upper part, something reddish, greenish, and brown was moving what seemed like thousands of tentacles. Some were thick, some as thin as fishing lines, and some resembled feathers. The lower part was darker. Sebastian took a step back and lost his balance on something dark and squishy lying on the floor behind him and fell. He swore something unintelligible when his eyes were just inches away from body parts floating in a reddish liquid, separated from him only by glass. Countless tubes connected the incubators to the glass container and ran in all directions in a black, tangled web.

Zoe slowly moved toward the incubators and hesitantly glanced inside. Gasping and holding her hand to her chest, she turned her pale face to Olesya, who caught up with her and peeked inside. A sudden wave of nausea overcame Olesya as she realized what was inside. A few-month-old human fetus floated, submerged in greenish, yellowish liquid, its little mouth connected to a tube filled with a black, slimy substance. Olesya stared at the fetus, fighting dizziness and nausea.

Zoe touched her shoulder. "Are you sure you want to do this?"

"They are making babies like me. Hundreds of them. We can't leave them here," Olesya said, her voice sounding convincing even though her mind was full of doubts.

"They are making an army," Sebastian said.

"They're like us. Is there another way?" Alexander asked.

"We can't rescue them, and we can't leave them here," Olesya said, deepening her voice to sound more assertive and convincing for his sake. "They're like us, Alexander, exactly like us. That's why we must save them from a horrific life ahead," Olesya said.

"Save them? You mean kill them?"

Olesya didn't answer. She pursed her lips and looked past him.

Zoe touched Alexander's shoulder. "We must hurry and get out of here before we cause a war," Zoe said. "We couldn't have prepared for this. This...this... this exceeds anything I could have imagined. Olesya is right, Alexander. We don't have a choice."

Olesya locked eyes with Zoe, and Zoe nodded. Olesya tugged Alexander's arm and pulled him toward the door. They left the room and continued walking through the building, opening more doors and finding similar incubators inside the remaining rooms.

Sebastian grinned at the sight of a safe in one small, dark room.

Mary sat by the safe to hack it open. "It won't take long," she said under her breath.

After a short while, she opened it, revealing a glass case full of dark, shiny fragments. Sebastian carefully removed the case and put it in his backpack. They exited the room and met with the other two groups, leaving the building together. They spilled from the building and, like dark warriors preparing for a battle, formed a line at the building's entrance. Olesya and Zoe exchanged glances, and Zoe gave a signal to her dark soldiers. Alexander stood in the back, blinking rapidly, watching the black-clad men and women thrust their arms at the building together as a terrifying, portentous force. The bluish-silvery globs of energy left their hands and combined into one giant glimmering ball. Then it burst into waves and hit the building. It separated in the middle, crumbled from the top, and then exploded into a million pieces as the dark silhouettes ran away along a hazy street illuminated only by stars, which just appeared to witness the spectacle.

Olesya sank into a soft leather seat of Zoe's private jet and, glued to the outside window, stared into the darkness. A black knit hat rested on her lap, revealing her bandaged head over the honey-colored hair. She saw Zoe's face reflected on the dark glass, and although she couldn't see her eyes, lost in the shadows, she sensed Zoe was watching her. Olesya kept thinking about what Zoe had said, regretting not studying dark matter with Sara before going to Italy as soon as she learned about Sergi becoming the president.

Learning to ski, speak Italian, and impersonate a high-end Italian prostitute, which, according to her uncle, Sergi indulged in during his skiing escapades whenever he accomplished something worthwhile, turned out to be the medicine she needed. Deeply focused on her studies, she thought less of the task ahead. Now that she had accomplished what she had planned, yet felt no satisfaction or relief.

Her stomach tightened, remembering the fleeting moments when

Sergi had tried to tell her something. Why did he hesitate when he had a chance to kill her? What was she not understanding or... remembering? And where was her Kevlar vest? Zoe claimed that the cleaning crew disposed of it. But did they? She now had to rely on Zoe to answer her questions, and that thought weighed heavily on her mind.

"How are you going to secure the black fragments?" she asked Zoe.

"I'll lock them in a safe."

"Your safe."

"You and Sara will have full access to the fragments to study them."

"Ah. You said something about going back to the darkness just before I passed out. Why did you say that? What did you mean by that?" Olesya asked.

"Sara is a better person to explain it to you in your nerdy scientific terms," Zoe said, yawning and disinterested.

Olesya stared out the window for a while, stewing over the strangeness of her relationship with Zoe and suddenly feeling alone and lost.

"It's connected to our research into dark matter, is it not? How?" Olesya asked, still looking out the window.

Zoe did not answer. Olesya glanced at Zoe and narrowed her eyes, noticing her head slumped to the side, fast asleep or pretending to be.

What are you hiding from me? And why?

Rising early, Olesya sat up in bed as the sun was just peeking from behind the horizon. She had a strange dream, but the details disappeared when she woke up. She vaguely remembered a girl with long blonde hair standing with her back to her and calling her name. Unable to respond or move, she desperately wanted to comfort the crying girl, but she could only listen, overwhelmed with sadness. Crying, the girl vanished into the black void.

The dream stirred a longing for the closeness of another human being with whom she shared her soul. Someone who loved her. Her parents loved her; she knew that, but the bond with her brother was unparalleled by anything she had experienced in her life before their reunion. She could share her feelings with him, and he would understand them as if they were his own. Olesya never even suspected that such a bond was possible. It was getting stronger the more time they spent together. Even just being in the same room seemed to have strengthened their connection, as if invisible waves bound them together into one being.

She sprang from her bed and knocked on Alexander's door. He opened it, still half-asleep, but his face lit up when he saw his sister. Sensing her mood, Alexander embraced her.

Olesya's eye was still swollen and bruised, and her arm rested in a sling. They sat on the bed while he gently unwrapped her bandages. His long, slender fingers moved quickly, separating her hair from the wraps.

"This may be your calling," Olesya said, chuckling, and then chanted. "Nurse Alexander. Nurse Alexander."

"Hold still. I am almost done, then you can make fun of me," he said, smiling. "Your wound looks much better. You healed fast."

"Is it healed enough for me to dye my hair?" Olesya asked.

"I'd wait a few days," he said, glancing at Olesya.

She sensed he knew why she wanted to remove the painful reminder. "I'm okay, Alex. Really. I'll be okay," she said, catching his worried glance.

She put her head on his chest, and they sat like that for some time, loving the closeness. Olesya felt his compassion and love penetrate her emotional tortoiseshell, soothing her innermost wounds.

"Did you tell your parents about me?" Alexander asked after a while.

"No."

"Will you?"

Olesya pulled out of the embrace, searching his face.

She considered it, then changed her mind. It had not occurred to her until now, seeing his face, that he yearned to belong to a family, having never had one. She admonished herself for being selfish.

"Yes. I will."

"What do they know?"

"They were aware Sergi was after me, wanting to dissect me, torture me, use me. I told them I shot him because I wanted us to be safe again. Now, they can go back home and back to their lives."

"How did they take it?"

"They knew Sergi was...a...monster. They don't know that he vanished Great Britain or about the army he was building, but they know enough. My Uncle Lech knew him well."

The conversation with Alexander brought back her doubts and unanswered questions. Something about the disappearance of Great Britain and Sergi didn't add up. She must talk to Sara. She wondered whether Sara had changed since working for Zoe. Would she be forthright with her, or would she conform to Zoe's orders and tell her only what she was allowed? She needed to know, but first, she had to talk to Peter.

50

FRIEND

JANUARY 2024

Olesya fiddled with her phone, sitting at her favorite corner table in a local café, sipping coffee and looking out the window. Her swollen face had turned to a less angry yellow-green, but her arm still rested in a sling. Shorter, but black again, her hair fell to her shoulders in waves. She dialed a number and cleared her throat.

"Peter. This is Olesya. Would you like to join me for coffee?" She listened for a while with her eyes closed. "I am okay. I'm at Café Kristina, next to your building. Come and join me if you can."

A few minutes later, Peter entered the café and walked toward her. "Olesya," he said, sounding out of breath.

"Good to see you, Peter."

Peter stood staring at her, unsure of what to say. Like a schoolboy, he acted shy, fiddling with his hands, which suddenly got in his way.

"Why don't you sit down? I need to tell you something," Olesya said.

Peter exhaled and sat watching her quietly, waiting for her to talk.

"I never told you how sorry I was about Laila. It must have been horrible, losing one of your own. I feel partly responsible for her death. They were after me, not her."

"Thank you," Peter mumbled. "Laila was not easy on you. And why were—"

"She was just doing her job," Olesya cut him off. "Anyway, the reason I wanted to see you is...the person responsible for her murder is dead. Laila and many other people were avenged."

"You mean Sergi?"

Olesya nodded. "How did you know?"

"I am a detective, after all," Peter said, smiling. "The entire world knows he disappeared. I traced your Uncle Lech's army days and learned he served with Sergi Orlov. When I found out that Boris was the one who followed your mother, I figured the Russian government was after you and your parents. I put the two together after seeing the article about Sergi Orlov usurping the presidency. The only thing missing was the motive. Why was he after you? When I saw you today, I had a hunch that you were involved in his disappearance. How did you—?"

"Don't ask me questions," Olesya interrupted, making a face. "I can't tell you anything. I just wanted to say I was sorry about Laila and tell you I was okay."

"I understand, but I don't care about what you did and why you did it, and I have a hunch he was someone that the world won't miss. I can see in your eyes that you've gone through a lot." Peter paused. "And I hope this is not the only reason you wanted to see me."

Peter searched her eyes, but she averted them quickly. Peter stirred up feelings she couldn't even perceive before she met him. But something had changed after Italy, and she wasn't ready to scrutinize her feelings just yet, sensing that might come at a price. Something happened to her in Italy. Something profound, but its meaning escaped her. Maybe she wasn't ready to face her demons yet, but she was now sure she possessed them. And Peter didn't deserve demons.

"I...like you, Peter. I like you very much, but there are some things I must do and figure out before...before..."

"Before you can have a friend to talk to?"

"That is just it. There are some things I can never tell you. I don't think a friendship like that would ever work."

"You don't have to tell me everything. Absolute honesty is overrated and not attainable. Do you think that even the best friends know everything about each other? No, this is what I learned on the job. Wives, husbands, lovers, friends don't know half the things about each other," Peter said earnestly. "I would never expect you to tell me everything. I think friendship is about letting someone talk about things they want to talk about and not feel pressured, and I would never pressure you."

"I wouldn't know. I don't have many friends, and it is difficult to even think in these terms," Olesya said, still avoiding his eyes.

"I understand. I just need you to realize that I'm here for you and will wait until you're ready to trust me to be your friend. I'm patient."

"I do, but...I'm different...and very confused right now. I don't want you to...to..."

"Judge you? Think less of you? I want to be your friend because I already like you. A lot. I love difficult. I love different. There is a connection between us. Don't tell me you can't feel it too."

Olesya glanced at him and found his eyes. They got lost in each other's eyes for a moment. Then, it was Peter who averted his eyes and left, holding back tears, leaving Olesya wanting to run after him.

But she didn't. She couldn't.

51

THE WORLD NEEDS YOU

JANUARY 2024

Olesya pressed the doorbell and waited. Sara came running to open the front door. She hugged her hard. Olesya winced; her arm still hurt.

"Oh, I'm so sorry. I'm an idiot," Sara said, moving away.

"It is okay. I am much better."

"I'm so happy to see you. Come on in. What can I get you?"

"Wine would be great. Red if you have it."

"You drink wine now?" Sara asked, laughing.

"Yeah. Zoe introduced me to good wine."

Sara and Olesya sat facing each other on orange velvet chairs by a large, wood-encased window overlooking Lake Washington. Lights shimmered in the distance, reflecting in the dark water. The muted lights of lamps placed artfully in all corners of the large living room softened Sara's new house, making it as comfy and warm as her personality.

"How are you doing, kiddo?"

"I...will be better. Some day."

"It must have been so hard for you," Sara whispered.

Sara put her hand on Olesya's, and they sat looking at the water and sipping red wine from oversized glasses. Olesya perceived no discernible difference in Sara's behavior. There was no awkward silence between them, and no hesitation in welcoming her to her new house. Sara was still Sara. Strong, optimistic, and open. A stab of shame for considering that Sara might conform to someone's will just because they paid her well passed through her chest.

"What are the black fragments?" Olesya asked, turning the glass of wine in her hand. She barely touched the wine.

"They are compressed dark matter."

"I had a hunch." Olesya smiled, the word reminding her of Peter. "But how? How is that possible? We were sure it only happened around black holes."

"That is what I thought at first…"

"Could they…be made by…aliens?" Olesya asked hesitantly.

Sara uttered a quick laugh, but her eyes were serious. "Not necessarily. But possibly. Wouldn't that be something?" Sara pondered, shifting her gaze to the window; her eyes got dreamy for a second. "I don't have enough fragments to figure out how they fit together and how they arrived on Earth. From what Zoe told me, one way was through meteorites."

"Do you think Sergi used the fragments on Great Britain?" asked Olesya.

"I believe so."

"How did he vanish the entire island?" Olesya asked.

Sara didn't answer at first, observing Olesya with an enigmatic smile. "You know the answer. You wrote a dissertation about it," Sara said after a while.

"Compressed dark matter dimensional explosion," Olesya whispered in astonishment. "No way! I wrote the paper, but it was just a theory that I could never test or prove."

"That is what I think happened. England, Scotland, and Wales were sucked into the dark dimension," Sara confirmed.

"So they still exist, but in a dark dimension. Could we extract it back?"

"I don't know. I wish I could talk to Zoe's dogs. They obviously know something we don't," Sara said, laughing.

"Zoe said something about going back to darkness. Is that what she meant?"

"Yup. This is the reversal of the Big Bang."

"You told her about it? Explained it to her?"

Sara narrowed her eyes, trying to remember. "Now that you mention it, I don't remember telling her that. Maybe she read it somewhere."

"Hmm." Olesya's suspicions of Zoe surfaced again. What Zoe had said about the US being Russia's enemy number one haunted her. Her stomach tightened when she recalled the ominous tone of Zoe's voice.

"How did they do it? How did they trigger the explosion? If they did it once, they might do it again. Any conflict between Russia and the US might escalate to the world's demise. We must understand it to prevent it," Olesya said and paused. "Does it have something to do with the disappearing dark matter?"

Sara deliberated for a second, then a tiny spark of understanding and a smile lit her face. She clasped her hands. "You might be onto something, kiddo."

"So how do we find out? Do you have any ideas? Is Zoe's lab equipped to handle testing our theory?"

"Equipment isn't the problem. I have a few ideas, but I don't yet know how to test them safely. I could use someone with keen perception, fire, and a healthy dose of doubt," she said and paused, looking into Olesya's eyes. "I need you. The entire world needs you right now."

"I agree, and there is nothing I want more, but I don't trust Zoe and am not convinced that she should be the one holding this power."

"Zoe has been holding this power for quite some time now. The physics lab is not the only lab she has going. She started cancer research using her DNA. She wants to distribute the potential cure for free. I can't tell you how many charities she's founded for people. For animals. And she is not doing it for tax breaks, fame, or recognition. She's doing it because she wants to. She's the only person I know who should hold this secret and protect it from the Sergis of this world."

Olesya pressed her hand to her chest, trying to massage out a sudden, overwhelming pang of despair and hopelessness that settled inside her. Was she wrong about Zoe? Maybe her mind had made up the constant feeling that something was amiss because there was something terribly wrong with her, not Zoe or anyone else.

Sara glanced at Olesya with concern, but continued talking after taking a large sip of wine. "Zoe went through some tough times. She tried to have children and got pregnant a few times, but lost the baby each time. And then she lost someone she loved in a plane crash. None of the seven remaining women in Zoe's group can have children. Their immortality and good health come at a price," Sara said, focusing on the view of the water.

"Misfortune transforms some people into demons and others into angels. She's the second, as far as I can tell." Sara added, not looking at Olesya.

Olesya sighed deeply. "You really mean it, don't you? If you trust her, that is all that matters. I'll be in the lab Monday morning, and we'll figure this out." Olesya sounded convincing, but felt otherwise. She couldn't understand her sudden, overwhelming sadness. She put the glass to her lips and grimaced when its aroma reached her nostrils, and set the glass on the side table.

"What's the matter? My wine is not as good as Zoe's?" Sara laughed.

Olesya shrugged. "I don't feel like drinking. That's all."

Sara patted her on her shoulder. "You'll be all right, kiddo. You just need some rest and...work."

～

For the next three weeks, Olesya and Sara worked on their research plans. Sara, more so than Olesya, who mostly wandered around the lab, looking at the equipment and not being able to concentrate. She complained about the lack of windows or poor ventilation, which was bogus. The state-of-the-art air circulation system made the air clear and fresh. Sara let her be, sensing her friend needed to get used to her new, unorthodox research surroundings.

52

FORGIVIE YOURSELF

FEBRUARY 2024

Olesya sat alone in the dark corner of Zoe's living room, looking longingly out the window and crying silently. Her hair came loose from the ponytail and surrounded her face in strings, wet from tears.

The lights came on suddenly; she jerked upright and quickly wiped her eyes.

The black dogs had materialized out of nowhere to greet Zoe and Alexander as they returned home together. Zoe entered the living room first, then Alexander. Laughing and holding hands, they were startled to see Olesya sitting alone in the darkness. Alexander rushed to her, brushing past Zoe, and Zoe followed.

"What is wrong?" Alexander asked.

"Nothing. I'm just tired," Olesya answered and tried to brush him off with a dismissive gesture.

"You're crying."

"Will you make us tea?" Zoe asked Alexander. He stared at her, not understanding, but then got it. "Of course."

"Forgive yourself," Zoe said. "You did what you had to and put yourself in great danger. We got him. It's over, done with. Time to move on."

"You don't understand," Olesya said. She felt her face crumple into a grimace and heard her voice choke with emotion.

"I think I do. I can't even imagine how it must've felt to have the creep touch you. Look at you now. You are miserable."

"You don't understand," Olesya cried out.

"Tell me then."

"I didn't hate it," said Olesya, throwing her fists into the air. "That is the problem. I didn't hate him as I should've. I told myself I had to seduce and kill him because it needed to be done right. But that wasn't the entire reason. Not at all. Ever since I saw his photograph, I couldn't stop thinking about him and had wanted to meet him. I was attracted to him, drawn to him like a moth to a flame. There is no logical explanation for it, only that there is something seriously wrong with me. Why else would I be attracted to a psychopath if I wasn't one as well? Tell me! I'm bad. I'm...evil. I'm probably as bad as he was, perhaps worse."

I really am a *monster.*

Olesya paused for a moment to wipe her face with her sleeves and looked Zoe in the eye with an intensity that made Zoe back up a step. "Here I go, telling myself that you're the wicked one, but I'm the wicked one. I'm the evil one and should've died in the snow with him."

Olesya finished her rant and fled the room, nearly bumping into Alexander, who had just returned, balancing a steaming pot of tea and a set of clinking porcelain cups on a crystal tray. He set the tray on the table and turned to run after his sister, but Zoe stopped him.

"Let her be. She needs time to herself," she said.

53

REGIS KNOWS

FEBRUARY 2024

Olesya woke up unusually hungry. She dressed hurriedly, opened her bedroom door, and jumped, startled by a dark shape lying outside her bedroom. It was one of Zoe's dogs. The dog got up, stretched, and greeted her with a big, sloppy lick on her hand. Baffled, Olesya stared at the dog, thinking the dog had mistaken her for Zoe and would discover his mistake in no time and run to find his proper mistress.

She trotted downstairs to the kitchen, and the dog followed her, wagging his tail and gazing at her with his black eyes.

When Olesya arrived in the kitchen, Alexander, fresh-eyed and alert, was already sitting at the kitchen island drinking milk and eating a good-looking pastry. Samantha, Zoe's long-term house-keeper, was a superb cook and an even better baker. Sebastian devoured her pastries as soon as they left the oven. Zoe had more control, but she gave in now and then and ate an entire plate of cook-ies. It mattered little. She was immune to weight gain, no matter how many buttery delicacies she consumed. Now, Alexander had joined the glutton team.

Zoe had a half-eaten pastry in front of her and was making an espresso. She glanced at Olesya. "Coffee?"

"Yes, please. Something's wrong with your dog. It keeps following me."

"Oh? Which one?"

"I don't know. I can't tell them apart."

"That is Regis," Zoe said, looking at the dog sitting by Olesya's side. His left ear is a little droopy.

"What are you doing, boy? Regis?" Zoe asked.

The dog gazed at Zoe and wagged his tail, but didn't budge. He stayed by Olesya's side.

"That is strange," Zoe said, but continued making coffee.

Olesya accepted a cup from Zoe's hand and sat by Alexander. She put her head on his shoulder. "Good morning, Alex," she said.

"Are you okay?" he asked.

"I'm good. Don't worry. I had a bad blue day yesterday. I'm going back to the lab today to work with Sara."

"The pastries are divine!" said Alexander with his mouth full. "I'm going to marry Samantha," he added.

Zoe glanced at him and couldn't restrain a smile. Olesya grabbed one scone with a mountain of glazing and a raspberry on top and started munching on it. Suddenly, she stood up and bolted from the kitchen, pressing her hand to her mouth. Afterward, she washed her face and shuffled back to her bedroom, where she fell asleep shortly after picking up a book to read.

Olesya went to the lab the next day but only lasted a few hours. The day after, she didn't bother getting up. Three days later, Olesya woke up and hurried to the bathroom. She vomited into the toilet for the third time in three days. Avoiding the mirror, she rinsed her mouth and brushed her teeth. With a sinking feeling, she left the bathroom and sat on her bed, clutching the sheets with both hands.

Later that afternoon, Olesya sat on the toilet, grimacing while holding a pregnancy test in her hand, extended as far away from herself as she could. After a few minutes, inhaled deeply and slowly brought the test within her view. The white plastic tester fell on the floor from her trembling fingers. The test was positive.

54

CHOICE

FEBRUARY 2024

Zoe knocked on Olesya's bedroom door. Olesya had locked herself in the bedroom and had not come out for two days. Alexander had tried talking to his sister but failed. She had told him she wanted to be left alone. He waited, sitting outside her room with his back to her door for hours. Slouching, he left when she shouted at him to go away. He couldn't even reach her telepathically. They just learned how to use this additional gift they had shared. But now, she had somehow locked herself out of his reach.

Zoe paced her living room in between checking on Olesya's door. It was already afternoon on the third day since Olesya had locked herself away. Setting her jaw, she marched to Olesya's bedroom.

"I'll open the door with a spare key if you don't open the door in five minutes."

No sound came out of the bedroom.

Zoe waited a few minutes and shouted again. "Time's up. I'm coming in whether you want me to or not."

She unlocked the door and peeked into the bedroom. The closed windows and drawn curtains created an oppressive darkness, thick with misery. Olesya's body lying on the bed was barely visible. Holding her hand to her chest, Zoe approached Olesya and, with a trembling hand, reached to check her pulse. She retracted her hand as silent sobs lurched through Olesya's body, and her fingers touched the wet pillow saturated by the tears rolling down Olesya's cheeks. Olesya was alive. Miserable but alive.

Zoe sat on the edge of the bed and touched Olesya's head, expecting to be brushed off. But she didn't react, so Zoe stroked her head. A few minutes passed with Zoe gently patting Olesya's head. Olesya stopped sobbing.

"Talk to me," Zoe said.

Olesya didn't answer at first but then glanced at Zoe with eyes so swollen from crying they resembled black slits, rimmed with crimson.

"Tell me what's wrong. Is it still about Sergi?"

Olesya pointed toward the bathroom, then she covered her head with a blanket. Zoe, guessing her intentions, walked to the bathroom. It didn't take her long to notice three pregnancy tests lying by the sink, and the fourth one, in pieces on the floor. When she reached for one from the counter and glanced at it, her shoulders arched back.

"Oh my God," she whispered. "This can't be. How could this possibly happen?"

Before she returned to Olesya, Zoe stood in the bathroom staring at the test.

When Zoe returned to the bedroom, the covers were off, and Olesya's eyes were open with a plea for help.

Zoe sat on the bed beside her, patting her hand. "This may seem like the darkest day of your life. It'll get better eventually, but you must face it, and the sooner you do, the less miserable you'll be in the end. I can help by listening and being there for you. I've been through this before and I believe talking to someone who has been through this helps."

"You don't know how I feel."

"Not quite, but I have been through some tough—"

"Sara told me. But I'm not you."

"You're right. I'm not you, but we can at least talk about it. Why don't you get up, shower, and join me for tea and something to eat?

You haven't eaten in a while. Please. You are not solving anything by lying in bed and making yourself miserable. Come on, let's figure this out. Sebastian and Alexander are not home. It will be just the two of us."

Olesya locked eyes with Zoe and nodded.

Samantha, Zoe's housekeeper, brought a tray of open-face sandwiches and a steaming pot of tea to the living area. She placed the tray on the coffee table and glanced at Zoe expectantly.

"Thank you, Samantha. That'll be all for today. Take the rest of the day off," Zoe said.

"Of course. Thank you, and have a good evening. Don't forget there are pastries in the pantry," Samantha said, leaving the room.

"Thank you!" Zoe answered. "Enjoy your evening."

Zoe paced the living room, glancing toward the stairway and listening, expecting to hear Olesya's footsteps.

At last, Olesya appeared. Showered, she looked better, although her eyes were still red and swollen. She'd arranged her wet hair in a chaotic ponytail and wore a comfortable cotton sweatshirt and pants.

"Good. Sit down and eat," Zoe said.

"I'm not hungry."

"Just try one. Sam's sandwiches are works of art. She puts her soul into these little heavenly things. They're even better than her pastries, melting in your mouth. You must eat."

Olesya sat on the couch, staring at the tasty-looking and masterfully garnished sandwiches and smelling the different herbs, eyeing the cheese and pastrami, cucumbers, and immediately her parched mouth started watering. Her brain did not register hunger, but her mouth and stomach did as she drooled, eyeing the food. She took one sandwich and bit into it. The sandwich disappeared into her mouth, then another, and another. Watching Olesya devouring the sandwiches, Zoe waited.

Olesya finished all the sandwiches. She stared at the empty tray in surprise.

"I'm sorry I didn't leave any for you. No idea what came over me. I never eat..." Olesya said and belched without finishing her sentence.

"That's okay. I already had my lunch," Zoe lied.

They sat in silence.

Zoe wanted to wait for Olesya to break the silence but couldn't wait and blurted out. "What are you going to do?"

"About what?" Olesya asked with a voice still hoarse from crying.

"You'll have to decide. Soon."

"What do you mean?" Olesya asked, but looking at Zoe's face, she understood, but was unnerved by Zoe's apparent impatience with her.

"I haven't thought about it this way," Olesya said, rubbing her forehead.

"Do you want to keep this baby? His baby?!"

"It is also my baby."

Olesya glanced at Zoe and was taken aback, seeing Zoe flash her eyes at her and grimace.

"Didn't Sara tell you?" Zoe continued. "None of us has ever carried a pregnancy to term. Decide if you want to end it or wait for it to happen," Zoe said, and seeing Olesya's expression, added in a softer tone. "It doesn't matter whether you want the baby. It'll still hurt and leave wounds that never heal. The longer you wait, the more it'll hurt, and the deeper the wounds will be."

"We're not the same. You and I were not created the same way. The outcome might differ from what you have experienced. I'm torn, like there are two of me living in the same body, arguing and growing further apart," Olesya continued. "One wants it more than anything in the world. The other one doesn't, but ending the pregnancy is not what either wants."

Olesya glanced at Zoe and stood up, seeing Zoe flaring her nostrils and flashing her eyes with anger and resentment at her again.

Zoe touched Olesya's hand and quickly assumed a slightly gentler expression. "Nature will decide for you eventually. You were made differently, but you're the same as me. It's your decision, but you'll regret it if you wait too long."

Zoe left, and Olesya sat staring after her and started having doubts. *Was Zoe right?*

THE MUMMIES

FEBRUARY 2024

A few days had gone by. Olesya stayed in her room most of the time but came out to eat and stopped crying. She stopped worrying about the pregnancy and stopped trying to decide, and as soon as she did, she felt immediate relief. "I'll let fate decide for me," she mumbled to herself and then immediately imagined Sasha's smiling face. *Yeah. Mama would be happy, and it wouldn't matter to her who the father was.*

The next morning, Olesya woke up peaceful and well-rested, as her night had been uncharacteristically free of dreams. With her subconsciousness free from disturbing and vivid premonitions, Olesya believed she could tackle any problem that came her way. In that state of mind, she checked her phone and realized she had a voicemail from Sara, recorded two days ago.

"Olesya, call me. I have something to tell you about what you asked me to do. My colleagues at the genetics lab have your DNA results," Sara said, and paused. "It'd be best if you came to my lab. I want to tell you this in person," she added without her usual laughter between words.

Olesya tilted her head and set her phone aside, shaking her head. She had never asked Sara to run her DNA, or had she forgotten? Sara sounded serious, and Sara always laughed. What was in her DNA test results that made Sara sound so serious?

She jumped out of bed and showered. Refreshed, she dressed and left her bedroom, stopping by the living room to talk to Zoe. But she wasn't in the living room or the kitchen.

Olesya shrugged and drove her Jeep to the lab. Now having unrestricted access to the lab, she glared at the electronic panel to scan her iris and slid inside the building. Longing for mental stimulation, her restlessness and curiosity grew, realizing her conversation with Sara concerning dark matter had just begun. She was looking forward to working with Sara, a welcome distraction from other issues and nagging existential questions swarming through her mind. The memory of Sergi's questioning expression at the ski resort that night and then just before she killed him stayed with her. Now, she had another reason growing in her belly she needed a distraction from.

She headed toward Sara's office but found only dark monitors in an equally dark room. Surprised (Sara was always working), Olesya looked around, searching for the other lab employees. She finally found a hunched man standing by a desk and walked toward him. Engrossed in the notes he was scribbling in a large notebook, he didn't immediately look at her. She cleared her throat, and only then did he reluctantly raise his balding head to glance at her. An old-fashioned leather belt held his khaki pants from falling off his thin frame, and his distressed brown leather shoes looked like they had survived centuries of shuffling.

He watched her through his thick-lensed glasses without hiding his displeasure. "Can I help you?" he asked.

"Yes. I hope so. I'm looking for Sara. Do you have any idea where I can find her?" Olesya asked.

"She's on vacation. Somewhere in South America, but don't ask me whereabouts." The man turned away, letting her know the prying was over.

"That's strange. She messaged me two days ago to come and see her. When did she leave?"

"I'm not her keeper. Now, if you'll excuse me," the man said without turning to face Olesya.

Olesya left the lab without thanking him. Confused, she called Zoe but only reached her voicemail with a laconic greeting: "You've reached Zoe Brie. Leave a message."

Olesya got into her Jeep and tried calling Alexander's phone next. She gathered, not without distress and disappointment, that Zoe and Alexander were in a romantic relationship and spending more and more time together. He answered on the third ring.

"Hey, Olesya. You are up and about," he exclaimed, sounding elated.

Olesya's voice sounded sharper than she intended. "Where is Zoe?"

"At home?"

"She's not home. Have you spoken to her today? She's not answering her phone. I need to ask her something important."

"What's so important? You sound agitated."

"Sara left me a message two days ago that she got the results of my DNA analysis and to see her in person. She said I'd asked her to run it, but I hadn't. She sounded off."

"So what did she say?"

"That's just it," Olesya sighed, as her rosy morning outlook on life turned sour. "Sara is not at her lab. Her colleague said she was vacationing in South America. She's not answering her phone either. I wanted to ask Zoe if she's spoken to her. Something is not right."

"Vacationing in South America? Why South America? Where in South America?"

"I don't know. That's all I got out of her grumpy colleague."

"Go home and see if Zoe is there. I am in New York now, but I am hopping on the plane as soon as we hang up and will be there this evening. I'll text her."

Seven hours later, Alexander ran into the house, looking for Olesya.

"Olesya, are you here? Olesya?" Alexander yelled.

"I'm here. I'm in the kitchen."

He walked into the kitchen and found Olesya sitting at the kitchen island with her back to him. He came closer and gasped at a plate full of pastries and a glass of milk in front of her. Olesya swallowed a chunk of pastry and wiped her milky mustache with her sleeve, glancing at him furtively.

"Sam knows how to bake pastries," he said, staring at her. She continued eating, so he grabbed one and sat by his sister.

"I've never seen you eat so much, but I'm glad you have an appetite."

They ate in silence until the pastries were gone. Olesya wiped her mouth again and burped.

"Miss Piggy," Alexander said, laughing.

Olesya shrugged.

"Are you going to tell me what's going on?" he asked.

"What do you mean?"

"Why did you lock yourself in the bedroom?"

"I'm out now, so drop it," Olesya snapped. "I'm okay now. I'll tell you later," she added, her stomach constricting after snapping at him. She wasn't sure why she didn't want to tell him about the pregnancy yet, but suspected it was the humiliation that stopped her. How could she, the pragmatic scientist, have allowed herself to get pregnant? She had time to learn how to ski and to speak Italian, but none to get contraceptive pills? She couldn't tell him until she understood it herself. But every time she tried to think logically about it, she saw Sergi's blue eyes. She couldn't understand why she kept seeing his blue eyes, not black.

"Whenever you are ready."

"Did you hear from Zoe?" Olesya changed the subject.

"Oh yeah. I enjoyed seeing you turn into a glutton and almost forgot. She texted me she went to—"

"South America," Olesya finished his sentence. "Did she say why?"

"Nope. She said she couldn't talk and that she'd call later."

"How can we find out where she went? Do you know where Sebastian is? Is he with her?"

"I doubt it. Sebastian and Henry left soon after we returned from Russia. Zoe sent him on a mission to Spain," Alexander said, and paused.

A mischievous smile flashed across his face, and Olesya couldn't help but smile too, her chest filling with love for this handsome being. *He is my brother. This wonderful man is my brother.*

She welled up with tears.

He stood and tugged on her sleeve, pulling her away from the kitchen. "Let's go. I have an idea," he said as he led her upstairs, skipping steps.

"Where are we going?"

"Zoe's room."

"Why?" Olesya asked, grimacing and stopping. "I'm not comfortable breaking into her room."

"You want to know where they went and why?"

Olesya nodded.

"Come on, then."

She remembered the strange voicemail from Sara and thought invading Zoe's privacy was a small price to pay for an answer. She followed him to Zoe's study. Alexander quickly found her laptop in a cabinet, and the screen lit up after he typed a password.

"You know her password?" Olesya was aware they were close, but she didn't think they were that close.

"Yup," he confirmed without explaining.

"Okay, I won't ask."

Alexander found Zoe's recent internet search history. A page opened, and the siblings stared at the screen in disbelief. They saw a picture of two mummified bodies—a teenage boy and a girl—wearing elaborate Incan clothes embellished with jewelry and beads. Their long black hair was bound in intricate leather straps adorned with jewels. A gold necklace rested on the girl's chest. Inside, a dark stone shone with an ominous luster.

The article below described the photo: "German anthropologist

Veronika Steinberg discovered two well-preserved mummies on the frozen mountaintops of the Andes near the Argentinian border of the Juncal Glacier area. The melting ice exposed the bodies of the children who had been sacrificed as part of an Incan ritual, capacocha, nearly fifteen hundred years ago. Before the priest left the children to die on the stone platform, he fed them maize alcohol to ease the pain and fear of dying. Sacrificing their offspring in the highest places humans could reach was the greatest honor, elevating the parents' status and immortalizing the children as deities. The sacrifice solidified the connection between the family and the Inca emperor, considered the Sun God. What is unusual is that someone enclosed them in a golden cage."

Olesya sat reading the article several times, as if reading more than once would clarify it. "Do you think what I think?" she finally asked.

"The necklace? Do you think it's the black shard?"

Olesya nodded. "I think Zoe went there to check it out. But why did she take Sara with her? And what does it have to do with our DNA?"

Olesya paused, mulling something over. And then her face lit up with an idea. "Do you want to go to Chile?"

"Wait. We can't be sure they are in Chile. Shouldn't we wait for them to return?" Alexander appeared doubtful. "We'll be chasing ghosts. We have no clue where they are. Let's try to get in touch with them again."

"We could try to contact the anthropologist," Olesya suggested.

"Okay, I'm on it."

He searched for the anthropologist's phone or email on the laptop. Olesya texted Zoe and Sara and asked them to reply ASAP, and not hearing from Alexander, she asked him. "How is it going? Did you find her?"

When he didn't respond, Olesya glanced at him and noticed his face drained of color as he stared at the monitor. She peeked over his shoulder and exhaled, seeing a *Santiago Times* article showing a mangled and burned car deep in a ravine. The Spanish headline read in large, bold letters. *A German anthropologist, Veronika Steinberg, died in an accident. The police speculate the driver lost control of the vehicle on a curvy road to Santiago.*

"Alex, what is it? Translate it for me," Olesya asked, even though she had already guessed what the article said.

"I have a bad feeling. We need to find Zoe. She might be in trouble," Alex said, massaging his neck.

"And Sara," Olesya said. "Since you're such a computer genius, can you hack into Zoe's email?"

"I think so." Alexander typed something, and Zoe's email opened. "What are we looking for?"

"Find the most recent emails from Sara," Olesya said, looking over his shoulder.

He opened an email from Sara from two days ago.

"Call me. It is important. It concerns Olesya's DNA. Sara."

"Our DNA. She found something in our DNA, and the next day they flew to Chile." Alexander sounded perplexed. "Looks like we are flying to Santiago."

"Can we take Zoe's plane?" Olesya asked.

"I don't see why not, but let's call Sebastian."

Alexander dialed Sebastian's number, and he answered on the second ring, as if expecting the call.

Sebastian spoke without waiting for a greeting. "Get ready. We are flying to Santiago."

"You know about Chile?" Alexander asked.

"I sensed Zoe was in trouble. Her pilot told me he flew her and Sara to Santiago, and then they took the helicopter somewhere high in the mountains. I was about to call you. I'll be back tomorrow morning, and we will fly at once."

56

THE CHAMBER

FEBRUARY 2024

Shortly after the plane landed at Aerodromo Tobalaba Airport in eastern Santiago, Sebastian, Elliot, Olesya, and Alexander raced out, each carrying a backpack, and headed for a chopper waiting for them in front of a hangar. Sebastian disappeared into the cockpit and talked to the pilot while the rest of the group sat in their seats and buckled up.

"All set. They will drop us off where Zoe had landed," Sebastian announced after he returned from the cockpit and sat across from Olesya. She's never seen Sebastian's eyes lose their shine and his lips not curve up in a smile.

"Did Zoe tell you she was going to Chile?" Olesya asked Sebastian.

"No, but I had a terrible dream about Zoe and then a persistent bad feeling. I texted her, and she didn't respond. It's not like her. When I saw the creepy mummies and the dead anthropologist, I had to do something. I'm going nuts worrying."

"What do you think about the necklace?" Alexander asked.

"Yeah, the necklace. I speculated that's why Zoe came here," Sebastian said.

The helicopter landed on a desolate plateau surrounded by

mountains that were partially hidden behind dark clouds. Dark gray with a tinge of red, the heavy clouds cast threatening shadows on the black, jagged peaks blanketed by snow and ice.

The icy wind blew in the faces of the small group as soon as they left the chopper. Casting heavy glances at their surroundings, zipping their jackets, and putting their hoods up, they hoisted their backpacks.

Olesya felt the wind go through her jacket and shivered from the cold and unsettling surroundings. She put her gloved hands into her pockets and glanced at Sebastian. "Where did her signal disappear?"

"This way," Sebastian answered, looking at his phone and pointing northeast.

They climbed through the unwelcoming, rugged terrain for two hours. The wind continued blowing, chilling them through their clothes despite the warmth generated by their bodies during the harrowing climb. They climbed, slipping and falling until they reached the closest peak. As they got closer, soil disturbance and yellow aluminum posts alerted them to recent activity in the area. The posts lay scattered on the ground, covering broken rock slabs. Olesya reached for a post and inspected it.

"University of Argentina," Olesya read the small print on the post. "This is not the place," she added. "A German team discovered the mummies, and the posts seem quite old, like they've been here for some time. Plants had already grown through the cracks in the rock," she said. "The one on Zoe's laptop was supposedly a new discovery."

While Olesya, Sebastian, and Elliot were inspecting the post, Alexander wandered away with his head low and eyes on the ground. He climbed higher and disappeared into the clouds. Bored with looking at the aluminum sticks, Olesya glanced around for more clues. She panicked, not seeing her brother.

"Where is Alexander? Alexander, where are you?"

"Come over here," he shouted back. "You've got to see this."

They followed his voice, climbed higher, and reached the peak. Alexander stood dangerously close to the edge of the cliff, looking down. He heard them behind him and turned his astonished face toward them.

"Come look," he said, pointing down.

They approached him and followed his gaze. Before their eyes stretched an enormous crater nestled between the sharp peaks of the mountains. Black, ominous-looking water filled half the crater.

"This is where Zoe's signal disappears," Sebastian whispered.

They looked at each other, guessing what was on everyone's mind.

"This looks like the one in Belyaska, except for the lake," Elliot said.

"Exactly. Isn't that strange? Let's go closer to the crater. Let's go down," Olesya said.

Climbing the northern side of the mountain, covered with a thick layer of snow and ice, proved a slow and arduous task. There was not much room for error. Each step had to be measured carefully to avoid slipping down the steep slope with black rock sticking its jagged fingers out of the ice and snow.

"Look!" exclaimed Alexander, pointing at something in the snow. Olesya traced his finger and saw an impression of a boot in the snow.

Olesya put her foot next to it. The imprint matched her size and had a large "A" in the middle. "It might be Zoe's," she said. "What do you think?" she asked Sebastian.

"That looks like her Asolo boot," Sebastian said.

They continued climbing down until they reached the edge of the crater. It seemed even more sinister, with its still, dark water looking like a molten lava bed. The area by the crater was alarmingly quiet and darker; the clouds stole the sun, casting dark shadows on the lake and the surrounding area. Complete silence enveloped them. Not even the sounds of birds or wind interrupted the eerie stillness. They stood silently, gathering their strength and wits to resume exploring the area.

"Should we walk along the crater?" Elliot asked, walking away.

"That is going to take forever, considering how huge this crater is.

We should start with the western border, which is dry now," Olesya said.

"Where did you go, Zoe?" Sebastian looked up as if he were asking the sky.

"I've got another footprint," Elliot exclaimed from a distance.

"Looks like the other one," Olesya said when she walked close enough to see it.

"It is pointing this way," Sebastian said. As he continued walking west, his pace increased and energized.

Elliot found another partial footprint that was different but appeared small, like it belonged to a woman or a child.

"This must be Sara's," Olesya said and sprinted forward.

At last, they reached the area the lake didn't capture. They stood at the edge, straining their eyes to see the bottom of the crater, but their view was obstructed by countless jagged edges protruding out of the walls, as if the crater were hiding a secret.

"There is something down there," Sebastian said, straining his eyes to see.

"What is it?" Olesya tugged his jacket impatiently.

"It's...It looks like a rope," Sebastian finally said.

"Okay, let's rappel," Olesya said. She threw her backpack on the ground with a sigh of relief and unpacked a climbing rope, a harness, and an anchor, while wondering how fortuitous it was that Sebastian had insisted on bringing climbing gear on the trip. Seeing her questioning eyes when he packed heavy ropes and anchors into their packs, he shrugged and then chuckled uneasily. "You never know when you'll need climbing gear. We're in the mountains."

Everyone followed Olesya and put their harnesses on in silence. Alexander and Sebastian secured the anchor and attached the rappelling device to the rope.

"I'll go first," Sebastian said, and started rappelling down. "I've got a hundred feet of rope. It should be enough. I don't think it is deeper than sixty or seventy feet on this end."

"It should be enough," Elliot said, glancing down.

"Do you know how to do it?" Alexander asked Olesya.

"I learned it in Italy."

"Sorry," he said, averting his eyes. "That was dumb of me."

Olesya shrugged. "It's all right."

They rappelled to the bottom of the crater. Resembling a nest of green snakes, a coil of green climbing rope greeted them from the ground. It didn't appear to have been there long.

"Is it Zoe's?" Olesya asked Sebastian.

"It might be," Sebastian said. "It probably is since she likes this color."

The bottom of the crater and the sides were dark, almost black, spiky rock. Alexander and Sebastian started walking, examining the rock walls. Olesya and Elliot stood still, taking in the strangeness of this place, while Olesya scanned the crater walls, searching for something with the odd sensation of having been here before. She couldn't remember, but she was certain of it, and more so with every passing second.

"Are you okay?" Elliot asked, glancing at her. "You look like you've seen a ghost."

"I am experiencing déjà vu. I've been here before, underground," she said in a dreamy voice.

"Underground?" Elliot asked.

"I don't know if it's a memory or a premonition, but I'm certain there's something under the crater."

"Okay, let's search for an entrance," Elliot blurted, glancing at her with an odd grin, as if what she'd said pleased him. He started walking alongside the walls, scrutinizing them, searching for irregularities.

The sensation of having experienced this situation before came stronger than ever and shot through Olesya like a titillating, tingling wave. She closed her eyes, and her arms shot out in front of her as if she were trying to reach for something. In her mind, she was walking in pitch blackness toward a distant light. She didn't know what the light was and why she felt its pull, but she sensed it was important.

"There is nothing else here," Sebastian said, walking back. "It's just rocks everywhere," he added, sounding disappointed. Then, he gasped when his eyes landed on Olesya standing motionless with her eyes shut tight. "Are you okay?"

She didn't respond because she hadn't heard him. Her vision now led her to the blonde-haired girl, calling her name and crying. The girl was in a dark passageway, and that passageway was here, underneath this forsaken crater.

"Olesya, open your eyes! Olesya!" he yelled at her.

She didn't respond. He ran up to her and shook her, shouting her name. She finally looked at him with glassy eyes.

"You gave me a scare, little sister," he said, and exhaled.

"We must find the entrance."

"Entrance to what?"

"I'm not sure. There's something underneath."

Sebastian scrutinized her as if assessing her mental stability.

"Don't look at me like that. There *is* something down there. Maybe that is where Zoe is," Olesya shouted at him. The déjà vu had gotten stronger. A sudden fright overwhelmed her, and she started panicking that time might run out for Sara.

"We must hurry. We must find them!" she yelled at Sebastian.

"Okay, okay. I believe you," he said, but he didn't seem convinced.

"Where's Alexander?" Olesya asked, looking around.

"He walked in the opposite direction I did. He should've been back by now."

Her pulse quickened. "I don't see him anywhere."

Olesya and Sebastian looked around, searching for Alexander. They saw Elliot still plodding along the wall, but then he disappeared from view when he stepped down to a lower area of the crater.

"Let's go!" Olesya shouted and ran in the direction where Alexander had gone and Elliot had disappeared. Sebastian followed, and they ran past the point where Edeeminglliot vanished and, not seeing him or Alexander, kept running, shouting their names.

Suddenly, they saw Elliot emerge from the rock wall, waving his hands enthusiastically.

"I found a passage," he said. "You were right, Olesya. There's something under the crater."

"Have you seen Alexander?" she asked.

"No, but I didn't go far. He might be ahead. This passage was open when I arrived, so I suspect Alex found it and went in."

Elliot stood by the wall and put his arm through it. His arm disappeared into the wall.

"Optical illusion," Elliot said. "But clever Alexander must have seen it, or maybe even opened it somehow."

Olesya shook her head. "Why didn't he wait for us?"

"Wow! Strange. How is that even possible? Someone went to a hell of a lot of trouble to conceal this so well," Sebastian said, examining the wall. "I wouldn't have noticed it walking by. Looks just like the rest of the wall. What does our scientist think? Olesya?" he added, gazing at her with a toothy grin.

Olesya put her arm through the wall and felt the cold air settling on it. She inspected the opening but found nothing conspicuous, so she rummaged through her backpack and found a headlamp. But she saw only darkness ahead of her when she shone her headlamp through the opening.

"I don't know what it is. I'm stumped. As far as I know, no one has this kind of technology. It might be some kind of natural yet unexplained phenomenon," Olesya said, then, imagining Alexander wandering the dark passage by himself and lost, barked an order: "We must find Alexander now!"

She entered the opening and walked forward. Sebastian followed. Her headlamp reflected on the smooth, seamless, glistening black rock. The passage led them down; the slope increased gradually.

Elliot stopped and grabbed Olesya's arm. "Wait," he whispered. "Listen. Someone is calling your name."

Olesya listened, hearing something, but couldn't discern the words.

"It's Alexander," Sebastian said. "I think he's yelling something that sounds like 'watch out' or something like that."

Elliot shone his flashlight down into the hole and whistled. "Holy shit! That is deep," he exclaimed. "And it stinks!"

A foul smell of ancient dust and mold oozed from the hole in the ground. Olesya kneeled by the black abyss in front of her. One more step and she'd tumble into the dark chasm below.

"Alexander, are you there? Alex? Are you okay?" she yelled into the dark void and then listened. She heard something. She still couldn't detect the words, but she recognized her brother's voice.

"What do we do?" She turned and glanced at Sebastian and Elliot.

"We've got to go down there," Sebastian said. "You and Elliot should still have a rope in your backpacks. We can rappel down."

Olesya laid the rope and anchors on the floor while Sebastian attached a monstrous drill bit and tried to drill a hole for the anchor in. But the drill did not penetrate the rock.

"This is not ordinary rock. The drill didn't even scratch the damn thing!" Sebastian said, scratching his head.

"Why don't you just lower me down there?" Olesya suggested. "I am the smallest. It makes the most sense," she added.

"You shouldn't go down there by yourself," Sebastian said.

"Do you have a better idea? We don't have a choice. If Alexander is down there hurt, I can tie him to the rope, and you two can pull him up."

"It makes sense," Elliot said.

"Okay." Sebastian gave in. "But we must keep in touch. Yell if you run out of rope or want to go back up for any reason."

"I will."

"We might not be able to hear each other clearly," Olesya said. "I will pull on the rope twice when I am safe on the ground and three times if I need you to pull one of us up."

Olesya hesitated for a second, imagining what she might find below—finding her brother injured and not being able to help him. She drew a deep breath, closed her eyes, concentrated, and sent Alexander a telepathic message: "Alex, I am coming."

They lowered her down. She shone her headlamp on the walls of the shaft, which were made of the same glistening black material. With trembling hands, she operated the rappel device, counting seconds, distracting herself from the fear of what awaited her below.

"Are you okay?" Sebastian yelled from above.

"I'm fine," she yelled back, surprised at how loud and crisp her voice sounded in the shaft. She finally touched the bottom with her feet, with just a few feet of rope to spare. She tugged on the rope twice and yelled. "I'm at the bottom and okay. I'm going to find Alexander."

She heard a faint reply that sounded like, "Okay."

Olesya untied the rope and shone her flashlight around and saw the same black and seamless material everywhere. She expected a musty, earthy smell, but the air seemed energized. There was a faint metallic taste in her mouth as she walked.

"Alexander! Alexander, answer me! Where are you?" she yelled, her voice sounding loud and sharp, as if the hollowness of the corridor amplified it. She walked for a few minutes until she noticed a faint light in the distance. With her heart racing, she walked faster until she reached a circular chamber and two ghostly figures in the distant corner, illuminated by a headlamp.

Recognizing Alexander, she ran toward him. When she was closer, she saw him kneeling by Sara, who lay motionless on the floor. Olesya kneeled by Alexander, and noticing Sara's chest rise and fall, she sighed. Her friend was alive. Alexander appeared unharmed, except for a few cuts and scrapes on his forehead and hands. She couldn't understand how he hadn't gotten hurt more by falling nearly a hundred feet.

"I bounced off the walls. There was a slope to the tunnel," he said, reading her mind.

"Where is Zoe?"

"I don't know. I tried to wake Sara to ask her, but she was not responsive."

Olesya tried to wake Sara by talking to her and shaking her shoulder. Pale and diminished, Sara appeared to be in a deep sleep. Olesya noticed something sticking out of her mouth, removed it, and examined it under her flashlight.

"It's some kind of leaf," she murmured. "Not sure what it is. I'm not that good with plants."

"Let me see," Alexander said, and took the leaf from Olesya's hand. "I think it's a coca leaf."

"Someone drugged her," Olesya whispered. "Just like the children were…just like the mummies."

"I don't know what to do now or where else to look for Zoe," Alexander's quivering voice sounded distant and hollow, and his wide eyes darted between Olesya and Sara.

"Water. Let's try water. Pour it over her face and chest," Olesya said while unzipping Sara's jacket.

Alexander poured a few drops of water from his flask onto Sara's face.

"More, pour more."

Alexander poured more water. Sara's face twitched, and her eyes opened and then closed again. Olesya slapped her face.

"Sara, wake up! You must wake up! It's me. Wake up, Sara. Please."

Sara opened her eyes.

"Sara, you must wake up now. Someone drugged you. Where's Zoe?"

Sara didn't respond. She parted her lips, but no sound came out, and her eyes shut.

"We must get her out of here," Olesya said. "She needs medical attention."

"Shouldn't we look around first?" Alexander asked.

Olesya agreed, seeing his worried look. "Okay, but let's be quick."

"Look for imperfections and indentations on the walls," Alexander said, stroking the smooth black walls with his hands.

"What kind of indentation?"

"Possibly a triangle. That is how I found the passage. I noticed a triangular indentation in the wall and pressed it. The wall wavered, became opaque, and the passage appeared."

Olesya glanced at Sara, and seeing her steady breathing, walked toward the wall to help Alexander. She inspected every inch of the wall and found nothing. The black walls were flawless—there were no imperfections; nothing stood out. There was a slight velvety sheen to them, creating an illusion of depth. Olesya stepped back, seeing her own reflection on the wall—distant, ghostly, and grinning back at her. Her heart leaped in her chest.

Alexander returned and asked. "Anything?"

"No, you?"

He shook his head. "There is nothing here except for this chamber. There are no other corridors; no doors."

"We can come back later," Olesya said. "We must get Sara out now."

"Okay," Alexander said, sighed, and looked up. His face changed. Olesya traced his eyes and looked up and gasped when she saw the outline of a triangle in the middle of the ceiling.

"We can't reach it," Olesya said, staring at the triangle. A few minutes passed while Alex and Olesya stood watching the ceiling. Then she thrust her hands toward the ceiling. They heard a low hum and felt a vibration, then it stopped and nothing happened. "Should we try together?" Alexander asked.

Olesya nodded. "On three."

On the count of three, they both thrust their hands, aiming at the triangle. A low hum and vibration, and nothing. They looked at each other, nodded, and did it again. Nothing changed; no door opened.

"We'll bring back a ladder," Alexander said.

"You said you opened the door by pushing the triangle?"

"Yeah, I just pushed it with my finger, and it opened."

"We've got to get a ladder," Olesya agreed.

Alexander picked up Sara and carried her through the dark corridor to the rope waiting for them. They put a harness on Sara and tied her to the rope. Olesya tugged on the rope three times.

After pulling the unconscious Sara out of the catacombs, they discovered they had a problem. They couldn't carry her up the mountain, and the satellite phone had no reception to call for help. Sebastian volunteered to climb to the top for better coverage. When he reached the top, he called for the chopper, giving the pilot the coordinates. Olesya wrapped Sara in her own coat to keep her warm. Alexander then covered Olesya with his jacket, despite her loud protests.

Half an hour later, the helicopter landed on a small, rocky plateau by the crater. They flew to Santiago to care for Sara, with plans to return to the crater the next day. Henry and Mary were on their way to join the search for Zoe.

They checked into one of the older hotels in the northern part of Santiago, per Sebastian's suggestion. He explained that they always traveled low profile so as not to attract attention, especially when they traveled in groups. In the older, middle-class hotels, they blended in with budget tourists, not raising any eyebrows. Well-cared-for and providing the comforts and necessities for out-of-towners, the Hotel Magnolia offered an incredible view of the city and the surrounding mountains and had friendly but discreet staff.

Olesya sat by Sara's bed and kept a cold towel on her friend's head, talking to her in a low voice to comfort her. Sebastian got phone instructions from Zoe's doctor to care for Sara until he arrived. Her breathing was steady, but her face was pale and hollow.

Meanwhile, Alexander and Elliot went into town in search of a ladder.

Sebastian paced the room, glancing at Sara. He asked the same question every few minutes: "There was nothing of Zoe's in the chamber?"

"No, there was nothing there," Olesya answered, guessing how miserable he felt not knowing where his twin sister was.

"Where am I?" Sara asked.

Olesya and Sebastian turned toward her and saw her wide awake.

"You're awake! You gave me a scare. We're in a hotel. We found you in the catacombs under the crater."

"Where's Zoe?" Sebastian asked.

Sara's eyes darted from Olesya to Sebastian as they waited for her to regain her cognizance. Sebastian leaned forward, watching every twitch on Sara's face while Olesya patted her hand.

"They took her," Sara said, with a shaky, barely audible voice.

"Who took her? Who took Zoe?" Sebastian asked in a breathy whisper.

"I don't remember. My memory is blurry."

"Give her time," Olesya scolded him. "She just woke up."

"They wore masks and hoods," Sara added.

Sebastian glanced at Sara, and a thought crossed his mind. "Brown said to give her coffee. I'll be right back," Sebastian said, and ran out.

After Sebastian left, Sara fell back asleep. Olesya took her hand and held it, waiting for her to wake up. Moments later, Sebastian returned with a steaming pot of coffee, creamers, and a sugar bowl on a silver tray. It seemed as if it had come straight from a restaurant.

"What did you do? Did you steal it?" Olesya asked.

Sebastian smiled impishly, setting the tray next to the bed. "They won't miss it. They had several of each and hardly any customers. Help me give it to her."

Sebastian and Olesya positioned Sara in a sitting position. Olesya mixed sugar and creamers into the coffee to cool it and started feeding it to Sara with a spoon. The first few spoonfuls dribbled out of her mouth, landing on the white sheets, but then she started swallowing. Her eyes twitched and then opened, appearing more alert. Then she grabbed the coffee mug from Olesya's hands and drained it in a few fast gulps.

Sebastian stood, wringing his hands as Sara stared at them, saying nothing. At one point, she exclaimed. "They kidnapped Zoe."

"Who?" Sebastian asked.

"The group of men who appeared out of nowhere. Zoe didn't stand a chance. They surprised us and threw something at her, and took her. Something shiny, like a gold blanket. They...they flew up carrying her." Sara looked at them and said, sounding unsure. "I realize it sounds crazy, but they really flew up carrying her. And that is the last thing I remember. One of them sprayed something in my face. Some type of...mist, smelling of...flowers and...alcohol. And I passed out."

"Why did you go there?" Sebastian asked, sounding angry.

Sara stared at him with eyes wide open, not understanding the question. "I can't remember."

She reminded Olesya of a scared child, the way she held her head and worked the sheets with her hands.

"It's okay, Sara. It'll come to you," Olesya said.

"What did the men look like?" Sebastian asked.

"They wore masks and hoods and moved so fast that everything disappeared in a golden blur. It happened so fast. I'm sorry, I'm not much help."

"Golden blur? What do you mean by that?" Olesya asked.

"That is what I remember. Gold, shining gold. They radiated gold."

"Hmm." It occurred to Olesya that her friend might still be intoxicated or drugged by whatever they gave her, because what she said made little sense.

"Do you have your phone?" Olesya asked.

"It was in my jacket. Where's my jacket?"

Sebastian fetched her jacket and passed it to her. Sara checked the pockets, her hands trembling.

"Not here. My phone is not here. Maybe in my backpack? We had them with us. I think."

"We didn't find your backpack," Olesya said. "Just before you left for Chile, you emailed Zoe about my DNA results and then immediately vanished. What is the connection between my DNA and your trip to Chile and the mummies in the golden cage?"

"I don't remember. I'm sorry. My head is fuzzy."

"The triangle on the ceiling. That is how the men must have gotten there and left with Zoe," Sebastian said to Olesya.

"The triangle!" Sara exclaimed. "That is how Zoe opened the door,"

"We are going there tomorrow with a ladder, and we'll figure it all out," Olesya said.

57

GOLDEN CAGE

FEBRUARY 2024

D r. Brown arrived, carrying a silver suitcase, and immediately started tending to Sara, prescribing rest and directing others to fetch food and fluids. According to his diagnosis, the drugs were wearing off, and the worst was over. He bagged the coca leaf, shaking his head, saying he'd never seen this kind. He couldn't recall any drugs with a flowery smell or alcohol that caused unconsciousness or amnesia, but drew Sara's blood for examination.

Mary stayed with Sara. Henry joined the group to help search for Zoe. They boarded the helicopter and flew back to the crater.

"Don't you think we need more people?" Olesya asked Sebastian. "Sara said several men kidnapped Zoe. Zoe is powerful and fast. Even when surprised, she should be capable of fighting them off—"

"This is just a reconnaissance mission. I have a few men on standby. They will join us when necessary."

"What I was going to say before you interrupted me is that the people who attacked Zoe were not ordinary people. Even if surprised, she would have fought them off. We need to bring more men with us. You realize we don't know how many of them might hide up there.

We're searching for your sister, Sebastian!" Olesya stopped her tirade, seeing his expression.

"What are you keeping from me, Sebastian?"

"I can't hide anything from you. You're just like her, like my Zoe. Too damned perceptive."

Olesya observed him closely and noticed how fatigued and worried he was. Suddenly, he appeared much older. For a moment, Olesya saw an old, wrinkled man sitting by her side. She closed her eyes, and when she opened them, she saw a young, vibrant Sebastian. His eyes, however, were sunken and dull.

"I couldn't get hold of anyone. This is it. It's only us. Only Henry and Mary replied to my message."

"What are you saying?"

"I don't know what to tell you, Olesya. I called everyone and got nothing. I called our emergency line and got nothing. I don't know what's going on. It has never happened before. We must find Zoe," Sebastian said, and gnawed at his lower lip.

Olesya nodded and took his hand. "We'll find her, big brother. Tomorrow. We'll find her tomorrow."

Sebastian kissed her on the cheek. "Little sister."

Henry and Elliot had just finished gluing an anchor next to the gaping hole with a fast-setting, super-strong epoxy that Alexander and Elliot had secured the night before, while Sebastian and Alexander were tying a foldable aluminum ladder to Sebastian's backpack. When they were all ready, Sebastian looked everyone in the eyes, opened his backpack, and handed everyone a semi-automatic gun. Olesya gasped, seeing the gun, and reached for it after a second of hesitation.

"Our powers need to recharge. We can use them only a few times before they diminish. You realize that, don't you?" Sebastian said, responding to her unease. "We need a backup. Do you know how to shoot?"

Olesya nodded. The cold steel of the gun weighed heavily in her hands and brought on memories of Lev teaching her how to shoot and how to load, and clean guns. He had taken her to a shooting range when she was a teenager, saying everyone should know how to handle a gun. "Just in case," he had said. To her surprise, Sasha, the adamant pacifist, didn't protest. After the shooting range, they would get greasy burgers and french fries and keep that a secret from Sasha. Olesya suspected Sasha knew their little secret, even though she never said so.

"Everyone be careful and stick together," Sebastian said.

They rappelled down the dark shaft in silence with their headlamps turned low. Once they reached the chamber, Alexander and Sebastian assembled the ladder and positioned it under the triangle. Then Henry, Olesya, and Elliot pointed their guns at the ceiling, ready for an ambush, while Sebastian climbed the ladder. He reached the top and drew a deep breath before pushing the triangle. Nothing happened. Sebastian pushed his finger deeper into the triangular depression. Again, nothing happened. He banged the triangle in frustration. Olesya tapped the ladder and motioned for him to stop. Sebastian kept hitting the ceiling, but eventually relented and descended with a disheartened look in his eyes.

"Why don't we try to open it together?" Olesya said, glancing at everyone. "There are five of us. It may work." She didn't sound convinced and had little hope it would work, but the look on her brother's and Sebastian's faces urged her to search for a solution.

They stood below the triangle and thrust their hands upward together.

There was a low drumming noise, followed by a distant vibration, just like before, but no door opened in the ceiling. They looked at each other, stumped and disappointed. It was apparent from his glowering eyes that Sebastian struggled to contain his frustration. Alexander sank into silent desperation, his arms limp as if disconnected from his body, his eyes downcast. The air filled with silence, pregnant with disappointment and apprehension, until Olesya broke it.

"I think we should go back up and look around more. There's nothing to do here."

Everyone except Sebastian agreed and nodded. Sebastian stood frozen with his eyes closed, seeming to be locked in a daydream.

Olesya touched his arm and asked. "Are you okay?"

When he didn't respond, Olesya shook his arm. "Sebastian, answer me! What is it?"

After a few shakes, Sebastian opened his eyes.

"Zoe isn't here," he said. "She is on top of a mountain. We must hurry."

Alexander seized Sebastian's arm. "What mountain?"

"I'm not sure. Let's go outside. I'll recognize it."

"Were you having a vision?" Olesya asked.

Sebastian nodded in response. "Zoe sent it to me. Let's go," he said, and rushed to the exit.

Alexander caught up with him. "What did you see?"

"I saw Zoe sitting on the mountain peak, enclosed in a golden cage. She seemed hurt and cold."

"Are you sure it was Zoe you saw in your vision?"

"I saw Zoe. I'm sure. We must move quickly," Sebastian said, and picked up his pace.

Sebastian was the first to climb and reach the top, scanning the surroundings in search of the mountain he'd seen. He closed his eyes and when he opened them, he squinted as the blinding sun peeked between the thick clouds. Everyone gathered around him. The atmosphere of the group had changed; everyone seemed more excited and hopeful. His vision had restored their hope of finding Zoe alive, even if it was just a vision.

"It's that one over there," Sebastian said, pointing at a peak partially hidden behind gray clouds.

"Are you sure?" Elliot asked. "We risk losing too much time if we don't find her there. It would take too much time to climb another peak if you are wrong."

"I am sure, but you are right. We can't risk it. They are so similar. It could be the one next to it."

"Why don't we split?" suggested Olesya. "We should have cell reception up there and can communicate and call a chopper."

"That's not a bad idea," Sebastian agreed.

The group split into two. Sebastian and Elliot went to the second peak, while Olesya, Alexander, and Henry climbed the peak Sebastian had pointed to.

Olesya and the others in her group put on their crampons, got their curved ice axes ready, and started climbing. It was a grueling, slippery climb, and with the air thin at this high elevation, it seized all the strength she had to labor up the slope.

At last, when they reached the peak, Olesya gasped at the sight. Zoe, dressed in traditional Incan clothes adorned with jewels and feathers, sat on a stone platform confined by a golden cage. Her eyes were closed, her arms crossed over her chest, and draped over her back was a thick wool blanket of Incan design. They ran to her side.

Olesya slid her hand between the golden bars and checked her pulse. Zoe was cold to the touch, and Olesya feared the worst, her own heart beating too loud to detect Zoe's heartbeat. She gave up and let Henry check her pulse. Henry kneeled by Zoe and put his fingers on her neck. Olesya and Alexander stared at Henry, frozen with anticipation. After two excruciatingly long minutes, Henry looked at them and gave them a nod.

"There's a pulse. It is weak but steady. We need to get her warm."

Alexander fell to his knees and cried out, inching toward Zoe on his knees. "She is alive. My Zoe is alive." He noticed something in her mouth, bent down, and took it out. "Zoe?" he asked in a high-pitched voice.

Alexander reached out through the bars and removed something from Zoe's mouth. "She has the same type of leaf in her mouth." Alexander said, holding his hand palm up to show the green leaf.

Henry investigated the three-quarter-inch-thick and seamless bars, which appeared glued or welded together, although with no obvious signs of glue or welding marks. "We must get her out of this cage," he said.

"You are right," Olesya said, eyeing the bars. "It looks like gold. Gold is super soft, and it should bend or break easily," Olesya added, searching for rocks.

She found a sizable one, approached the cage, and whacked it. The bars didn't budge. Henry found an even bigger rock and whacked the bars with it. The bars did not sustain any damage. Not even a mark.

"This is not gold. It might be an alloy," Olesya said, and grabbed the bars with her bare hands. Her eyes became two wide, crazed black marbles. She staggered back, screaming in pain and surprise.

"What happened?" Alexander asked.

"This thing shocked me."

She examined the cage, searching for the source of the electric shock, but found nothing. She sat on the ground, gawking at the golden prison. Zoe's eyes twitched at the sound of the stone hitting the cage but remained closed.

"I've never seen anything like it. There doesn't seem to be a source of electricity. The bars look like gold, but they're not. I have no idea what kind and how to break the goddamned thing with no tools," Olesya said and added, looking at Zoe. "But we'll figure something out, I promise. Just hold on a little longer."

"Maybe if we insulate the bars with something to avoid shock and see if we could bend them," Alexander suggested.

Alexander and Henry glanced at each other, stripped off their jackets, wrapped them around the bars, then grabbed the bars through the jackets and tried to bend them. They didn't get shocked, but the bars didn't budge.

"We'll transport her in the cage and then figure out how to cut it," Olesya decided and said to Henry. "Call Sebastian and have him bring the chopper."

58

OPEN

FEBRUARY 2024

It was dark when the helicopter carrying the golden cage landed in front of Zoe's house. It had been a long, emotionally and physically exhausting journey from Chile, having to transport the cage from helicopter to her private jet, where they reunited with Mary and Sara, and then to another chopper once they landed in Seattle. Sebastian and Alexander took turns by the cage, watching the unresponsive face of their sister and lover. The wind blew heavy smoke from the east, where forest fires had raged for the past week. The full moon behind a brownish haze appeared menacing, casting its eerie light at the cage.

Zoe sat motionless inside like a zombie; her long black hair spilled over her shoulders, catching the ghostly moonlight as they carried the cage.

Inside, they positioned the cage in the central part of the living room on the huge, multicolored carpet. Dr. Brown, who came with them on the chopper, tended to Zoe. He injected her with epinephrine to counteract the effects of the drug. He seemed optimistic about Zoe's chances of survival, saying that her vital signs were strong.

Sebastian sat by Zoe, telling her something in a muted voice, while the others in the group gathered in a circle to brainstorm how to open her prison. There was another very concerned being near her cage: her dog, Louis. He waited by the door while they carried the cage inside and then sat by it, gazing into Zoe's eyes and whimpering. The other dog, Regis, lay by the cage, panting, but his eyes were glued to Olesya as he watched her every move.

Sara, who had regained her wits sat by Olesya, inspecting the bars.

"Not sure how it shocked you. I can see no apparent source of electricity."

"It must be inside the bars. They are thick enough."

In the meantime, Zoe started responding to the epinephrine. She opened her eyes and stared blankly at them without blinking. At first, they were delighted with the signs of awareness; they showered her with questions. But she just stared at them silently, motionlessly. The doctor carefully reached through the bars and listened to her heart with a stethoscope, nodding with satisfaction.

"Her heart is beating strong and steady, but we have to extract her out of this cage so I can examine her," he said, scratching his black, wavy hair and glancing at everyone imploringly.

Mary and Alexander sat near the cage, holding Zoe's hands. Zoe's blank expression was taking a toll on Alexander. He was pale and despondent, making little sense, repeating the same words as if he were chanting a prayer.

With his hands rolled into fists, Sebastian paced the room, murmuring to himself, stopping occasionally to glance at Zoe's blank expression. At one point, he collapsed to his knees by the cage and cried out. "Zoe! Zoe, come back to me!"

Sara and Olesya stood up.

"Okay, everyone, listen up. We need an ultrashort laser to send a proton beam at this thing and short the circuit while slicing through the bars. Let's see…" Olesya paused. "We will also need a fiber laser to cut it. Someone needs to get it from the physics lab," Olesya said in a calm and commanding voice.

"I'll do it," Elliot volunteered.

"They may be heavy. I'll go with you," Henry said.

"We'll need heavy rubber gloves to hold the bars while we cut them and rubber mats to protect Zoe. Do you think you have something like that in the house or the garage?" Olesya asked Alexander, wanting to snap him out of his worries by getting him out of the room and making him feel useful.

"Why is she this way?" Mary asked the doctor. "Sara snapped out of it quicker. Do you think they gave her something to cloud her mind?"

"I don't think so," he answered, though he didn't sound sure. "Her pupils seem normal now, and her heartbeat strong. I don't see any obvious external injuries."

Just as Elliot and Henry were leaving, Olesya stopped them. "Wait. I think Zoe is trying to say something."

Zoe was moving her lips. Mary put her ear as close as she could to Zoe's lips and listened.

"She said, 'not laser.' She is saying…'ichor,' or something sounding like that," Mary said and put her ear closer to the cage. "Yes, it is definitely 'ichor.'"

"What the hell is 'ichor?'" Sara asked.

"Ichor is the legendary golden blood of gods or immortals in Greek mythology. Toxic to humans," Sebastian said, then added when he got surprised glances from everyone. "What? I like Greek mythology."

"So she is saying not to use the laser," Sara said to herself, patting her chin. "She is comprehending, but unable to interact. Golden blood of gods or immortals…does she mean the bars are made of ichor? It doesn't make any sense."

"Why don't we use the black shards?" Olesya asked, glancing at everyone.

Alexander listened to Zoe's whisper and then nodded. Sebastian ran to fetch a fragment from the safe. He came back with a crystal box that contained several black shards.

Olesya approached him, seeing his hands tremble. "Let me do it," she said. "You're a mess."

Gazing into her determined, calm eyes, he agreed and handed her the box. She touched his cheek and seized the box, touching his hands with hers and looking into his eyes. "It'll be okay."

She took one shard out and approached the cage. After a blinding blue light and a high-pitched whistle, the cage shuttered and scattered on the colorful Persian carpet into tiny golden pieces.

Olesya stood frozen until Elliot touched her arm.

"I saw...a void," she said, her voice breaking.

"You saw what?"

"An endless black void. I've seen it before in my dreams. A girl is calling my name. I couldn't see her face, but her voice sounded familiar, and so does the...void. I don't know if I'm dead or imprisoned somewhere in a dark place. I can't move or say anything."

Alexander rushed to her and snatched her into his arms. She exhaled deeply and whispered in his ear. "You've seen it too, haven't you?"

She pulled back and searched his eyes. She guessed right.

59

YOU ARE BACK

FEBRUARY 2024

As soon as the bars of Zoe's prison collapsed, she regained her strength and wit. At first, she shifted slowly, groaning, her body stiff from being stuck in a sitting position for hours. Alexander and Sebastian, overjoyed at seeing her move, hurried to her side, desperately wanting to touch her to confirm she was okay. They ended up in a three-way awkward embrace.

"Zoe, you are back," Alexander said, burying his face in Zoe's hair, hiding tears of joy.

"What did the bastards do to you?!" Sebastian cried out, wiping his tears with his sleeve. "Who are they, and what do they want from you?"

"Shush," Zoe murmured. "I'll explain everything, but first I need water and...food."

"Give us some room. I need to examine her," Dr. Brown asserted, holding his stethoscope, motioning for them to step away.

In the next few minutes, the doctor examined Zoe, asking her questions, while everyone else gathered on the other side of the living room to give them privacy. When he was done, Dr. Brown smiled at Sebastian.

"Your sister will be okay. Tomorrow she'll be as good as new. She wasn't in the cold long enough to suffer major damage. All she needs is food and lots of fluids. She doesn't need me anymore," Dr. Brown said, packing his bag and getting ready to leave.

"Sorry, I'm a fool for not thinking about it sooner. I'll get food and water," Alexander said, and ran to the kitchen.

Sebastian stood still, observing Zoe silently. "How are you?"

"Fine. Just weak and sore from sitting for two days straight," Zoe answered and stretched her back, grunting and avoiding Sebastian's eyes.

Sebastian nodded, not convinced, and followed Alexander to the kitchen. A few minutes later, they returned carrying a pitcher of water, glasses, and sandwiches. Zoe drank water, one glass after another, water spilling over her Incan clothes. She wiped her mouth and grabbed a sandwich, eating ravenously, practically stuffing her mouth, moaning with contentment. After she had wolfed down two sandwiches, she regained her manners and slowed down.

Alexander beamed at her unrestrained display of appetite. No one said a word until she had satisfied her thirst and hunger, but they kept their eyes on her the entire time.

"We must talk. I have things to tell you. But first I need a shower, and I must lose these scratchy, filthy rags. Must burn these damned things! Wait for me," she said.

"We are not going anywhere," Olesya said under her breath.

Zoe left, stuffing another sandwich into her mouth as she walked away. Louis followed his mistress, wagging his tail, reminding her he could help her finish the sandwich. Zoe glanced back at Regis. He wagged his tail but stayed by Olesya.

Sebastian collapsed on the sofa while Alexander paced the room, not in the mood for talking. Elliot and Henry joined Sebastian on the sofa, waiting for Zoe's return.

Sara and Olesya bent down on the floor, scrutinizing the golden pieces.

"It is solid metal. Solid gold, or is it something else?" Olesya asked. She picked up one piece with a rubber mat and stared at it, shaking her head.

"We'll figure it out. We'll take it to the lab and examine it," Sara said, sounding confident, but her hands shook.

Olesya swallowed hard, seeing Sara scared and insecure. "Sure."

60

ISHTAR

FEBRUARY 2024

Zoe returned wearing a cotton jumpsuit and with a towel wrapped around her head, holding a bottle of wine and several glasses. She seemed healthy and radiant, as if nothing had happened.

"What? Brown said I need fluids. Don't give me that look, Sebastian. I need it. Instead of glaring at me, offer everyone drinks and food. Join me," she said, looking at everyone and pointing to the glasses and the bottle.

She sat on a chair opposite Alexander and Olesya. Sebastian busied himself getting drinks for everyone, mumbling to himself. All eyes were on Zoe, who sipped her wine, peered out the window. "How much do you remember?" she asked Sara.

"Not much. They drugged me as they were taking you away. I passed out. I remember they wore masks."

"They ambushed us," Zoe said, nodding at Sara. "They threw something on me, incapacitating me. I couldn't move, couldn't make a sound, as if I were paralyzed. Not being able to take deep breaths, I passed out."

"The golden blanket," Sara whispered. "I thought I had imagined it."

"Yes, the golden blanket," Zoe said. "I regained consciousness when they dropped me down. Then they strapped me to a chair with golden chains and removed the blanket. Just like the blanket, the golden chains paralyzed my body. I could only listen. After they lifted the blanket off, all I could see was smooth black rock, just like in the chamber and the corridors. Then I saw them, standing still and silent, observing me. They wore dark clothes and masks. I could only see their dark outlines and a golden glow escaping through their clothes." She paused, remembering. "It was as if golden waves flew through them."

"Were they...people?" Sebastian asked.

"Yes," Zoe nodded. "They were changed just like we were, but a very long time ago. Thousands of years ago," she said.

A heavy silence enveloped the room while everyone stared at Zoe with astonishment.

"Thousands?" Olesya asked, doubtful. "How can you possibly know that?"

"They told me."

"And you believed them?"

Zoe ignored her, but not before sending a murderous look in her direction.

"Were they changed the same way?" Mary asked. "With the black shards?"

Zoe didn't answer. She looked around the room and held everyone's gaze for a few long seconds before she finally spoke. "Not exactly."

"What does that mean?" Olesya asked. "Was it the black shards, or wasn't it?"

"Let her talk," Alexander said, sounding annoyed.

"It happened ten thousand years ago in Mesopotamia," Zoe began. "A nomadic family traveling to trade goods across Mesopotamia came upon an underground passage during a torrential rainstorm. The stone road gave in, undermined by the rain, and they plunged into a dark corridor, which in no time filled with wet dirt and rocks, blocking their light and their way out. They walked until they reached a dead end. At least, that is what they believed. Terrified, imagining their imminent death in the dark, they sat on the cold stone, discouraged, ready to give in and die on the spot. But not Ishtar, the youngest boy. The twelve-year-old started exploring the dark passage with his hands, trying to find an opening, a slit, something, anything he could pry open. And he found a triangle on a wall and pushed it, opening a door."

Everyone had their eyes fixed on Zoe as she told the story. She was an excellent storyteller, telling it as if she had seen it happen. She paused to collect her thoughts, but mostly to take a sip of wine.

"What was behind the door?" Elliot couldn't wait.

"A shrine."

"A shrine? What kind of shrine?"

"To a deity. A golden deity," Zoe said, and continued with her story. "The boy went in and saw a golden statue of a man holding a boy in his arms in the heart of a circular room made of black, seamless stone. Both the man and the child were naked except for a gold necklace containing a golden stone on the boy's chest. Despite the absence of light, the room remained bright. Golden blades of light radiated from the statue, laying golden patterns on the walls. One beam swept across Ishtar's dazzled face as he stood still, spellbound, admiring the scene that lay before him. He didn't notice when his father and uncle entered the room."

"What's this thing?" His father asked in fear.

"It is gold," his uncle whispered. "This is worth a fortune."

The rest of the family entered the room, gawking at the statue. The uncle's wife entered the chamber and proceeded straight for the necklace but failed to grasp it. His uncle went to her aid, but the boy's father stopped him.

"Wait. Let's not touch anything here. This is a sacred place. Taking anything from here will only bring bad luck and misery."

The father gazed at the boy, who remained unmoving, fixed on the statue.

"Ishtar," the father said to the boy.

The boy didn't respond, mesmerized by the statue.

"Ishtar, look at me, boy! Wake up. We need to leave this place," his father shouted.

The boy stared at his father with a vacant stare. Suddenly, without warning, he darted to the statue, climbed like a cat, and grabbed the necklace.

The father looked at the necklace in the boy's hand. His brother and his wife stood by and gaped at the necklace, but didn't dare touch it. As the leader of their clan, Ishtar's father commanded respect and obedience.

"You shouldn't have taken it," his father whispered.

Ishtar glanced at him with a peculiar, distant expression and fastened the necklace around his neck. Letting out a frightened scream, he collapsed to the ground, groaning in pain. His hair and eyes changed to gold, and the boy was not a boy. He was much taller and stronger, and his body glowed gold. Thus, the golden people were born. Ishtar changed his family with the necklace and created more golden people to help him rule over the common folk.

Zoe finished her story and observed everyone to gauge their reactions.

"So they shared with you the story of their beginnings and then left you out to die on the mountaintop?" Olesya didn't care that her face contorted in leery grimace and that her voice sounded sharp. "It makes no sense. Why?"

"I don't know why. I couldn't ask them questions. All I know is that they're extremely dangerous and powerful. We must leave this place and disappear if we want to live. They'll come for us. They've already tracked and killed the rest of our people."

"No!" Henry cried out. "They killed our people? Why?"

"We disrupt the balance," Zoe said.

"What balance? What are you talking about?" Olesya snorted. "And what about the DNA? You two went to Chile because you found something about my DNA, and then you got kidnapped. And now, according to Sebastian, all your people—except for the ones in this room—are missing. You are hiding something, or you're still under the influence of the drug they gave you. Tell us what's going on!"

"Your DNA matched that of the twins bound in a golden cage on the mountaintop," Sara said. "To be honest, when I plugged your DNA into a worldwide database, I didn't expect to find a match. And then I got an email from Veronika Steinberg, who said she got pinged when there was a match to her mummies. That's why we traveled to Chile. We never met the archeologist because she never showed up to meet us."

"She's dead," Alexander said. "Supposedly, she died in a car accident."

"Supposedly?" Zoe asked.

"Well, that is what the article said, but we never followed up," Alexander explained.

"What balance, Zoe? I don't understand why they want to kill us all," Olesya asked.

"The balance of the universe. We disrupted it when we were changed with the black shards. There is only a limited amount of dark matter converting to normal, visible matter since the beginning of the universe at a constant rate. When we change with the black fragments, we alter the conversion rate and disrupt the delicate equilibrium. They have been searching for the black fragments, destroying them, and destroying the people who were changed by them."

"I'm not buying any of it," Olesya said. "It sounds like a bunch of crap! And how would they even know this? Either they lied to you or..."

"I'm with you," Sara said, glancing at Olesya and then focusing her gaze on Zoe. "Delightful story, but it makes little sense. If dark matter has been converting to normal matter since the conception of the universe, how is that maintaining the balance? Something must be replenishing dark matter."

"Right," Olesya said, expecting a response from Zoe.

Zoe, however, cast her eyes down and sat with her hands folded on her lap, her thoughts elsewhere.

"Zoe?" Alexander prodded.

"The dead..."

"Dead people?" Sara asked with an incredulous look on her face. Olesya shook her head.

"I don't know. That's all they said. When people die, they replenish dark matter." Zoe answered, sounding unsure, not looking at anyone. Eyes lowered, she seemed glum and exasperated.

"That's all I've been told. They threatened to find and kill all of us and then drugged me. One of them sprayed something in my face, and I was out."

"Why go through the trouble of bringing you all the way to the top of the freaking mountain instead of just killing you?" Olesya asked.

Zoe shrugged. "I don't know. I don't understand how it all fits together."

"How sure are we that they killed our people?" Alexander asked.

"Because they are not responding," Sebastian said. "I've called and emailed repeatedly, and no one has responded."

"We should check. Drive to their houses," Henry said.

"It could be a trap," Sebastian said.

"I agree," Zoe said and added after a brief pause. "We should get out of here. They will find us."

"From your description of them, I doubt they will parade in cities for fear of being found. Just imagine them walking around, shimmering in gold. People would find the strange people suspicious and film them with their phones. You'd see them all over on social media," Olesya protested.

"They'll find us!" Zoe shouted.

"How would they know where you live?" Olesya asked incredulously.

"They found out where the rest of us lived, didn't they?" Zoe snapped.

"I have a cabin in remote Montana that no one knows about. We could stay there until we figure out what to do next," Sara said, looking at Zoe. "Olesya and I will examine the golden fragments in the lab, and we'll meet you there," Sara suggested.

Olesya nodded absentmindedly, preoccupied with the story of the golden people, the cosmic equilibrium, and most of all, the kidnapping. At the end, she concluded that Zoe's story didn't make a lick of sense. She glanced at Alexander and caught him glancing suspiciously at Zoe as if he was struggling to reconcile her story.

Good. Zoe hadn't completely bewitched and brainwashed him.

61

***

DOG TRICK

FEBRUARY 2024

S ara and Olesya sat at a workbench that was connected to an impressively tall metal tube as part of the transmission electron microscope setup. The large screen displayed an image of a thin slice of the gold bar with subatomic precision. Gold waves emerged from a structure resembling a closing and opening seashell, repeating like a kaleidoscopic image.

"It is not gold. It is not even metal," Olesya said, squinting and rubbing her eyes, stinging from looking through the lens.

"I have seen nothing like it," Sara said. "It's incredible."

"What is it?"

"I don't know. It fluctuates in a repeating pattern, but it doesn't appear to be a living...cell. Is it a mechanism? I don't think so, but I have no idea what it is. At all."

"Let's try the black shard now," Olesya said.

"I've already tried," Sara said. "It behaved nothing like this. It was black and uniform. Maybe we need higher magnification, but our microscope is the best there is."

"What if we put them near each other and see what happens?"

Sara nudged Olesya's arm with her knuckles. "Brilliant. Let's."

Working together, they prepared several new samples and positioned them under the microscope. After a while, a new image appeared. They were staring at a black screen—the first image was of the black shard itself. Sara manipulated the microscope levers, showing the golden sample on the left screen. The kaleidoscopic image started to shift and shatter into an array of uncoordinated dots as Sara pushed the slide with the black shard closer. As the black shard fragmented the golden shards, it emitted a burst of blue light and the golden dots merged into two tiny golden spheres.

"The black shard modified the golden shard," Olesya said. "I wish I knew how and what it means."

Over the next few days, Sara and Olesya worked every day, sometimes even nights, to learn the secrets of the shards but were no closer to an answer. Neither the black shard nor the golden one interacted with other materials or forces. They found no source of electricity in the gold substance either.

Sebastian disappeared somewhere, not telling anyone where he had gone. Zoe and Alexander moved into a hotel on the edge of town. When Zoe came to check on their progress, she seemed distant and indifferent, surrounded by a dark cloak of suspicion and distrust, which deepened her eyes even more.

With her heart sinking, she watched her brother grow pale and less talkative and throw furtive glances at Zoe. The next day he came alone and lingered, glancing at Olesya as if he had something on his mind but didn't want to say it in front of Sara. Olesya stretched, groaned, and pointed to the break room, saying. "I need a break. Come on, Alex, say hello to Regis."

Alex sat by Regis on the couch and scratched the dog's huge, soft ears. The noble creature seemed too dignified to acknowledge how much he enjoyed it and sat still, staring at Olesya. But she could tell that he liked it by the way his eyes narrowed into slits. She had noticed his eyes narrowing when she had shared a New York steak with him in the past.

"What is on your mind?" Olesya asked.

"Zoe. She changed. Ever since she came back from the mountain, she's been acting strange, suspicious, angry. She used to tell me everything. But now... I have a feeling she is hiding something from me. That is not the worst. She sometimes looks at me...as if she hates me. I don't know what to do."

"I perceive a difference in her behavior since the incident with the cage. Maybe she's just scared of the golden people?"

"She is scared of something or someone."

"You doubt her story?"

Alexander rubbed his face, then looked at Olesya with eyes full of distress.

"I don't know what to believe anymore. I want to, but...I can't," Alexander said and paused. After a while, he continued. "The other day, I wanted to ask her something and ran into her hotel room, expecting her to greet me with a smile. Instead, she slammed her laptop shut and screamed at me. Screamed! 'Get the hell out of my room! Don't you fucking know how to knock?' I left. She apologized later, saying that she was upset and tired, but her apology was hollow and insincere."

"I am sorry, Alex. I don't know what to say. Maybe she is in shock after what she's been through?"

Alexander glanced at her with a strange expression on his face. "Before she closed her laptop, I saw what was on it."

"What?"

"The chamber. It resembled the one we found, except it had some sort of console emitting something resembling a three-dimensional image...a hologram."

"A hologram? Are you sure?"

"I saw a transparent image of a woman resembling you."

"Me? Can't be. Not possible."

"I keep replaying it in my head, and I am sure it was your image."

"Did you ask Zoe?"

"Of course not. That is why she screamed at me. She didn't want me to see it."

Alexander and Olesya sat in the break room for a while but couldn't come up with a logical explanation. The more they tried, the more perplexed and frustrated they became, so they decided to wait for an opportunity to break into her laptop. Olesya embraced Alexander, walked with him to the exit, and whispered in his ear before he left. "Give her time. Maybe she will get over whatever is worrying her and explain everything," Olesya said, trying to sound convincing, even though she could not convince herself.

Exhausted, Olesya felt defeated by the mysterious nature of the golden and black shards. They seemed no closer to understanding how they worked. As they sat exasperated, hoping for a new idea, Olesya noticed Sara had something on her mind but was reluctant to say it. Olesya encouraged her with a look.

"We should try to see what it does when it interacts with humans," Sara said.

"How?" Olesya asked, but looking at Sara's expression, she understood. "No way, Sara. Even for science. You can't sacrifice yourself."

"It wouldn't be a sacrifice. Not really. I'm getting older. Zoe asked me once if I wanted to change and be immortal, and I said I needed time to think about it. Well, time's up, and I'm ready."

Olesya studied Sara's face. Sara's eyes glimmered and her chin jutted forward.

"Before we even entertain the idea, we must be sure you won't disappear."

"How do you propose we do that?" Sara asked, and then, tracking Olesya's gaze, added. "Do you mean ask the dog? Both dogs licked my hand when they first met me. Regis licks my hands and my face every day. By the way. Why's Regis with you? Is Zoe okay with him following you everywhere like a shadow?"

"I guess so. I don't really know what to make of it," she said and rubbed her forehead. "Anyway, I want to see it for myself. If you think about it, it doesn't seem so far-fetched. In certain cases, dogs can sense people's diseases better than blood tests or instruments." Olesya said and whistled for Regis, who came running, tail wagging and tongue sticking out, staring at her.

She was still getting used to Regis taking on the role of her follower and protector. Having not grown up with dogs, she knew little about them, but his loving demeanor and wise eyes had grown on her. Regis had a knack for disappearing and reappearing at just the right moment, giving her time to adjust to him.

Regis approached her, and she touched his head. He responded by looking into her eyes with love, and she melted with affection for this magnificent creature. She caressed his ears, surprised at how much she enjoyed touching the dog.

"Regis, I need to ask you a favor. You must tell me if Sara can be changed safely," Olesya said, pointing at Sara. "Do you understand what I'm asking?"

As a scientist, Olesya realized how silly it was, but her instinct whispered otherwise. She glanced at Sara, who observed her with a healthy mix of skepticism and amusement.

"Do you know any other way? Scientific way?" Olesya asked.

"By all means, don't mind me. Do your dog trick."

Olesya walked toward Sara and stood by her side. "Come on, Regis. Do your magic."

Regis walked toward Sara, glancing at Olesya. He sat in front of Sara and stared at her for a considerable time, his black nose moving fast in all directions. Then he got up, licked Sara's hand, and gazed at Olesya, wagging his tail.

"There you go. I told you. I'm safe," Sara exclaimed, laughing. "Good boy, Regis."

"Thank you, Regis," Olesya said. "You *are* a good boy."

62

KEEP IT TO YOURSELF

FEBRUARY 2024

Sara took the black shard in her hand and closed her eyes. She fell to the floor, crying in pain. Olesya sat by Sara, watching. Part of her, curious about the process, observed every little twitch and change in Sara's face and body with fascination. Then it was over, and Sara just got up, gazed at Olesya with her black eyes, and grinned, wiping her bloody hand with a towel.

"No worries, Olesya. I feel great. Come on, let's get back to it."

Despite the countless questions she wanted to ask, Olesya followed her lead and helped prepare Sara's blood samples they had collected before the change. Sara put the slide inside the microscope and moved a thin slice of the black shard toward it. The sample quivered and rotated when they positioned it near Sara's slide, releasing a thin, black strand, which then shot across into the slide with Sara's cells. The cell closest to the shard opened its walls by creating a small notch, and the strand entered the nucleus and became part of Sara's cell, bonding to her DNA and most likely altering her genetic makeup.

"So that happens. I wonder if I have it in my DNA. I probably do, but there is no way to tell. You didn't have to do it. We could've just looked at the slides."

"I decided it was time. I have no regrets. And I was getting older and tired. I couldn't keep up."

"How was it?" Olesya asked.

"It was painful at first. The pain infiltrated every fiber of my body and intensified until it reached a point where I no longer perceived anything. I felt as if my body had broken into a million pieces. At one point, I was certain I had died. Then, after a jolt, I woke up pain-free, blissful, and whole."

Sara paused, glancing at Olesya before she continued. "I'm absolutely certain that what I did was right. This is how I was meant to be. At birth. The crystal-clear thoughts, the fluidity of mind, the ability to recall everything you ever wanted to remember, and the knowledge combined into a cohesive sense of the world around me. People describe the effects of hallucinogenic drugs as having a sudden revelation and an understanding of how the universe works. I feel like a young goddess. There are no aches and pains, only limitless energy and confidence. I didn't know a human being could feel this way. Is this how you feel all the time, Olesya?"

Olesya hesitated in answering. It never entered her mind that other people perceived the world around them differently. "I can't compare. I was born this way."

"You're right. You don't know what inferiority feels like," Sara said, laughing.

Olesya observed her for a moment. The new wrinkles that appeared after her ordeal were gone; her tiredness had evaporated. She radiated energy and health. But when she looked into her black eyes, she knew she'd miss Sara's blue eyes, surrounded by a web of tiny wrinkles.

"Any downsides?"

"Not so far. Right now, I feel fantastic. Ask me tomorrow," she said, laughing.

"To summarize," Olesya said. "The black fragments integrate into our nucleus, changing our genes...but it looks like the golden ones can't get inside our nucleus but form new organelles in the cell. So how can we explain the golden people, then?"

Sara listened, nodding her head. "We should try it on cells from different people. Perhaps some people have an affinity for the golden fragments. Maybe it is like with the black fragments when people without an affinity for black shards vanish into a dark dimension."

"We should," Olesya said, and yawned. "Tomorrow. I'm tired and starving."

Olesya got up from her chair and stretched, showing her tiny bump.

Sara gasped.

Olesya dropped back in her chair. "I didn't want to tell you yet."

"Is it...?"

"Yes, it's Sergi's."

"Will you...end it or wait?"

"I'm going to wait and see what happens. Zoe was strangely adamant that I should abort to avoid pain later. But I can't, Sara. It's a girl. My daughter, my baby girl. It doesn't matter who the father is. I'll take all the pain in the world if there is even a slight chance she'll be born."

"I'm not sure what to say. The only thing I can think of is congratulations. I will do anything to help. Anything. And you are right—it may be different for you. You look amazing. You're glowing."

"Keep it to yourself for now, please."

"Wear loser clothes for now. I think it's time to go to the cabin and tell everyone what we've found, or rather not found."

63

CABIN FEVER

FEBRUARY 2024

"I wonder what happened to the necklace the girl mummy wore on her neck?" Olesya asked Sara while driving her Jeep to Sara's cabin.

"The archeologist, as you know, never arrived to show us the mummies or told us where she stored them. After scrutinizing the photos, Zoe concluded the shard was not real, but a symbol and a warning."

"By the golden people?"

"We speculated it was part of an Incan tradition, revolving around the golden people. The Incas worshipped the sun god, believing he was their ancestor."

"Sara, I don't remember asking you to run my DNA. Alexander said he didn't either. Did Zoe ask you to run it?"

"Well, yes. She said you had talked about finding your roots. She wanted to surprise you."

"Did you talk to that archeologist yourself?"

"No, I forwarded her email to Zoe, and she took over the communication and set up our appointment with her."

The nagging suspicion returned, holding her stomach hostage in a tight grip.

Olesya parked her Jeep at the end of a dirt road, and with Sara's help, she covered it with branches. They packed their supplies into backpacks and hiked to the cabin. Sara opened the cabin door and inhaled deeply.

"What're you smelling?"

"My father's pipe still lingers in the air, or perhaps only in my imagination."

The log cabin could accommodate eight people for a while, with two small bedrooms and several cots.

"We'll be cozy," Olesya said, glancing around as Sara unpacked the groceries from the backpack.

The mantel above the stone fireplace held a few photos of Sara and her father. Teenaged Sara, skinny and wearing overalls covered with dirt, huckleberry stains, and holes, stood smiling ear to ear, her arm wrapped around her father's waist. Seeing the photo, Olesya sighed, wishing she were in her father's arms.

Shortly after, Alexander, Henry, Mary, and Elliot arrived, each carrying a backpack with provisions and a few belongings. Uprooted from their lives, they carried only what was important and cherished. They brought vivacity into the cabin, laughing at an overused old joke.

Everyone somehow knew that Sara was one of them. They glanced at her but said nothing. Sara laughed when Henry started taking things out of his backpack. "Scotch? Chocolate-covered cherries? We were supposed to bring only necessities," Sara said, giggling.

"These are necessities. You'll see. You'll be begging me for one or the other."

Although Sara had felt reasonably comfortable among Zoe's people before the change, they were oddly distant, as if there was a void between them. She wondered how different her experience might be surrounded by people she shared something with. Olesya didn't count. She shared a special bond with her already, and nothing could affect it. She sensed a connection to Henry, Alexander, and Elliot when they arrived and sensed their energy reaching her in gentle waves that felt warm and feathery. Not expecting it, she shuddered, realizing she would have to understand and get used to many new sensations and emotions.

"I was an adult when Zoe and Sebastian changed me. I can help," Henry whispered. "If only to talk about it."

Sara smiled and nodded.

As soon as Henry, Sara, and Olesya had unpacked and got comfortable on the sofa and chairs, Zoe and Sebastian walked in. Louis came running to greet his brother Regis, and they both settled under a table, one gazing at Zoe and the other at Olesya.

Zoe observed Olesya from across the room. Having seen her own transformation in the mirror, Olesya knew she was beaming with health and had already put on a few pounds. Her complexion, which normally had a Mediterranean tint, had developed a peachy tinge and was even smoother and softer now. Zoe's frequent stares and heavy sighs unnerved her.

Zoe seemed moved from chair to chair as if trying to find a comfortable place to sit while flashing her eyes at anyone who looked her way. The surrounding air seemed to thicken, but Alexander didn't seem to care, wrapping his arms around her and inhaling the scent of her hair.

"Nobody will find us here. It's going to be okay."

"Will it?" Zoe spewed the words slowly and then pulled out of his embrace. "Are you sure nobody knows about this cabin?" she asked Sara.

"No, nobody knows I own this cabin. It's still under my father's friend's name. It's safe."

"It's not like you to be pessimistic, sister," Sebastian said. "We'll figure this thing out."

"How are you guys doing?" Alexander asked Elliot and Mary, who were masking the IP address on the satellite internet to avoid detection during their research.

"Almost done," Elliot answered.

"Did you hide all the fragments?" Olesya asked Zoe.

"Yes. I hid them in different places. You'll each receive the locations of several fragments. Do not share it with anyone. You should move them to another safe location, telling no one about it. A precaution in case any of us get caught," Zoe said.

"I still think we're being too paranoid," Sebastian said.

"Perhaps we should track them down and take care of them," Alexander said.

"You mean kill them?" Olesya asked.

"They want to do the same to us."

"We don't know that for sure."

Olesya sensed Zoe's stare and glanced at her, recoiling at seeing her face contorted with hate and anger. The glimpse lasted only a split second, and Olesya wondered if she had imagined it.

"We need to understand all this. Sara and I researched the fragments and know more about them now," Olesya continued, glancing at Zoe, who had suddenly lost interest in the discussion and was staring out the window. Olesya had expected Zoe's worries would ease as soon as she re-engaged as the leader, but she seemed to have lost interest in leading.

Olesya continued, taking the leadership role upon herself. Zoe did not object.

"We should start researching tomorrow. We'll keep watch outside, switching every four hours. Sara will give details of what we learned in our research on the black and golden fragments."

Sara explained the results of their research and the superiority of the black fragments over the golden ones. "Maybe that's why they attacked us. They wanted the black shards."

Olesya suggested the next step was to make something disappear using the black fragment. "On a small scale, of course and with inanimate objects. Now, let's talk about what we are doing here. Our goal is to find other chambers like the one we found in Chile. Elliot, since you are our research genius, why don't you perform your 'Slavic witchcraft' and help us get started?"

Zoe suddenly perked up and nodded

"Sure," Elliot said and cleared his throat. "We should start with religions across the globe, and specifically Egypt, Mesopotamia, Greece, and then the rest. Each person should focus on one religion, and then we can compare notes."

"Why religion?" Mary asked.

"All religions hold some truth, embodying the belief in unusual, supernatural, godly entities when people could not explain the universe in any other way. Religion often becomes tied to economics when a society experiences sudden prosperity or a loss. The golden shards were part of the Incan religion and became embedded in the traditions. I am thinking there might be religions based on dark or black gods. We will search for references to dark gods, gods of shadows, blackness, and immortality, and civilizations ending suddenly without an obvious cause. Or new civilizations emerging out of nowhere. Look into legends and stories, references to black shards, amulets, dark gods."

With a plan in place, everyone relaxed, got comfortable, and told jokes to get their minds off the task ahead, the golden people, and being trapped in this cabin indefinitely. Zoe sat on a chair by a window with a glass of wine in her hand, not paying attention to anyone. Alexander kept trying to involve her in the conversation, but she ignored his efforts. Sebastian at one point uttered a frustrated sound and stormed outside.

The following day, the group of fugitives delved into old religions and tales of gods and monsters, stories, legends, and historical accounts and made copious notes, which they shared with the group. After a while, Sebastian couldn't concentrate on the research but kept staring out the window or pacing the room. Then he announced the need to expand the sentry duty to areas further from the cabin to make sure nobody watched them. A restless spirit, he struggled with confinement and ached to get away. Patrolling the area outside calmed him, and he soon returned to researching and reading old stories and legends, which he enjoyed well enough.

"I may have found something," Elliot said quietly. He went unnoticed, as everyone was deeply absorbed in their research. He coughed and spoke louder. "I've got something interesting."

"What did you find?" Olesya asked, getting up from her chair and facing him.

"The construction of a new highway near the city of Al Amara in southern Iraq resulted in the unearthing of an old but well-preserved temple with many artifacts inside. A subsequent archeological dig recovered the fullest and oldest collection of Sumerian clay tablets. They decoded part of the text." Elliot stopped.

"And?"

"It is about a Sumerian god of shadows and eternity, named Urukksan. He came to Sumer from somewhere northeast of Eridu, carrying a bag full of black...something—they didn't translate the word—and built a pantheon for gods to rule over Earth. He mixed the black stuff with clay and created people out of the black clay, bestowing upon them strength, health, and immortality. Together, they created the flourishing city of Eridu. For centuries, the gods ruled over Earth in peace and prosperity until the feud with the golden clan, who worshipped the sun instead of the dark gods."

"Where did the golden clan come from?" Olesya asked.

"It is not clear. The translation is not complete in places. They've been having trouble translating the old words, and many tablets broke and were missing pieces. It hasn't been published yet," Elliot said.

Alexander tilted his head. "So how did you find it?"

"I hacked into the email of the Iraqi anthropologist who oversaw the dig and found the tablets, then I went online and hacked into their files."

"Clever Elliot. I could kiss you now," Olesya blurted out and then blushed.

Elliot shrugged as if he didn't care for the praise, but smiled. "It was easy; they didn't protect the files."

"What else does it say?" Olesya asked.

"A war ensued, caused by religious differences. Then came greed, cruelty, and disobedience. Urukksan banished the golden society and rescinded his gifts of strength, health, and immortality from his people. He left carrying his bag, promising to come back with the gifts he once gave them if they became worthy of them."

"I take it he didn't come back?" Sebastian asked.

"I don't think so."

"So what does this give us? We have a story that may or may not be significant. Now what?" Sebastian asked.

"We have a location," Olesya said.

"We have two locations. Eridu and northeast of Eridu—where Urukksan came from," Elliot added.

"Northeast is just too vague. It could be anywhere," Alexander said.

"That is something. Elliot is right. We have one location and should explore it. Maybe we can find more clues there," Zoe said, looking at Olesya.

Surprised to hear Zoe take part in the conversation after hours of silence, Olesya nodded eagerly.

"Perhaps we should look for dark stone passages with triangles," Sara suggested.

"Good idea," Zoe said, adding. "It suits you."

"What?"

"The hair."

Sara smiled, shaking her head, sending her black waves into rebellion. The black hair did indeed look good on her, complementing her creamy complexion.

A while later, Olesya approached Zoe, who sat alone on the

bench outside, reading from the laptop in front of her. "What are you not telling me?" Olesya asked.

"What do you mean?"

"You're hiding something. I can feel it. You're behaving differently."

"Nonsense. I'm preoccupied with this, just like everyone else, and haven't been myself."

"Alexander told me he saw a photo of me inside the chamber on your computer."

"He was upset and imagined things," Zoe snapped and got up from the bench, signaling the conversation was over.

"No, he didn't. I will find out what it was," Olesya said, more to herself than to Zoe.

Zoe shrugged and walked back to the cabin.

ERIDU CHAMBER

MARCH 2024

F ollowing Elliot's discovery, everyone except for Sara, who stayed in the lab, traveled to Nasiriyah, the current name for Eridu. They had gone there with fake credentials as American anthropologists and rich benefactors, who were also extremely generous donors to archeological research. In this way, they bypassed the heavy security imposed by the Iraqi army.

It helped to have the support of Zoe's high-level Iraqi government insider, who vouched for them and even briefed Zoe on the history of the shrine. According to him, two years ago, a group of teenagers had discovered it while searching for a hiding place to do recreational, and not-so-legal, testing of local marijuana. Underground caves seemed like the perfect place to hide. The cave floor, undermined by the water seeping from the river, caved in under the teens, trapping them in the dark tunnel with no way to escape. Lucky for them, they had matches for their bongs, and after two days and nights, they clawed their way out through a small opening in the rocks; their fingers and knees scraped raw. Because of the mysterious nature of the chamber and its potential military application, the government kept it locked and restricted access to it. American benefactors' generosity opened doors for Zoe and her team for a limited time.

Elliot led the group deep into a tunnel, stopping at several security checkpoints. The somber guards stared at them while checking their credentials and grudgingly opened the doors. Three, armed guards stood by the third and final door leading to the chamber, and each checked their documents and reluctantly let them in, staring at Olesya's large backpack suspiciously. Once they were inside and the door behind them closed, Zoe whispered, "Not to worry. They know nothing, but it's their duty to make us feel like villains. I was promised nobody would bother us for an hour."

The phony archeologists turned on their flashlights and walked around the chamber, examining its walls, which looked just like the walls under the Chilean crater.

"Look for triangles," Olesya whispered, looking around the room and trembling at the sight of the familiar spooky walls.

"We know," Sebastian said.

"I found it," Alexander whispered.

He stood, pointing at the carved triangle on the ceiling.

"It looks identical to the one in Chile. The chamber is the same. Whoever built this one also built the one in Chile," Elliot said after examining the triangle.

"How many more are there in the world?" Alexander wondered.

"What I don't understand is why we could open the entrance door by pressing the triangle, but not the one in the chamber," Sebastian observed.

"Should we try?" Olesya asked, looking at her companions.

"It is too high. We can't reach it," Mary said.

"We can with this," Olesya smiled, taking out a drone from her pack. Olesya attached powerful suction cups to it. Next, she pulled out a nylon rope with knots and attached it to the suction cups. She sent the drone up with a remote, and when the drone reached the ceiling, she pressed the remote, and the drone flipped and attached the cups. The rope hung from the ceiling, ready to be scaled. The obedient machine returned to the ground as Olesya pressed the remote control.

"You came prepared," Zoe said, looking at Olesya with a puzzling, wintry smile.

Alexander stood by his sister as she put on gloves and ascended the rope. She didn't have any trouble pulling herself up. Her strength increased with Alexander near her.

"Here goes nothing," she said before pressing the triangle with her finger. And nothing happened.

"Just like the one in Chile. We can't open it," Olesya said, frowning.

Alexander approached Olesya and embraced her, whispering in her ear, "You'll figure it out. I'm sure."

"Well, there is not much we can do here," Mary said. "Let's get out of here. This place is giving me the creeps."

"How did the kids get here? Someone must have opened another door with a triangular notch. Would it be possible to talk to the children?" Olesya asked Zoe.

"No. Ever since they considered this place valuable for the military, they relocated the children and their families somewhere safe. Safe means nobody can find them. I suspect there was a door that the children accidentally stumbled upon and opened it," Zoe answered brashly.

"We are back to square one. We've made no progress," Sebastian said.

"I disagree with you. We know there are two chambers like this one and possibly more. We must figure out how to open it," Olesya said.

"I doubt they'll let us come back here. Our cover will be blown by then," Alexander said.

"There is the chamber in Chile."

"We're not going back there!" Zoe bellowed.

"We look for others then," Alexander said, glancing at Zoe. "If there are two, there are more. Who knows, we might even find ones that no one has found yet."

"I suspect there are," Elliot said. "We've got more research to do."

"That's just great!" Sebastian. "I hoped we were done with the cabin."

They returned to the cabin, but they didn't stay there long.

Once they arrived at the cabin, the caretakers sent Zoe a message informing her that someone had broken into her house and that part of the building had suffered major fire damage.

"They found us, Sebastian!" Zoe shouted. "They attacked our house!"

Sebastian, after an initial bout of anger, tried to lessen her worries, assuring her they were safe in the cabin and started cracking jokes. But she didn't listen or pay attention to his humor. Her frustration oscillated between outbursts of anger and withdrawal and hours late, Zoe stormed out of the cabin and checked into a hotel.

Olesya thought something entirely different was stealing Zoe's sleep. With each passing day, she grew more certain that Zoe was keeping something from them that concerned the golden people, and the image on Zoe's computer only increased her suspicions. Alexander couldn't help anymore—Zoe had changed her password and kept her laptop hidden.

Olesya dove into finding the secret of the chambers. What had started as an unnerving curiosity had ended in an obsession. Her first waking thought was of the chambers; she dreamed about them at night. She spent her time researching, obsessing, and cursing them. A few times, she felt she had the answer. It was so close she could almost see it. But in early September 2004, her obsession with the chambers evaporated with the birth of her daughter. She named her Emery, which in Old English meant powerful. The spooky chambers still haunted her in her dreams, but they couldn't compete with her love for her daughter. From the moment Emery was born, Olesya was preoccupied with her, and nothing else mattered. So she swept the chambers back into the corner of her mind.

Olesya spent less time in the lab and more time with Emery and Alexander, who was heartbroken over losing Zoe. Soon after Emery was born, Zoe abandoned her home state and traveled across the continents. Sebastian followed his sister everywhere. Alexander accompanied Zoe on the first few trips, but in the end returned to be with his sister and his newborn niece.

Zoe continued to change, Alexander told Olesya. She became a ghost of her former self and seemed to have lost her confidence as she became more obsessed with finding answers to questions only she knew. When he asked her, she brushed him off.

He would wake up at all hours of the night, crying out Zoe's name. He told his sister he felt like a selfish coward, leaving Zoe when she most needed him.

"She's the one who abandoned you, Alex. She is the one being secretive and aloof. You've tried to help her and comfort her, and what did she do? She isolated herself from you."

"I left because I couldn't help her, but I knew Sebastian would take care of her as he always had. Zoe's eyes are never indifferent toward her brother; their bond is unbreakable and impenetrable to outsiders. Like ours, or perhaps stronger because of all the years they spent together."

"You're not an outsider!"

"Sometimes I think Sebastian understands Zoe more than she understands herself and senses her every thought and wish. I understand their bond, but I resent it. I can't help it. Their bond shrouds them in a protective cloud and isolates her from me."

"I'm sorry."

65

THE TRIANGLE

2024-2030

During the next six years, only Sara persevered in the quest for answers to what had caused Great Britain's disappearance. She carried a small black shard with her everywhere she went, trying to make things disappear. She no longer had concerns someone might spot the black shard as she tried it on random inanimate objects and then ants, flies, mice, or even small birds whenever she went. And then, the lab became her home. There, she spent all her time working, sleeping, and eating whenever she remembered to eat. And it showed on her sunken and pale face, eyes staring into the distance, and her bony hands with oversized veins pulsing whenever she moved them.

Without Olesya's unexpected visit to the lab in March 2030, Sara could have spiraled downward rapidly. Having not been in the lab for more than a month, Olesya gasped, seeing Sara's pale face and fevered eyes. She immediately blamed herself for her diminished involvement in the research in the last few years.

After a long conversation, she persuaded Sara to leave the lab for a while and go on vacation while promising herself and Sara that she would be more involved in the research from now on. Emery, growing like a weed, now spent the mornings in kindergarten, meeting and playing with other children, much to Olesya's joy.

"Promise me you'll leave the lab for a while."

Sara sighed. "Fine, I promise."

∾

On a whim, Sara booked the first ticket she saw on Expedia. That is how she ended up in Sierra Leone, where, following Olesya's advice, she behaved like a typical tourist. She visited local beaches and historic sites, discovered local gastronomic treasures, despite her initial contradictory mindset.

One day, a charming old church with exquisite mosaics in the small town of Lakka sparked her interest. She had not been in a church since she was a girl, taken by her great aunt, who took it upon herself to fill in the gaps in her spiritual education. It was not a fond memory for her; having to kneel on the hard ground and listen to a long sermon she didn't understand as her aunt threw stern looks her way. The smell of burning candles and old stone forever etched itself into her memory, and it was not a pleasant recollection.

But this was different. She went of her own volition and ended up enjoying the quaint little church. As she was leaving it, a small boy ran inside, bumping into her. She thought nothing of it until she noticed he had snatched her bag. When she glanced back, she caught sight of him emptying the bag right there onto the floor. And that is when it happened. The contents of the bag spilled, and the black shard hit the stone floor, breaking out of the glass case. A blue, blinding flash filled the church, and then the church disappeared in front of Sara and the boy with it.

She stood paralyzed.

Soon, people started gathering around her, asking questions, so she fled and returned to her hotel in Freetown. Terrified and heartbroken that her stupidity and recklessness had caused this tragedy, she cried for hours. She would never forgive herself for disappearing a boy and the old building that held such significance to the town.

But this tragedy led to her understanding of what caused the disappearance of Great Britain and the realization that it wasn't what Sergi used with the black fragment but where he used it.

The place held the secret. She noticed her phone did not work afterward. It would not turn on.

Over the next two days, Sara delved into the history of Lakka and its church, uncovering both miraculous and cursed stories. Several articles described the spontaneous breaking of a wooden statue. Believers attributed it to God's wrath. Scientists tried to explain it in scientific terms, discussing the properties of the wood, the surrounding air, and the atmospheric pressure. None were correct.

Coincidentally, Sara had just finished reading an article about an Austrian team of scientists who found out that in certain places on Earth, the collision of heavy ions causes an electromagnetic field stronger than a neutron star. The collision was impossible to detect and measure from a distance because it only happened for a split second. To detect and measure the collision, the monitoring equipment must be set up near it ahead of time. That's why no one had devised a theory explaining Great Britain's fate.

Sara returned to the lab and resumed experimenting, creating a strong electromagnetic field and finally vanishing a few granules of salt and pepper. She searched for other places where extraordinary things happened, or where things broke spontaneously, or phones stopped working. She traveled to those places but discovered they were just tales to lure gullible tourists.

Then, one late summer afternoon, Elliot showed up, and everything changed. He seemed equally absorbed in discovering the secret of the triangles and chambers, just as Sara was obsessed with Great Britain's disappearance. High with feverish excitement, he told Sara that he had figured out the triangles. Sara immediately called Olesya, and it wasn't long before Olesya and Alexander came running into the lab. Olesya's shirt bore signs of recent baking; flour and chocolate stains covered her T-shirt.

As soon as they arrived, Elliot pulled out a world map and spread it on the table. He had covered the map with his notes, marks, and a giant red triangle. One corner rested on China, one on Iraq, and one on Russia.

Seeing the triangle, Olesya gasped. "How did I not see that before?"

"How? I still don't understand," Sara said.

"Pressing all three triangles simultaneously opens the chamber," Olesya said, and Elliot nodded, smiling.

"But if you orient the triangles differently, you will end up in different places. How could you have pinpointed the exact locations if you only have one location?" Alexander asked.

"We have two locations. We've always had two locations," Olesya said and paused, waiting for Sara and Alexander to figure it out.

"Is that where...Belyaska is?" Sara asked.

"Northeast of Eridu...the crater..." Olesya whispered, not taking her eyes off the map.

66

THE HERBAL BOUTIQUE

OCTOBER 2030

The tip of the triangle rested on Chamdo, China, a prefecture-level city in the eastern part of the Tibet Autonomous Region and Tibet's third-largest city. Hoping to use one of Zoe's jets to travel to China, Olesya, Alexander, and Elliot drove to Zoe's airport. Alexander kept his trembling hands in his pockets on the way to the hangars, staring out the window. Olesya guessed he was hoping to learn Zoe's whereabouts from the pilots, whom he knew well.

It had been a while since Olesya had flown anywhere on Zoe's jet, so she wondered whether she had disbanded her airport as she had her home after the fire. Much to her surprise, the hangars were still operational and filled with even more planes. The crew, as busy as ever, if not more, scurried around the planes, cleaning and maintaining them. A new hangar held a new plane that was shinier and larger than the others. They walked into the office near the main hangar. Steven, the airport manager, stood by the desk talking on the phone, his back to them when they entered. They waited for him to finish his conversation before approaching him. Alexander eavesdropped.

"How are you guys?" Steven asked, smiling. "Haven't seen you in a while."

"Was it Zoe on the phone?" Alexander asked.

"No, it was my parts' supplier. Zoe, last I heard, is in Africa."

"Where in Africa?" Olesya asked.

"I don't know."

"Are you supposed to keep her location confidential?" Olesya pressed him.

Steven averted his gaze and bit his lip.

"Thanks, Steven. We want to use Zoe's jet to fly to China," Elliot said.

"Of course. All the planes are at your disposal. If you're going to China, you will need the Challenger 850. It should be ready for use by tomorrow. Let's talk to the guys," Steve said, leaving his desk and leading them toward the hangars.

While they walked to the hangars, Olesya noticed several luxury cars in the parking lot. *Zoe pays her employees well*, she thought. *No wonder they keep secrets for her.*

After a long, twelve-hour journey, the jet landed at Chamdo Airport, where they rented a Haval—a common Chinese car—to avoid attention. On their long flight, they tried unsuccessfully to reach Zoe or Sebastian on their phones. Olesya left a cryptic message hinting at recent developments, but gave no specifics. She kept glancing at Alexander, who sat engrossed in his thoughts, checking his phone for messages, looking dejected. Seeing him depressed again angered her. Her hands rolled into fists. *She should at least fucking tell him it's over so he can move on.*

"What is the plan?" Sara asked after they had settled into the car. "How will we locate the chamber in this city? I found nothing about secret chambers or passages in Chamdo when I searched the internet."

"I'm not surprised. The Chinese are secretive, but I found something interesting when I researched the town," Elliot said.

"What did you find?" Olesya asked, relaxing her hands.

"See for yourself," he said, handing her his silver tablet.

"Elliot, you're a genius," she praised, gazing at the tablet image. "I couldn't find anything when I searched. How did you do it?"

"I'm a research genius." He smiled. "If I reveal my secrets, I won't be a genius anymore."

"Not very humble, but geniuses seldom are," Olesya said.

Sara grabbed the tablet from Olesya's hands. "Let me see, let me see."

They stopped the car in front of a shop that sold ancient homeopathic remedies. Elliot had found it while researching historic sites, stores, hotels, and businesses in Chamdo during the flight. Only a few of them had photographs. How lucky it was that this one did.

It was a while after they had entered the store before their eyes adjusted from the sunny street to the dark room illuminated only by a few flickering candles. The candles provided just enough light to see the walls behind the red shelves, which stored colorful jars full of indiscernible floating objects, ointments, and dried herbs. Olesya exhaled, recognizing the black, seamless walls. They had found the chamber!

The store owner, a small old man sporting a long, thin mustache, greeted them in his language, bending his little body in a polite, deep bow. Elliot surprised everyone, including the store owner, when he spoke fluent Chinese. Although they didn't understand the conversation between the store owner and Elliot, they recognized its politeness. Trying not to cause suspicion, they inconspicuously scanned the dark, seamless walls in search of the triangle. Elliot ended up buying a few jars of dried herbs, which the little man wrapped in colorful paper before handing them to him. Before they left, they engaged in a bowing competition with the store owner, bowing deeply and smiling, not understanding a word he said.

Back in the car, Elliot summarized his conversation with the shopkeeper. He was not aware of how the store ended up in his family years ago, but he recalled his grandfather mentioning that it used to be a temple for a goddess a long time ago. The government destroyed most of it to discourage superstition and magic, leaving only the black, seamless stone intact. Customers never questioned the strange black walls, assuming they were part of the store's décor. The store owner himself thought the walls strange, but not enough to forgo his thriving business.

"I wasn't aware you spoke Chinese," Olesya said.

"I learned it when I discovered the triangle pointed to China. Don't look at me that way. I have a knack for languages."

"Has anyone noticed the triangle?" Sara asked.

"On the ceiling, like Chile," Alexander said.

"Has anyone seen a security system in the store?" Olesya asked.

Sara and Alexander shook their heads. Elliot said "no".

"Now what?" Sara asked.

"We'll come back at night," Olesya said.

"Have you been in touch with Mary and Henry?" Olesya asked Elliot. The familiar black seamless material reminded her of them.

"They are in Europe somewhere. I have their new phone numbers and can contact them if we need them. But not until we absolutely need them." Elliot seemed unwilling to discuss his friends.

When they returned later that night, they found the streets abandoned. Only a few streetlights were lit, providing little illumination, which suited their purposes perfectly. Elliot fumbled with the lock for a few seconds before it opened with a loud clank, and they were inside the chamber, tracing the walls and the ceiling with flashlights. The triangle stared at them from the ceiling like an evil eye, exactly like the ones in Chile and Eridu.

The store door opened as they stared at the triangle, and the owner walked in, holding a huge shotgun that was as old and nearly as big as himself. With surprising agility, the small man pointed the gun at them, shouting. Elliot spoke calmly to appease him and convince him they were not robbing the place, but he wasn't convincing enough. The man now shouted repeatedly, swinging his gun in uncoordinated movements, his voice turning into a fearful shriek. Olesya thrust her hands as gently as she could to stop his shouts, and the man fell back. His gun went off, hitting the wall.

Alexander sat the storekeeper upright, and Elliot spoke to him to calm him down and reassure him they meant no harm to him or his business, but he stared past him with crazed eyes, not comprehending and shaking.

Olesya and Sara inspected the walls to check for any damage, but found none. The walls remained smooth and perfect. With nothing else to do in the store, they returned to their hotel on the other side of town, leaving the man sitting on the floor, staring into space.

"How did he know we were in his store?" Alexander wondered once they were back in Olesya's room, sitting on the couch.

"Maybe he lives somewhere nearby, and our flashlights alerted him," Olesya said. "Are we still on to fly to Belyaska tomorrow?"

"I thought that was the plan," Elliot said.

Olesya grimaced, not looking forward to reliving her nightmarish experience in the strange town full of odd people. But she also couldn't wait to find another chamber, verify their theory, and satisfy the intense desire to know what secrets the chambers held. Every time she thought about opening the door, her breath stalled.

The next day, they flew to Belyaska. Elliot had arranged land transportation on their way here. A dented, rickety old van was waiting for them when they arrived.

"Splendid!" Sara laughed at the sight of the van.

Although Olesya had mentally prepared for the town's sinister atmosphere, she was still overwhelmed when she set foot there for the second time. As if a heavy shroud, the town's creepiness settled on Olesya's shoulders. She hunched in her seat. As she kept staring out the window, the town seemed to darken. Sara's pale face showed she shared Olesya's impression. The town's eeriness only intensified as they drove through it and experienced the unnerving glares and baleful grins from the locals. Sinister clouds stole the sunlight from the streets of the hellish little town in the middle of nowhere, exposing the town's dark soul. On top of that, a foul, stomach-churning smell made its way into the car through the vents as they drove. Olesya wondered why she had not noticed it before.

They drove to Olesya's parents abandoned house to take the path to the crater from there. When Olesya saw the sad old house, her eyes filled with tears of sorrow for the crumbling structure. She didn't remember this house, and yet it seemed familiar somehow.

Sara tapped her on the shoulder. "Let's go," she said. "The sooner we do it, the sooner we get out of this forsaken place. No offense, kiddo. I realize this is your parents' house, but there are strange vibes here."

Teary-eyed, Olesya began her journey into the forest where her parents had found her. This magnificent old forest had given her life; thus, in a sense, it had also been her parent. With each step, her connection to this place grew. Alexander walked alongside Olesya, admiring the enormous trunks and crowns that almost reached the sky, experiencing similar emotions. Olesya clutched his hand, and the eerie yet peaceful sensation of being part of this forest intensified.

They stood at the edge of the gigantic crater in silence before taking the climbing gear from their backpacks as if the task seemed too tough to even attempt. They took turns rappelling to the bottom to search for an entrance to the chamber. The crater's depth forced a midway halt for multi-pitch rappelling as the hundred-foot rope fell short. Getting everyone down required time, concentration, and skill. Only when they landed at the bottom of the crater did they shake their heads at its enormity, as if realizing the task ahead of them was even more daunting than they feared. It would take at least a week to inspect the crater's walls. Even then, nine days had passed before they examined the entire perimeter of the crater. On the ninth day, they gathered, tired and disappointed, not having found the chamber's door.

"What're we going to do now?" Alexander asked.

"We explore the town," Olesya said.

"I'm so looking forward to it," Sara blurted out.

"What about the government building Zoe found? I imagine there was a reason to build it there. Shouldn't we search it?" Elliot suggested.

"I've thought about it, but how do we unlock the doors without alerting anyone?" Olesya asked.

"We'll just break them," Alexander said. "That seems like the next obvious place."

"I think we need to involve Mary," Olesya said, looking at Elliot. "Let's call her. This is important. Breaking down the door may bring unexpected guests. If Mary could unlock it without causing an alarm, we could search the buildings longer."

"I agree wholeheartedly," Sara said.

Elliot called Mary, and she responded an hour later, saying she and Henry would join them in two days.

To avoid ghostly stares from the locals, they stayed in their dingy hotel rooms.

Mary arrived two days later, as she had said she would. Henry, who accompanied her, had tears in his eyes when he embraced Elliot and the others. Henry hadn't changed much, but his eyes were duller than before.

Mary's black hair was short. Looking noticeably thinner and paler, she wasted no time and started working on the locks as soon as she arrived.

"Yeah, nothing I can't handle," she said, smiling lightly. "Good to be back at work," she added quietly, more to herself than for anyone else to hear.

Mary opened the lock and assured everyone she had disabled the alarm before opening it.

Olesya sensed Mary and Henry had lived through difficult times but didn't pry. Mary's eyes shone with excitement when she opened the lock.

A sinister darkness and the stale stench of ancient air, trapped underground for years or perhaps centuries, ambushed them when they opened the door, as if it were guarding the building from unwanted visitors. They cast the darkness away with powerful flashlights and entered.

Inside, the building seemed much smaller than it appeared from the outside and was mostly empty, with just a handful of dirty shelves, heaps of bent and broken wire, and pungent garbage littering the floor. Their first impression revealed nothing of interest. Dirty gray paneling covered the walls, floor, and ceiling. Something indistinguishable and filthy covering the floor made squishy sounds when they walked.

Just as they were leaving, disappointed at not finding what they had come for, Alexander tripped over a wire and sent a heavy metal shelf falling to the floor, breaking on impact.

"Are you okay?" Olesya asked.

He didn't answer, so she shone her flashlight at him. Alexander sat on the floor with a flashlight in one hand, tearing up the gray flooring with the other. When she approached him, she understood what he was doing. Underneath the dirty gray floor panels, there was the black seamless stone, which she recognized too well. The shelf broke the gray paneling, revealing the black material below, which the observant Alexander noticed right away.

Energized, everyone started peeling panels from the floor, unveiling the familiar seamless black stone and the triangle. Olesya felt her fingernails give under the sharp-edged paneling, but she didn't care, peeling and tossing the pieces of dirty paneling to keep up with her pounding heart.

Once they cleared a large area, the pounding in her chest suddenly stopped, leaving her lightheaded. She dropped to the floor, whispering, "We found it!"

"This must be the entrance," Elliot pointed to the triangle.

Alexander pressed it. The door opened, revealing a deep black hole resembling the one in Chile.

The ancient smell of dust and old metal hit Olesya in a biting gust from below, restoring enough of the energy to pull herself from the floor. "We should split. Three of us will stay here to keep watch while three will go down to investigate."

"You're going down?" Alexander asked Olesya. "Then I'm going with you."

Henry, Mary, and Sara stayed to keep guard. Alexander, Olesya, and Elliot rappelled and disappeared into the black hole. They were gone much longer than expected. But just as the guard group began to glance at each other with worried looks, the rope started moving.

Sara sighed with relief. "Well? Did you find it?"

"Yup," Alexander said. "We'd found the triangle on the ceiling and tried to open it. But guess what?"

"It didn't budge?" Mary asked.

Olesya and Alexander shook their heads.

"Can we please get the hell out of here?" Sara asked.

They locked the door behind them and returned to the plane.

On the plane, Olesya was already planning and discussing the trip back, shivering with the realization that she'll finally learn their secrets. One person would return to Belyaska, the second to China, and the third to Iraq, and they would press the triangles at the same time and open the chambers.

Olesya worried that without Zoe's financial and political influence, they wouldn't be able to go back to the Iraqi chamber. And that's when Elliot jumped in and assured her it was no longer guarded by the army and no longer locked. The Iraqi government had grown bored with it and left it to the locals to do whatever they wanted. It now stood open to gawkers and omnipresent tourists whenever they stumbled upon it, however, its novelty wore off. You could stare at the black walls only for so long.

Olesya glanced at Elliot as he was talking, but quickly averted her eyes to hide her sudden suspicion that he had a hidden agenda. He was always ahead of everyone. Always found information others couldn't. He claimed he didn't know where Zoe was. Olesya had never doubted him until now. As quickly as it had appeared, the suspicion faded. She couldn't find a reason for Elliot to deceive them or act on Zoe's behalf. Zoe, it seemed, had lost interest in finding the chambers.

Since the Iraqi chamber was the safest to enter now, Olesya volunteered Alexander. Elliot, as the sole Chinese speaker, would fly to China accompanied by Henry, while Olesya adamantly insisted, despite Alexander's protest, that she had to be the one returning to Belyaska. Mary volunteered to go with her and received a grateful look in return.

"I'm coming along," Sara informed Olesya. "Yes! Do not protest."

"You said the place gave you the creeps."

"Your solitary trip to that place is even more unsettling."

"Not solitary. Mary is coming with me."

"Three is better than two. The more, the better, in that shitty little town."

And a few weeks later, Olesya, Sara, and Mary booked one hotel room for the three of them for safety reasons. In the evening, the three women sat in their hotel room, each holding a glass of wine. Olesya confided in them about her dreams of floating in the dark, alone and scared. Emery was calling her name, asking where she was, begging her to find her. She couldn't see Emery, but she recognized her voice. She sounded desolate and scared. Olesya associated her dreams with the chambers because they always happened when she was close to one. Emery's golden hair floated in the dark in long strands, leading Olesya toward her daughter's voice.

Olesya had finished telling her dreams and had fallen into a sullen silence. Sara patted Olesya's hand.

"I've had a similar dream," Mary blurted.

Olesya looked up, surprised. "You dreamed of my daughter?"

"I didn't know she was your daughter. I saw a girl with long blonde hair waving at me but calling your name. As in your dream, I floated in darkness, alone."

"When did you have the dreams?"

"Just after our return from Chile and before..." Mary hesitated to continue.

"Before what?" Olesya asked.

"Before I was attacked."

"I didn't know. Who attacked you?"

"I'd been shot. It was a close call, the doctors said. The bullet missed my heart by a hair and ravaged my lungs. Two years passed before I regained the courage to go outside without fear. Henry saw the man who shot me flee from the scene, and he swore he'd seen a golden glow emanating from him. Henry wanted to catch up with him and kill him, but he stayed by my side instead."

"A golden man shot you? When did this happen?"

"Right after our cabin trip. He was waiting outside our house in New York."

They sat shrouded in leaden silence for the rest of the night, sipping their wine. Olesya's thoughts revolved around Zoe and Sebastian and the golden people. The unnerving sensation returned that something was amiss. The golden people had returned to haunt her again.

When they arrived at the chamber in Belyaska, Olesya's hands trembled holding the flashlight.

They extended the folding aluminum ladder and set it under the triangle. Before climbing up the ladder, Olesya wiped her forehead and glanced at her watch, and waited for the timer to beep. When it beeped, she drew a deep breath and pressed the triangle. Alexander in Iraq and Elliot in China pressed theirs at the same time.

THE HOLOGRAM

FEBRUARY 2031

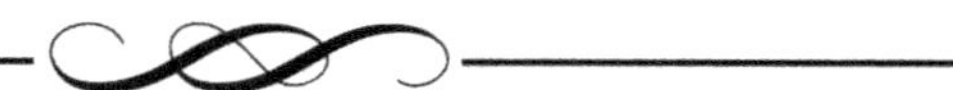

Olesya's heart raced as a deafening humming sound and a strong vibration filled the air. The hum turned into the roar of a raging river, followed by a gust of wind on their faces. Olesya lost her balance on the ladder and was flailing her arms to stabilize, but she was out of time—she was already falling. Sara rushed toward the ladder to catch her, but discovered her movements were sluggish and uncontrollable. But Olesya didn't fall. Wide-eyed and mouth agape, she floated, looking down at Sara and Mary, who watched her in amazement as she hovered awkwardly in midair.

As Mary and Sara observed Olesya floating in the air, the door above Olesya's head opened soundlessly, revealing a round dark hole in the ceiling. Mary and Sara exchanged cautious glances; meanwhile, Olesya floated up and disappeared into the opening.

After she floated into the hole, it lit up with a pale blue light. Mary and Sara followed and drifted through the opening in the ceiling into another chamber, where Olesya hovered over a console with blue light emanating from its center. The same black, seamless stone covered the walls, ceiling, and floor. At one end of the room, there was an upright, empty crystal capsule.

The triangular opening in the center of the console emitted blue light, pulsating at a steady pace. Olesya hovered over it, mesmerized by the light. Mary, drawn to the capsule, inspected every inch while Sara made her way toward Olesya. Unable to control her body in the weightless environment, she bumped into her friend. Bounced out of her blue daze, Olesya looked at Sara with astonishment, her mouth agape.

"What is this?" Sara asked. "Microgravity, operating on a trigger? How is that possible? It would require a vast amount of energy and sophistication. And that capsule looks...like something you lock people in if you want them to disappear."

"You think it is alien technology, don't you?" Olesya asked.

"Either that or a sophisticated extinct civilization. Or both?"

"Where is the power source?" Olesya asked, scrutinizing the circular room. "There is nothing here."

"Hidden within the walls."

"What do we do now?" Mary asked.

"We'll try the triangle," Olesya said and drifted to the console. She had her finger on the triangle, pulsating with blue light, ready to press it, but Sara stopped her.

"Are you sure about this? Imagine if those golden people suddenly rushed in—three of us, no weapons."

"I'm sure. I don't quite believe in the existence of the golden people. This doubt has been on my mind for a while now."

"But I've seen them floating in from somewhere above in the Chilean chamber with my own eyes, and Zoe later confirmed it. And they attacked Mary."

"I have a feeling they won't harm us."

"A feeling?" Sara said, frowning. "We are risking our lives because you have a feeling."

"Trust me," Olesya said, and pressed the glowing triangle.

The blue triangle expanded and emitted a holographic image of a man seated in a golden chair. Olesya gasped, seeing the man's face.

"What is wrong?" Sara asked. "You look as if someone painted your face with chalk."

Olesya pointed at the man from the hologram, who was a perfect likeness to Sergi Orlov.

"Sergi?" Olesya said in an unsteady voice.

Sara tried to convince Olesya that the hologram's resemblance to Sergi was just a coincidence, nothing more. But Olesya's insistence eventually convinced Sara that the man was Sergi Orlov or his clone.

"But how could that be possible? The Russian government couldn't have built this chamber or the ones in China, Chile, or Iraq. They don't have the technology."

"But they could've discovered it."

Sergi sat motionless, with a blank look on his face. Olesya pressed the triangle for the second time. The hologram became brighter, and he spoke.

"Olesya, listen to me first. You can be angry and yell at me all you want later, but listen to me now. It is important. We created a special girl who can return what we lost long ago. We can be strong again and immortal, and Emery is the key to it all. She is the only one who can traverse the dark world and return, bringing back what we've lost. This is how it was in the beginning. When only a few hundred of us existed on Earth, we possessed immortality, strength, and immense power. We never succumbed to disease or old age. Born this way, we never questioned our uniqueness. Until we discovered there were others, known as the Meekers, who didn't live long and surrendered to diseases. And malice.

"Weakness consumed them, fueling their insatiable greed, violent tendencies, and growing resentment toward us. We didn't consider them a threat, as they were weaker, disorganized, and frightened. Instead, we helped them. We showed them how to make tools out of metal, grow food, and heal themselves.

"They always wanted more, desiring what we possessed and never being satisfied. Even though they considered us gods, they hated us with all their might and soul. We lived together for centuries until Ishtar—the Meekers' sun god—arrived. We didn't know of his existence until it was too late. In hindsight, we should have known something was wrong when the Meekers' demeanor changed. Their cowardly expressions diminished, their shoulders straightened, and they became bolder and scheming. We should have seen their sly and hateful smiles.

"One day, they announced a celebration in our honor and appreciation of our help. They told us they had prepared a feast and festivities, promising us the time of our lives. Well, we did, but not in the sense we expected it. Hundreds of us arrived at a magnificent hall with tables adorned with flowers and lit candles.

"As we sat at the tables, they started bringing us wine in copious amounts. Several groups of musicians came, playing harps and singing. The wine and the music did the job. We relaxed and enjoyed ourselves, laughing and singing along with the musicians and didn't see it coming. The musicians disappeared, but we paid no attention. The hall doors closed, but we didn't notice. When the flower-scented mist descended upon us, we thought it was part of the festivities and, amused, we laughed.

"I don't remember when I became unconscious. When I woke up with my wrists and my ankles tied with golden strings, I couldn't move, but I could see the great hall in flames, while I lay in a field of tall grass and wildflowers, watching my brothers and sisters burn alive. Bound and crying for my family and friends, I didn't notice when a flaming globe landed on my chest, burning a hole in it. It missed my heart only because the golden string on my bound hands resting on my chest deflected it.

"The burning globe broke the restraints on my hands, and I could remove the burning globe and relieve the pain. I've never experienced such horrible pain. I considered giving in to end the pain. But the desire to avenge my brothers and sisters wouldn't let me. The anger at what happened to them fueled me, and I threw the fiery ball toward my feet to break the golden string. It broke, and I was free. Clenching my jaws not to scream in pain, I dragged myself away from the flames.

"I was unsure of how I ended up outside the burning building. Did someone try to save me, or did the blast throw me out through the window? With a scar on my chest and a bigger one inside, I hid from the world for years. The need for vengeance grew, but I couldn't defeat the Meekers alone. Hiding underground, I traveled the world and became an expert in finding hidden tunnels like this one without realizing why they existed and who made them, although I sensed there was an important reason for them. As you know, I couldn't open the chambers alone and discover what was inside. Centuries passed before I figured it out." Sergi paused and smiled woefully.

"After years of wandering, I returned to the place where the Meekers massacred my people. I became skillful at hiding in plain sight and observed them to find their weaknesses. That is how I discovered Ishtar and his powers. Ishtar became their new and only god. A powerful god, but not a loving, helpful, or forgiving one. He gave power and longevity to the Meekers, but took back more, requiring sacrifice, and offerings that exceeded their means. But they obeyed him. Fear of the golden god appealed more to them than our goodwill.

"The fortunate Meekers who received the gifts of good health and power differed from the rest—they had a golden glow. Revered, but also resented, the golden Meekers prospered and, true to their nature, wanted more.

"Eventually, the golden Meekers revolted against their god. They found the place on Earth he called home and ambushed him, demanding more power and immortality. He laughed at them, calling them spoiled children. So they picked up their axes and swords, trying to kill him. Instead, Ishtar decimated them with his fiery golden globes. Only a few smarter ones escaped and hid around the world, hoping to escape Ishtar's wrath.

"I don't know what happened to Ishtar afterward. Perhaps he grew tired of humans and left, or hid from their view. The golden god avenged my people and left me with nothing else to do or wish for. Thinking I was the only one of my kind left, I felt utterly alone. My fate sent me back to the underworld, where I wandered for centuries until I found more of my people who had avoided the bloodbath. They didn't take part in the festivities, exploring faraway lands when it happened. With a renewed interest in life, I dove into uncovering the secrets of the underworld, where I found the chambers.

"When we opened the first chamber, we experienced what you are experiencing now. Weightlessness and awe at the brilliant technology and sophistication that created it. Years filled with questions, but answers never came. No hologram greeted us when we opened our first chamber. It wasn't until I found the black shards in the Belyaska's crater that I could start uncovering the significance of the chambers. Only when I carried the shard with me did the hologram deliver a message to me, carrying the history of our people.

"That's how I learned about you and your future. I stayed in Russia and became a powerful force in the Russian government to get my hands on more shards. The invention of contact lenses and hair dyes provided me with a disguise that allowed me to blend in with my Russian countrymen. I fell in love with Russia and the welcoming and passionate inhabitants, their melancholic art, heartbreaking music and literature.

"You will appreciate what I am about to tell you. This is what the hologram showed me. Dark matter has existed forever and was the beginning and end of everything, the creator of everything. It created, shaped, and supported our universe multiple times, trying to forge one that would last. But the new universes were unbalanced, as though the dark matter acted on trial and error, concocting the universe with a flawed recipe. The universe expanded too fast as normal matter interacted with light and collapsed on itself into massive black holes. Only after creating our kind did the dark and normal matter achieve balance, with only insignificant fluctuations.

"Until Ishtar discovered our world and had fun destroying it at our expense, entertaining himself by wreaking havoc on Earth. Pitting us against the Meekers and the Meekers against us, using our differences and strengths to start the conflict. We were immortal, but our immortality came at a price. We couldn't have children. The Meekers envied our immortality and health. Though we envied the Meekers for their ability to have children, our desire for peace never led to ill will or violence against them.

"Stronger and smarter, we won all the wars. So the golden ones turned to clandestine tactics, such as the one that befell me. Who is Ishtar? You are probably wondering. Ishtar, an ageless being as ancient as the universe, personified a sun deity for many peoples. For millennia, that role satisfied him. But then, the monotony and the power demoralized him. Being someone's god and being immortal just wasn't enough anymore. He craved something else. Something beyond death and the universe. Something that perhaps only he knew.

"He stopped desiring life and planned on ending it by collapsing the universe again. That is why he started disrupting the balance by creating his golden children, his golden slaves, the last time he came. Ishtar instilled fear in his golden minions. To appease him, his golden clan had to kill the dark people. He lied to them, telling them the dark people had created the imbalance in the universe. Ishtar promised them immortality for their children if they killed all of us.

"I dedicated my final years to locating and eliminating the golden people. I killed many, but many remain. Great Britain didn't disappear because it was the enemy of Russia. The reason for its removal was its large population of golden people. Ishtar must have gone there recently to restock his golden minions.

"In Yorkshire, there was a place with a peculiar past. Sculptures broke for no apparent reason. Electronic devices stopped working; people felt strange vibrations. Since the early 1900s, the abandoned church has been in ruins. This is where I sent the black shards with a drone. I've done it before on a much smaller scale. I've played with the shards since I gained access to the Russian government's laboratory. Millions of innocents died in the course, you'd say. Yes, but the price is low when you consider the entire universe. Sure, the universe will be created again. But will we? Life in the universe is uncertain, as it's a matter of chance.

"We must stop Ishtar and return the balance to the universe. Every chamber I visited worldwide had identical recordings. When I listened to the first one, I dismissed it as a fable. When I listened to the second, I couldn't wait to find the next chamber to hear the message, curious if it was the same as the first one. All the recordings talked about a girl named Emery, whose mother was born to the Siberian forest enhanced with black shards from a meteorite explosion and whose father was a man saved from Ishtar by the Sun. The message said that the girl would return the balance by unlocking the black shards and the gift of immortality to all people. Emery was the only person capable of escaping the darkness. Other dark people tried before but only managed to send back a handful of black shards to the Earth through meteorites, not able to escape the dark hold. I recorded this message before I went to the Alps, knowing I would die there. I didn't want to die, but I felt the inevitability of my approaching death at your hands. I never intended to harm you, but I had to make it look real.

"You must have the black shard to open the capsule, and you will travel to the dark dimension. Emery will pursue you, hoping to find you and protect you, but she must not know until she is an adult. Only then will she be ready to follow you into the dark world.

"I realize you don't believe me yet. Maybe some of it rings true already. Seek truth before then, but be cautious. The golden people wear many disguises, and they are everywhere, spying on us, hunting us. I know you'll do what's right. The world depends on you and Emery. No one else can save it."

Sergi smiled, and the hologram faltered and disappeared. Only the strange blue light on the console remained as the only memory of the recording.

Olesya stood staring at the console, shaking. Sara touched her shoulder, and Olesya exhaled deeply, as if holding her breath for the entire recording.

"Are you okay?" Sara asked her.

Olesya slowly turned her head toward Sara and searched her eyes. "Do you believe his story?" she asked.

"I don't know," Sara said. "It seems far-fetched, but certain facts add up. We should do what he suggested and seek the truth for ourselves."

"We should leave now," Mary suggested.

"I agree," Sara said, glancing at Olesya.

Sara and Mary began working their way back to the lower chamber, but Olesya lingered, inspecting the console and the capsule. This place evoked a powerful memory, stronger than her occasional déjà vu. She'd been in this chamber before, more than once, and had been certain she was connected to it. Sergi's message evoked neither a vehement denial nor an acceptance, but something in his voice and the way he said certain words bothered her. He never once called her his little forest girl. He resembled Sergi, but was he?

68

IGOR

FEBRUARY 2031

Olesya learned from Alex and Elliot that the other two chambers had identical recordings of Sergi telling the same story, so she couldn't listen to the older recordings Sergi had mentioned. Maybe he erased them before the new recording, or maybe he lied and there was no other recording. She had no way of knowing, and that drove her mad because her daughter was now involved. She threw herself into a search for the truth to repudiate Sergi's story and put an end to the madness reaching for her with wrathful tentacles.

Elliot volunteered to help with the research. She agreed, aware of his special talents, and ended up spending hours reading stories about the golden people. He even found recent anecdotal evidence of golden people spotted in London and other British cities before England disappeared, and a short video of a man shimmering with golden streaks. Instead of finding it suspicious, onlookers cheered him, asking where he held his magic performances.

The more research Elliot conducted, the more he bought Sergi's story. Olesya noticed his curious glances whenever he'd bring her a new story or video. He didn't try to convince her, but she sensed his growing impatience with her reluctance to accept it, and her search for something to disprove it. The thought of sacrificing her daughter or even herself without absolute certainty seized her stomach in a painful grip.

Sergi's story contained believable facts, unverifiable claims, and puzzling inconsistencies.

Sergi couldn't have known that Olesya had already encountered the golden people. One fact bothered her more than the others. How did he know of the existence of her daughter or her name? Sergi had died before she was born, or even before Olesya realized she was pregnant. Every country had covered the news of the discovery of Sergi's body two years after Zoe cut his throat. He couldn't possibly be alive, yet she wondered.

Olesya continued asking Elliot for more research, but the more she read, the more doubts she had, even though the stories sounded believable. Until the golden one attacked Elliot after he left a restaurant in a remote part of Seattle.

It happened on a starless evening during a downpour. The raindrops were so big and heavy that Elliot, caught without a raincoat or an umbrella, protected his head with his arms and hands, thus unknowingly exposing his torso to the attacker. The golden followed him from the restaurant and jumped at the opportunity when it presented itself. He plunged a knife into Elliot's abdomen and turned around to run. Elliot grabbed his arm and didn't let go. With a knife embedded in his abdomen, he held the attacker with one hand while searching his pocket with the other. Finding what he was looking for, Elliot extended his hand and pressed a taser into his assailant's arm. The golden one cried out in pain and collapsed on the pavement.

Elliot called Olesya and Dr. Brown for help. When Olesya and Alexander arrived, Elliot was lying in an alley, hiding behind a dumpster, with a knife sticking out of his stomach. His attacker lay near him, unconscious. Dr. Brown was already by his side, imploring him not to remove the knife until he got him to his clinic.

Elliot stayed at Dr. Brown's clinic for a few days, but his injury wasn't life-threatening. The knife didn't harm any major organs; the doctor explained. Olesya and Alexander transported the golden one to the cell under the headquarters and kept him there. He was awake when Olesya and Sara paid him a visit the next day, and glowered at them through the bars, his golden eyes filled with loathing. There was a slight golden glow emanating from under his clothes. He noticed Olesya's stare, covered his chest with his hand, and averted his eyes. He turned around and didn't say a word to them.

Olesya recognized this unfortunate event as her chance to discover if Sergi's story was true, provided she could get him to talk. With Elliot still in the clinic, she waited to interrogate him, hoping the imprisonment would break his spirit. She would let the golden one stew until Elliot returned, and Henry and Mary arrived to help with the questioning. Henry, Elliot told her, would get him to talk. Olesya dreaded it, as torturing someone, even a golden one who had tried to kill her friend, seemed unbearable.

Her worries about torture proved unwarranted.

Elliot came back from the clinic, energetic and glowing as if nothing had ever happened to him. Hearing Olesya's unwillingness to torture the golden one, laughed. "Not to worry, Olesya. Brace yourself for the amazing display of Henry Motivator's skills. He has mastered the art of information gathering from unwilling participants so that they don't even realize that they're telling him everything and more, including their life stories, with no need for torture. He convinces them they are being liberated by unburdening themselves of secrets they've kept for reasons they have forgotten. Henry gives them the gift of relief. In some ways, he acts as a priest." Elliot chuckled.

Olesya was skeptical. With an uneasy feeling, she sat at the imposing wooden table, observing Henry do his magic. And he did. As if he were an artist, he performed in front of his friends and his unsuspecting victim. As she watched, her jaw dropped in amazement and a great deal of disbelief, speculating that Henry was hypnotizing him. With his angelic facial expression and his penetrating eyes, he created an immediate response from the golden one. With merely a few words and even fewer gestures, Elliot's attacker sat with his eyes fixed on Henry; his mouth was ajar.

"Tell me your name," Henry asked.

"Igor. My name is Igor," he said, with a strong British accent.

"Good. Igor. I am Henry. Now that we're acquainted, can we chat?"

"Yes." The golden one lost his edge and stared at him with child-like fascination.

"Tell me, Igor. Why did you attack my friend Elliot?"

"I had to. Ishtar will grant my children everlasting life. Each kill saves one of my children from dying before me."

"Did Ishtar tell you that in person?"

"Yes."

"When?"

"Hmm...fifteen years ago."

"Where did you see him, Igor?"

"In Yorkshire. In a cathedral. He said the more dark souls we kill, the healthier and wealthier our children will be. Killing more ensures safety by restoring the world's balance you disrupted. If we kill you all, we'll live forever."

"And you believed him?"

"Yes. He is our God. We don't question what our God tells us."

Olesya shifted in her seat, hearing this. People always question their gods. That is part of their nature. She kept her suspicion to herself.

"How did you find us?"

"We saw her picture online," Igor said, pointing at Olesya. "When the lab blew up."

"Long ago," Henry said.

"We were not to kill her."

"Why not kill her?"

"Ishtar told us to capture her alive and not to hurt her."

"Why?"

"He didn't tell us. He said she was the key to destroying the dark people, but he didn't say how, only that she must not die."

"Where is Ishtar now?"

"I don't know. We don't know."

"Do you have a way of calling him when in need?"

"No, he always knows."

"Thank you, Igor. Anything else you want to share?"

"Let me go. I promise not to kill anymore. I swear on the lives of my children," Igor said, teary-eyed.

"We will. But not just yet," Henry said, and got up from his chair. He knocked on the double wooden door, and the guards came in and escorted the attacker back to his cell. His defiance disappeared. Henry had robbed him of his courage, integrity, and rage. The golden one appeared drained of emotions and thoughts, even any guilt he might have had by telling Henry everything and betraying his god. He walked out with the guards, shuffling his feet with his eyes on the floor.

As soon as he left, everyone clapped at Henry, the magician. Or more of a hypnotist, Olesya thought as she and Sara sat staring at him in disbelief. Without coercion or torture, the golden one had told him everything he knew.

"How did you do it?" Sara couldn't wait for an explanation.

"Magicians never reveal their secrets," Henry said, smiling. "Just kidding. I have a knack for this sort of thing. My friends used to tell me their deepest secrets, and my girlfriends told me if they cheated on me. That is one reason Zoe recruited me," he said, chuckling.

"Does it work on everyone?" Sara asked.

"So far. Would you like to try?"

Sara blushed and shifted in her chair so violently that she almost fell off. He just laughed, and everyone else joined him.

"You look pale, Sara," Olesya said. "You must have many secrets," she added, laughing.

69

YOU DIDN'T PROTECT HER

MARCH 2031

The next day, Olesya was looking forward to questioning the golden one alone, having prepared a set of questions to trick the golden one into admitting he was full of shit. And she was excited to investigate the golden glow, planning to ask the guards to hold him while she examined his chest. However, when she returned to headquarters to speak with him, she found his cell empty and him gone. The guard informed her that Elliot had requested his release early that morning.

"Why would you release him without asking us first?" Olesya asked Elliot on the phone. For the first time, her tone was icy toward Elliot, whom she had always liked and admired for his knowledge and amiable personality. She wasn't the only one. Everyone liked Elliot.

"Relax, Olesya. We got everything we needed out of him and had no reason to keep him. I thought you, of all people, would be pleased."

"You should have asked me first," Olesya hissed through her clenched teeth and ended the conversation. Alexander and Sara were the only two people she fully trusted now.

She tried to talk to Alexander, but he seemed to be on the verge of a nervous breakdown and couldn't bear the mention of the golden people. When she looked into his dull and distant eyes, she thought someone had kidnapped her brother's spirit. Imagining Zoe roaming free somewhere out there, unperturbed while her brother suffered, she folded her hands into fists, wishing she could sink them into her chin.

Zoe was hiding somewhere for some strange reason, and Olesya doubted Elliot would tell her where she was. He claimed he didn't know, but she now doubted his truthfulness. She decided she would follow him, hoping he would lead her to Zoe. She slept like a baby after deciding.

Everything changed the next day, when Emery, a perceptive six-year-old, noticing her mother's anxiety, asked if she'd done something that upset her. When Olesya looked into her sad blue eyes, an intense wave of guilt pierced her heart. Her priorities shifted instantly, realizing she was stealing Emery's childhood and missing her opportunity at motherhood. She locked the golden people and the chambers in a secret compartment in her brain and hid the key, promising herself that from now on she'd be a mother to her again, but this time fully—with her entire soul.

She recognized she had to decide eventually. But she had many years. Until then, she would bake cookies for Emery, take her on hiking trips, and teach her what she knew about stars.

For the next six years, Olesya was happy being a mother to Emery, pushing her worries aside. They spent more time with Sasha and Lev. Alexander loved Olesya's parents. Once they learned he was Olesya's brother, they asked no questions but welcomed him to their home as if he were their son and lived with them forever. Alexander and Lev bonded playing chess and spending time in the garage, where Lev taught his new son how to fix cars and build wooden furniture, which he built in his spare time and donated to charities.

And so the family lived for six happy, fulfilling years. Until one sneaky day in late summer of 2037, when the nightmares, the questions, and the impending doom of the decision she would have to make returned with a vengeance, furious at their imprisonment. From that day on, all she thought of was the dreadful decision she'd have to make before Emery grew up. Sergi's words, "The world depends on you and Emery," haunted her every night, depriving her of sleep and appetite. After the last nightmare, she couldn't postpone her decision anymore.

In her nightmare, Emery and Olesya hiked up a mountain slope. They were tired and covered with dust, but smiling. Gold and black dots sparkled intensely in Emery's blue eyes. Then Emery's eyes widened, and her mouth opened while she stared into the distance. Olesya followed her gaze and saw a mountain collapsing and disappearing. The clouds above the mountain started disappearing. The valley below the mountains started swirling and disappearing. Olesya looked back at Emery. She was disappearing too. Olesya tried to grab her daughter, but her hands went through her disappearing body. She couldn't scream. Everything turned gray. Out of the grayness, Sergi's face appeared.

"You didn't protect her. You didn't protect our daughter!"

The next day, Olesya packed her backpack and went on a backpacking trip to sort out her feelings before making a decision of a lifetime.

70

DECISION

AUGUST 2037

Olesya, covered with sweat and dust and wearing a backpack, hiked uphill on a narrow mountain trail. The switchbacks got shorter as the trail got steeper. It had been a while since she had backpacked in the wilderness alone. She hadn't told Emery she was going on a trip by herself, knowing the girl would be heartbroken, despite important teenage issues occupying her mind lately. Emery's inquisitive mind and gregarious nature, matched by a striking appearance, made her many friends at school. Olesya's heart melted, although not without some worry, discovering Emery's interest in things other than school. She noticed boys, and they noticed her.

Olesya walked the trails unburdened by other hikers, as this area was one of the hardest to hike. Unpredictable weather, dumping snow in August or extreme heat and dryness, made the climb unbearable. Few people dared to come here, let alone by themselves. She reached the top and dropped her backpack. She stood at the edge of a cliff, overlooking a valley full of wildflowers, surrounded by emerald forests and snowy mountain peaks. The sun low on the horizon bathed them in warm light. Overwhelmed by the view, she felt transported into a dream or a fairy tale. With teary eyes, she marveled at how the sight of a row of trees or snow-covered peaks could elicit such intense feelings, causing her chest to tighten. At that moment, she gained absolute certainty that she must act to preserve this magnificence. For Emery. For her children. She inhaled deeply, extended her arms, and screamed at the top of her lungs.

Olesya came down the mountain path to the trailhead area of the Pasayten Wilderness. She tossed the backpack onto the back seat of her old Jeep. Covered with a thick layer of dirt, the Jeep looked as tired and dirty as its owner. She had hiked for ten miles straight from her last stop; her muscles ached, but her mind was light, relieved at reaching a decision. Maybe because she was a child of nature, the wilderness helped her focus on what was most important to her.

She drove to the nearest town, hoping for phone reception, and called Sara. After she finished her conversation, she drove straight home. She needed Emery's skin cells before going to the lab. Last night, she couldn't sleep. Tossing and turning, she had stared at the sky full of bright stars when a powerful vision of Emery appeared before her eyes. She had a hunch this was more than just a vision, and she had to verify it, sensing it would bring her closer to discovering the truth.

Later that evening, Sara and Olesya hunched together over the microscope, manipulating a slide with a cross-section of one of Emery's skin cells. When the sample was ready to view, Olesya exhaled and nervously glanced at the screen. The image showed a dark spot where the dark matter joined Emery's nucleus and DNA, and two golden organelles guarded the nucleus from both sides.

"Oh my God," Sara whispered. "She has two..."

"I suspected she had one like me, but I didn't," Olesya whispered. "I should have checked her blood sooner, but I didn't want her to be... I didn't want to..."

"You didn't want to know," Sara finished. "It's totally understandable. I wouldn't have either."

"The black is so pronounced you can actually see it. Why does she have two?

"Sergi?" Sara asked. "You? I've admired her beautiful blue eyes so many times, remarking how unusual the golden and black spots were. Emery has two, you have one…Sergi must have had one too. Emery inherited one from you and one from Sergi."

"You know what that means?" asked Olesya.

"Sergi was telling the truth?"

Olesya shrugged. "That's what it looks like."

"But your face says otherwise. What are you thinking?"

"I can't shake off the impression that someone is lying, but I don't know who and why. I am still doubtful whether it was Sergi who recorded this message. He didn't quite sound like himself. I have no explanation for this. This is only my gut feeling. My mother ingrained in me to trust my gut feelings before I trust anything or anyone else. And my gut feeling tells me something is off, but it also says everything will be okay. I'm one confused woman," she said and sat quietly for a moment.

Sara's face clouded with worry as she observed her friend.

"You and my brother are the only ones I trust," Olesya continued. "I never fully trusted Zoe and still don't. I used to like and admire Elliot, but after Elliot released Igor, I started remembering how he was the only one who found all the stories entailing the golden people and the dark deities. I tried, but could never find what he found. And there is that feeling, a memory, a premonition that I am linked to the chambers. More than linked. It is as if I should know who made them. It sounds crazy; I know. But the feeling is over-whelming."

"I've known for a while you've been struggling with trusting Zoe and her people. I trusted her completely after I understood why she destroyed the lab and kidnapped me," Sara said, looking at Olesya thoughtfully. "My trust has not wavered. However, a lot has happened since. Although I agree with you that Zoe did a shitty job of explaining all this, I always ascribed it to her fear of golden people. I also suspected she might have been jealous of your ability to keep the pregnancy and have Emery. And for stealing her dog."

"It occurred to me, too. Zoe kept looking at my belly all the time. It was unnerving."

"Regardless. I am your friend first and foremost. I love you and will do everything I can to help. And I trust you more than I trust Zoe."

Olesya nodded, her eyes downcast, her fingers tapping on the desk.

"Do you believe people can be completely selfless?" Olesya asked. "Wanting nothing for themselves, thinking only of others?"

"That is a tough question," Sara said, exhaling. "In my humble opinion, people are too complex to have just one defining quality. Everyone wavers on their path. But I believe that people have selfless moments, momentous moments when they do brave things, shitty moments when they do stupid things, and selfish moments when they hurt others. All of us have those moments, but some have more selfless moments than others, and some have a lot more shitty moments."

"Do you believe we all deserve immortality?"

"Huh! This question is even tougher than the first one. Well, the first thing that popped into my mind was yes. So I guess my answer is yes. Why do you ask?" Sara looked into Olesya's eyes and sighed in despair.

"No, please don't. The hell with the world! Let it end! I don't want you to go! Think of Emery!"

"I am thinking of Emery. That is why I must do it."

When 2037 was ending, so was Olesya's life as she knew it. Sara would never stop regretting her decision to help her plunge into the dark dimension all by herself.

71

MARCY

WHERE TIME DOESN'T EXIST

Olesya blinked and saw nothing but darkness. Darkness so deep and thick that it weighed on her, sinking her. She had been falling fast for a very long time when suddenly a light lifted her. When the light embraced her, carrying her, she felt at peace, but she started forgetting everything little by little. She forgot where she was, how she got there, and who she was.

Then something grabbed her and pulled her away from the light. At first, she didn't know what had gotten a hold of her, but as the force moved her further from the light, she saw dark, shadowy hands holding her. She discovered with a shock that she no longer had a body. Instead, she morphed into a gray, cloudy shadow floating in the endless, heavy darkness. The hands dragged her inert gray being. She couldn't get free, having no control of the gray substance that was now her flesh.

The further they dragged her away from the brightness, the more she remembered of her life and who she was. Her memories became clearer, and she wished she could cry, remembering how she had ended up here and what she had left behind. But she was also relieved that she was still herself and still had coherent thoughts.

Maybe she was not truly alive, but able to remember and perceive her surroundings.

The hands stopped pulling and left her alone, motionless, floating in the infinite darkness that surrounded her. Olesya lost perception of time, floating for what felt like an eternity, not knowing whether it was hours, days, or years. And then she saw something moving in the distance. A gray shadow moved toward her, getting bigger as it got closer. It stopped in front of her and morphed its oscillating, shapeless being into something resembling a human shape, and kept hovering over her, waving long arms back and forth.

The being inched closer and touched her, passing a jolt of energy through her being. It wasn't a powerful jolt, and not unpleasant, but it went through her entire gray essence, making her realize how insubstantial her body was in this world. The strange blob touched her again, and another shock of energy traversed her. Hovering around her, the gray entity appeared to want to engage Olesya. Suddenly, the being's body blurred as it whipped into a frenzied spin. Its gray substance fluttered, vibrating with energy.

When it stopped moving, she saw two eyes appearing on its roundish top, which vaguely resembled a human head. No, they were not eyes, but glowing, vibrating white slits focusing on her face, while the being recklessly waved its gray appendages at her, madly wanting something from her. Olesya, unable to say anything or move, floated motionless. The being drifted away and flew at Olesya fast in a gray blur, swinging its arm to hit her. That was when she moved, trying to avoid it.

Was that thing trying to make me move?

As if in confirmation, the being bowed its head in an approval gesture and waved its arms, pointing somewhere in the distance.

It wants me to come with it?

She tried to remember how she had moved her body and concentrated on repeating the movement, but failed. The being swayed its arm at her again, and she scurried to avoid it.

Aha, she felt triumphant. *I get it now.*

Olesya started moving, but she only rolled slowly, her body

changing shape as she rolled. The being followed her, waving its arms as if her clumsy movements annoyed it. At last, she made a few coordinated shuffles that resembled a slow-motion waltz. Her companion floated ahead of her, waving, encouraging her, and pointing the way. She followed the gray form, getting more coordinated as she waltzed.

Her movements improved as she mimicked the figure's more graceful movements. They waltzed, gliding through the vast black landscape devoid of smells and sound. Olesya followed her gray guide, who led her to a destination it alone knew. She believed the being was friendly, as it beckoned her to follow, glancing back at her with its bright slits that feigned eyes.

Olesya started noticing structures in the distance. Once they got closer, Olesya recognized the structures as houses, churches, streets, unlit streetlamps, and scattered, motionless cars. Everything was made of the same gray, shape-shifting, shimmering substance as Olesya herself and the being she followed. She watched her appendages with fascination when they flopped by her side while she waltzed in undulating movements.

The gray companion steered her through the streets, which became narrower, and the buildings appeared older as they traveled deeper into the city. Curious about what the gray substance was, she tried to touch a building, but her shapeless hand went through as if she were a ghost. She couldn't shake the impression that she recognized these streets, even though the buildings were just gray shadows. It was not until she saw a clock tower she recognized the city. The marvel of Victorian architecture, the recognizable Big Ben, as it stood at the north end of the Palace of Westminster in London. Her gray friend glanced back at her, and Olesya swore it smiled at her despite not having a mouth.

So this is what became of England, Olesya thought. *A shadowland*.

She continued following her gray friend. They traversed many cities and an ocean and stopped at a small gray house. Olesya recognized the house. It was her friend Marcy's childhood home where they had spent many afternoons reading and talking while hiding in the attic. Marcy's parents were always absent. Is it possible that the gray figure was her Marcy? As soon as the idea popped up, vivid memories of their afternoons together in this house materialized in front of her as quick flashes.

Then the house disappeared, but her friend still hovered before her. Olesya hobbled closer to the gray being and touched it with her gray appendage, which looked nothing like a hand but more like snakes extending and retracting. A powerful jolt passed through her gray being, and she saw fifteen-year-old Marcy smiling. Astonished, she backed away, and the vision faded. She touched her again, and the image of Marcy reappeared. And then Marcy spoke, and as she did, silvery waves escaped her gray body and moved toward Olesya. "I found you, but I thought you'd be older. Much older."

Olesya tried to respond but didn't know how.

"You'll learn to talk with time," Marcy said. "Follow me. I'll show you my favorite places."

Marcy's favorite places proved to be variations of gray, wavering cities scattered throughout the vast black emptiness. Some towns appeared ancient and unknown to her; others reminded her of the ageless Roman cities with copious Corinthian and Doric columns and old statues. Lavish and elegant in their former lives, the statues were full of cracks and lacked limbs or heads; most lay on their sides, a poignant reminder of the once rich and lively cities they had adorned.

Olesya followed Marcy through the towns and villages, which bore no resemblance to anything she'd seen before—an endless array of windowless boxes connected by closed passageways, like a maze or a twisted puzzle. When they glided over them, they could see they had created a recurring pattern resembling an ever-unfolding and refolding seashell.

Among the favorite places where Marcy guided her were the gray mountainous slopes, the river gorges, or the clearings in the forest, where they'd lie on the gray grass and stare at the gray trees swaying in the gray wind. Moments like that reminded her of the times she had spent with Emery. They used to lie on the grass, staring at the trees for hours with Emer's head resting on her belly. In those moments, she missed her daughter the most and tearlessly wept, lamenting over their lives, cut short by their destiny, and the grandchildren that she would never know and love or see her daughter grow old (if she ever did).

Olesya wondered if the places Marcy was showing her shared the fate of London, collapsing into darkness and forgotten, but she couldn't ask. She couldn't create a single sound, even though she had tried countless times.

On their journeys, gray beings passed them by, but Marcy didn't seem interested in interacting with other beings. She saw them, but then would glide past them without acknowledging them. Olesya wondered if they were people who had died, like Marcy, and why they didn't interact with each other like Marcy and she did? The question she wanted to ask her foremost was how she had found her and how she knew she was here, desperate to find Emery in this endless darkness. But she would have to wait until she could ask, or until Marcy would guess her question and tell her. Sometimes, Olesya suspected Marcy didn't want to tell her. If Marcy found her, could Sergi find her?

72

PAYBACK

AUGUST 2047

Emery waited for the text from Elliot and Henry and then pressed the triangle, just as her mother had ten years before. The ceiling opened to reveal a dark hole, and Emery and Zoe floated to the upper chamber. Emery surveyed the chamber, finding it exactly as Sara had described, yet she was still astounded by its eeriness. The console in the middle with the blue pulsating triangle drew her to it. Her finger flexed, ready to press the triangle, when Zoe appeared before her and snatched her hand.

"What are you doing?"

Emery glanced at her and detected angst in her eyes. "I want to listen to the message myself."

"Why? Didn't Sara tell you all about it?"

"It is not the same. I'm about to commit suicide, and I wanna listen to this goddamned message!"

"Waste of time. We must hurry before more golden people come."

"Why do I sense you don't want me to listen to it?"

"You know what the message said. Don't waste time. Let's get you into the capsule," Zoe yanked Emery's hand.

Emery narrowed her eyes, pulling her arm out and pushing Zoe away. Expecting stronger resistance, Emery watched in amazement as

Zoe floated away, waving her arms and legs. Grinning, she pressed the triangle and saw the blue hologram unfold into a life-size image of her mother before her.

"Mom? What the..." Emery started saying when Zoe thrust her hands, pushing her toward the capsule. The weightlessness absorbed most of the attack, and Emery, ignoring Zoe, returned to the console and pressed the triangle again. Her mother spoke: "This is Dr. Olesya Solensky. This message is to..."

Zoe came at full speed and thrust her hands at Emery with all the power she could amass in such a short time, pushing Emery toward the capsule for the second time. Emery tumbled toward the capsule, fearing the end was coming, but then she glanced at the hologram, and her mother's eyes spawned a burst of immense power. With it, she thrust her arms up and stopped moving. Then she propelled herself toward Zoe.

"You fucking bitch! You pushed my mother into the abyss! Didn't you? Guess what? Today is your lucky day! You're going in there instead!"

"Emery, I'm not your enemy. The golden people are. I didn't push her. I didn't have to. She went in there on her own. Believe me."

"The golden people? Really?" Emery spat. "I might be young, but I am not gullible. Do you want to know when I figured out there were no golden people? You are getting careless in your old age. Why did you bring the doctor with you? I'll tell you why. Your people in disguise kidnapped and drugged Sara. I had a good look at them when you went outside, scheming with Sebastian. They were just your people in disguise, with some kind of contraption underneath their clothes to make them glow. That is why you showed up with the good doctor in tow, knowing Sara was drugged, because your people did this to her. How did you know we were here? Elliot informed you of everything, didn't he? No one killed your people. They were hiding and pretending to be the golden people. Hiding from my mother and Sara. Because you kept Sara, like my mother, in the dark. You tore the last pages from my mother's letter to me. You or Elliot. She probably warned me about you. She never trusted you."

Emery saw her mother talking on the hologram but didn't hear her voice as she yelled at Zoe. She heard only a few isolated words between the shouts. She heard "travel...past...glitch...future". Separately, they made no sense, but Emery couldn't pay attention as Zoe hovered around Emery, waiting for an opportunity to push her into the capsule. Emery made sure not to have her back to it.

Zoe attacked first, but Emery saw it coming and somersaulted in the air and pushed herself at Zoe, presuming that she had already exhausted some of her power. She grabbed her and shoved her toward the capsule, then threw her hands at her. Wide-eyed, Zoe waved her arms frantically to stop moving, but Emery's thrust was so powerful she couldn't fight it. Zoe's body slammed into the capsule on the side where she kept the black shard in her pocket. The capsule opened on impact, but Zoe grabbed the rim of the opening. Emery worried she would escape the capsule, so she pushed her body closer and pushed Zoe inside. Anticipating it, Zoe grabbed Emery's arm and pulled her into the capsule, holding on to her with all her remaining power. Emery tried to push with her legs to get away, but the capsule closed on them.

Emery wrapped her arms around Zoe to keep her inside with her. A sudden noise cut through their heavy breathing. The noise started as a shrill harmonica and escalated to a chaotic, cacophonous string orchestra, lacking a conductor for coordination. Emery wished she could muffle her ears with her hands, but her hands were busy holding Zoe in an embrace. She glanced at Zoe and saw that in her fear, awareness had abandoned her, and in its place, her now-enormous eyes and mouth wide open conveyed the stench of humanity and bottomless horror.

After a few excruciating seconds, the sound ended abruptly, replaced by a flash of blue light. Then, they started falling fast. Emery felt her stomach dangerously near her throat, and she panicked when she couldn't lick her numb lips or close her eyes, and she remembered the one time she had experienced similar sensations—skydiving with a friend a few years back. But this was worse. She was falling much faster and questioned whether she had imagined it, whether she was still conscious because of how gravity worked differently here. And here was nothing but darkness. They were no longer in the capsule. After a while, which seemed like an eternity, their falling speed decreased. Emery thought the worst was over and let go of Zoe.

She stared at her hands in horror as they started losing definition and color, changing into black, cloudy globs sparkling with golden dots, endlessly shifting shape. Zoe's body changed into a gray glob as she drifted away from Emery, unable to hold on, having only blurry blobs for hands. Emery saw black holes where Zoe's mouth and eyes used to be, getting smaller as she drifted away.

Bye, bitch. This is payback for my mother.

Emery, unable to control the direction or speed of her movements, drifted into the dark space surrounding her. Her entire body was now a black blob teeming with glowing golden dots. Not being in control of her movements, she panicked. Though certain she no longer possessed ears, she felt and heard something thumping in her black body. As her fear increased, the thumping sped up, and at that moment she moved her body. Realizing it was fear that made her move, she focused on harnessing the energy of fear and anger to move and slowly learned how to control and move her body to drift through the dark space.

She didn't know where to go, surrounded by dark nothingness. Everywhere she looked seemed the same. Her perception of time blurred. One moment she was certain she'd been floating in the darkness for years, and the next, as if she'd just arrived. She felt so alone and lost, wondering if she was the only black, cloudy figure in this endless darkness, and she wished she hadn't let go of Zoe.

Until she saw dark shapes gliding against a distant gray mist. The figures passed quickly, and she lost track of them but tumbled in the direction they came from. This was her first sight of anything other than darkness, and her cloudy body energized, shifting its shape out of control, moving in all directions, elongating, widening, or clumping together.

As she got closer, she recognized the gray background as buildings and streets, resembling a small American town from the fifties. She drifted through streets lined with old cars, looking through the gray windows of the buildings and seeing nothing behind them. She sought signs of other black shapes like her, but found none. But she kept searching, drifting through space, finding other cities, forests, deserts, mountains, and even oceans. Occasionally she would glimpse gray shadows passing in the distance, and she wondered what or who they were. Was one of them her mother? Her uncle? Too slow and clumsy to catch up to them, she waited for an opportunity to find closer ones.

Once, when she was drifting through the city, admiring its unusual architecture of slanted houses, she didn't see when several dark shapes had surrounded her. She had only spotted them as they inched closer to her. Much faster than her, the figures surrounded her in a dark, tight circle before she even considered escaping. And suddenly, they snatched and pushed her forward with their long, dark arms. She thought their intentions could only be sinister.

Scared, helpless, and full of rage, Emery uttered a sound. Surprised, she saw something gray in front of her—that was her voice, spinning away from her in grayish-silver waves. She uttered another sound, calling her mother's name while being pushed by the dark shapes.

73

UNBORN

WHERE TIME DOESN'T EXIST

Olesya kept guessing how much time had elapsed since Marcy found her, if any. She lacked time awareness in this dark world, guessing time did not move forward like an arrow here, and wondered whether it stood still, rolled backward, or folded upon itself. As a scientist, Olesya was fascinated by this world and thrilled she could observe it, secretly wishing she had access to a lab to study it.

Olesya still couldn't speak, but Marcy, unfazed by her friend's chronic inability to speak, continued to show Olesya her favorite places. And there were many haunting places to see.

Her movements had improved so much that they now matched those of Marcy and the other gray entities they passed on their journeys. Adjusting to her surroundings, she effortlessly glided through space with her old friend. It seemed unreal, like a dream—and perhaps it was, she sometimes pondered.

As she watched the gray figures passing them by in the distance, she wondered if one of them was Emery and if she would recognize her daughter among other indistinguishable gray beings.

Occasionally, she caught glimpses of darker shapes passing them by. At first, she thought she'd imagined them, but as she got used to her surroundings more, she could discern the black shapes better. She couldn't ask, but pointed her gray appendage toward the shapes, hoping Marcy would explain what they were. Marcy ignored her.

One time, Olesya noticed the black figure before they passed, and, hoping it would trigger a reaction out of Marcy, she thrust her gray body in its way and wished she hadn't. An intense, incapacitating electric shock pierced her, shattering her gray body into a million pieces that spun around and away from her in a gray fury. For the second time, the memories of her life and her loved ones faded as pieces of her dispersed into the infinite darkness. But Marcy did not let it happen. Gliding around her, she gathered the scattered pieces tirelessly together, not missing one. Olesya regained her body and memory. Marcy finished and glided away, not checking if her friend was following as she typically did.

"Is she mad at me?" Olesya wondered, following Marcy.

Marcy led her friend through areas she had never shown her before, passing through darkness so dark and dense that it slowed their movements, or so it seemed to Olesya. There were no other gray figures around, no gray towns, trees, or ocean beaches. At one point, Olesya stopped, not wanting to go further, having the harrowing darkness pressing in on her from all sides, afraid if she went just a little further, the darkness would crush her. Marcy looked back and disappeared. Lost and confused, Olesya didn't know how to escape the tormenting darkness. She spun, seeking something other than darkness to guide her, but found nothing else. The horrifying reality that she was alone in this black hell forever overwhelmed her, crushing her hope of finding Emery. Never had she felt so lonely and scared. At that moment, she found her voice ripping out of her gray body. She could see her voice as a faint silvery streak flowing away from her in silvery-gray waves.

"Marcy! Marcy, come back! Where are you? Please come back to me. Don't leave me here alone. I beg you."

And Marcy reappeared in front of her.

"You scared me! Stay away from those dark shadows! This is where they'll take you," Marcy said, pointing toward the darkness.

"There is no escape from there. The darkness is so thick, you won't be able to move. It will swallow you, and you will stay here forever."

"Why? Who are the dark shadows?"

"Let's get out of here. I'll tell you when we're safe. Come on, hurry."

Marcy led Olesya onto a gray mountaintop.

"What was that place? I've never been so terrified. I never knew the darkness could be so painful and oppressive."

Marcy didn't respond to Olesya immediately.

"Marcy?"

"Never go back there. This is where evil comes from!" said Marcy. "Sorry for frightening you, but it was the fastest way to learn how to talk in this place. That is how I learned how to talk, by being scared shitless and lonely."

"What is this place?"

"I don't know. This is where the dark shadows come from if they break free."

"What are the black shadows?"

"They are...the unborn."

"What?"

"The dark shadows are the unborn. They break free of the darkness and go toward the light, desperate to be born. But they can't get through the light, no matter how hard they try. The light destroys them, scattering them into pieces, which sink back into the blackness. When one of them scatters back into the darkness, there is this horrible noise that starts as a menacing whisper and then turns into a shriek. The noise reverberates everywhere in the darkness. There is no escaping it. I wish I had ears I could cover to muffle the sound."

"How do you know they are unborn?"

"Someone told me, just as I am telling you now."

"Who?"

"You will know soon enough. He will find you."

"Who will find me? Marcy, tell me."

"I can't. You must wait."

"Is this how people are born? Do the dark shadows make it through the light?"

"No, the dark shadows can't make it through, but some of their pieces make it through the light when it blinks. But I don't know what happens when the pieces go through the light. Maybe nothing."

"The light blinks? Marcy, I don't understand any of it. You are not making any sense."

"The dark pieces make it through the light when it blinks. I saw it."

"That's right. I saw a light when I first came here. I felt a force lifting me, but then dark hands seized and dragged me away."

"The light was pulling you?"

"That is how it seemed. I started losing my memories when it happened, but regained them when the black hands pulled me away from the light."

"You were being reborn. That happened faster than usual. The black shadows didn't want you to be reborn. You are lucky they didn't drag you into the darkness."

"Reborn?"

"Yes. Some of us will be reborn. Some will not. At least, I don't think so."

"Are all gray shadows like…you, Marcy? People who died?"

"I think so. I can talk to some of them. Those who have been here long no longer talk. Not to me, anyway."

"How did you know I was here? How did you know how to find me?"

"I felt you, Olesya. I felt your presence when you arrived. You were not like the other kids. You never made fun of me or bullied me. I felt smart and normal when I was with you. I loved you, and that is probably why I sensed you."

"I loved you too, Marcy. If you sensed my presence when I arrived here, would I be able to sense my daughter when she comes here?"

"If you love her."

"Of course I love her. She is supposed to come here to find me."

"You want your daughter to come to this hell to find you? What's wrong with you?"

"I don't want her to, Marcy. I didn't want to be here, but it happened. Now my daughter will come to find me."

"Why the hell would you do that? You'd have your daughter stuck in this endless black hell? What possessed you?" As Marcy grew more agitated, her voice grew in intensity, and the waves became thicker. Her slits narrowed even more as her anger grew. "What's wrong with you, Olesya?"

"My daughter is the key…"

"The key?"

"I'll tell you my story and everything, Marcy. You may not believe me, but believe in me, please."

Marcy said nothing, circling Olesya in chaotic movements. Olesya shared with her everything that had happened to her since the explosion at the lab. Marcy listened and kept silent, asking nothing throughout the story. Even after Olesya finished, Marcy was still silent.

"Marcy, say something."

"I believe you."

"But?"

"I would do everything in my power for my daughter never to be aware of and never to find this place."

"I realize I made mistakes along the way. But perhaps our sacrifice will help all people."

"How can you be so dumb? Didn't history teach you anything? You sacrificed your daughter's life and your own for something humans can't handle and, therefore, should never have."

"We don't know that."

"Don't people always get greedy and violent? I can't even imagine what the world would be like if they all were immortal. They couldn't handle it, and they will end the world themselves, with no help from Ishtar or any other golden freaks."

"People can change."

"You are an optimist, Olesya. What you are offering is perfection.

And perfection is not in our nature. You'd have to genetically engineer us first. Change us somehow so that we're not so power-hungry. We will always have conflicts, wars, and greed. We fuck everything up. You can't give humans immortality and that kind of power."

"You were an optimist once, Marcy. Everyone deserves a choice, and Emery will provide it for humanity. Besides, if we don't find dark matter, the universe will collapse, and my daughter will with it. I need to find her. I need to find my daughter."

"Do you think your daughter is already here?"

"I don't know, since I don't know how much time has elapsed since I came here. I can't feel her. Would you help me find her, Marcy?"

"I can't help you, Olesya. You're the only one who can find the ones you truly love. Your voice can find her, but you must do it alone."

"Why can't I feel her presence, like you felt mine?"

"I don't know. Maybe she's not here," she said and added after a pause. "Yet."

"You are not telling me everything, Marcy. I can sense it."

"Your daughter could have been reborn as soon as she got here. You almost were." Marcy shrugged.

"Everything would have been in vain. What have I done? My baby. No, it can't be. I will find her."

"I hope you do."

"Maybe she's not here yet. Maybe she hasn't read the letter yet...or maybe she will not get the letter if my mother never tells her or if Sara forgets to put it in the cabin."

"Maybe," said Marcy, turning away from Olesya.

74

THE LETTER

APRIL 2047

A young woman in her early twenties sat on a wooden chair in a small mountain cabin, reading a letter from her mother. She had been sitting in the same position for hours, reading her mother's story. Her thick blonde braid rested on the wooden table as she read. She read the last sentences repeatedly, unwilling to sever this connection to her mother, even if it was just words in a notebook.

This is how you were born, my daughter. You came to me when I least expected it. I couldn't tell you any of it before because it wasn't the right time. I know it is unfair. I also felt that way for a long time, and then one day I understood. You are the one who will forever change the world for yourself and the ones you love. The burden is yours to carry. I am sorry, dear Emery, my beloved daughter. The decisions and steps ahead are yours to make. You will understand everything soon enough. I love you.

By the time she finished reading the handwritten letter, tears made their way down her cheeks and landed on the wooden table. She saw her blue eyes reflected in the teary puddle. She was closing the notebook when she noticed several torn pages from the back.

"That is strange. Maybe she tore them even before she wrote this letter," she wondered aloud while closing the notebook and pressing it to her chest. When she stood up, a dark shape stood up with her. Regis was ready to follow his young friend wherever she went.

One last time, Emery surveyed the cabin and noticed a sweater hanging on a hook. She pressed it to her face, inhaling the scent of mother. *Mother. You should have told me. What am I supposed to do now?*

Regis touched her hand with his cold nose. She glanced at her black companion. "Come on, Regis. Let's go back. We need to talk to Grandma," Emery said, and pushed the door open.

Emery left the Bear Paw Mountains cabin and hiked on a dirt road to where she had parked her solar two-person plane. Flying to Helena, she intended to charge her plane and find something to eat. Her stomach painfully reminded her it had been a while since she had eaten. Food had been the last thing on her mind when her grandmother told her that a letter from her mother was waiting for her at a cabin in Montana. Numb, she had hopped into her plane and taken off, saying nothing to her grandparents.

Emery had returned to her grandparents' house for her spring break from university. She studied mathematics at the University of Washington and was in her final year. She had spent most of her breaks with her grandparents after her mother and uncle had died in a car accident ten years ago. That's what she was told. After reading her mother's letter, she now questioned everything her grandparents had told her and wondered what they had not told her.

The time following her mother's death was fuzzy in her memory. Emery remembered little from that time—the loss stunned her, deadened her senses. She spent three years in a daze. She functioned, ate, and studied in a state of emotional anesthesia. Immediately following the accident, she couldn't cry. The tears would not come.

After her mother's death, she lived with her grandparents. Sasha, understanding the healing properties of tears, tried to make her cry and grieve. She showed her photograph after photograph and talked about Olesya often. But Emery stayed numb.

Emery and her mother had been inseparable. They were best friends, a loving mother and daughter. Olesya had passed on to her daughter her love of nature and adventure. Emery had experienced her first backpacking trip with her mother as a five-year-old girl. It was an easy hike, and she had walked most of the six-mile trail on her little legs. At one point, the girl seemed tired, and Olesya picked her up, only to put her down quickly because Emery threw a fit, wanting to walk by herself. From then on, they would pack their backpacks and take off on an adventure on a whim. They would explore the most challenging and difficult to get to mountain trails in remote parts of the country to be rewarded by the splendor of mountainous landscapes untouched by human hands.

Her uncle, Alexander, sometimes joined them on their trips. He was the male version of her mother, but smiled more than she did. She and her uncle shared a strong connection. So strong, she sometimes swore she could hear his thoughts. But then she dismissed it as something she'd made up, as was her habit. During sleepless nights, she conjured up stories and got lost in them for hours. The stories transported her to many strange places, faraway lands. Emery didn't share her stories with anyone, not even her mother, but suspected that her mother and her uncle knew about her overactive imagination. Once, when she was twelve years old, she ran back into the house to get a schoolbook she had forgotten and found her mother and uncle talking in low voices.

"...she can see it. She travels to it in her dreams," Alexander said.

"We can't be certain of that," Olesya answered. Emery backed out and then dashed back into the house, announcing loudly, "I forgot my math book!"

They both looked at her, mortified, but Emery pretended she hadn't heard their conversation. "How does Grandma say it? If you don't have it in your head, you'll have it in your legs?" Emery asked Olesya.

Olesya smiled. "Yes. It is a Russian idiom that doesn't sound as good translated. It means if you are forgetful, you will have strong legs running back and forth looking for things you've lost or forgotten."

Emery grinned, ran to her room, grabbed her book, and left the house. She forgot that conversation, having more important teenage stuff to worry about. Now that she had read her mother's letter, she remembered it. And in that instant, it occurred to her she might have special abilities, like her mother. She grew up thinking she was just a typical American girl without too many worries until her mother died.

Emery stopped at a recharging station in Helena, Montana, and plugged in her plane; then she entered the waiting area to recharge herself. Gazing at her food options, she chose the biggest omelet, a stack of pancakes, and the largest blueberry milkshake on the menu. Besides that, she also got coffee and a pastry with lots of powdered sugar. She ate healthy foods most days, but sometimes the fat girl inside her desired something more, and she gorged on fat and sugar, like a bear before entering its winter rest. She retrieved her AI tablet and the letter from her backpack and searched for Brie Industries: Zoe and Sebastian Brie. Not surprisingly, she found nothing.

She opened the letter and read it for the second time, looking for anything in her mother's story she could verify on the AINET—the artificial intelligence internet. If it existed, the AINET would find it. She searched and found information concerning the explosion at the physics lab in 2023. But no one questioned the unexplained explosion or connected it to dark matter as the reason for the explosion. Dark matter theory had died when a team of scientists from the University of Ottawa found a better explanation for the missing mass in the universe—the tired light model. This model explained how the forces of nature decreased over cosmic time and light lost energy when it traveled a long distance. Tested, it matched observations and was now an accepted standard for most scientists, and the concept and the mystery of dark matter had been forgotten.

She searched for Belyaska, Russia. What she found confirmed her mother's story, or at least a part of it. She read a brief paragraph describing the history of Belyaska as the AINET's spat out the information she had requested from its search system.

"Belyaska was a small rural town in the former USSR with five thousand inhabitants. Following a local gravel mine accident in 2001, the town experienced a significant loss in population. The accident led to the mine's decommissioning, costing locals their jobs. The final blow to the town occurred in 2037 when an unexplained, devastating explosion obliterated the gravel mine and the whole town of Belyaska."

Emery sat at the table, processing this information. Not finding anything about Zoe or Sebastian and not knowing the last names of Zoe's people, she was stuck. Her uncle was dead. Her grandparents could only answer some of her questions. She'd have to ask them, but with extreme caution not to divulge facts about her mother that would shock them.

While thumbing through the letter, another thought occurred to her, and she searched her AI tablet for Peter Amberlite. She stumbled upon an article portraying a retired detective who had coordinated a rescue mission for lost mountain wanderers. The face of a handsome man in his sixties with a full head of silver-laced hair and the most incredible blue eyes she'd ever seen stared out at her from the tablet. His face was that of an energetic man fulfilled in his life, but his melancholic smiles and deep blue eyes betrayed him, hinting at a broken heart and unfulfilled passion. The photo made her wonder if her mother had gotten together with him.

Emery searched her AINET for Sara Mowen, but except for the article that mentioned the discovery and her disappearance, she found nothing else. Sara had vanished, too.

Emery had one more search she needed to do later. Much later. For now, her father, Sergi Orlov, would remain in the darkness until she found the courage to look into his eyes.

75

BABUSHKA

APRIL 2047

Emery parked her plane at a small airport for passenger airplanes in Walla Walla and picked up an electric bike with an extra cargo area for Regis. Accustomed to traveling by bike, Regis eagerly hopped into the cargo basket. She looked into his bottomless black eyes. "How is it I never noticed your eyes before or questioned your age? You've been with me since before I can remember."

She biked to her grandparents' house. It was still the same house where her mother had grown up and returned to whenever she missed her grandparents. They would never sell the house where they still felt Olesya's presence, and memories of her resonated from every corner of the house. Nothing had changed since the day she left. Emery's heart overflowed with gratitude—she felt her mother's comforting presence in this house. Sasha told her she felt it too, and just like her granddaughter, she would sit on the couch on which Olesya once sat, taking deep breaths, trying to inhale her essence.

Emery unlocked the door with her key and entered

"Babushka, Grandpa! Are you here? I'm back," Emery shouted, and Regis barked.

"Emery! Baby! You're back!" Sasha exclaimed, running to the door to greet her. "I was so worried when you left so abruptly," Sasha added, wiping her flour-coated hands with a kitchen towel.

Emery hugged Sasha and teared up.

"I'm sorry, Babushka. I didn't mean to worry you, but I couldn't talk. I was overwhelmed," Emery said, trying not to cry. "I don't even remember leaving here."

"It's okay, baby. I'm just glad you're back. Come on, I'm baking your favorite."

"Chocolate chip?"

Sasha nodded, grinning.

"As if you knew I was coming."

"As if," said Sasha, smiling; her face lit up. There were a few extra wrinkles and many more silver hairs in her blonde braid, but Sasha stood as straight as she did when she was in her twenties.

"Where is Grandpa?"

"In the garage. Pretending that he is working on something to get away from me," Sasha chuckled. "Come on, baby. Let's put the cookies in the oven."

Later in the early evening. Emery and Sasha sat on the couch, holding steaming cups of hot chocolate with homemade whipped cream, which was Emery's favorite. A plate of cookies, still warm, sat on the coffee table, giving off a sweet chocolate smell.

Lev poked his head into the living room door. "Are you girls okay? I'm going to Mark's now unless you need me for any reason," Lev said.

"No, we don't. Have fun. Good luck!" Sasha said.

"Is he playing chess again?" Emery asked.

Sasha nodded. "He'll enter another competition this winter. He's practicing with Mark."

"Grandpa has always loved chess. I'm glad."

Emery hesitated to inquire about her mother, aware of the pain it would cause, but she also suspected Sasha envisaged the time would come when she would have to answer tough questions.

"Tell me how you found my mother in a forest," Emery blurted out, avoiding eye contact with Sasha. She felt her face redden.

Sasha told Olesya's story, beginning with finding her in the forest, omitting nothing. Emery listened, sipping her hot chocolate. Her eyes glistened with tears as Sasha told her about a quiet girl fascinated with stars and with a passion for science. Hearing Sasha describe her mother's childhood, she sensed her mother's presence, convinced she could smell the flowery scent of her mother's hair. It was the first time Sasha had talked about her mother so openly. The relief she experienced in telling the entire story for the first time in her life showed on her face as it slowly relaxed and her eyes regained their shine.

What Sasha told her aligned with the letter, except Zoe and Sebastian were missing from Sasha's story. Sasha mentioned Olesya had help from her friends in dealing with Sergi, but didn't mention their names or who they were. Sasha didn't know her daughter's secret life or her powers. Emery dared not ask, not wanting to change Sasha's perception of her only daughter.

"Did you know the friends who helped her?" Emery asked.

"I knew of them, but no. I never met them and figured she had her reasons not to tell me more. She didn't want to talk about the time she had spent in Europe or the people she had gone with. I trusted my girl with all my heart and was absolutely certain she did what was necessary, and that she didn't want to worry me."

"How about Peter? Peter Amberlite?" Emery asked.

"The detective? What about him?"

"Did my mother ever...get together with him?"

Lost in her memories, Sasha sat with a sad smile on her face, and when she spoke, her voice sounded hoarse. "I suspected she liked him. I don't know if she got together with him, but I don't think so. Your mother was...different after the Sergi thing happened. She no longer confided in me as much as she used to. She was more secretive. And I wouldn't pry."

"Do you know who my father was?" Emery asked, hearing her voice as if someone else had asked the question.

"No, I never asked, sensing she didn't want to talk about it. Did the letter—?"

"No," she lied, not knowing why. She inched closer to Sasha and put her head on her lap.

Sasha stroked Emery's head.

"Sing me a lullaby. The one about the sun in Russian."

"Okay, baby," Sasha said, and began singing in the pleasing voice of someone who derives joy from singing and sharing it with others.

Emery loved Sasha's Russian lullabies, even though she didn't understand the words. Her soft voice and the way she sang were comforting but also magical, transporting her to a different world, and since she didn't understand the words, she made up her own stories to fit the songs' melodies. Emery's story depicted a sun saddened that nobody appreciated it. And the sun desired appreciation. Not getting the recognition he craved, the sun became more desolate and moodier. Crying, the sun lost its strength and stopped shining. Sun gone, crops diminished, hunger came. The people prayed to the sun, promising offerings and everlasting worship, but it was too late. The sun retreated into the darkness of self-pity and sorrow. People begged the sun to forgive them and save them. Still cross with them, the sun didn't respond.

A young boy, tormented by the sight of his little sister crying with hunger, volunteered to travel to the sun in person. He hurried to the sun, crying for forgiveness and pity, and in his eagerness, he got too close, burned, and died. The sun wept for the boy and wrapped his burned body in a golden blanket. The golden god forgave the people for not worshipping him. It shone even more brightly from then on and sent colorful and tender sun rays toward the boy's sister. The crops grew, and people were thankful to the sun for returning, but nobody remembered the boy or his name. Emery wept for her imaginary boy every time Sasha sang this song.

She fell asleep on Sasha's lap. Regis fell asleep on the floor by his mistress, relaxed, running in his dream. When Emery woke up an hour later, she had a clear idea of what to do next.

76

SPYING

APRIL 2047

Through the window of her solar car, Emery stared at Peter instructing his students to arrange the manikins on the gurney during the mountain safety education class in Issaquah. Time had been kind to him, or perhaps he fooled it with his boyish demeanor and grin. He was over sixty but looked and behaved twenty years younger. Emery realized the appeal the handsome detective had held for her mother.

The article in the newspaper praised Peter for his high success rate in rescue missions. Teaching had unexpectedly entered his life when he agreed to substitute for an ill colleague, but he developed a passion for it and became a sought-after teacher, delivering his lessons with modesty, ardor, and humor.

Emery observed as his students followed his every move and seized his words with hunger. Watching him infused her with a spark of optimism, and at that moment, she was certain she had made the right choice in finding him, even if it was just to look at him for a while. Watching him somehow made her feel closer to her mother. She wanted to talk to him and ask countless questions, regardless of how insignificant they might seem, to know more about the woman who was her mother and whom she seemed to know so little about.

However, she sat with the key in her ignition and hands on the steering wheel. The courage to speak to him ticked away the closer the end of the course loomed. She had discovered the existence of a man her mother liked and maybe even loved. Was she ready to share her memories with him? After all, he was a stranger to her.

The class ended, and the students poured out of the building and spread out, going to their solar cars, bikes, or buses. She waited, still unsure. Peter came out and proceeded straight toward her car, deciding for her.

In a deep and mellifluous voice, Peter asked, "May I help you?"

Emery sat speechless, trying to think of a lie.

Leaning down, Peter gave her a curious look. "Who are you?" he asked, and his voice trailed off. He paused, and hesitating, he asked, "Olesya?"

"No, I'm her daughter," Emery answered. "I'm Emery."

"You are the spitting image of your mother." Peter recovered quickly from his initial shock.

Moments later, Emery and Peter sat at an outdoor table at a bar in Issaquah, with a beer in front of each of them. He chose this bar because of its spectacular view of the Issaquah Alps—the unofficial name for the Issaquah Highlands—and the friendly and unassuming atmosphere. He sometimes came here after his class to grab a beer and a bite to eat. Peter had proposed they grab a beer after he found Emery spying on him from her car, and she immediately agreed and then felt angry with herself for agreeing so quickly. *He'll think I'm a stalker.*

They were quiet, studying each other with quick, stolen glances. Neither volunteered to start the conversation. Emery dreaded where it might lead or that it might stall to a dead end, but needed to hear from someone other than family how they perceived her mother, now that she had found out she was different. She broke the awkward silence, telling Peter about the letter her mother had left for her in a cabin Emery never knew existed. She proceeded carefully, sharing only select letter details, unsure of what he already knew and what he suspected, and avoiding telling him what happened between her mother and Sergi. Above all, she didn't want to embarrass or make Peter uncomfortable, sensing he had suffered and believed her mother was to blame.

Peter listened; his blue eyes fixed on hers. As she neared the end of the story, she glanced at him, and his sad eyes pierced through her eyes and into her soul.

"I wanted to ask if you and my mom ever got together," Emery asked and regretted it soon after, puzzled why she had asked this question and not something less intrusive and personal. She wished she could take it back.

But Peter didn't mind and answered with a woeful smile. "No. Your mother came to me saying that she couldn't burden me with her wretched life and that she was not worth my attention. I pleaded with her, but she just stared at me, distant and dejected. She said she had been tainted by what she did, that her guilty conscience would make my life pure hell, and she would never hurt me in that way. I responded by telling her she would hurt me more by running away, and I didn't care what she did."

"What did she say to that?" Emery breathed.

"She said nothing more. She left and never looked back. I have not heard from her since. When I heard she had died in a car accident, my life changed. I lost hope, realizing she wasn't coming back. Soon after, I quit my job and retreated to live like a monk in a mountain cabin," Peter said, and paused. "I didn't know she had a daughter. When I saw you, I thought she had returned," Peter said, his voice breaking.

"I'm sorry for bringing it all back. I'll leave you alone," Emery said and got up.

Peter shook his head. "It hurts, but not as much as it did. I gathered the shattered pieces of myself a while back, and now I am whole. Scarred but whole. Stay, please, if you want, and ask anything you need to ask."

Emery nodded and slid into her seat, staring into the distance, deliberating what to ask next. Peter observed her discreetly, studying every feature of her face, but keeping his stare to a minimum.

"I'm not sure what I wanted to ask you. I guess I haven't thought this through. Maybe I just needed to meet you to find out if you knew something about my mother that I didn't. After reading her letter, I realized I knew her less than I thought I did. She kept secrets from me I didn't know she had."

"Olesya was brilliant, determined, and the most beautiful being on Earth. In and out. She was serious, but I could see the spark of humor in her eyes. I think only Sasha truly knew that side of her," Peter said as he began telling Emery everything he remembered, understood, and sensed about Olesya. As Emery sat and listened to him talk, she wondered why her mother had left him. He told her everything that transpired between them in extraordinary detail, as if it had just happened yesterday.

Her heart warmed when he said her mother's name. No one could pronounce her Russian name with perfect intonation. Coming from his lips, her mother's name sounded as melodic and magical as she was.

Why would she leave this man? Because of Sergi? Because of me? Emery could only guess.

From that day on, Peter and Emery met regularly at local bars or parks. They shared stories. They laughed when Emery recalled Olesya's blunders at social gatherings and wept when she recalled the time of her death. She told him about Olesya's childhood friend. The only friend she had in school. A girl named Marcy. Marcy was a big girl. She was tall and stout, with a head full of unruly curls that always stood up in all directions, no matter how she tried to tame them with lotions and hairsprays. It didn't help that her upper lip was covered with a layer of thick black hair. They kept their friendship a secret, not wanting her classmates to know the fat, weird girl had befriended another weird girl who never smiled. The girls feared enduring double the bullying if their friendship became known.

Marcy was the only one who shared Olesya's dream of flying in space someday.

"Marcy was her soulmate. She was gentle, smart, and funny, my mother said."

"She never mentioned her. Sasha said Olesya didn't have any friends," Peter said.

"Marcy died when she was fifteen years old."

"That's terrible. How?"

"Leukemia."

In just a few months, Emery and Peter grew inseparable. At ease with each other, they found unexpected solace in one another's company. They had grown closer, and their meetings became more frequent. To Emery, their three-hour rendezvous felt like three minutes. When they sat across from each other at a table, one moment the table between them seemed as large as a mountain, and another like a feather that might blow away with a breath at any moment. Whenever they met, the surrounding air electrified with anticipation and possibility.

There wasn't a single time they met that Emery didn't fight the urge to bring up her mother's death and the unclear circumstances of her death. According to the police report, her mother's car had plummeted into a ravine, getting severely damaged and burning after the gas tank exploded upon impact with the rocky bottom. At the time, she couldn't put a finger on why she had questioned the accident. But a few years later, she learned that the likelihood of a gas tank explosion on impact was not that high, which intensified her doubts. Peter could help her find out the truth. Despite leaving the police force, he continued to keep in touch with his former colleagues, often meeting them at a local tavern that was a favorite hangout spot for active and retired cops. Once, when Emery and Peter met there, she witnessed his friends come and pat him on the back; their boisterous camaraderie was full of warmth and respect.

Emery dreaded asking Peter to investigate her mother's death, realizing he'd have to relive the nightmare, but the need to know intensified. And soon, she couldn't hide the tension in her body, or her fingers drumming, or her foot tapping. One time, sitting in a booth across from her, Peter simply asked, "What is wrong?"

She kept her eyes on some distant target and didn't answer, weighing hurting Peter against uncertain results.

"Tell me. Whatever it is, it is okay."

"I don't even know if it is possible," she said. Her voice cracked. After a pause, she added, "I want to be sure that…that my mother really died in the car crash." She spat out the last few words fast, as if she wanted to get them out before she changed her mind.

"I see," Peter said and stared into the distance with an odd expression on his face.

A loaded silence ensued. She sat glancing at him, worried he might crush the beer bottle with his white-knuckled hand. In that instant, she regretted her question, and there was a hollowness in her chest when she imagined him walking away, never to return.

"Why?" asked Peter. "Why do you think she didn't?"

"I don't know. It is just a gut feeling, a suspicion I've always had. Something didn't seem right. The exploding gas tank. My grandparents' reaction was strange. It was almost as if she had left and would come back someday. I realize how stupid that might sound to a detective, but I can't help thinking about it and reliving it. And it's not getting better. The uncertainty had only increased since I read the letter."

"It's not stupid. I felt uneasy about the accident. Your mother was an excellent driver, and she didn't really drink alcohol. I couldn't imagine her losing control of a car. Something was eating at me, but I attributed it to my bad habit of being a cop and always suspecting foul play." Peter paused. He worked the coaster with his long-fingered hands and gazed intently at the beer bottle as if trying to find the answers inside. "I'll look into it. You deserve to know how your mother died."

Emery looked at him and realized that he meant it.

77

CAR CRASH

JULY 2047

Peter sat in a booth at Seattle's Pike Place Market bar. Sipping a beer, tapping his fingers on a manila folder on the table in front of him, Peter waited for Emery.

Emery arrived at the bar and searched for him. When she saw him, her face lit up, but her smile faded and her eyes turned listless as she got closer and saw the manila folder. She sank into the booth across from Peter and looked at him.

"Just tell me," Emery said, noticing he was struggling to find words. "I am stronger than you think."

"I know. You are as strong as your mother." He paused, observing her. "Perhaps stronger."

"What did you find?"

The bartender brought her a beer, which Peter had ordered for her, asking him to deliver it cold when she arrived.

"There is not much in the file. Statements of the couple who found the car in the ravine when they stopped to take their dog out. And... photos."

Emery's face dropped when she heard the last word. "What else?"

"That's all."

"There was no investigation? What about identifying the bodies or DNA?"

"They decided there was no need. The car was registered to your mother, and after questioning your grandparents, they established that Olesya and Alexander were driving home from the airport."

Emery bit her lip. "So there's no proof that my mother and my uncle burned in that car?" Emery said and glanced at the folder, letting Peter know she was ready to look inside.

Peter put his hand on the folder. "Are you sure?"

Emery nodded and put her hand right next to his, touching his fingers. The touch felt electrifying and familiar.

Peter lingered and then released the file.

She placed her trembling hands flat on the yellowed folder, as if trying to sense what lay inside. When she opened it, she was composed and calm. She scanned through the photos, showing no emotion, but when Peter observed her flipping through the pages of the report, his face twitched with compassion. The charred and mangled bodies lying on a steel morgue table would give many experienced cops stomach twists.

She finished reading and looking at the photos, closed the folder, and pushed it back toward him.

"I felt nothing," Emery said after a pause. "Is that normal?"

"What do you mean?"

"The bodies. They are horrible to look at, but...I didn't feel a connection to them. I expected to feel something, but I didn't. My heart did not ache. A bolt of lightning didn't strike through my body or my soul. As if...they were strangers. Is that normal? How do people behave when they see the bodies of their loved ones?"

"People react in different ways. Sometimes it takes a while to realize the irrevocability of death, so you postpone the emotions, not being able to process them at that moment."

"So I'm still no closer to understanding what happened, why it happened, and if these bodies belonged to my mother and my uncle."

Peter nodded. For a long moment, they didn't try to fill the silence and stared out the window at the busy market where residents and tourists strolled through the street, gawking at displays, buying food or flower bouquets from the vendors. If there were only two things the vendors did well here, one was creating and selling extravagant flower arrangements, and the other was excelling at showcasing and selling fresh fish. Emery observed the animated display of life while she felt less than alive at that moment.

"I read a while back that gas tanks rarely explode on impact. Is it true?"

"It's true. They normally don't unless the gas tank gets severely damaged. Page twelve of the report mentioned the lack of a crumple zone around the tank. Your mother's Jeep was an older model and didn't have one."

"Oh," Emery breathed and traced the wood patterns on the wooden table. "Can we do anything to find out?" she asked.

"I've thought about it," Peter said. "It depends."

"On what?"

"Were your mother and uncle cremated or buried?"

"Cremated."

"What happened to their ashes?"

"We scattered them in the mountains," Emery whispered, dropping her chin. A cotton-like, unsettling sensation shrouded her thoughts as she realized she'll never know the truth. But then she remembered the heart. "Is it possible to test the ashes for DNA?"

"It's not impossible. Depending on the cremation temperature, some DNA might remain in the ashes. They have developed strong DNA enhancers, allowing the detection of minuscule amounts," Peter said and glanced at Emery, tilting his head. "I thought you said you scattered the ashes in the mountains."

"We did most of them, but I asked my grandma to save some, so part of her would stay with me forever. My grandmother portioned some ashes from the urn into a small porcelain heart that was actually a salt shaker that my mother and I bought at a Russian festival."

"Where is the heart now?"

"In my apartment in Edmonds."

"Let's go get it."

"Now?"

"Do you want to know or not?" Peter asked as he glanced at his watch. "We have time to swing by the lab and have the analysis done today."

"Really?" Emery observed Peter questioningly. When she saw the answer in his eyes, the cottony sensation faded. She stood up and straightened her shoulders. "Okay. Let's go."

78

THE HEART

JULY 2047

Small, bright, and modern, Emery's apartment had the newest self-cleaning technology, granting carefree living for a busy individual who despised housework. The white eco-furniture, floors, and bathroom cleaned themselves once a week with a UV light that popped out of the ceiling when prompted by the apartment's maintenance computer. When finished, it filled the rooms with the scent of lilacs, Emery's favorite. A few colorful pillows and throws enlivened the apartment.

Regis sprang from the sofa and greeted Emery with a graceful dance and a vigorous tail wag. He had met Peter a few times and greeted him friendly, but not as ostentatiously.

An oil painting that her Uncle Alexander had made to express his Bohemian mood just before the accident occupied one wall. He ended up hating it and threw it away. Emery rescued it from the dumpster and saved it, not knowing why. The painting wasn't great. It was not awful either, but Emery couldn't look away. It depicted a winter landscape with a forest in the background and a leafless oak tree in the middle. A boy sat by himself, facing away from the tree. Emery left Peter in the living room and went in search of the porcelain heart. He stood staring at the painting.

"Do you like it?" Emery asked, returning with a blue porcelain heart painted with tiny red roses. "Or you can't stop staring at it?"

"Not sure. Probably both. You found it?"

"Yes. I knew exactly where it was," she said, pressing the little painted heart to her chest. "Come on, Regis. Let's go."

"This is my friend, Emery," Peter introduced Emery to an older man with a curly mustache and wearing blue scrubs. "Emery, meet Doctor Gary Lawson, a dear friend who can't stop working. He postpones his retirement every year. Pretty soon, he will be a permanent fixture in this sad facility. Thanks for seeing us on short notice, Gary."

"Anything for you, Peter. What do you have?"

"We've got cremated ashes, which we want to compare to Emery's DNA to see if they match."

"I see," Gary said and looked at Emery with his keen eyes. "You want to make sure it is your mother?"

"Yes. How did you know?"

"It's obvious just looking at you that you are her daughter. I remember the case and remember wondering why they didn't test the DNA. I'm sorry. It must have been horrible not having certainty."

Emery nodded. Gary pulled a syringe out of a packet and put on surgical gloves. "I'm going to take your blood, Emery. Sit here, dear," he pointed to a stool.

Gary tied Emery's arm with a rubber tube and drew a syringe full of her blood.

"Forgive me if I hurt you, dear. I am not good with the living, dealing mostly with ones who can't feel anymore."

"I'm okay, Gary. It doesn't hurt a bit."

Peter cocked his head and grinned. It was apparent that Gary had trouble with the vein by the way Emery bit her lip.

"How long will it take?" Peter asked after Gary was done with Emery.

"An hour?" Gary said.

"We'll come back in an hour," Peter said to Gary, and then glanced at Emery. "Do you want to get some coffee?"

"Yes, coffee sounds good."

"There is a coffee place around the corner. We could wait there."

Peter's face tensed when he opened the door to Café Kristina.

Here is where he last saw and spoke with Olesya. This is where she told him she couldn't be with him. It was the last time he had set foot in this place.

"Are you okay?" Emery asked. "Do you want to go somewhere else?"

"No, it's okay. What can I get you?"

"Cappuccino. Why are you smiling?"

"No reason," Peter answered and ordered two cappuccinos from the barista.

Sitting at a table, sipping her coffee, Emery remarked, "This hour will be the longest of my life."

"What are you studying?"

"This and that," Emery said. "I don't know what I want to do with my life. I dabbled in science, psychology, and political science, and nothing calls to me. Nothing worthwhile. For a while, I even tried cyber history, finding the failed attempts and catastrophic results of creating humanoid AI fascinating. I get into it, learn what I want, and then lose interest. My current major is math, but I have no clue what I'll do with that."

"Maybe you want to be a cop?" Peter joked.

"It is not as funny as you think. I've thought about it." She looked at Peter seriously. "I think of it as gratifying and honest work."

"It can be, but it also could be dirty and discouraging."

"Why didn't you try harder at convincing my mother to be with you?" Emery whispered the question, looking down at her hands.

"Because she meant it when she said it. Pressing her would have killed her love and respect for me. At least I knew she loved me in her own way."

Emery and Peter entered the lab and saw Gary sitting at a desk, staring at the screen.

"We're back," Peter announced.

Seeing Gary's troubled expression, Peter's face scrunched. "Just tell us, Gary."

"There's no relationship between Emery and the person whose ashes I analyzed," Gary blurted out.

"Are you sure?" Peter asked.

Gary just nodded in response, resting his kind eyes on Emery and nervously sticking his hands in the pockets of his not-so-clean blue scrubs.

Emery searched for a chair to sit on as her knees developed a similar cottony sensation as her brain did before. She had suspected it, but now that it was certain, the realization hit her hard, flipping her world upside down. Again. Peter lowered his head and clenched his teeth while Gary tapped his fingers on the desk as Emery collapsed in on herself. Neither one tried to console her.

Peter touched her gently on the shoulder. "Let's go, Emery."

She looked up at him, but couldn't say anything. Her mind was stuck in a loop, questioning her entire life and wondering where her mother was.

Peter grabbed her hand and led her out of the lab. She didn't object.

He then glanced at Gary and mouthed a "thank you."

Gary nodded.

While Peter drove his car to his apartment, she sat straight up, frigid, looking ahead onto the busy street with unseeing eyes, not concerned where they were going, not responding to his questions, like an empty shell of herself.

Peter's apartment was on the top floor, overlooking Lake Washington. A true bachelor apartment, it lacked softness. There were no blankets, no pillows, no decorations, only the necessary, useful gadgets a single male needed. To his benefit, the apartment was squeaky clean, smelling of leather and sandalwood, and organized, except for a few scattered clothes and a few open books on mountaineering.

Peter led Emery to the sofa, and she sat without dissent. Her furry friend jumped on the sofa and curled himself up by her side.

"Make yourself comfortable, dog." Peter chuckled.

Peter fetched her water and then sat opposite Emery, observing her for a while as she sat motionless, held captive by her shock. After a while of looking out the window and going over and over the accident, her mind suddenly stilled, as she felt the hot breath and the softness of Regis's tongue on her hand. She shifted her gaze to Regis and touched his ears. Soon after, her breathing steadied, and she looked at Peter, pacing his living room, then suddenly smacking his forehead and fetching his laptop.

He opened his laptop and started researching. Besides his mountain rescue work, he freelanced as a private detective finding missing persons, opting to stay busy to avoid dwelling on the past. He excelled at finding people; his nose always led him to clues others had missed. For the second time in his life, he started the search for Sara Mowen. His fingers tapped the keyboard faster and faster, while his eyes grew steely sharp, focusing on the screen.

"What are you doing?" Emery asked, leaning over his shoulder.

Peter jerked.

Emery saw the prompts for Sara Mowen in several open windows on his laptop.

"You're looking for Sara?" she asked, surprised. "Why?"

Peter swiveled his chair back and studied her for a moment. His features relaxed. "I'm not sure. Just had a hunch that she might know something."

"A hunch. Hmm. That is interesting."

"Why?"

"Because I was about to ask you to find Sara. I remembered something. She called my mother shortly before the accident. My mother was taking a shower, so I picked up the phone. Sara, sounding incensed, shouted on the phone. 'Fine, you win! I will go with you.' Curious, I asked where. 'To your part of the woods. Where else?' Sara answered. Only when I asked, 'What woods?' did Sara guess she wasn't speaking with my mother. The very next day, my mother and my Uncle Alex left, supposedly for a work conference. I want to ask Sara about the woods because I think my mother went there."

"Did you know Sara well?"

"Not very well. I visited the lab with my mom a few times and played video games or read while she and Sara worked. They never talked about their work in front of me, which seemed odd, but when I read about the—" Emery stopped suddenly, remembering that Peter might not be aware of her mother's...special powers and the black shards.

"You read about what?" Peter sighed. "I know there is something you are not telling me. Your mother kept something from me, and I was fine with it, but now I'm not. I need to know everything if I'm to find out what happened."

Emery regarded Peter, hesitating. He deserved to know the truth after years of suffering, not knowing the reason her mother couldn't allow herself to be with him. However, it was her mother's truth, her story. She must have had her reasons for not telling him. So why should she tell him now? Because she didn't want to lose him. Not showing him the letter would signal a lack of trust, and she trusted him with every inch of her soul. It occurred to her that her hesitation might have been born out of fear that her mother was ill and had concocted the story. She quickly dismissed the scenario. Her mother had been as healthy and sharp as it gets.

Emery pulled her mother's letter from her bag. She clasped the paper in her hands and pressed it to her heart.

"She wrote to me but never said not to share it with anyone. I can't think of a better person to share it with. It's long, and you may end up with a different perception of her and...me. I'll leave you alone with it while I go home and take care of Regis. Call me when you're ready."

Emery handed Peter the letter. Their hands trembled as the letter passed between them. Before she left, she threw him a quick, furtive, but affectionate glance. Regis ran to her, wagging his tail, but then turned around and winked at Peter.

79

PAMELA

JULY 2047

The next day, Emery knocked on Peter's door. Ever since she'd given him the letter, her heart raced as she imagined the worst reaction from him. She tried to calm herself down, telling herself that Peter couldn't hate her or her mother. But her heart didn't listen and kept thrashing in her chest as if it were a scared bird wanting out of a cage.

Peter opened the door immediately after she had knocked. Despite his impenetrable face, Emery found solace in his eyes. They held no hate, no anger, no judgment. She entered without saying a word. Her furry companion made himself at home, curling up on the sofa.

"Regis," Emery said, trying to reprimand him, but her voice betrayed her. Regis glanced at her with one eye, then glanced at Peter, unmoving.

"He's fine. I love dogs," Peter said and added under his breath. "Especially the ones that wink."

Peter and Emery stood eye to eye in an awkward silence. Every inch of Emery's body wanted to know his reaction, but she couldn't ask, fearing pushing him might make him say something that might crush her. With Peter not volunteering to talk about it, they were at an impasse.

Emery shifted her weight.

Peter cleared his throat. "Emery, I know I'm the one who called, thinking I was ready. I don't want to talk about it just yet, but I wanted to tell you I found Sara. She changed her appearance and her name, but it's definitely her." Peter stumbled over his words.

"That is great," Emery exclaimed. Part of her was relieved as she fathomed it would be one of the toughest conversations of her life. "We...I'll talk to her. Well, you can come...if you want to."

"I want to," Peter said eagerly. "When do you want—"

"Now?"

Peter flew Emery's plane, while in the backseat, Regis watched the trees and hills going by beneath, panting happily (he loved flying), and Emery read about Sara on Peter's AI tablet. Sara Mowen was not Sara Mowen anymore. She had changed her name and appearance, but Emery recognized her from the snapshot taken of her leaving a grocery store. She lived in Oregon as a retired nurse, Pamela Harrison. How Peter found this, she didn't ask. They were on their way to her house in a small town in Oregon.

"Were there more pages?"

"What?"

"The notebook that contained your mother's letter."

"Oh, I noticed that too, but thought she might've had something unrelated at the end, like her work notes. But I thought it was strange," Emery said and glanced at Peter. "No, I didn't tear them up, if that's what you're asking."

"Thanks," he muttered.

An uncomfortable silence fell between them. Peter pursed his lips and focused on the controls. "It'd be okay if you did. After all, Olesya wrote the letter to you, not to me. You had every right to tear pages you didn't want me to read."

"But I didn't. Either it was my mother or someone else. But as thoughtful and meticulous as my mother was, I doubt she'd have written such an important letter in a notebook containing anything else, or that she'd have torn pages out of it."

"Who else knew about the letter besides Sasha?"

"I don't know."

"Could Sasha have done it?"

"I doubt it. My grandma believes in personal choices and freedom to make her own decisions."

Peter nodded.

"I wonder whose bodies burned in the car?" Emery asked after the long silence. "And who put them in there?" Emery didn't want to believe her mother or her uncle had killed someone to stage their own deaths. But who else? Zoe?

"Sara might know."

Emery sighed, leaned back, and stroked Regis's ears. "Do you think she'll tell us anything?"

"Hard to say. I've never met her. But she was your mother's best friend. I can't imagine she wouldn't tell her daughter everything she knew."

"You have arrived at Prineville Municipal Airport," the plane navigation assistant announced.

Sara's house sat in a remote area outside the city, on a hill overlooking a valley peppered with uncanny rocky formations. The sparse vegetation scattered throughout the valley consisted mostly of hardy shrubs and curly trees, sturdy enough to withstand the dry conditions, winds, and several feet of snow every winter. They drove the car to a gate with an electronic security system. Peter glanced at Emery and pressed a button. After a few moments, the screen lit up, and Sara's face, just as Emery remembered, appeared.

"The gate will open momentarily," Sara said. Her voice sounded strangely distorted by the speaker. "Drive to the front and park in the garage." The screen blackened, the gate opened, and then closed behind them as soon as they drove through.

Peter parked the car in the garage. The pair exchanged glances and spoke at the same time. "She was expecting us."

As soon as they approached, the door between the house and the garage opened, and Sara came running.

"Emery. My dear Emery," Sara said, opening her arms.

Emery slid into them naturally, without hesitation, as if she'd done that a thousand times before. After they hugged, Sara appraised her at arm's length.

"Look at you, all grown up. You look very much like your mother."

Emery was at a loss for words. She had not seen her in so many years. The last time she saw her was at her mother's funeral, at which Sara appeared for a few minutes, glanced at Emery, then left in a hurry.

"Regis, my boy! So good to see you." She kissed Regis on his head. He licked her hand, looking a little embarrassed.

"Peter," Sara said, staring at Peter intrusively. "Glad to meet you."

"How do you know me, and how did you know we were coming?" Peter asked.

"All in good time. Patience, my good detective. Patience," Sara said, laughing. Emery now understood why her mother loved her and her laugh. "Let's go inside," Sara said, beckoning them in.

80

DON'T LET GO

JULY 2047

"Make yourself comfortable. What are you drinking?"

"Water would be great," Peter said.

"Same here," Emery said.

"Sit down, kids. I'll be right back."

Emery looked around Sara's house, finding it warm and comfortable. They sat on the sofa, waiting for her. Regis plopped himself on the floor at Emery's feet. Peter kept shifting in his chair and rubbing his chin.

"What's wrong?" Emery whispered.

Peter whispered back. "Something about Sara's appearance bothers me, but I can't figure out what. It had been a while since I had investigated her disappearance."

Sara reappeared with glasses and a crystal pitcher of iced water and lemon. "Don't look so gloomy and nervous, you two. I don't bite."

"We just want to know about the woods and what happened to my mother," Emery blurted.

"I know you do. I'll tell you what I can."

"What do you mean? Why couldn't you tell us everything you know?" Peter asked, agitated.

"What I meant was, I can only tell you what I know." Sara

observed Peter with her deep black eyes and, without looking at Emery, she asked her. "I assume you read your mom's letter?"

"Yes."

"And you?" Sara asked Peter.

"Yes. I did," he said, pinning her eyes under his blue stare. "When I investigated your disappearance years ago, your eyes had been blue and your hair lighter. You could've easily dyed your hair, and you could be wearing contact lenses, but you couldn't fake your age. You were in your fifties when you disappeared. And that was twenty-three years ago. You're in your seventies, but you look like you're in your forties."

Sara held his gaze, smiling. "Yes, I've been changed. Didn't Olesya put that in her letter?"

"How do you know about the letter?" Emery asked, after a heavy pause, "Did you tear the pages from the end?"

"Why would I do that? I am about to tell you everything. Yes, I knew about the letter because I put it there. Your mother asked me to, and I knew when Sasha would give it to you. So, answering your question, Peter: I expected Emery, but I didn't expect her to have help," she said in a slightly sarcastic tone, observing him.

"And you didn't notice pages missing?"

"No, but I didn't look inside either."

"She ended the letter when she found out she was pregnant with me. I remember you with black eyes and hair, so it must have happened before my mother disappeared."

"Disappeared. Why did you say that?" Sara asked.

"We've had the DNA from the car crash analyzed and compared to Emery's. We know she's not related to whoever those ashes belonged to, so we assumed it was not her mother that died in the car," Peter said in his detective voice.

"DNA? Where did you get Olesya's DNA? It was supposed to be scattered in the mountains. That's what she wanted."

"My grandmother saved some for me."

"Well, the secret is out," Sara sighed. "It doesn't matter, anyway."

"What do you mean?" Peter asked. His eyes were flashing, and his fingers tapped the armchair.

"It's too late."

"What's too late? What the heck do you mean by that?" Peter asked.

"The capsule was destroyed."

"What capsule?" Peter asked.

"Sara, just tell us everything, please. Start with what happened to my mother." Emery realized she sounded agitated, but she didn't care. She didn't come here to play games.

"I will. You deserve at least that much. I'm sorry."

Sara told them everything that happened after Olesya found out she was pregnant up to the time they found the chambers. Emery couldn't wait any longer and asked. "What does it have to do with my mother? Where is she? And what did you mean when you said you were going with her to the woods? What woods?"

"I will get to it, dear." Sara paused. She kept glancing secretly at Peter and Emery while telling the story, observing their clandestine interactions.

Sara stopped her story and got up from her chair, stretching. She glanced at Peter and Emery, who watched her like hawks, expecting more.

"I can't talk anymore. Ugh. Telling the story brings all the memories back and is more difficult than I thought it was going to be. We can continue tomorrow."

"But you still haven't told me what happened to my mother!" Emery protested.

"I will. Tomorrow. I promise. Where are you two staying in town?"

"Nowhere. We haven't talked about it," Emery said, glancing at Peter.

"Why don't you stay here tonight, and then we can jump back to the story in the morning? The house is large enough for ten people, and I make killer pancakes," Sara said, laughing. "Look at Regis. He is happy here," Sara added, pointing at the dog, who was stretched on the couch by the window, sticking his enormous pink tongue out, appearing very relaxed. "I can find something special in my fridge for Regis, my old friend."

Peter gazed at Emery, and she returned his stare, shrugging, trying to look like she didn't care. But she cared. She didn't want him to leave. The thought of him not being by her side suddenly terrified her.

"Up to you. I don't mind, but if you need to go anywhere..."

"I don't mind either. I don't have anywhere else to go," Peter said. "If Sara truly doesn't mind us staying here, she can finish her story sooner."

"It's settled, then. How about drinks?" Sara asked, smiling.

"Beer would be great if you have it," Emery said, and Peter nodded in agreement.

After Sara left to get the drinks, Emery glanced at Peter. "You think my mother is dead, don't you?"

Peter opened his eyes wide in shock.

"It's okay, Peter. You can be honest with me. Tell me what you think."

"It is just a feeling I've had since I heard about the accident. A premonition that she was gone and never coming back. And I don't know if it means she is dead or somewhere far away. Like you, I want to know what happened to her. I had no idea the police hadn't veri-fied her identity at the time of the accident."

Emery woke up early and tiptoed into the kitchen, expecting to find it still empty. But Sara was up, making coffee. She offered one to Emery, and they sat at the kitchen table, sipping in silence before Sara spoke.

"I wonder what Olesya would think of her daughter falling in love with the same man, forty years her senior. I sensed neither you nor Peter had disclosed your feelings for each other yet, so perhaps it's not too late to add a word of caution before you jump into something you'd regret."

Emery's pulse quickened, but she kept her voice steady and her eyes on Sara's. "Being my mother's friend doesn't give you the right to butt into my life. I don't need a word of caution from anyone."

"I'm only doing this because I care about you."

"You do? Then where have you been for the past ten years?"

"You're right. I have no right," Sara said and grew quiet.

After Peter walked into the kitchen a few moments later, she made them breakfast and coffee. As she promised, her pancakes were amazing. Full of flavor, crispy on the outside, holding a heavenly sweet and soft secret inside. They sat in the breakfast nook with wraparound windows overlooking the valley. Sipping her coffee with her eyes focused on her coffee cup, Emery, torn between wanting to hear the rest of the story or delaying it, realized what Sara would tell her would be final and might not be what she hoped for. After she found out that the body in the car wreck was not her mother's, she had hoped for a miracle. Maybe her mother was still alive somewhere. She shivered at the thought that Sara would soon reveal the truth.

"So you're retired?" Sara asked Peter, scrutinizing him openly, shamelessly.

"Yes, for a while now."

"What do you do with yourself, then? You look...good for your age. Fit," Sara said in a cheeky tone while glancing at Emery with an inscrutable smile.

Emery looked at Sara, surprised at first, but then she understood what she was doing. Sara was trying to discourage her by pointing out his age. Emery considered intervening, but hesitated upon hearing his calm response. He could handle himself.

"I'm teaching mountain rescue classes."

"Impressive. Beats frying in Florida," Sara said, laughing.

His lack of reaction didn't fool Emery; she saw in his eyes that he understood Sara's intentions too. From the forlorn look on his face and eyes that grew a shade darker, she sensed Peter not only understood, but he also agreed with Sara. He was much too old for her.

Emery avoided analyzing the relationship unfolding before her, dreading the implications. Age mattered not. Only her guilt at falling for a man her mother loved, especially now, knowing that she might still be alive. Drawn to him from the start, she couldn't stop glancing at him, but she had attributed it to him being interesting, intelligent, and Olesya's friend. But only in the beginning. Later on, catching the gleam in his eyes, it became clear it was more, but she lied to herself. Her infatuation had morphed without warning, without her knowledge or will, and grew into something she couldn't and didn't want to stop. She realized when she caught his quick, pilfered glances that he felt the same. The gleam in his eyes was unmistakable. When she caught his eyes gliding over her face and body, her chest filled with a cotton-like cloud that expanded into her entire body, robbing her of control.

Sara, in revealing their secret, hinted at its repugnance and wickedness. Worse, she hinted Peter's only option was to leave here now and never see Emery again.

Emery clenched her teeth and considered intervening again, but changed her mind after Peter's reply.

"It sure does. That's why you are here?" Peter asked.

"Touche," Sara said, laughing. "Okay, you probably want me to continue the story."

"Please," Emery said.

Sara continued her story of opening the chamber and finding Sergi's hologram.

"My father?" Emery asked in a shaky voice. "My father was one of the dark people and recorded the hologram?" She asked in disbelief.

"That is what we thought at first. The man in the hologram resembled him, but your mother insisted that he sounded different and pronounced words differently than the Sergi she knew. The discrepancy haunted your mother. She suspected and later became convinced that someone who looked like him recorded it, or that someone generated it with AI."

Peter interjected. "AI was banned years ago and its use heavily prosecuted."

"If there's will and money, nothing is unattainable. I'm sure unofficial copies of AI software exist on the black market."

"Who do you think did that?" Emery asked.

"I don't know. We never figured it out. She entertained the idea that the recording, or even his nerves, might have altered his voice. Despite the inconsistency, the story concocted by Sergi or his looka-like itself was so preposterous, and yet, she believed it must have been what happened because of...how preposterous it was. She oscillated for years, not knowing what to believe; one day she was ready to jump into the capsule, another dismissing it all as a fairy tale."

"What convinced her?"

"You."

"Me? How?"

"She had a dream or a vision, as she said that you were the key, as you possess both black and gold in your body. Your cells have golden organelles, which other people do not, and your DNA contains dark fragments."

"What? No, you are making this shit up as you go. I don't believe you," Emery said, stood up, and started walking to the door as if she wanted to leave. Peter glanced at her and got up too.

"I'm not making anything up, and I can prove it. Ever wondered what's with those golden and black spots in your eyes that pop out and spark when you're angry or when you're happy? Your mother collected your skin sample, and we examined it under an electron microscope. There was no mistaking it. After that, she became convinced that at least part of Sergi's story was true, despite the inconsistencies."

"So what did he say?" Emery exclaimed.

Sara finished the story from the hologram while Emery stood glaring at her.

"So she went into the capsule?" Emery whispered at the end.

Sara nodded.

"But you had no certainty," Peter hissed. "All you learned from the golden one is that the golden people existed and Ishtar's goal was to kill you all. He told you that the dark people caused the imbalance. You had no way of knowing who was telling the truth. She might have sacrificed herself for the wrong reason. Why did you let her go?"

Peter glanced at Emery and stilled.

Sara tried to reassure her. "It wasn't only the organelles, Emery. Your mother came to this conclusion because she had never witnessed the dark people killing the golden people. It was always the other way around. To this day, I am not sure if she fully believed in the golden people or Sergi's story, but she believed in saving the world for you. We knew dark matter was disappearing from around us."

"For Emery?" Peter sounded sarcastic and angry. "How would it save the world for Emery to follow her mother into some kind of capsule and sacrifice herself? Nowhere in your story do you mention the origin of the chambers or the capsule. Who built them and why? Where exactly did the capsule send her?"

"Those are all good questions, Peter. But I have no answers for you. I asked her those questions myself. Olesya seemed to think she was linked to the chambers. She had visions and dreams and a memory of having been in all those chambers before. I couldn't convince her otherwise. I tried arguing she was risking her and her daughter's lives for a vision."

"What did she say to that?" Emery asked.

Sara hesitated, making a dismissive gesture.

"What did she say?" Peter asked; his voice could cut through stone.

"The more I argued, the more adamant she became that she'd be safe in the capsule. One detail Olesya was sure about was that Emery would prevail and return from the darkness."

"How could she be so sure?"

"She said Alexander saw her in the future. Once she decided to go into the capsule, Alexander had one of his visions and told her Emery would be okay. He saw her grown up and happy in the future."

"A vision? She sacrificed herself, and now you, for a vision?" Peter stood up, set his lips, and started walking up and down the living room. When he returned, his blue eyes shot icy daggers at Sara.

"What about my uncle?" Emery changed the subject, seeing Peter tense with each passing second. "Did he go with her?"

"Not with her. A while after she went. I suspect he couldn't bear losing your mother after losing Zoe and followed in your mother's footsteps."

"And now I must find them," Emery whispered.

"Well, that's just it. You can't," Sara said.

"Why not?"

"Belyaska's chamber doesn't exist anymore," Sara said.

"What happened?" Peter asked.

"Zoe returned just before your mother disappeared into the capsule. She was with your mother in the chamber when she entered the capsule. Alexander wanted to go with Olesya into the chamber, but Zoe sweet-talked him into staying and waiting for her. She told him she had returned to be with him and that Olesya would return with Emery. He believed her—or wanted to—and obeyed her."

"Zoe was the last one to see my mother," Emery said. "She came back just to see her off. How fortuitous was that? How did she know?"

"I learned over the years never to underestimate Zoe, but I guessed that someone had told her."

"Did you?"

"No, by golly. I didn't know where she was. I stopped trying to contact her years before because she never replied to me. Maybe your uncle did, hoping this would make her come back, even if it was for a short time. But anyone could have told her. Possibly even your mother? I have no idea, kiddo. I never had the chance to ask."

"What happened to my uncle?"

"He asked Elliot and Henry to help him open the chamber so that he could listen to the hologram, as he claimed he needed to do desperately, and he never came out. After that, I didn't care to learn what happened to Zoe, Elliot, or anyone else. I was heartbroken after your mother had gone into the capsule and I left."

"Zoe didn't return to get back with my uncle. She came back to see my mother off," Emery said pensively.

"I don't know. It is hard to tell. When Zoe found out Alexander had gone after Olesya, she came unglued and started tearing up the town of Belyaska in a furious rage. Her anger turned her into a dark demon. She tore down houses, sending debris flying around at high speed and killing everyone in close range. Then she used every explosive imaginable to finish what she started and blew the town to pieces. Only black, foul-smelling ashes, rubble, and dark clouds—much like the soot that blanketed the ground—serve as a reminder of the town's painful past. When she was done, she disappeared again." Sara said and paused, leaving a heavy silence lingering in the air.

Peter, lost in his thoughts, stared at the floor. Emery had also drifted away, remembering her mother's last days, her frequent travels, hushed phone conversations, and her mother smothering her with hugs and kisses as if there were no tomorrow. There was no tomorrow.

"That would mean that my mother sacrificed herself in vain. We must find another chamber."

"Emery, I don't know where the other chambers are," Sara said.

"Well, we must find them. We can replicate the process. Can you... call Elliot?" Emery asked.

Peter sat quietly, observing Sara, and responded to her reticence to resume the search for other chambers with a tiny smile and a nod.

Sara got up, stretching. "We've been talking for hours. Let's get something to eat and stretch our legs. We'll talk about it some other time."

"No! I must find my mother! And save the world."

"As you said before, we are not even sure you'll be saving anyone. Are you certain the world is worth saving?" Sara's face suddenly changed and darkened. Her black eyes got even darker, and Emery wondered how it was possible.

"What do you mean?"

"Look around you, Emery. Everywhere you look, you see widespread malice, greed, worthless technology, never-ending conflicts, lack of empathy, injustice, not to mention ignorance and apathy. There is a reason I live in the boonies and avoid news and people. I think we're doomed, and this imbalance might have happened for a reason. To get rid of failed experiments. We are the Meekers, if you believe what Sergi told us. What good did we ever do except kill each other, steal from each other, or hate each other? How do we deserve everlasting life and happiness?"

Emery pinched her eyebrows, listening to Sara's tirade. Olesya had portrayed Sara as an ever-positive optimist who had the ability and the disposition to always find something good in anyone or anything. This woman sounded bitter, tired, and pessimistic. Emery glanced at Peter pleadingly, asking with her eyes to convince Sara otherwise.

Peter dithered before speaking. "That is one way of looking at it. I believe many selfless people work hard and love others, harming no one. They don't deserve to die, even if they are the Meekers."

"I don't want Emery sacrificing her life for the few virtuous souls. We must face the fact that we are losing the battle. We've lost our ideology, replacing it with technology, games, and instant gratification. Young people lack the fire to fight for what's right, as if they lost the will to choose for themselves and instead opted to follow the norm, desiring only the fastest planes, fastest cars, and designer clothes."

"Sara, I realize what you're doing. No matter what you say to me, you're not changing my mind. I'll find my mother and uncle, with or without you," Emery casually stated as she stood up.

Sara sighed. She left the living room, saying nothing and not even looking at them.

Emery and Peter exchanged baffled looks.

"Is she coming back?" Emery asked.

"I'm sure she is. Maybe she needs time. Perhaps you need some time to think about it?"

"No, I don't need time. I have no time. I must find my mother. She's been waiting for me all this time. Is she alone or with her brother? She is probably suffering immeasurably, waiting for me."

"Emery, don't go there."

"It's true."

"I don't want you to sacrifice yourself for anyone else, even for Olesya."

"You are as stubborn as your mother," Sara said, returning to the living room. "Elliot will be here in two days. There's no assurance you can even find her or make her come back, right? Even if we find the chambers? You might find her if she is still your mother."

"What do you mean, still my mother?"

"We know nothing about the place she had ventured out to. Only that there lies a secret to getting a balance in the universe and eternal life for a few. Supposedly."

"I will bring them back with me when I find them," Emery said with conviction, but when she looked at Sara's face, her voice faltered. "What is it? What are you not telling me?"

"It is nothing. It is merely an intuition that Sergi's message was simply a scheme to lure your mother into reaching the capsule to exile her permanently. Perhaps there is no dark dimension, and the story he told us was all made up." Glancing at Emery's face, Sara changed the subject. "Don't put too much faith in my ramblings. I'm going to prepare something for us to eat. Since living here like a nun, I've developed mean culinary skills. I can whip up a gourmet dish out of nothing."

Sara left the living room. She felt guilty she had alarmed Emery, but secretly she was glad she had, hating the idea of Emery disappearing. She still hadn't gotten over Olesya's disappearance. Her pessimistic view of the world started soon after she left. Her only friend, her brilliant Olesya, was gone. Sara had never had many friends, despite her outgoing personality and her dazzling laughter. She just never sought friends, finding sufficient contentment in her own skin to enjoy solitude when not at work. Her work meant everything to her and absorbed most of her time.

When Olesya started working at her lab, their spontaneous friendship gave them both wings. *Friendship at first sight*, Sara laughed to herself. She missed Olesya more than she thought she would, and since losing her friend, she had lost her vivacity and ability to find enjoyment in anything. Now, her dilemma was to help Emery find Olesya or to thwart her efforts to protect her friend's only child.

With her arms wrapped around herself, Emery stood looking out the window. Acting on impulse, Peter touched her shoulder. She turned toward him and immediately sank into his arms. In that instant, magic happened. She'd never felt more herself than now. The certainty that she'd reached her destination overwhelmed her to the point of near unconsciousness as she melted into his arms. Peter stroked her hair and kissed her on the head.

"Are you okay?" he asked.

"I am now," Emery replied in a dreamy voice. "Don't let go of me."

81

MORE TRIANGLES

JULY 2047

Elliot arrived two days later, as promised. Henry and Mary were on their way. Emery appraised Elliot, liking what she saw.

Tall, dark, and handsome. Chuckling to herself, Emery admired the old-fashioned look of Elliot's pocket square and perpetual suntan of an outdoorsy, mysterious, and masculine male. Intelligence and humor beamed out of his penetrating black eyes. Emery liked him instantaneously.

Emery felt Peter's gaze on her when she was appraising the handsome Elliot and grinned to herself. *Is he jealous?* Then she felt guilty and smiled at Peter.

After the introductions, Emery accosted Elliot right away. "Any idea where we can find the other chambers?"

Elliot looked at her and laughed. "You're just like your mother. To the point. Yes, I have some ideas. I've been contemplating this for years."

"And?"

"I realized that if we kept the size of the triangle the same, we would not have too many options in South America because of its size and geography. It could only fit in one way. So it was really simple. It had been staring me in the face for years. I just couldn't see it."

Elliot spread out a map of South America on Sara's desk. Everyone watched the red triangle drawn on the old, tired-looking map. One corner rested on Chile, one on a small coastal town in northeastern Brazil, Grossos, and the third one on a tiny town, Utivé, in Panama.

Sara regarded the map and made a face. "How can you be certain that the geographical triangle is the same size?"

"The triangles in each chamber were all equal in size. It is just an assumption, but it makes the most sense. At least to me."

"A hard-copy map. I didn't think you could get your hands on one," Emery said, touching the map with the tips of her fingers.

"I've had this map forever and wouldn't trade it for anything, but I confirmed the locations electronically."

"When are we going to check it out?"

Elliot smiled mysteriously and said, "No need."

"Why not?" Emery asked, crossing her arms.

"I've done that already."

Emery looked at him with admiration. She caught Peter's darkening eyes and pinched lips. As if reading his mind, she knew Peter was struggling to see Emery engage so naturally with Elliot, who seemed to be closer to her age. She nearly snorted out loud that Peter was still a child, compared to Elliot, who must have been approaching two hundred.

"What did you find?"

"The chambers. I found them both. One was under an abandoned metal processing factory in Grossos, serving as junk storage."

"And the other one?"

"The other one gave me some trouble, but I eventually found it. It took me only a few weeks to find it in the tiny town. It would've been quicker if I hadn't missed it initially. I explored Utivé and its surroundings, even entering people's homes by pretending to be dizzy and in need of water. Luckily, the people in town were an easy-going bunch who suspected nothing, even if it stared them right in the eyes. It was the second time I visited the little hair and nail salon that I finally noticed the triangle on the ceiling. The owners had painted the walls bright red and covered them with photographs of famous actresses to showcase their haircuts."

"You've been a busy bee, Elliot," Sara said, not without a slight reproach in her voice. "Why didn't you tell me?"

"I didn't want to open any wounds, but I had to satisfy my curiosity. The urge to find it was eating at me, not letting me rest."

Emery sat engrossed in her thoughts. Now that they had located the triangles, an incapacitating panic descended, and an epiphany that it was all preordained and decided for her by someone or something else. For a moment, self-pity overwhelmed her, and she had to fight hard to suppress the tears for her brief life that had barely begun and was soon to be cut short.

"You don't have to do it," Peter said; his face turned ashen. "There is no assurance you'll find your mother or that you'd save the world. You achieved your goal and discovered what happened to your mother. This is what you wanted. Now, you can walk out of here and go on with your life."

"You're wrong. I must act quickly as time is running out," Emery said, and as she said that, she suddenly felt calm and at peace with her decision. "You can't persuade me otherwise. I'm sorry, Peter. I'm sorry, Sara. I must do it because it's my destiny."

A heavy silence fell upon the room. Sara opened her mouth several times but never articulated her thoughts. She finally said under her breath. "I've always known this day would come."

Peter kept clearing his throat.

82

VISITOR

JULY 2047

Peter was packing a suitcase when Sean Connery's voice announced, "You have a visitor."

He had programmed his electronic house assistant with his favorite actor's voice. So far, he hadn't tired of it yet. Sean's voice always amused him and elicited a smile while the assistant performed domestic chores, such as opening the windows or cooking his dinner.

He glanced at his watch and saw an image of Emery standing in front of his door. He hadn't been expecting her. They were not meeting until tomorrow at the airport before flying to Chile. She seemed tense and had a strange expression on her flushed face. His heart started beating fast. Was something wrong? He ran to the door, yelling at Sean to open it.

Emery walked in carrying a small backpack. She threw the backpack on the ground, looking forlorn, and stood for a while, lost for words, wriggling her hands nervously.

"What is wrong?"

"Nothing." Emery's voice cracked, and her lips trembled as she spoke.

She gazed at him with a pained expression. "I am on the verge of diving into a dark dimension where I might die or be lost forever. I want to be with you before I go. This feeling that I have for you... makes my chest hurt. Literally. I can't breathe. I want to experience this before I go. When you pulled me into your arms, I felt that fate had put us together, even though I don't believe in fate. Well, I didn't believe in fate. Now, I'm not sure what I believe. But there's this powerful feeling of inevitability that got hold of me, and I can't shake it off. Peter, I want to make love to you more than anything I've ever wanted in my life."

Peter stood listening to Emery, resisting the overwhelming desire to hold her. But he fought the urge and endured the pain that held his chest in a powerful clasp. He couldn't breathe. "You are so young. Almost a child. Do you realize I could be your grandfather?"

"I am not a child. I'm a grown, strong woman; not a virgin, just so you know. And I know what I want. I want you. I have never been so certain about anything in my life as I am now. The prudish small-town mentality does not suit you. I know you want the same thing. I see it in your eyes and in every move you make. We have very little time together. Let's not waste it."

As she spoke, her trembling voice became steady. Her blue eyes shone intensely, golden speckles sparkled, and then she smiled at him with a smile that held the entire world and pulled him close to her. At that moment, he could only embrace her, and as soon as he did, she folded into his arms. He held the precious cargo to his chest tightly, but with the gentleness his arms and six-foot-two-inch muscular frame allowed. But she pulled back and stared boldly into his eyes, then searched for his lips. When she found them, it was too late for Peter or Emery to let go. There was no force strong enough in the world to pull them apart.

83

GROSSOS

AUGUST 2047

When Sara glanced at Peter and Emery on their journey to the airport, her eyes narrowed, but she bit her lip and kept her mouth shut.

Peter might just be the reason Emery could change her mind and not go through with her plan. A lot could change between now and then.

Peter and Emery sat in their seats, solemn and quiet, holding hands. The long flight wasn't long enough. Emery gripped his hand tight, realizing fate would rip them apart after the journey ended. The anticipation and dread of their impending separation numbed her.

She no longer feared going into the capsule. Instead, the dread of losing Peter weakened her willpower, and she feared she might stay if he asked her to. She didn't look at him, sensing he was restless beside her, battling his thoughts, perhaps figuring out how to ask her to stay. At the end of the sixteen-hour flight, her tired eyes closed, and she fell asleep for the last hour.

Meanwhile, Peter fought with his emotions, watching her. He considered begging her to stay or even destroying the chamber as a last resort. But then, the thought of betraying her shamed him. This is what she had to accomplish, and he would help her, including going to the chamber and the capsule with her.

Once they arrived at Aerodromo Tobalaba Airport, they went their separate ways to catch connecting flights to their destinations. Mary and Henry traveled to Panama, having had fond memories of time spent there together. They wanted to revisit their old stomping grounds. Elliot immediately volunteered to stay in Chile. Emery thought it was strange, but it suited her purposes well because she wanted to spend the last hours with Peter and didn't want others with them. Sara, however, insisted on going to Brazil with Emery, ignoring Peter's unfriendly glare.

Emery guessed Sara's hopes of changing her mind were fading, and she wanted to cling to her in hopes Emery hesitated even for a moment. She knew that both Sara and Peter watched her constantly, and if they saw even the slightest vacillation, they would take advantage of the situation and do everything in their power to deepen her doubts.

A tiny hotel in Grossos offered them refuge until nightfall, when they would drive to the abandoned factory to open the chamber. Peter and Emery checked into a room together. Sara opened her mouth to protest, but Peter didn't even look at her. Ignoring her, he grabbed his suitcase and headed for the elevator with Emery, who sent Sara an apologetic smile.

In their room, Peter and Emery did not talk as they had intended. Once alone, they blended with each other, staying that way the entire day and night, making love greedily, knowing it was their last time. When it was time, Emery got up and dressed, evading eye contact with Peter despite the pain that felt as though someone was clawing her chest open. Peter dressed and acted as calmly as his broken heart and body allowed him to, but his entire being wanted to scream. *Stay! Stay with me!*

They packed, left the room, and waited in the lobby for Sara. She was late. Emery kept glancing at her watch impatiently. Ten minutes after she was supposed to meet them, they headed to her room. They knocked several times but did not get an answer.

"Is she sleeping?" Emery asked.

"I doubt it. Let's check with the receptionist. Perhaps she went out to get food?"

The receptionist, a young girl with a head full of golden-brown braids, smiled at them. Yes, she had witnessed Sara depart immediately after their arrival, and she didn't remember if she had returned. Emery and Peter exchanged worried glances, and afterward, Emery called Sara. No answer.

"What now?"

"We could just go to the chamber ourselves," Emery shrugged. "She doesn't want me to go and is playing games."

"What if she is in trouble?"

Emery sighed with resignation. "You're right."

"It's a small town. She couldn't have gone far. Let's search the restaurants and bars."

There were just a few restaurants and bars, and after an hour of unsuccessful searching, they had only one bar left to search.

They showed Sara's photo on their phones to the bartender. He shook his head, not speaking English. They headed for the door, but an old man stopped them, speaking perfect American English.

He studied Sara's face staring at him from Peter's phone and nodded. "Yeah, I've seen her. I went out to have a smoke cause they got all new-agey in there and don't let us smoke in there and saw her leave. She had a few in her and was kinda walking funny."

The old man's face hinted at a long and difficult life, laced with misery, alcohol, and perhaps regrets. His face was a hundred years old or more, with deep wrinkles covering his face, neck, and hands. Strangely, the mop of wavy white hair cascading to his shoulders, alert black eyes, colorful beads on his neck, and vibrant but worn-out clothes reminiscent of Woodstock, gave him an exotic and youthful vibe that contrasted with his face and the rest of his hunched and bony body.

"When was it?"

"Not that long. Half an hour ago."

"Which way did she go?" Peter asked.

"She left with her friends," the old man answered.

"Her friends?" Emery asked.

"Yeah, she went with them in the dark sedan that pulled up right in front of her. I thought it was kinda cool for them to pick her up like that. You know, so she wouldn't have to walk far. You know, being drunk and all," the old man said, glancing at Emery.

Peter transformed into a detective. "Did you see them? Her friends? What did they look like?"

"Not really. Couldn't see their faces or anything. They wore way too many clothes for this part of the world. Long, dark coats and pants and stuff. Kinda weird, if you ask me."

"Did you see the direction the car went?"

Pointing southeast, the old man said, "That way. They weren't her friends, were they?"

"Thank you for your help," Peter said, walking away.

"Wait," the hippie shouted. "Lady! Do I know you?"

Emery turned around and studied him curiously. "I doubt it. I am Emery. Thank you for helping us."

The old man kept staring at Emery as she was leaving. She turned around, sensing his glare, and waved at him, smiling. When he saw her smile, the old hippie breathed out a tiny shriek and staggered.

Emery bit her lower lip. "That old man looked so familiar."

"I didn't notice. We need the car," Peter said while they ran.

"Where would we go? They could be anywhere. Who were they?"

Emery paused and gripped his hand. "Do you think the golden people kidnapped her?"

"I don't know, but I have an idea of where they were heading."

"Do you think they are heading for the chamber?"

"That's my hunch."

They drove thirty miles southeast of town. Peter drove lightning-fast, as he did when in pursuit as a cop. Emery watched the road blur in front of her, clutching the seatbelt, studying his handsome face as he maneuvered the corners with precision and ease. He was back in his element and apparently loved it. And she loved how the little smile danced on his lips and his jaws moved, and his keen eyes watched the road. She was certain he missed nothing.

Peter parked by a black bus in front of the old factory, which was now a graffiti-covered, windowless ruin. Emery saw him retrieve something out of his coat pocket and gasped when she understood what it was.

"Where did you get that thing? And that driving? What was that?"

He put his finger to his lips, and they tiptoed to the front door, which barely held onto the doorframe and was riddled with bullet holes. They entered and saw several silhouettes in the silvery light that shone from the ceiling.

Sara, with her back to them, sat in a chair. It was too dark to see whether she was hurt, but she was motionless, and her head slumped to one side. Three dark silhouettes walked around her. One of them was tying her to the chair.

Peter and Emery sighed with relief. If they were tying her, she must still have been alive.

Peter motioned for Emery to stay behind while he pointed the gun at the silhouettes.

With enormous eyes, she tugged on his sleeve, rocking her head, and pointing to the door. With his eyes assuring her he'd be okay, Peter inched closer to the silhouettes and waited until one of them ventured out by himself into a darker corner. Without a sound, Peter attacked him from behind, choking him until he became uncon-scious. The body slumped to the ground, and the two figures glanced toward the sound and went to investigate it.

Seeing one of them on the floor, they readied their guns and searched the area, pointing their weapons with outstretched arms. Peter was nowhere to be seen. As Emery poked her head out of her hiding spot, one man pointed his gun at her, ready to fire. She ducked behind the door and ran outside, her heart pumping blood to her brain too fast for her to think. Considering she lacked weapons and fighting skills, she was like a sitting duck in there, but then she remembered the letter, and it occurred to her she could be like her mother and have the same kinetic powers. She ran back inside without hesitation.

The man pointed the gun at her. She straightened her back and threw her hands forward, closing her eyes tight, prepared to die in this forsaken factory. But she heard no gunshots. She slowly opened her eyes and saw the man who had pointed the gun at her lying on the floor, motionless. When her eyes found him, she looked at her hands and became lightheaded.

"Did I just do that?" she whispered and approached the men to check their pulses. When she couldn't see their chests rising or feel their pulses, she gasped in horror and started searching for Peter. Lifeless, he lay on the floor, his face pale and eyes closed.

"What did I do? Peter!"

Emery kneeled by him, who lay with his arms spread out and mouth partially open. She panicked, not seeing his chest move. She pressed her ear to it, searching for a heartbeat, but with her own heart beating violently, she heard nothing else.

"Peter, wake up! Wake up, please. I'm sorry. I didn't think it was going to work."

"You are your mother's daughter. You are even more powerful than she was. Of course, it was going to work," a woman's voice sounded behind her.

Emery turned her head and laid eyes on the most stunning and imposing woman she had ever seen in her life. She couldn't take her eyes off her, forgetting everything else, even Peter lying on the floor. A man, looking like the spitting image of the woman, appeared and stood by her side, staring at Emery.

"Is that Emery?" he asked the woman. "She looks just like her."

"Are you...Zoe?"

"Smart as your mom. Yes, I'm Zoe, and this is Sebastian. We are just in time, I see."

"How did you find us?"

"Later, Emery. Let's take care of Sara if it is not too late," Zoe said, walking over to Sara, who lay on the floor, still tied to an overturned chair. Sebastian kneeled by Peter, listening to his pulse and heart and examining his eyes. Emery sat, afraid to breathe, afraid to look at Sebastian.

"He'll live. Lucky for him, he was further away from the line of fire, so to speak." He picked up Peter as if he weighed little, whereas Peter was tall and muscular. He sat him up against a wall and sprayed water on his face. Meanwhile, Zoe untied Sara and attempted to wake her, but her head rolled from side to side.

"Goddamn it. Those bastards drugged her! They will pay for it!" Zoe yelled.

"They already did," Sebastian said, glancing at the corpses while slapping Peter's face. "The little one is strong. I can't believe the old cop is still alive," Sebastian said. "Oh, he is waking up. Talk to him, Emery, to check if he still has his wits."

She sat by Peter, who opened his eyes. She took his hand and peered into his eyes. "Peter. I'm sorry. I didn't know I could do that. I wouldn't have done it if I had known."

"You did that?" he whispered. "How?"

"I don't know. I have powers like my mother, I suppose."

"You saved us," Peter said. "Is that Zoe?"

Emery nodded and buried her head in Peter's chest. Zoe threw a surprised glance at her; Sebastian smiled.

"Why are you here?" Emery asked.

"Guess."

"To stop me from going?"

Zoe laughed. Sebastian's smile slowly faded, and his face became solemn.

"Quite the opposite, child. To make sure you go."

"Why?"

"You are the savior of the world. Besides, if there is even a slight chance you might bring your mother and Alexander back…"

The way Zoe said her uncle's name implied she still loved him, but Emery was mistrustful. She narrowed her eyes and hissed. "Aren't you bossy? You can't just waltz in here, expecting everyone to obey you as if you're some queen. Where were you when we found this place? Where were you when my uncle ventured into the darkness by himself, heartbroken? You didn't even have the guts to say goodbye to him, but went on a rampage, destroying the other chamber. If it weren't for Elliot, I couldn't follow my mother." Emery stood up, straightened her back, and faced Zoe.

Zoe studied her for a while, not responding. Then, the corners of her lips started twitching, and she laughed. Wholeheartedly, with her entire body and teary eyes.

Emery stood, glaring at Zoe. The laughter dispelled her anger, but not her suspicions.

Zoe laughed for a while, tears running down her cheeks. "It's been a while since I laughed like that. You are just like your mother. Don't take shit from anyone. She'd be so proud of you. You're right. I acted stupidly and wasn't there for the people I cared about, but paid for it dearly, losing them. But we haven't lost everything. You're going to bring them back."

"How can you be so sure this can be done?"

A mysterious smile appeared on Zoe's lips.

Sebastian, who had been listening in on their conversation, shook his head in disapproval. "She got this idea from an old African tablet we found in Kenya. We sponsored an archeological dig where we were told there once was a temple for dark gods. And sure enough, we found tablets carved in the same black material the walls of the other chambers were made of. Zoe had them translated."

"What did the tablet say?"

Sebastian glanced at Zoe, and she nodded.

"The girl named Emery, born to dark parents, was the key to reclaiming immortality for humankind and restoring balance to the universe. I kept saying it was just a story, a meaningless coincidence, but Zoe insisted."

Emery grimaced as she listened to Sebastian, but then shrugged and said, "You are telling me you found an ancient tablet that fortuitously had my name on it. I suppose it's not any crazier than Sergi's story."

Movement in the doorway alerted them to new arrivals. Dr. Brown and his assistant came through the door, carrying a stretcher.

"Poor woman," the doctor said, glancing at Sara. "She keeps getting into trouble. Don't worry, I'll have her up and running in no time."

Together with his assistant, the doctor placed an unconscious Sara on the stretcher, giving the assistant a sign to roll her out to the van parked outside, as he walked to Peter to examine him. While Zoe had gone outside with Sebastian, Emery kneeled by the man she had killed and opened his jacket. She gasped and closed it quickly, then walked over to Peter's side. He sat against the wall, pale and looking exhausted, and as hard as he tried, he couldn't keep his eyes open. Beads of sweat covered his forehead as he clutched his chest.

"He'll be fine, but I must bring him to my clinic. He might have suffered a heart attack."

"Oh, no!" Emery exclaimed.

"He'll be okay," the doctor said with certainty.

"He's in excellent hands, Emery," Zoe said, returning.

"I'll need a minute," Emery said.

The doctor nodded, then scurried to the van to check on Sara and get another stretcher. Emery sat by Peter and whispered in his ear. "My heart and soul were hollow before I met you, and now my chest is filled with you. And I will carry you in there forever." His eyes remained closed, but his lips twitched as if he heard her. Then she tried to deceive time, kissing his lips. When she stood up, she was pale, but her eyes were clear. She turned and walked away, while the doctor and his assistant placed Peter on the stretcher and rolled him toward the van.

"Are you ready?" Zoe asked.

"Why do you want to go with me?"

"You can't go without me, silly girl."

"Why not?"

"I don't imagine Sara has given you a black shard, has she?"

Emery bit her lip, trying to remember what Sara had told her about the chamber. Zoe was right. Sara mentioned the shard in passing in relation to the chamber, but she never gave her one.

Emery hurled an indignant glance Zoe's way.

"I didn't think so. See, I can be of use to you then," she said, smiling and showing her a bulge in her pocket. "You can't open the capsule without the black shard."

"I see," Emery said through her teeth.

"Let's go then."

84

THE LAB

WHERE TIME DOESN'T EXIST

"**D**id you hear that?" Olesya asked Marcy.

"I heard a woman's voice."

"There it is again! It sounds like Emery. She's calling my name," Olesya said, listening to the distant voice. "It is my baby calling me. She sounds older, but that's her voice. Let's go," Olesya tarted floating toward the voice.

Marcy drifted along.

"Emery! Emery! Where are you? It's your mother! Say something!" Olesya shouted.

"Mother! Is that you? Where are you?"

"That way," Olesya said and pointed at the silvery waves, guessing they were Emery's voice. She followed them, crying Emery's name. When she saw the dark figures pushing her, she wanted to go faster, but Marcy kept stopping and gesticulating as if she wanted to say something. Olesya kept following Emery, glancing back at Marcy, surprised and annoyed at her friend for not showing more enthusiasm to help her daughter. *Why is she slowing down? What's wrong with her?*

"Olesya, wait. Stop for a second, for fuck's sake! I have to tell you something!" Marcy yelled.

Olesya stopped, surprised. Marcy rarely swore. "What? I must get to Emery. You are slowing us down."

"They are taking her to the black space. We can't go there, or we will be stuck there forever."

"You don't have to go with me, Marcy. But I must go to save my daughter."

"And how do you propose doing that? You can't move there. You'd be stuck."

"What else can I do? I must try. If I get stuck along with Emery, at least we will be stuck together."

"I thought you wanted to help her?"

"What a dumb thing to say, Marcy. Of course, I do."

"Then listen to me. We can't go there, but we can ask for help."

"Ask for help? What are you saying, Marcy? Ask whom? The other gray shadows who always avoided us or the black shadows that took my baby? There's nobody else in this hellhole!"

"Are you done? Can I talk now? There's someone who can help."

"Who?"

Marcy hesitated with an answer, testing Olesya's patience as she longed to go after Emery.

"Marcy, speak for fuck's sake!"

"Okay. I'll call him," Marcy said and shouted. "Alexander! I am here, and I need you!"

"What did you just do, Marcy? Whom did you call?"

Marcy didn't answer.

"Did you just call my brother? Marcy! Answer me now!"

Marcy nodded.

"You called my brother here? Are you mad? What's wrong with you? Alexander is not here. You made me waste so much time when I could have gone to find her. I thought you were my friend."

Olesya turned and started searching for Emery's voice, furious with herself for listening to Marcy and disappointed in her friend.

"Olesya, wait. Alexander is here. He came right after you did."

Olesya tried to ignore Marcy, not believing her and not wanting to believe her. Propelled by her anger, she drifted as fast as her gray, shapeless body allowed her, trying to catch up with Emery while ruminating over Marcy's actions. Her devoted friend, Marcy, had betrayed her and her daughter. How would Marcy know Alex was here or know anything at all, stuck here in the darkness by herself? Her old friend Marcy appeared unchanged, but something in her friend's behavior had been bothering her, and it finally came to light today when she openly and deliberately slowed them down, thwarting their efforts to find Emery. In anger and frustration, her pace increased, and she flew after Emery, hoping with her entire gray body she would not be too late.

"Mother! Can you hear me?"

Olesya saw the faint silvery wave of Emery's voice coming her way. She assumed it was Emery's voice because of the golden dots sparkling inside the waves.

Good, I'm closer. Maybe I have time, Olesya thought. "I'm coming, Emery," Olesya yelled.

"Don't! Can you hear me? Don't follow me! Please! Listen to me! I'll be okay. I know what to do now. I love you. Find your brother!"

Olesya thought she had misheard. Why else would she implore her to stop following her, and why would she tell her to find Alexander? Maybe the dark shadows forced her to say that? Emery's words made little sense to her, so she ignored them and continued following her voice. Then she saw a gray figure drifting straight at her. She drifted toward the figure, ready to fight with her clumsy dark body.

When he came closer, his size disappointed her. From a distance, the figure had seemed large, floating like a huge gray cloud. But up close, the gray blob was not much bigger than she was. Once he stood before her, his shape started taking on a more human form. Soon, from a shadowy and shapeless body, a gray image of her brother, Alexander, appeared.

Alexander smiled at her with his gray mouth. "Olesya, you called me at last," he said.

"I didn't call you. Marcy did," Olesya said, drifting away from him with tiny, imperceptible movements. "And you're not my brother. You can't be."

"Marcy? You called me, Olesya. I heard your voice. And *I am* your brother."

"Marcy did," Olesya said, looking around. "She's here. At least she was here until you arrived. If it's you, what are you doing here?" Olesya asked.

"I had to warn you."

"About what?"

"I need to show you something. It would be easier for you to understand."

"It'll have to wait. I must save Emery now," Olesya said, searching for a trace of Emery's voice.

"Olesya, wait! We must talk. You can't help Emery."

Olesya stopped and looked at him impatiently. "Why not?"

"You can't pass through the black hole. You'd be stuck there forever."

"Black hole? Okay, Alexander...or whoever you are. You just look like my brother, but I don't believe you are. The golden people made you look like him. I am done; I am leaving. Go away," Olesya said and thrust her gray blobs at him. But she accomplished nothing. Her powers were no good here.

"Olesya, you never believed in the golden people, and you were right. There are no golden people, and never were."

Olesya ignored him and resumed the search for her daughter, but Emery's voice disappeared. She had little choice but to talk to the strange gray blob that had taken on Alexander's shape.

"You made me lose her, you son of a bitch! Was that your ploy all along?"

"You can't help her," Alexander said. "No one can."

"What the fuck do you mean, no one can help her? And what do you want from me?"

"I want to show you something. You came here so that Emery could save the world. If you don't want her to have wasted her life in vain, you must stop following her and come with me. Stop fighting me. I'm your brother, and I came here to help you remember. You'll understand soon enough."

"How do you know my name? Or my daughter's? Did Marcy tell you?"

"I'm glad you had Marcy here with you, but you know it wasn't Marcy who called me, Olesya. You called me."

"No. It wasn't me. It was Marcy who called you. You're still in the real world."

"Okay, where's she then?"

"I don't know," Olesya said, looking around. She hadn't noticed when Marcy had stopped following her.

"Come with me, please. Once you see what I want to show you, you'll understand and hopefully remember. I'm your brother. I always wanted to protect you, remember? Even from across the ocean?"

"How do I know you will not throw me into the darkness?"

"Then why would I want to stop you from going after Emery? You'd be stuck in the darkness if I hadn't stopped you. Come on, Olesya. You can ask me anything you'd like that only you and I would know the answer to."

The man who called himself Alexander turned around and started drifting away. He didn't bother to see whether Olesya was following him. Olesya hesitated, torn between trying to find her daughter and following the shape who claimed to be her brother. *What if he really is Alexander?*

Emery's voice was long gone. Olesya followed him as he guided her through gray cities that appeared indistinguishable from each other. She stopped in her tracks when the city they were passing through suddenly faltered. Not in its typical shape-shifting, shimmering way, but more violently, as if it were breaking, dissolving. Alexander stopped and looked back at her. The city stabilized itself quickly, and Olesya thought her imagination had concocted it.

"What was that?" Olesya asked. "Have you seen it happening before?"

"No. It's probably nothing. Come on, we're almost there."

When they reached their destination, the city that spread before her would have taken her breath away had she had one. It was a city like she'd never seen before. The skyscrapers reached unimaginable heights. If one stood on the street, one wouldn't be able to see the tops of the skyscrapers because they hid in the clouds. The enormous towers and other buildings were made of the same gray material and yet they seemed different, more translucent. They were connected by convoluted arches, circles, triangles, and every other known shape interlocked in a three-dimensional web that made her think of a kaleidoscopic image the longer she stared at it.

Alexander plunged low and circled the buildings, stopping in front of an enormous structure, waiting for Olesya to catch up. He waited at a door, then slowly opened it for theatrics, revealing a state-of-the-art, futuristic physics lab.

85

I KNOW

AUGUST 2047

Peter sat in an uncomfortable metal chair by Sara's bed in Dr. Brown's clinic. Sara, propped up by pillows, sat glaring at a plate of untouched food on a tray in front of her. Private or not, the clinic's hospital food inspired neither hunger nor confidence. The mound of mashed potatoes and unidentified piece of meat sailing through the lake of sad, brown gravy smelled and looked not the way food should smell. She grabbed a remote from the shiny white nightstand on her left side and lowered the volume of the big-screen TV broadcasting the news. An enormous bouquet of artfully arranged flowers sat on a table by the window overlooking the busy city street.

"No appetite?"

"I haven't even gotten a chance to say goodbye to her," she murmured, shoving the plate of untouched food away. "What happened to you?"

"Nothing really. Minor heart issue. I'm all cleared by Brown. I just wanted to stop by before I leave," Peter said and asked after a moment of hesitation. "Did you know Zoe was coming?"

"No. I've not heard from her in years. I was shocked to find out she had come and had gone into the chamber with Emery."

"I planned to go with Emery."

"Really?" Sara observed him with interest. "She might not have been able to save you."

"It didn't matter. I'll be leaving now, Sara. Emery asked me to take Regis from her grandparents' house and bring him to you if you'll have him."

"Of course, I'll have him. I'll be going home tomorrow."

"I'll bring him in a few days. Take care."

"What will you tell her grandparents?"

"I haven't decided. I want to tell them the truth, but I doubt Emery or Olesya would have wanted that."

"Good luck."

Peter got up and headed toward the door, but stopped and asked. "How would we know if she succeeded?"

"No idea. I guess we wouldn't, unless…if the world doesn't end?"

He nodded and left.

Peter knocked at the door of the house he had become so familiar with. Sasha opened the door and stood in the doorway. Showing no emotion, she stared at him for a while and opened the door wide. Regis ran to greet him, wagging his tail vigorously, jumping on his chest, and sloshing his face with his tongue. Sasha watched the display of affection between Peter and the dog with interest.

"He likes you. Regis can tell the good ones from the bad ones. Come on in and make yourself comfortable. Can I get you some tea?"

"Water would be great if it's not too much trouble."

Sasha appraised him, looking him up and down, and then a faint smile appeared on her lips. "I'll be right back."

Peter was on the verge of tears when he looked around the house and realized it had stayed the same since his last visit twenty-three years ago. The photo of Olesya, Emery as a baby, and her parents surprised him, seizing his heart with a sudden ache. He clutched his heart and stood staring at the photo as tears rolled down his cheeks.

That's how Sasha found him when she returned carrying a pitcher of ice water with floating lemon wedges and two glasses. She studied him for a while, then she coughed lightly and set the water on the coffee table by the couch.

"Sit down for a while. My husband is away competing in a chess competition. I'm sure he'll bring home yet another trophy."

Peter sat on the sofa, across from Sasha, who sat on a chair. Regis plopped himself in the middle, observing them both as they sat in silence. Peter rolled the glass in his hands, staring into the distance.

"I know about you and Emery," Sasha said eventually, breaking the silence matter-of-factly.

His face flushed as he tried to avoid Sasha's gaze. Expecting to see resentment and disapproval in her eyes but finding only kindness and understanding, Peter was at a loss for words for a long moment before he whispered. "How do you know?"

"She told me. She called and told me everything," Sasha said, and glancing at Peter's flushed face, chuckled.

"Come on, Peter, I'm too old to be a prude. Love doesn't give a hoot about age. You've made my little Emery happy. Even if it was just for an instant, she experienced love. As popular as she was in school, she never cared about anyone much."

Peter coughed. The lump in his throat grew thicker as Sasha spoke.

"Emery told me Olesya didn't die in the car accident, and that she knew how to find her. I knew all along that my daughter hadn't died in that car that day. She was too good a driver to roll off the road, and she didn't drink, as the detectives tried to imply. I realized early on that my daughter had secrets she wouldn't or couldn't share with me, mainly because she didn't want to cause me concern or pain. And I never pushed her, but I wished I shared her pain."

"She was too selfless for that."

Sasha nodded. "In the last few months before her disappearance, Olesya was consumed with worries. She was always serious, but I've never seen her so forlorn. I've always known the day would come when I would lose her. And on the day she left for the work conference, she hugged me so tight I could barely breathe. And then she said that if I were to hear that something bad happened to her, not to believe it, but to keep on believing she was still alive."

Peter and Sasha sat for hours talking about Olesya and Emery. At one point, he brought up the fact that Olesya's only childhood friend, Marcy, had died at such a young age.

Sasha had a strange expression on her face. "Marcy wasn't real."

"What do you mean?"

"Marcy was her imaginary friend. I knew about her and played along. I even talked to her and brought her cookies. Olesya needed someone her age to play and talk to, but she didn't make friends easily. One day, she came into the kitchen where I was baking cookies and said her friend, Marcy, had come to visit, and she asked me to meet her.

"I was so happy that she had made a friend; I followed Olesya to her room, only to discover it was empty. She pointed to an empty chair and said, 'Marcy, this is my mama. Mama, this is my friend Marcy.' She seemed so happy, so I bit my tongue and smiled at the empty chair. 'Nice to meet you, Marcy. Would you like some cookies and milk?' I asked her. 'Yes, she would. She loves cookies,' Olesya replied for her friend."

"Since that day, Olesya had a friend and was happier. So I pretended with her."

Peter closed his eyes for a moment, then rose from his chair. "Thank you, Sasha. Take care. If you ever need anything…"

Sasha hugged them both before Peter left with Regis.

86

REMEMBER, OLESYA

WHERE TIME DOESN'T EXIS

Olesya drifted into the lab, looking back at Alexander. "What is this place?" she asked.

He didn't answer. He just watched her with a mysterious and slightly apologetic smile.

Not getting an answer, she started exploring the futuristic lab. Amidst the monotonous gray substance, she identified familiar equipment, yet the rest remained unknown.

"Why did you bring me here?"

"Look around. Try to remember."

"Remember? What the hell are you talking about? This is some kind of futuristic lab. No idea what most stuff is; never seen it before in my life."

Alexander pointed toward something in the distant corner of the lab and disappeared.

Annoyed, she floated around the unfamiliar lab. She stopped by a door, and her whole gray being shook when she saw a gray sign on the door: *Olesya Solensky, President of the Department of Darkness*.

"What the hell?" A sudden wave of intense anger came over her as she imagined someone was manipulating her when her daughter needed her. With that anger, she burst the door open with her gray body, finding herself in a large office with gigantic windows and a massive desk. On the desk lay a model of a multi-level structure with interconnected rooms and complex instruments and items she didn't recognize.

But she recognized the rooms, which looked exactly like the chamber she had come from. She stood staring at the model, trying to find a sensible explanation. It must be a different Olesya Solensky. This wasn't real. Or was it the future? Her future? But how could that be? Was this man, alleging to be her brother, doing this to prevent her from going after Emery? But why show her this strange lab? And the feeling of déjà vu, the echoes of the past, returned, tugging at her gray body.

As if he had read her mind, just as he had in the past, Alexander floated into the office. "Do you remember now?" he asked.

Olesya did not give in easily. "Remember what? This is a futuristic lab and the three-dimensional schematics of the chambers. Obviously, it hasn't happened yet. How can I possibly remember the future? Are you insane?"

"You're right. It's the future."

"Why tell me to remember, then?"

"Because it's also the past."

"You think I am stupid?"

"Olesya, you know what I think. You are the smartest person I know."

"So what are you saying?"

"I was hoping you'd remember, but I'll have to tell you myself. The chambers here," he said, pointing at the model, "were your invention and your creation, the culmination of your long career."

"I invented the chambers? Why would I do that? To be stuck here?"

"You invented the capsules for time travel to get back in time to unlock dark matter. The dark dimension was something you stumbled upon by accident, but you had never actually come here yourself before because it was too dangerous."

"So is this the future, the past, or what?"

"In the dark dimension, there is neither the future nor the past. Time does not exist. Not in the actual sense. Zoe tricked you into coming here by lying about Sergi's intention to destroy the world."

"It was Zoe who vanished Great Britain, wasn't it?"

Alexander nodded, continuing. "Zoe was the one who inferred you were a freak by providing you the details of your birth. Then she helped you save me and earned your gratitude. Zoe, an excellent judge of character, knew you'd feel shame that would rot your soul, but grateful to her..."

"...and she figured out it would eventually lead me to self-destruction, sacrificing my worthless life to save the world," Olesya finished his sentence.

"The AI-created hologram of Sergi was just one mechanism to get you to do what she wanted you to do—"

"I knew it wasn't Sergi!"

"You did what she'd expected you to do almost to the end. She knew you'd be the hero and go after Sergi. And Sergi did what she told him. Well, almost."

"I suspected her, but wasn't sure until she pushed me into the capsule. Why would she devise such elaborate plans just to get me into the capsule? What would she gain from sending me here?"

"Prevent you from eventually traveling back in time."

"Why?"

"Dark matter, Olesya. After the discovery of the nature of dark matter, you became an expert, learning its benefits and applications. And with Sara's discovery of the golden substance when combined with the dark matter—"

"Sara's discovery?"

"She was the one who apparently discovered it. I don't know more —your holographic message didn't include details, only that you planned to give humanity the ultimate utopian world where people were free of diseases and lived for centuries or more. More importantly, the golden substance and the dark matter combined would give human bodies what they lacked and eliminate their violent tendencies."

"Why would she be against that? Why would anyone?"

"Zoe didn't want you to succeed. If everyone were like her, she would no longer be special or in control. Fearing she'd lose the power she had worked so hard to achieve, she became unhinged. Zoe, made only with the black shard, lacked the golden substance to balance her. But Zoe is not evil. She's merely a human being who couldn't give up her power once she had gained it, and her mind convinced her she had no choice but to get rid of you."

"How did you find out?"

"After you and Zoe had gone into the chamber, I hacked into her laptop and figured out what she was up to."

"I built the time machine to go back in time and release dark matter that was locked in the past by an ion explosion," Olesya said slowly. "So what happened? The time machine didn't work?"

"The machine worked, but not in the way you envisioned it. Despite your efforts, you could travel only into the future. And by doing so, you created an endless loop, and now we are stuck in it."

"Closed time-like curves. How did Zoe find out about the loop and the capsule?"

"The hologram. You set up holograms in the chambers describing your progress with time travel, the plan to unlock dark matter, and the schematics of the chambers and manuals for operating them. Your holograms served as record-keeping journals and as a warning to avoid the dark dimension. This time, Zoe discovered the chambers and the holograms and, learning about the dark dimension, designed her plan. Knowing you felt something for Sergi—"

"She did? How did she?"

Alexander hung his head. "It was my fault. I sensed it and mentioned it to her. When I saw her expression, I immediately recognized my mistake. I'm so sorry."

"Don't blame yourself. I know you meant well," Olesya said, fixing her gaze on the model. "So, it was Zoe who, thanks to my obsessiveness with record-keeping, added a new hologram AI Sergi telling the story."

"Yeah, but she got sloppy and didn't delete your original message from all the chambers. And that was her biggest mistake because I was able to listen to the original holograms."

"Why didn't she just kill me? Why go to all the trouble of sending me here?"

"She did. That is what she did. Repeatedly, she had you murdered on the slopes of the Italian Alps, but it was too late because you had already created the loop."

"You mean she had Sergi kill me each time? How come he didn't this time?"

"This is the new and unexpected part of the time loop, an unsolved puzzle in this story. He must've changed his mind. He shot you with a rubber bullet and tried to stop you from following him. Emery's existence was a spontaneous glitch within a glitch. In no other loops did you have a daughter. Emery's existence not only put a wrench in Zoe's plans but also created a crack in the time loop, changing it. I suspect that is why Zoe found the chambers this time. Finding the hologram and discovering the dark universe, she convinced herself that to prevent your success and keep her power, she must send you here and break the loop forever."

"Let me guess, Elliot, crucial in Zoe's scheming, made up old myths and legends and presented them to gullible me."

Alexander nodded. "But she also had to plan for Emery, the new and unforeseen part of the loop. To send Emery after you, she made up the story of Emery saving the world by unlocking dark matter. Poetic justice, I'd say. She sent Emery to the dark dimension, lying to her she could save the world, not knowing that she had sent her to do exactly that."

"It must've been hard on you. Knowing what she planned and yet loving her."

"Not as hard as losing you. I suspected her since I saw the hologram on her computer; she recorded it with her phone. I think she was afraid her plan would fail if I found out anything, and that is why she behaved so strangely: why she left and didn't want me around anymore."

Suddenly, everything around them blurred. The chambers, the

equipment, the entire building faltered. Olesya glanced at Alexander and saw in horror that he, too, was faltering.

"What's going on?" Alexander gazed at his gray hands that blurred in and out of view.

Olesya had an epiphany: "Alex, how is Emery going to save the world?"

"Emery, possessing golden and black elements, can pass across the black hole, travel back in time, and release the dark matter. Why do you ask?"

"Because something is happening here. How can you be so sure Emery is going through the black hole?"

"That's what your hologram predicted as part of your research. After the failed attempts to go back to the future, you researched the golden and black fragments on the black hole you've created in your lab and discovered that mice with black and golden fragments had gone through them."

"This is just getting better and better. I created a black hole—to create a utopian society for people who do not deserve it, maybe don't even want it, and who will eventually squander it."

"It's too late now. Emery is on her way to the black hole."

"Her presence inside the black hole might be what is disrupting the dark dimension. We may not have much time here before we disappear."

"What do you mean, disappear?"

"After Emery goes through the black hole, the dark dimension might implode. I'm so sorry, Alex. I shouldn't have—"

"You're starting to remember?"

"Bits and pieces..."

"There is a different way out of here. Not through a black hole, but through the light. When I came here initially—"

"Initially?"

Alexander nodded and continued. "Yes. This is the second time I have come here looking for you. The first time I came here, I searched for you and stumbled upon the light. Awed and curious at the bright, pulsating light, I drifted toward it, and when I was near it, the light pulled me in, and there was nothing I could do to withstand its pulling force. And that is how I ended up back in our dimension."

"Marcy said people are being reborn by going through the light."

"You realize there is no Marcy, right?" he asked softly.

"I do," she sighed with resignation. "So, how did I know about the light, then?"

"Maybe you remembered it?"

"Where did you end up?"

"On the shore in Grossos in northern Brazil, as an old hippie, whose body washed up on the beach. I found myself in an old body with no memories of my previous life. I ended up doing odd jobs for people in town and got room and board at the local bar. For years, strange dreams haunted me. I dreamed of you and Emery, but didn't know who you were until I saw her in person."

"You did? Where?"

"In Grossos. That is where the chamber was in South America, and that is where Emery went. When I saw her, I was immediately drawn to her and followed her. That's when I saw Zoe and Sara, and all the memories resurfaced. I couldn't do anything to protect her. I had no powers and was just an old hippie. But everyone ignored me, so I spied on them unhindered by suspicion. After Emery and Zoe entered the chamber and didn't come back, I guessed Emery had figured it out and brought Zoe with her to the dark universe. I found two people to open the chamber to save you and to make sure Emery succeeded."

"Why didn't Zoe stop Emery from going into the chamber?"

"She didn't know Emery possessed both golden and black fragments, and having never been to the chamber in Grossos, she didn't know of the last hologram you recorded on the possibility of traveling into the past using the black hole and that the black hole existed within the dark dimension."

"Where would Emery go? How far back into the past?"

"You've speculated dark matter was locked by a powerful ion explosion, which happened forty thousand years ago...approximately."

"Forty thousand years ago? How would she survive alone?"

"She's as strong or stronger than you. She'll survive."

The futuristic lab blurred, but this time, it also shattered briefly and then slowly reconfigured itself, but it seemed darker and more subdued. Olesya glanced at her hands and noticed they, too, appeared fainter. Alexander drifted to the exit and signaled for her to follow.

"I think it is time you went into the light," Alexander said.

"What about you?"

"I'll be right behind you. Going through the light and into a different dimension, you may not remember everything, or you may remember nothing. You will still be you, but your life may be different. Or similar. When I saw glimpses of you in a different life, you were happy. You smiled a lot."

"Is it really what happens in the light? We will end up in a different dimension?" Olesya asked, following Alexander. He increased his pace.

"I'm the proof. Come on, hurry! I'll show you the way."

"I'm not going without you!"

"I can't go yet. I must stay here in case it doesn't work. Don't worry. I'll be okay. I'll go up in a while and see you in another life. I promise. Trust me."

"You're not going with me because you want to find Zoe?"

Alexander didn't answer.

"Are you going to take her to the light?"

He shook his head. "The opposite."

"No. You can't go there. I need you. Don't you dare disappear into the black hole! I forbid you! You come with me! Do you hear?"

"I must take her to the black hole so she'll never threaten you again."

"I'll help you then."

"No. I must do this one alone. You need to go now."

Olesya stopped trying to convince him and remembered her dreams of her brother pulling her out of the darkness. When Alexander saves her from Zoe for the last time.

"Was Sebastian in on it?"

"Not sure. I thought he genuinely liked you like a sister and never wanted to hurt you, but he would do anything for Zoe. I don't know."

Alexander led Olesya to the light, staying closer to her than before, almost touching her, and she was aware it was to make sure she ascended safely. It was his plan all along. He didn't foresee that she had a plan of her own. Olesya opened her gray arms in a loving gesture, and Alexander drifted even closer. She grabbed him with all the strength her shapeless arm possessed, held him tight, and pushed toward the light. Alexander tried to pull out of her grip and yanked his arm away, but expecting it, she grabbed the other one as he turned. He tried to kick away, but the light pulled them both up. Afterward, they simply drifted into it. As they ascended, they slowly started forgetting who they were and what had happened, drifting into a blissful oblivion.

87

THE LOOP

WHERE TIME LOOPS

A woman with black eyes and short black hair walked along the sidewalk, holding her four-year-old daughter's hand. Her daughter's dark blue eyes sparkled with gold and black specks when she gazed at her mother with admiration.

"I want to go to your laboratory again, Mommy. I want to see that shiny machine that makes golden spots. Can we go? Can we go, please?"

"I will take you, but not today. Today is Sunday, and the lab is closed. The people who work there need some rest. We'll go some other time, okay, Emery?

"Yes, Mommy. Daddy said you're the smartest person in the world."

"And you believed him?"

"I don't have to. I know you are the smartest person in the world. You're my mommy."

"You know what I think?"

"What?"

"I think you are the smarty-pants. But the cutest smarty-pants in the world."

Olesya bent down and tickled the girl's belly. Then she picked the giggling girl up and carried her down the street. It was a glorious afternoon. The sun shone through the colorful glass buildings, so tall that they disappeared into the clouds. Glass walkways connected the buildings high above the ground. Trees and shrubs and emerald-green fields radiated greenness from inside the glass structures.

"We've got to hurry. Daddy is waiting for us at the ice cream store, remember?"

"Yeah! Let's go to Daddy."

Olesya walked into a pink and blue building, and an elevator transported her upstairs to the ninth floor to the ice cream parlor, where people were eating ice cream, floating in multicolored clouds resembling ice cream cones. Emery giggled and slid down from Olesya's arms, then immediately ran to a cloudy table where a man sat with outstretched arms and a proud smile on his handsome face. His blue eyes had black and golden spots that sparkled the same way as Emery's when he smiled at her. The girl ran into his arms and disappeared into them as he hugged her. He kissed the girl on the head and smiled at Olesya.

"Done shopping, girls?"

"We didn't go shopping, Daddy. We were in the library of secret books with Uncle Alex."

"Oh, you did, did you?"

"Come on, Sergi. Get us some ice cream."

"Yes, madam. Any special orders today?"

"No, the same as usual," Emery said and burst out laughing.